Midnight Rainbows
Over The Little Village

Midnight Rainbows over the Little Village

ELLA COOK

A Broclington Romance Book 4

Choc Lit
A JOFFE BOOKS COMPANY

Choc Lit
A Joffe Books company
www.choc-lit.com

First published in Great Britain in 2025

© Ella Cook

Cover art by Jarmila Takač

ISBN: 978-1781898277

*To all the people walking Imogen's path, fighting pain,
fatigue and chronic illness every day. This one's for us . . .
because it's not often we're seen in fiction.*

*And to the loved ones who walk alongside us — sometimes
carrying us — and always keeping us strong. Thank you, always.*

*And for Brin — one of those strong people, who may
well have inspired some of Kai's better characteristics, and
definitely gives great hugs — still the very best man x.*

CHAPTER ONE

Kim was restless. She'd looked at Jake's filing, shuddered at the complexity of the system and abandoned it. She grabbed the cordless phone, settling on one of the waiting-room benches by the window. She may as well take advantage of the afternoon sun streaming in as she sketched.

She enjoyed the peace. Working from memory, her fingers chased the pencil across the paper to spin out a flurry of speckled feathers, sharp claws and intelligent cold eyes set over a vicious beak — the same one that had slashed at her fingers earlier this morning when she'd held the little owl for Jake to examine. The tiny tawny had been fine, just stunned from colliding with a car — the driver had brought him in. A few more hours in Jake's care, and he'd be packed off to Angela — and Ryan — at the animal sanctuary, get fed for a few days before being released.

She switched pencil for eraser and used the sharp edge to add glints of light to the eyes, bringing the picture to life. Her hair fell forward as she worked, and she paused to tuck it back, sighing as she did. The pink she'd dyed it was already fading, so she'd have to redo it soon, or she'd end up with orangey-peach streaks, making her look like a pastel, cartoon pony — or worse, a teeny-bopper — definitely not looks she was going for.

She'd first dyed it — bleaching the brown from most of her hair — a couple of days after breaking up with Clark. Honestly, she should have known better, dating someone called *Clark* — the goody-two-shoes, boring version of Superman. So she'd stripped the natural colour out of her hair and turned it green, then red, then blue, before the current, rapidly fading pink. Maybe she'd try purple next.

She'd craved a change — needing some edge or excitement in her life, and instead found herself back in Broclington, sleeping in her childhood bedroom, working as a receptionist in her brother's vet practice, covering someone's maternity leave. Hardly setting the world on fire as she'd planned when she'd insisted on doing an expensive art degree so many years ago.

She looked up when the door clanged, and blinked in surprise. Not only was it someone she didn't recognise — not all that uncommon in Broclington, with its tourists and hikers, but the woman certainly didn't look like either of those. Curly, dark hair had been dragged away from her face, pinned with what looked like twigs from a garden behind a bright purple bandana. She wore a massive, dirt-stained turquoise sweatshirt over star-speckled leggings, and boots that looked like original Docs, but had been re-laced with multi-coloured ribbons, topped off with mismatched socks.

Kim grinned, thinking she was the most interesting-looking person she'd seen in weeks. But then again, outside of Santa visiting in Summer, nothing all that exciting ever seemed to happen in Broclington. At least, not to her.

The woman looked around for a second, shot a bright and oddly familiar smile at Kim, then leaned over the desk to reach for the bell.

'Oh, you don't need to do that. I'm here.' Kim closed her sketchpad, rolling to her feet. 'Can I help?'

'I'm hoping so.' The woman's smile was warm, but seemed slightly shy, which Kim didn't get. If she was half as gorgeous as the woman stood in front of her, she wouldn't be shy at all. 'The thing is, I don't have an appointment. But I was hoping I could get away with being cheeky, if I asked really nicely?' Her shrug was apologetic, but her dark eyes — framed by heavy lashes — were bright with mischief.

'Let me have a look.' Kim stepped behind the desk and opened up the calendar for the day. She knew a good receptionist would probably have memorised the day's schedule, but she definitely didn't class herself as good at the admin side of her role — she much preferred working with the patients. But, for the first time, she kinda cared about it, and really hoped this new customer wasn't judging her for her general uselessness. 'What was it you were needing?'

'I'm not totally sure.' The woman shrugged again. 'I know I'm being dreadfully rude, but I hadn't exactly planned this. But often I find that the most interesting things are the ones we don't plan . . . like this little man.' She reached into her bag and pulled out a sleepy, grey tabby kitten, who mewled in complaint.

'Oh, how gorgeous!' Kim leaned forward and held her fingers out to the tiny cat. 'Is it yours?'

'No. At least, I don't think so. I found him curled up in the garden when I was clearing it. He seems a bit little to be out by himself, and was far too scruffy and skinny-looking. I cleaned him up a bit, and he's kept down some tuna, but I thought it was worth bringing him to the vet in case I'm wrong, and someone is looking for him. I would have taken him to Angela and my brother, but I'm pretty sure I remember them saying they didn't have one of the microchip scanner things . . .'

'You're Ryan's sister?' Kim felt her eyebrows raise. 'Ryan, as in better-known-as-Maverick, Ryan?'

'If I answer that honestly, will you promise not to hold it against me?' The woman smiled at her again. Kim found herself smiling back as the woman leaned in closer. 'I promise I'm much nicer than he is. And less trouble too. Usually.'

There was something in the way she said that, and her cheeky grin, which made Kim wonder exactly what type of trouble she was getting into, and whether she might want a partner in crime. Because she really thought she might want to be it.

'So, what do you think?' Again that hopeful, cheeky, lip-biting smile.

Kim thought quickly, finding herself wanting to be more helpful to this stranger than she had any of Jake's paying customers all week. 'Jake — the vet — is in surgery now, but should be finishing up soon. I know where the scanner is, so we'll see if we can find this little guy's home — if he has one. And while you wait, we could check the National Pet Register to see if anyone local has reported a cat missing that matches his description. I mean if you're OK to wait. Though you're probably not, because you probably have better things to be doing.' *Shut up, Kim!* Why was she rambling like an idiot?

* * *

Imogen hid another grin as the brunette with pink streaks in her hair, which almost perfectly matched her lipstick, wittered on, obviously flustered. Well, that was very interesting. She let her carry on for a few more seconds until she started to repeat herself, before gently interrupting.

'I don't mind waiting for a bit.' Imogen continued cradling the kitten against her chest.

'OK.' Blue eyes sparkled at her from beneath a heavy fringe. 'If you wait here, I'll grab the scanner.'

'Sounds good.' Imogen couldn't keep the smile from her face. After half a day in the garden, digging and tugging up weeds, sweating and being scratched to bits by thorns, she was hardly feeling — or looking — her best. But the vibes she was getting from the receptionist were really interesting. And it looked like she had good taste. 'I like your T-shirt, by the way.'

4

'Thanks.' The receptionist tugged at it self-consciously.

'Great A'Tuin, right?' She eyed up the giant space turtle and glowing disc. 'From the *Discworld* books?'

'And films. Although I think some of them were better than others. You're a fan?' Those blue eyes lit up again.

'Obviously. All the most interesting people I know are.'

'Favourite character?'

'Well, I like the witches . . .'

'Who doesn't?' The receptionist laughed, her bright blue eyes twinkling.

'But favourite, favourite? Gotta be Angua the female werewolf.' And she definitely wouldn't mention that it was because she'd had a full-blown literary crush on that character for years. 'What about you?'

'Angua's cool.' The pink hair bobbed and swayed with her nod. 'But I kinda like Susan.'

'Death's granddaughter?'

'Yeah, she has some of the best lines. Like the one about "a room without books" being like . . .'

'"A body without a soul". Yeah, I know that one,' Imogen finished off, eliciting another stunning smile from the other woman, whose eyes locked with hers. Damn, she was pretty.

'What was I . . .'

'The scanner?' Imogen looked down at the kitten wriggling in her arms.

'Yeah. Are you OK to wait here?'

'Sure,' she answered honestly. 'I've nowhere else more important to be.' She watched as the other woman left the room, forcing herself not to look down and check out her arse. She wouldn't — she had more respect than that — but it was very tempting.

'Well, isn't that interesting?' she murmured to the kitten, now pawing at her arm and trying to bury himself in the crook of her elbow. 'Just a couple of days after I started thinking about getting another cat, you turn up in my garden, and introduce me to someone like her. If I didn't know better, I'd suspect something odd was going on.' The kitten just peered up at her, blinking his golden eyes. 'Even if you knew, you're not saying anything, are you?'

'Mweep?' He butted at her fingers, demanding attention.

'Yeah, that's what I thought.'

'I got it.' The woman returned holding up the machine. 'And Jake's just finishing up, so should be with us in a few minutes.'

'It's OK, I'm not in any rush.'

'Great. Can you hold him while I scan? It won't hurt, but sometimes they don't like it that much. I think it's the radio frequencies or something.'

'Of course.' Imogen followed her to the seating area, cuddling the cat on her lap. 'To be honest, I don't think I'd be terribly upset if he didn't have a microchip. He's quite cute.'

'Planning on becoming a cat owner?' The woman leaned in, giving Imogen a whiff of delicious scent, somewhere between honey and fresh apples.

For a moment, Imogen struggled to focus. 'Sorry, what was that?'

'I asked if you were thinking about keeping him.'

'Maybe I might be.' Imogen smiled sadly. 'I lost my cat not that long ago. I mean, to be fair, she was nineteen. Renal failure.'

'I'm sorry. That's a really good age, though.' She stopped fiddling with the scanner and rested her hand over Imogen's. 'But it doesn't make it easier. It's the worst thing about having pets . . . that we have to say goodbye.'

'Yeah.' Imogen looked down at the warm hand that rested on hers, the bright pink nails contrasting starkly with her garden-grubby ones. 'It really is. But they're so worth it the rest of the time. And it's such funny timing. I'd just started thinking that, now I'm a bit more settled, it might be a good time to think about another pet . . . and then this little guy turns up, mewling his head off from inside a bramble patch. It took me five minutes to dig him out. I'm still not sure how he got himself so well tangled.'

'Let's see, shall we?' She clicked on the scanner and ran it over the cat's back. She did three slow passes while Imogen fussed with the kitten, keeping him distracted. 'Nothing. Fourth time to be sure?'

'Yeah.' Imogen held her breath.

'Nothing.' She smiled up at Imogen. 'No chips. But we should still check the database for any kitty matching his description.'

'It's going to be clear.'

'You sound pretty sure about that.'

'Just a feeling.' Imogen had learned long ago that her instincts were right more often than they weren't.

A few minutes later, the bright blue eyes looked up from the computer screen and locked with hers. 'You're right.'

Imogen grinned and offered her hand to the cat. 'So, do you think you might want to come back home with me to live?' The kitten butted against her fingers, tickling her with his whiskers as he made chirruping noises.

'I think that might be a yes.' Blue eyes smiled at her.

'Yeah, I think so too. Maybe you should register me as a client here? If you've time now?'

'Sure, I can do that.' The woman glanced down at the screen, letting Imogen look away. 'So, you said you're "more settled" now. Is that in Broclington or one of the neighbouring villages?'

'Yeah, as of last month, it's Broclington.' And she hoped it would be for a while, at least. She certainly had a good feeling about the village. It had been there since she'd first visited to see the place, to meet the woman who'd stolen her brother's heart.

'Welcome then.' Another warm smile. 'So, name?'

'Imogen Finnegan. Two Ns.' She waited for the typing to stop. 'What about you? What's your name?'

'I'm Kim. Macpearson.'

'Hi, Kim. Nice to meet you.'

Kim's hand was warm and firm in Imogen's, the skin incredibly soft. 'Yeah, it's nice to meet you too.' Those bright blue eyes locked on hers again — and lock really was the word. Imogen wasn't sure she could have looked away if she wanted to.

'So, um . . . do you need my contact details?'

'Right, yes please.'

Imogen found herself grinning like an idiot — yet again — as she rattled off the address she'd learned by heart over the last few months. Every time she thought about it — what she'd achieved, all her hard work coming to fruition — she experienced a huge flush of pride.

'Oh, it's *you*.'

'Me?'

'Yeah, you're the one who's taking over the old model shop?'

'I am.' Imogen nodded, a bit surprised. She hadn't formally announced anything. In fact, she had left the front of the store untouched while she worked to get the flat above cleaned and painted before moving in. She hadn't realised that giving the flat's address would give away the shop too. She supposed it made sense the locals would know it. But while she'd ordered her shop sign, it was still a few weeks away. She'd planned it like that deliberately, hoping to sneak in with a soft opening to establish things before making a huge fuss. Apparently that wasn't working.

She must have pulled a face, because Kim burst out laughing. 'Yeah, don't set your heart on trying to keep anything even a little bit secret around here. One of the biggest problems with living in a place like this is everyone is always in everyone else's business. We've all known the shop lease was taken over — finally — but no one seemed to know what for, because you haven't submitted any change-of-use plans, so it couldn't be something like a bakery or takeaway. Which is actually a bit of a shame. I would have welcomed a few more cuisines. I do miss a decent curry . . . So, what will you be selling?'

'Do you really want to know? I had planned on keeping it a bit of a surprise, to be honest.'

'You can trust me.'

8

Yeah, Imogen was pretty sure she could. 'It's an extension of my existing business, only this time with a fixed base.'

'Oh come on, you have to tell me what it is now. I promise I won't tell anyone until you're ready.'

'I'm a complementary therapist.'

'Complementary? You don't mean like the social media craze of butthole sunbathing or drinking silver water, or juicing to cure cancer . . . do you?'

'No, definitely not. What you're talking about are alternative therapies, and some pretty contrived ones.' Imogen pulled a face. 'Complementary ones are a lot more holistic, looking at the person as a whole, and treating them in that totality — including working in line with any clinical treatments they're undertaking and with medical doctors.'

'That makes a lot more sense.' This time Kim's smile looked a bit relieved. 'Right, back to this little guy.' She rubbed the cat's ears. 'I need a name to register him.'

'Well, I found him in a bramble patch, so what do you think of Bramble?'

'I think it's adorable.'

'There we go then.' She gently caught one of his front paws in her fingers. 'Nice to meet you, Bramble Finnegan.'

'Hello. I hear we have a stray kitten?' Imogen looked up as a man in blue scrubs joined them.

'Not anymore.' Kim greeted him cheerfully. 'While you've been faffing around in the back, I arranged his adoption. Mostly. This is Bramble Finnegan. And his new person, Imogen.'

'Nice to meet you.' He held out a hand. 'I'm Jake Macpearson, the vet. May I?' He pointed to the cat.

Imogen felt a slight pang of disappointment when he introduced himself — which was silly. She had no reason to think that Kim was single, or interested in women, or that the vibes she thought she'd felt were anything more than polite friendliness. She gave herself a mental shake, thankful that she hadn't said anything to make an idiot of herself, then handed over the cat.

Jake tickled the cat as he rolled him onto his back, briskly peering into his eyes and ears, checking him all over. The kitten yowled as Jake prised his mouth open to check his teeth and throat. 'Well, he's got good lungs on him. Feels a bit skinny though. I'll just go pop him on the scales. Kim, I take it you didn't find any chips?'

'Nope.'

'And you checked the database too?'

'Yeah.'

'I'll just double-check him for chips while I weigh him.' He scooped up the kitten and scanner.

As soon as the door closed, Kim groaned. 'I swear he still acts like I'm a stupid seven-year-old.'

'Wow, you've known your husband since you were children? That's kind of sweet.'

'What?' Confusion crossed Kim's face before she burst out laughing. 'Ewww, no! Jake's my brother.' Her laugh was deep and contagious.

Imogen couldn't stifle her own giggles. 'In my defence, it's not like it's a common name. Seemed like a pretty safe assumption.'

'I know, but that's just the funniest thing.' Kim wiped her eyes. 'Sorry, it's just . . . you probably don't know what it's like living in Broclington. Like I said, everyone is constantly in everyone else's business, and half the village really has known you since you really were a stupid seven-year-old.'

'Who's a stupid seven-year-old?' Jake came back out, the kitten tucked under one arm.

'You are. At least mentally.' Kim stuck her tongue out, and Imogen had to bite back a smile.

'Only around you. I swear you drag me back to childhood.' He rolled his eyes. 'And if we can try being professional again for a few minutes in front of the client . . . It's hard to tell because he's a bit malnourished, but I think he's around ten weeks old. And you're right, that's too young to be out really. He's probably a stray.'

'Oh, you mean you didn't find a chip either? What a huge surprise.' Kim pulled a face.

'As I was saying—' Jake shook his head '—he's probably a stray, so we have to assume he's not had any of his vaccines. I'd recommend doing that pretty urgently. I can't see any fleas, but would suggest giving him a flea treatment and worming him as well. If you've got a few more minutes, I can do both now. If you are, indeed, sure about adopting him.'

'I am.' Imogen nodded. 'It just feels like he's supposed to be with me. And he's not the first cat I've owned. But he will be the only one I've got now. At least for the time being.'

'Her last cat was nearly twenty when she lost her,' Kim added.

The fact that she was on her side gave Imogen a warm feeling.

'Sounds like he'll be in good hands.' Jake smiled. 'I can get him vaccinated and wormed then.'

'Yes, please.'

'Run up as a new pet wellness check?' Kim asked.

'Yep. Right, come on then, Mr Kitten.'

'Bramble. She's calling him Bramble.'

'Come on then, Bramble, let's go make you dislike me.' Jake picked him up again. 'Do you want to come? Or would you like me to be the bad guy, then bring him back to you for cuddles?'

Imogen was really tempted by the offer. 'Does it make me a wimp if I want to say yes to that?'

'He's a stray. He's been through enough already,' Jake replied. 'If this helps make it easier for him to bond with you, and make it so that you're his safe space and person, then I'm all for that. I can be the "baddy" this time.'

'Then yes please.'

'I can schedule your follow-up appointments. He'll need booster shots in a few weeks,' Kim offered.

'That would be good thanks. I guess I need to go get some supplies in. As much as I'm sure Bramble would like it, he's not going to be living on tuna.'

A few minutes later, when Bramble almost threw himself into her arms, she knew she'd made the right decision.

'Thank you for your help.' She gave them both a bright smile. 'Guess we'll see you in a couple of weeks.'

'Yeah.' Kim smiled at her. 'If not sooner.'

Imogen was still smiling all the way back to her car, and as she tucked Bramble into her bag and strapped it in. Not ideal, but it would have to suffice, and she wasn't going far.

* * *

Imogen let Bramble loose to wander around his new home while she called her brother.

'Moggy!' Imogen knew Ryan was grinning just from that one word. Even if it was the least favourite nickname he'd ever come up with for her — which was probably why he liked it so much.

'Hey Ry-no. Got a min or two?'

'For you? Always. What's up?'

'I need a favour.'

'Go on.'

'I sort of just adopted a kitten.'

'Really? I didn't know you were looking.'

'I was thinking about starting to look, and, well, he just turned up.'

'Turned up?'

'Yes. In a patch of brambles at the shop. I had to cut him out. And by the time we'd both been attacked by the bush I think we were a bit in love with each other.'

'You are looking after yourself, aren't you? Not overdoing things and making yourself ill?'

'Nagging already, Ry-no?' She adored her brother, but he did fuss at times.

'Can you blame me for worrying? Anyway, you said you wanted a favour?'

'Yeah. Like I said, I seem to have adopted a kitten, but I don't have anything I need, and I don't really want to leave him all alone while I go shopping to try and find the basics . . .'

'So you thought you'd come on the scrounge and see what you could steal from me and Angela?'

'I was going to go with beg and borrow, while possibly guilting you over the fact that I had to rescue him from being shredded up by a truly mean plant, and hoping a donation would suffice? Because he *is* a rescue and that *is* what you do at the sanctuary, right?'

'I'll have a word with Angela. I'm sure we can pull together some bits. Do you need me to drop them off?'

'No, it's OK. I can try and wear him out now and pop by later, if that's all right.' She knew how busy the animal sanctuary got, and already felt guilty for how much of her brother's time she'd taken up, helping her to get the shop ready.

'You know, this really is too perfect. It's just too funny.' Her brother laughed.

'What is?'

'You, with all your witchy-woo ways.'

'Ugh, would you stop with that? You know I'm a trained physiotherapist, and a pain management specialist to boot. Just like you know the complementary work I do supports that. And that it helps me too.'

'I do. But I also know it's fun to wind you up. And that you can't complain too much when you want a favour from me.'

'Honestly, sometimes it's hard to remember that you're actually older than me. You act like a twelve-year-old!'

'But you still *luuurve* me!'

'I really do. Otherwise I'd have turned you into a frog years ago.'

'Nah, I don't believe you can really do that. Like you said, you're a pain management specialist — not a wizard.'

'You were going to tell me what was funny?'

'Well, you claim you're not a witch, but your wished-for cat has just turned up in a bramble bush in the middle of your new garden. You going to tell me that's not just a little bit fairy tale magic?'

Imogen regarded the kitten, who chose that moment to let out a huge, stinky fart. 'Eww. Nope. Definitely a normal cat.'

* * *

A couple of hours later Kim parked outside of Bill's Sanctuary and grabbed a box containing the little owl, taking care not to joggle him too much. She headed up the side of the building, clanging the brass bell by the gate.

It swung open a couple of seconds later. The squeak of the gate startled her charge. She looked down to try and calm the bird.

'Fancy meeting you here.' The smile in Imogen's voice caused a smile from Kim when she looked up.

'Yeah. I . . . um . . . I'm dropping off an owl.' She held up the box.

'An owl! Oh, can I see? I love birds. Even Mallow and I get on.' Imogen leaned down to peer in the basket.

'You mean Ryan's actually found someone else that cranky cockatoo likes?'

'Well, she does still swear at me.' Imogen giggled. 'But she doesn't try to rip off my nails like with some people, so I'm assuming we're friends. Hello, little owl. You been in the wars a bit?'

'Hit by a car. Nothing too serious, thankfully,' Kim explained. 'Angela will feed them up a bit before release. I'm just the taxi service.'

Imogen stood back, holding the gate open for her. 'I'm afraid I'm not doing anything even nearly as altruistic. I'm just on the scrounge.'

'How do you mean?' Kim kept a firm grip on the owl as she walked through the gate, then set the cage on the floor.

14

'I didn't really want to leave Bramble alone in a strange place for too long. This place is much closer than the big pet store, so I thought I'd beg and borrow some immediate supplies from here.'

'Who is it?' Angela called from the office, her voice echoing across the courtyard, followed by a series of ear-piercing wolf-whistles.

'It's Kim, from the vets,' Imogen called back. 'She's brought you an owl.'

'You know, to anyone else in any other place that sentence would be nonsensical.' Kim wasn't sure why, but the fact that Imogen had remembered her name made her feel warm and happy.

'And yet, here, it makes perfect sense.' The dark-haired woman with eyes the colour of dark chocolate smiled as warmly as she had in the vet's a few hours ago.

'I hear the cockatoo's in fine form. As usual.' Kim laughed at the torrent of swear words and growls now echoing across the courtyard.

'Yeah.' Imogen grinned as she bolted the gate behind her. 'She's kinda cute.'

'Maybe to you. She still tries to crack Jake's knuckles like nuts every chance she gets.'

'Poor Jake.' Imogen laughed. 'But then I suppose it's like he said — if he's the "big bad vet", then at least us pet owners get to remain innocent and give snuggles and sympathy afterwards.'

'Yeah, he can be pretty smart when he's not being annoying.' Kim winced as soon as she said it. 'Sorry, that probably makes me sound really bratty or something.'

'No.' Imogen shook her head and reassured her. 'Just like someone with an older brother. I love Ryan, but sometimes he drives me crazy.'

'Hey, Moggy, will this do for your moment of madness?' Ryan asked. 'Hey, Kim.' Holding up a small animal carrier and a cat basket, the sight of Ryan made Kim realise why Imogen's smile was so familiar.

'Moggy?' Kim couldn't resist asking.

'As I said—' Imogen shook her head '—I know what it's like to have a brother. Thanks *Ry-no*. Any chance I can get you to stop calling me that?'

'You've only been here a couple of weeks. Give me a chance to get bored.' He grinned again. 'Or maybe not. Can I take the owl?' He dumped the things in Imogen's arms and took the box from Kim. 'Laters, sis.'

Kim grinned when Imogen rolled her eyes.

'I see what you mean,' Kim said. 'And I know it well. I've got two brothers — both of them older.'

'I can't decide if that's better or worse.'

'Worse. Jake you've already met, and the other is one of our local GPs.'

'Wow, no pressure at all then.' Kim stared at Imogen, who turned bright pink under her gaze. 'Sorry, that was out of line.'

'No, it wasn't. It was just . . . surprisingly accurate.' She wasn't sure how someone she'd known for a handful of minutes could understand her better than her own family seemed to at times. It was like those dark eyes that locked on hers could see right through, to thoughts so deep that she didn't share them with anyone. But, while it should have made her feel uncomfortable, she wasn't sure it was a bad thing. She was still pondering the thought as Imogen called out her thanks, waved and left.

CHAPTER TWO

'Auntie Kimmy?' Sarah tugged at her sleeve, pulling her attention away from the conversation her parents and brothers were having at the kitchen table. She wasn't entirely upset about it, to be honest — she'd already tuned out of the conversation Liv and Evelyn were having about wedding stuff. 'Do you want to come and play fairies with me and Summer? Nanna bought us a new fairy playhouse that looks like a tree.'

'I know, I've seen it.' Kim leaned forward and added in a whisper, 'I've been wanting to play with it all week, but I wasn't allowed to until you were both here.'

'Will you come help us build it? Please?'

'Please? Auntie Kim?' Summer added her own pleas.

'I'd love to, but you better both ask permission.'

'Please, Mum, can we get down and go play?' Sarah asked.

'Yeah, Mum, please?' Summer echoed.

'Yeah, Mum, please?' Kim grinned as her own mum, Julie, swatted at her.

'Clear your dishes and yes, you *may* all get down from the table.' She caught Kim's arm as Kim jumped to follow her nieces. 'You know you can say no to them, right?'

'Yeah, but given the choice between surgery budgets and wedding-breakfast seating charts — and the

17

oh-so-important-and-difficult choice between ivory and cream table linens — I'll take building fairy tree castles any day!'

'You off to play with the kiddies, sis?' Jake grinned at her.

'Not my fault my nieces are more interesting than their dads!' She stuck her tongue out at her brothers.

'Still avoiding growing up, brat?'

She refused to let Callum's jibes get to her. 'Yup. Just call me Petra Pan.' Though she sometimes wished she did have her life a bit more in order, and a bit more sorted, like most of her peers did. 'Don't you have a home of your own to go to?'

'Yeah, unlike you. How long are you crashing on the parental's couch this time before you flit off again?'

'Well excuse me for taking Mum and Dad at their word when they said this was always home to us,' she snapped back.

'Stop it, the pair of you.' Julie shook her head. 'Honestly, I really do think Summer and Sarah are more grown-up than you both some days.'

'She started it,' Callum grumbled.

'And I'm finishing it. Whether Kim wants to stay here another six days, six weeks or six months, she's more than welcome. All of you children are.'

Kim was just about to retort she didn't want to be there another six minutes if it meant staying around her annoying older brother that long, when Sarah's timely shout rang out. 'Auntie Kimmy!'

'I'm coming.'

Her dad caught her wrist on the way past. 'Don't ever change, love. You're perfect as you are.'

'Thanks, Dad.' She kissed him on the cheek.

'Auntie Kim!'

'All right. I'm coming!' She shrugged. 'Duty calls.'

* * *

Imogen leaned up against the trunk of the ancient oak. The night was mild, and she wasn't cold, but she knew that wouldn't last long now she was sitting still. She opened up her backpack and pulled out a glass bottle, along with the boxes she'd packed earlier, and settled back to wait. She'd scouted out the position earlier in the week. It was an ideal spot, and in about half an hour or so she was pretty sure the moon would be perfectly framed by the branches. Once she was comfortable, she pulled out some of her favourite crystals and arranged them in a circle around her, then turned off her torch to let her eyes adjust.

She knew there wasn't any guarantee she was going to get lucky, but it looked like it could be a good night for it — and it would be utterly magical if it did appear on midsummer's night. As much as she didn't want to get her hopes up, she did have a really, really good feeling. Good enough that she'd spent a couple of hours doing her best to wear out Bramble before tucking him into bed, and then trekked across the village in the dark.

She knew she'd be tired tomorrow, and nowhere near as productive as she should be, so close to opening — but the nagging feeling that tonight was the night to come out here had been too tempting to ignore. She'd learned the hard way to trust her instincts, and now she was glad she'd listened. The air almost thrummed with energy, and she was tingling with anticipation. She didn't know what was going to happen tonight, but she had a feeling it was going to be good.

Trying to be patient, she settled — closing her eyes, and focussed on breathing in the cool scents of the Summer night. After a few seconds, she pulled off her jumper, and hiked her skirt up her legs. It was still warm enough that she could get away with it. She twisted to stretch out across the blanket she'd brought with her — one of her favourites, coloured in blues and purples, and patterned like a mandala — and closed her eyes again. It wasn't the same as sunbathing, but it was pretty close as she let the silvery light wash over her. It was somehow warming even as it drew goose pimples over her skin.

She sighed happily, relaxing fully for the first time in . . . well, she didn't know how long. Her life lately had been wonderful, and exciting, and filled with colour and light and passion . . . but it hadn't exactly been calm or restful, and she was feeling ready for some peace. And she was pretty sure she'd found it in Broclington.

She'd felt it the very first moment she set foot in the village. She hadn't entirely figured it out yet, but there was an energy about the place, almost a form of magic in the air and earth. It was a little like the sense of awe she felt standing in a cathedral, or at the bottom of the Gaping Gill Waterfalls, or sunrise at Stonehenge — only the feeling was softer and more welcoming.

She'd known immediately that Broclington was where she should be — at least for now. After that, everything had happened so easily that it was like fate had cleared a path for her. A well-located shop, perfect for the expansion of her business, with a good-sized flat above it, had just dropped in price, bringing it easily within her budget. With a bit of love and attention, it would be an ideal home. Bramble turning up, almost as soon as she'd thought about opening her heart to another cat, seemed like another perfect omen.

She was pretty sure that Broclington was a place where she could be happy.

The sound of footsteps coming closer pulled her back into the present. Imogen knew who it was before she saw her, and sat up, grinning. 'Third unexpected meeting in a week. Some people in this situation might ask if you were following me.'

* * *

There was enough light from the moon for her to see, but Kim recognised the voice instantly. For the first time since she'd finished reading her nieces' umpteenth bedtime story, her smile didn't feel forced or fake. 'Or maybe you're following me.'

'How do you figure that? I was here first.' Imogen's voice was teasing. She sat up, tugging her skirt back into position.

'I think I beat you by quite a lot of years. This has always been one of my favourite spots.'

'Oh, now I feel like an interloper.' Imogen apologised as she pulled on her jumper. 'I can move if you want — if you came here looking for peace and quiet. I wouldn't want to deprive you of that.'

'No. I don't really know what I was looking for, but I'm happy to share this spot if you are.' Kim hoped Imogen would stay. Something about this woman just made her smile.

'Thank you. Well, as I'm trespassing, can I make it up to you with the offer of mead?' Imogen held up a bottle that glinted amber in the moonlight.

'Sure. It's alcoholic, right?' Kim squinted.

'Definitely. This one's got more of a kick than wine, but less than most spirits. It's honeyed and spicy.'

'Sounds good.'

'Unfortunately, I didn't think to bring cups. Do you mind sharing?'

'Doesn't bother me.'

'Good. Because it sounds like you could use a drink, if that's not too cheeky of me.'

'I don't mind cheeky.' Kim shoved her hands into her pockets. 'Besides, you're right.' When Imogen didn't answer, she ploughed on, wanting to fill the silence. 'It's silly. Nothing major, not like we've had an argument or anything, it's just family can get a bit much, you know? I just needed to get out of there for a bit. To escape.'

'To your favourite spot?'

'Yeah.'

'Well, you might as well get comfy then. It is your spot.' Imogen gathered up her crystals, shuffling them and herself over on the blanket.

'You're sure I'm not disturbing you?' Kim worried as she looked around. 'I mean, obviously I am . . .'

'You're not. I'm just waiting. And moonbathing. Come and sit.'

'Thanks.' Kim settled next to Imogen, mirroring her position, stretching her legs out in front of her. 'You know I'm going to have to ask. I'm too curious not to.'

'Go for it.' The smile in Imogen's voice was clear.

'What are you waiting for, and what is moonbathing?'

'Well, moonbathing is just like sunbathing, only at night.' Imogen made it sound so obvious and matter-of-fact that Kim almost felt silly asking her next question. So much so that she wasn't sure she wanted to.

'It's OK to ask, you know. I've always believed the only really silly questions are the ones you don't ask.'

Kim could feel Imogen's eyes on her. She'd never really understood that phrase, about feeling the weight of someone's gaze, until that moment — but she thought she liked the feeling. 'How did you know I wanted to ask something else?'

'I don't know. A feeling in the air. An air of anticipation, I suppose. What else do you want to know?'

'Is moonbathing really a thing?'

'Of course! You could try it and see for yourself. Take a drink, sit back and relax.'

'Sure. Why not?' Kim took a swig from the bottle and was immediately hit by the heady mix of honey and florals. 'Wow, it's like Summer in a bottle.'

'Yeah, with a good helping of alcohol.' Imogen giggled as she took it back.

'So . . . what are you waiting for?'

'Something magical, and really rare. Which probably won't happen, but I'm hopeful that it *might*. I have a good feeling that it will.'

'Now you have to tell me!' Kim looked over to Imogen, who had stretched out next to her.

'I'm hoping for a moonbow.' She handed the bottle back to Kim.

'A what?'

'It's like a rainbow, but it's formed by the moon's rays instead of the sun's. And you need a combination of factors

22

to all come together at the same time, under the perfect conditions.'

'Which are?'

'You need a clear dark night, in a location away from light pollution. The moon needs to be full — or close to full. Ideally you want one of the points in the year where the moon is closest in its orbit to Earth. And it needs to be the right time — a couple of hours after sunset or before sunrise — and when the moon is low in the sky, less than forty-two degrees.'

'Wow.' Kim was fascinated.

'You also need water in the air, but not so much that it obscures the moon, like rain clouds would.'

'And all of those things are happening tonight?'

'Yeah, or at least most of them are.'

'You know a lot about this.' Kim handed her back the mead.

'I love this sort of thing,' Imogen admitted. 'And I've been wanting to see one for years.'

'You've never seen one? How rare are they?'

'At least ten times rarer than a solar rainbow. And lunar rainbows are rarer in some countries and latitudes than others.'

Kim laughed, then took another drink as the bottle came her way. 'And I'm guessing the UK is one of those unlucky places?'

'Of course it is.' She laughed. 'I've only seen one before. And that was when the moon was higher, so it was quite faint. But I've got a really good feeling about tonight, and it would be so perfect if we saw it.'

Kim smiled at that, liking how Imogen had automatically included her. 'Why is tonight so perfect?'

Imogen leaned closer to her, her arm pressing warmly against Kim's, as she pointed through the tree branches. 'Because that, up there, is the Mead Moon. The full moon closest to the Summer solstice . . . which just so happens to be tomorrow.'

'And that's important?'

'It is if you believe in things like energy healing.' She twisted to look at Kim.

For a second, Kim missed her touch. 'Which you do.'

'Yes, very much so.'

Kim took another swig. 'Thanks. This is really delicious, by the way.'

'I've always liked mead. You can see why they've made it for thousands of years.'

'Yeah. Will you tell me about it?'

'What, mead?'

'No.' She handed the bottle back, twisting to face Imogen. 'The energy thing.'

'You really want to know? Some people find it a bit . . . out there.'

'I don't mind things that are a bit "out there". The moonbow thing is really interesting.'

'I think so. And I certainly find it interesting. I'd have to, to have studied it for years.' She must have seen the face Kim pulled. 'But the short version is that everything and everyone are all basically made of the same energy and matter — the same atoms and electricity that make up you and me, the tree we're sitting under, the air we're breathing, the mead we're drinking, even the moon we're sitting under — it's all the same. And a lot of cultures believe similar. Whether it's yogis from South Asia, reiki practitioners, faith healers, witches and pagans, voodoo priests or countless others around the world, many of their core beliefs are very similar. That magic, or rituals, or energy, or a combination of them all, can be used to affect or change things or people.'

'So you're saying spells and stuff like that really work? That magic is real?'

'Yes, I think so. But maybe not quite in the way that fairy tales would have us believe.'

'So what way is there, then?'

'Well, think about Broclington. I know I'm new here, but Ryan's told me a lot of stories about this village. And it does have a nice feeling. There are some strong ley lines running through here.'

'Ley lines?'

'Energy lines.' Imogen's explanation sounded like it made sense to her, but didn't really help Kim understand. 'Haven't you ever noticed how many strange things, how many coincidences, happen here? How often things seem to work out just the way they're supposed to? Sometimes in ways that shouldn't really work, that probably wouldn't anywhere else?'

'Maybe . . .' Kim nodded slowly, thinking about all the times that exact thing had happened. 'So do you think we should read anything into the fact that this is the third time we've bumped into each other in a week?'

'In a place like Broclington, on a night like this . . . I think it's probably just a bit of coincidental magic.'

'Coincidental magic,' Kim mused aloud. 'I like that. Do you really think your "coincidental magic" means we'll get lucky and see this super rare midnight rainbow?'

'Midnight rainbows? That's a nice turn of phrase.'

'Thanks.' Kim laughed. 'I do try. So what do you think?'

'Maybe.' Imogen drummed her fingers on the bottle before taking a swig and offering it back to Kim. 'I know I have a better chance sitting here with you — sharing honey wine — than I would at home. All in all, I think I'd rather be here.'

'I guess that's true.' Kim looked at Imogen as she handed back the bottle. Even in the semi-darkness, those molten chocolate eyes found hers, and Imogen smiled, sending a weird shockwave through Kim. The moonlight painted her skin luminescent, throwing her features into stark relief. She really was stunning. Kim shook her head, wondering where such an odd thought had come from. Maybe there truly was some strange magic at work.

'Besides,' Imogen added, her eyes sparkling, 'I'm having fun with you.'

'Yeah, me too,' she replied honestly. 'This evening has turned out a lot better than I'd expected.'

* * *

Imogen gasped with laughter, trying to catch her breath as Kim finished telling the story about how she'd dressed up as a fairy one Christmas, then somehow convinced her brothers to help her "fly" off the shed roof, using nothing more than looped-up washing line, an old hammock and sheer childish ingenuity, so she could spread fairy dust everywhere.

'You're lucky you didn't hurt yourself!'

'I broke my arm.' She leaned closer to Imogen, treating her to that sweet honey-apple scent. 'Look. You can still see the scar.'

'Ouch.' She winced in sympathy. 'How old were you?'

'Five or six. I think that was the closest Mum ever came to actually bashing my brothers' heads together — though she threatened it often enough!'

'My mum used to say the same about me and Ryan.' She sighed, swallowing back the sadness that still flooded her when she thought of her mum and dad. 'It's nice you're still close with your parents.'

'You're not?'

Imogen shrugged, not really wanting to ruin what was otherwise a good evening. 'Not so much. You know how some families are . . . they just drift a bit.'

'That's kinda sad still. I mean, my family drive me up the wall at times, but I still wouldn't change them. Most of the time.' She rolled her eyes. 'That said, I'm not sure how much longer I want to work for Jake — I'm losing the will to live a bit.' She clapped her hand across her mouth. 'Sorry, forget I said that.'

'It's fine.' Imogen chuckled. 'I'm not going to tell on you. You can trust me.'

Kim studied Imogen for a few moments. 'You know what? I really believe you when you say that. It's weird. We've known each other for less than a week and . . .' she twisted her wrist to peer at her watch '. . . a few hours total, including the time we've been sitting here tonight. But I feel like I've known you for years. Is that as stupid and cheesy as I think it is? I've drunk too much.'

'No, I feel it too.' Imogen was quite glad Kim had said it. 'Like we could carry on talking for the rest of the year and still not run out of things to say — but at the same time, it's like I already know you.'

'Exactly. Weird.'

'I'm fairly used to "weird".' Imogen giggled.

'Yeah, I suppose you would be,' Kim agreed. 'But I think it's cool.'

'Me too.' Imogen sighed. 'But I have to admit, I'm starting to get a bit cold.' And that was something she needed to avoid, otherwise she'd really pay for it tomorrow. It was annoying that even in midsummer she had to stop and think about things like that. But she counted her blessings — there were a lot of people with similar conditions who were far worse off. At least she could manage hers most of the time. Shaking off the grumps, she reached for her bag and pulled out a blanket.

'Any chance you feel like sharing that too?' Kim grinned.

Imogen hesitated. 'You want to cuddle up?'

'Well, we've already shared spit.'

'Thank you for that lovely image, Kimberly.' Her arch tone sent the other woman into a fit of giggles.

'Sorry.' Kim couldn't stop giggling. 'That mead's stronger than I thought, and it went down way too easily.' She shifted closer to Imogen. 'You know, if you were a guy, I'd be a bit suspicious you were trying it on. What with the romantic setting, moonlight and alcohol, cuddling up with blankets.'

Imogen laughed, but edged away, a little unsure of how Kim was going to respond to what she was about to say. Kim certainly hadn't said or done anything to suggest it was going to bother her — but if experience had taught Imogen anything, it was that you could never entirely tell how someone was going to react until it was too late. She'd hate to ruin a new friendship, but it didn't feel fair to not tell her. 'Kim, I'm not the type of person who'd take advantage of someone when they're drunk — it's definitely not my style. But I do think you should know I'm gay.'

27

'Oh.' Kim hesitated for a second or two — which felt far, far longer to Imogen — before nodding and reaching for the corner of the blanket. 'But we can still share this, right? I mean, I know I'm hot — probably close to irresistible — but I'm sure you can manage, can't you? To resist me, I mean.'

Imogen stared at her wordlessly, not having a clue how to react. Of all the responses she might have guessed at, that was nowhere near the top ten.

'Gotcha!' Kim cracked up laughing. 'You looked so serious I thought you were going to tell me something terrible. Like you were into bestiality or something, in which case — me being a veterinary receptionist — I'd probably have to report you to the NSPCA or whatever.'

Imogen stared at her for a few moments, her brain working. 'Do you mean the RSPCA?'

'I never said I was a good vet receptionist. Anyway—' Kim pulled the blanket around her shoulders, pulling them closer together '—you said you don't feel up drunk chicks. So it sounds like I only need to keep an eye on you when I'm sober.'

Imogen finally cracked up too. 'You, Kimberley Macpearson, are absolutely terrible!'

'And now you know why my parents have grey hair. And why my brothers despair of me. Seriously though, thank you for trusting me enough to tell me. I get the feeling you were expecting me to react differently?'

'Not expecting, really, but . . .'

'But in the past it's not always gone well?'

'Yeah, that's pretty fair to say.'

'I'm sorry some people are such arses.'

'Yeah, me too. Thanks for not being one of them.'

She felt Kim shrug next to her. 'No worries. I've never been much of the arsey type. Now bitchy, on the other hand, I can pull off really well.'

'I don't believe it for a second.'

'Oh, you should.' Kim grinned mischievously. 'When I'm pissed off, I can have a really nasty streak. You don't want to know what I did to get back at my ex.'

Imogen relaxed. 'You realise that now you've said that, I'm obviously going to ask.'

'Well, it may have involved some *creative* storage of food products. Particularly potatoes.'

'Potatoes?'

'Yup. Thinly sliced and sewn into the mattress. Potatoes really, *really* stink when they go off. And they're cheaper than prawns. And vegan. He claimed to be really, really big on being vegan. And I believed him, right up to the point where I walked into our bedroom and found him eating cream. In the bed I paid for too.'

'I'm guessing it wasn't vegan cream, was it? And I'm guessing not from a bowl.'

'You would be right. Up until that point, I'd thought *she* was a friend. And that he loved me.'

'I'm so sorry.' Imogen squeezed Kim's hand beneath the blanket.

'Honestly, I'm over it now, but at the time I'm not sure what annoyed me most. The fact that I'd been duped by both of them, the fact that it was my favourite bedding, or the fact that I'd gone vegan for him for six whole months.'

'Wow. I don't think I'd give up eggs for anyone. I make a mean soft poached egg on toast. With garlicky mushrooms on the side, it's pretty much the perfect lazy breakfast.'

'I'll see your poached eggs—' Kim grinned '—and raise you with eggy bread, served with cherries, cinnamon and chocolate sauce.'

'Oh, wow. Dessert for breakfast. That sounds so good.'

'It really is.'

'So eggy-bread deprivation led to you sewing sliced potatoes into your old mattress?' When Kim blushed, Imogen laughed.

'And the pillowcases. And curtain hems. If it hadn't been a rented place and unfair to the landlord I'd have stuffed them under the floorboards too. But the stuff we'd bought? That seemed fair game. And there may have been some creative recycling of some clothes . . . Particularly the football shirts.' Kim buried her face in her hands.

'You are absolutely brilliant,' Imogen told her. 'So what do you do when you're not being a bad receptionist or creatively storing potatoes?'

'I'm already regretting telling you that!'

Imogen nudged her, laughing. 'If you can tease me about being gay — which I'm not sure is politically correct, by the way — I can definitely tease you about your troublesome tuber storage!' She tugged Kim's hands away from her face. 'But seriously, you know what I do for a living. What about you? What do you want to do?'

'I know you're a complementary therapist who is setting up a shop. I have a lot more questions about that still. It sounds fascinating.'

Imogen rested her elbow on her knee, staring at Kim. 'What?'

'Just wondering why you'll happily tell me about how you "recycled" your ex's football shirts, but are cagey over what seems like a pretty standard question.'

'Are you psychoanalysing me?'

'Wouldn't know how, beyond online personality quizzes. I'm a physiotherapist, Kim, and the complementary work I do is alongside that. I'm not a psychiatrist or anything like that. I'm much more likely to crack open a bottle of wine and talk stuff out than try to counsel someone.'

'Or mead?'

'Nah, that's for special occasions. But you're still avoiding the question, which makes it even more intriguing.'

'I'm not really avoiding it. I just don't have an answer. I've been temping. You know, offices, shops, bars and the like. Not exactly big plan stuff.'

'Well, what do you want to do?'

'Promise not to laugh?'

'I promise not to laugh any more than I did at improperly stored potatoes, or the image of you flying off a roof in a hammock. How's that?'

'OK, I guess.' She took a deep breath, making Imogen wonder why she seemed so nervous. 'I want to do something artistic and creative, and just make beautiful things.'

'I don't know why you'd think I'd laugh at that.' Imogen felt genuinely confused. 'It sounds like a lovely idea to me.'

'That's just it.' Kim sighed hugely. 'All it's ever been is "a nice idea". People don't really make money from that — not real, normal people, anyway. Or if they do, it's not enough to live on. It's just such a silly, shallow thing.'

'Why would you say that?'

'It's hardly like it compares to other jobs, does it? I mean, it's not like saving lives or something.'

'You know not everyone does that, right?' Imogen replied gently.

'My mum and dad run the GP surgery in the village — that is, when they're not in some war-torn, drought-ridden or otherwise struggling part of the world, helping build hospitals and clinics.'

'Well, that's their choice and their lives. I don't think that means your dreams are any less important or worthwhile.'

'Then there's my brothers. Callum runs the surgery when Mum and Dad are away, and he'll be taking it over. He's engaged to Liv — another doctor — and between them they're pretty much turning the way community healthcare works on its head.'

'Yeah, I might be aware of their work.' Imogen nodded carefully, not wanting to emphasise that the local focus on community support and care was one of the things that had helped her decide on setting up in Broclington.

'And you've already met Jake. Badger's Hospital is his, by the way. He doesn't just work there. He owns it. And Evelyn, his fiancée, is a community nurse. And then there's me. Yet another screwed-up relationship to add to my tally, and back living in my childhood bedroom, while probably messing up all of Jake's filing systems in a job I'm pretty sure our mum made him offer me.' She pulled her knees up and rested her

31

head on them. 'It's a lot to live up to. And most of the time I feel like I'm falling pretty short.'

* * *

Kim didn't look up, not wanting to see the look of disappointment on Imogen's face. She was so used to seeing it from her family — and hearing the phrases about "Kim and her different paths" and "Kim trying to find herself" — that she should be used to it, but she really didn't want to see that look from Imogen. So she didn't notice the other woman move until she had already wrapped her arms around her, hugging her hard.

The gesture was so surprising, and so sweet, that for a moment it brought a lump to her throat. 'So, this is what not being groped by you feels like?'

'Shut up.' Imogen giggled and gave her another squeeze before gently releasing her.

'You're stronger than you look, you know.'

'Told you I trained as a physio. Got to be pretty strong when you're supporting a whole patient's weight. And I think you're completely wrong about art and creativity not being important. Beauty and colour is important in life too. I wouldn't want to live in a world that is only clinical and sparse and plain. I did that for many years, working in hospitals and traditional clinics, and I feel much happier and healthier with colour and light in my life. I think it's hugely undervalued, and I envy people who understand it and make it work.'

'How do you mean?'

'I just don't really seem to have any sense for it. Like, right now, I've spent weeks planning the shop, my consulting room and working on the flat above it, and turning it into a home. I even adopted a cat!' She laughed, making Kim smile. 'But I still haven't managed to pick my paint colours or wallpapers, or anything other than some cushions and curtains. And I'm not even totally convinced they look any good.'

'What's the problem then? You just match things to what you've got.'

'That *is* the problem.' Imogen shrugged. 'I've been trying to pick my paint colours for over a week. I know what I want, and the feeling I want to create, but I just don't know how that translates to colours and patterns and stuff.'

'I could help you.' Kim made the offer without thinking.

'Really? That would be amazing.' Imogen looked delighted.

'I'm not doing much tomorrow. I'm only part-time with Jake. I could stop by in the morning?'

'Is there any chance that could be later in the morning? Given that it's already close to midnight. I can throw in brunch, if it helps swing your decision at all. My famous poached eggs?'

'You know I'm not going to say no to that,' Kim teased. 'Guess you really do know what girls like.'

'You'd hope so. I'd be a fairly rubbish lesbian if I couldn't please a woman.' The look she gave Kim was so frank that she couldn't stop the very unladylike snort of laughter from escaping.

'Now who's being cheeky?'

'What? You can make jokes about it but I can't? That's just hypocritical.'

'Do you want my help or not?'

'Yes please. Sorry.' Imogen managed to look contrite for all of three seconds.

Kim laughed again. 'It's OK. Probably my fault, anyway. I'm a bad influence.'

'Hey, that's my friend you're bad-mouthing. Stop it,' Imogen scolded.

Kim was so touched that Imogen felt that way — for a moment she didn't know what to say. She grinned, then froze as something caught her eye. She grabbed Imogen's hand. 'Oh my God, is that what I think it is?'

'Yeah.' Imogen's voice was hushed as she looked up. 'Wow.'

'A midnight rainbow over our little village. Just magical.' Kim stared up at the pastel, almost ghostly rainbow that glowed across the sky and among the stars, encircling the moon and stretching out over Broclington.

'It's so bright,' Imogen whispered, her hand tight around Kim's. 'Almost like it's made of crystal. It's perfect.'

'Beautiful.'

CHAPTER THREE

Imogen woke up as she usually did — slowly and reluctantly, and feeling slightly apprehensive. She started cautiously, wriggling her fingers — they were a little stiff, but not too bad. Hands and wrists came next, and they behaved well. She forced her eyes open, grateful not to be greeted with a stab of pain that often accompanied the bright morning light. She wriggled her toes and rotated her ankles gingerly, and was relieved when nothing grated or hurt. Slowly raising her knees, she winced slightly as her lower back gave a warning tug. Not great, but not dreadful either. She rolled her shoulders, arched her back and let her ribs expand in a deep yawn. There was definitely some stiffness on her left side, and the usual tenderness in her sacroiliac joint, but nothing that some heat, stretching and maybe some targeted vibration therapy shouldn't sort pretty easily. She might be a bit slower than usual today, but she'd still be OK to get on with everything.

Her assessment completed, and the results a lot better than she expected, she flopped back into her pillows, grinning to herself. She'd been careless the night before, not avoiding triggers as she usually did, and drinking way more than she'd planned. But she'd enjoyed every single minute, and finally seen a good, bright moonbow — or midnight rainbow, as Kim put it.

Thinking of Kim made her smile again. She'd come away from the evening, which had ended so late that it was technically early morning, with a new friend, and one who was going to help her out with her decorating dilemmas. Definitely not a bad start to midsummer, the rest of the year or her life here in Broclington.

She'd been bouncing around, picking up locum physio jobs, short-term contracts and similarly short rentals for so long that she'd almost forgotten how nice it could be to stay in one place. And the village Ryan had found had such good energy, an almost magical feel to it, that it felt like she was being urged to stop and put down some roots.

As much as she was tempted to stay in bed and nurse her aches while daydreaming, she knew that wouldn't get things done, and there was plenty that she wanted to do to celebrate the day. She'd already missed sunrise — which she usually would have tried to greet, but that was the sacrifice and pay-off for last night, and she didn't mind that much. There would be plenty more midsummer sunrises, many, many more than there would be lunar rainbows. Or first nights with new friends.

As tired as she was, it was one of the best possible days of the year to reflect on everything she'd achieved so far, to spend some time being grateful, and refocus her energies on her goals for the coming months. And she had a lot of them, so every bit of extra help was going to be incredibly valuable to her in the coming weeks and months.

One more deep breath, and she shoved back the heavy covers and swung her legs round. She winced, and slowly lowered her feet to the floor, guarding her back against more pain, but if she didn't move and work through the ache, she'd seize up. It was a careful balancing act between causing herself more pain and using up her energy too quickly, and actually doing everything she needed and wanted. It was going to hurt — there was no way to escape that fact, but it would only be brief, and it wasn't causing any actual damage, and it would ease.

And there was tea waiting to be made, and tea made most things better. It was just the few minutes between the moment she rolled out of bed and the tea being ready that could really, really suck. She gave herself a mental shake, stuffed her feet into her slippers, and dragged a baggy shirt over her head.

Mercifully, the usual rule about watching pots boil didn't seem to slow down the kettle from its steaming, wakeful chortling, and she was soon able to sit, sipping caffeine, letting the heat soak into her hands and ease the ache in her fingers. She grinned when Bramble stumbled into the kitchen and head-butted her feet sleepily before curling up on her slippers. In a little while he'd wake up and be bouncing around like a stripy little pinball, looking for mischief, but at least he seemed to take as long as she did to wake up. The perfect little furball for her lifestyle and needs.

He stayed there, quietly purring against her ankles, while she finished her tea. When she was finished, she started her stretches — easing the stiffness out of her hands, then her back. After a few more minutes she leaned down and scooped him up, tickling him under the chin. 'Hello, sweetie. Shall we get you your breakfast?' He chirruped at her and pressed his nose against hers. 'You really are the perfect little gift from the universe.'

He chirped in agreement before pawing at her, wanting to be put back on the floor. 'Yes, yes, you're awake and ready for your breakfast. And while Prince Bramble enjoys his stinky turkey and salmon casserole, his loyal servant — *moi* — will be going to shower, put on some clothes, and then head out to pick some midsummer herbs and find some flowers. Then you can help me unpack the rest of my crystals, and bathe them in sunlight. It is midsummer, after all. That might not mean much in the feline world, but it does in mine. And then—' she smiled as she put his dish down '—Kim, who you met at the vet's, is coming to visit.'

She didn't really know why she talked to him so much, except that it seemed rude not to explain to him what would happen in his life each day, and he seemed to like listening. Or, at least, he didn't object too loudly, and he hadn't yet mastered the disdainful stare and walk off that so many cats did. But then again, he was young — he probably would before too long.

* * *

Kim paused at the shop door, running her fingers through her hair before straightening her top, then knocked loudly.

'Come on in, it's open.'

She pushed the door, and couldn't suppress her surprised gasp.

'I know, sorry, it's a terrible mess. You must think I'm an awful hostess. I didn't forget, I promise . . . I just lost track of time, and had forgotten how much longer some things take with a kitten who wants to "help" with everything.'

'No, it's not that.' Kim looked down to where Imogen was sat on the floor, surrounded by a chaotic mix of plants, flowers, crystals and bubble wrap. 'It's just . . . this place is amazing. It must have been years since I've been in here, but I always remember it as being quite dark and dusty, and . . . well, a bit dingy.'

'Yeah, I've been getting a bit of work done.' Imogen shrugged.

'A bit of work?' Kim looked around the bright, airy space, taking in the light from the huge window, the way it played with the wrought-iron, ivy-patterned banister, which spanned the staircase up to the second floor. 'I don't think I even knew that staircase was there — it's beautiful.'

'Isn't it?' Imogen grinned, and Kim couldn't help but think what a beautiful smile she had. 'This was all partitioned off into storage and an office, which didn't help with the "dusty, dingy" feel that you mentioned, but it was all just plasterboard really, and I got permission to take it all down as part of the lease agreement. So long as I don't do anything to the actual building, I've got pretty much carte blanche to do whatever I want.'

'That's brilliant. I can't believe you've done all this in a month.'

'I've had plenty of help. I bullied Ryan, and the landlord had a list of contractors ready almost as soon as I'd signed the lease. I think they were pretty glad to get a tenant in here. I was quite surprised to hear the last two leases fell through. It seems well-positioned enough to me.'

'Maybe it was waiting for you.' Kim wasn't sure where the words came from, and immediately felt a bit silly, until Imogen treated her to another stunning smile.

'Maybe it was.'

'What was it you called it? Coincidental magic?'

'Yeah. Or maybe a bit of fate, lining everything up so it happens just as it should.'

'Do you think that's really a thing? That it's true of everything?' Kim liked the idea that a lot of the bad things that had happened to her might be for a bigger reason.

'I think sometimes things seem to work that way.' She stretched and stood, and for a moment Kim thought she winced, but before she could ask the smile was back in place. 'Hey, do you want a tour?'

'Yeah, that'd be good. Then you can tell me a bit about what it is you want to achieve, and where you're struggling, and hopefully we can figure something out?'

'Perfect. Then maybe we can talk over brunch, and you can pretend you haven't just walked into chaos. I promise the kitchen is much more organised. Poached eggs, wasn't it?'

'Yes please.' She grinned, pleased that Imogen had bothered to remember. 'And copious amounts of tea.'

'A woman after my own heart.' Imogen grinned back at her.

'So we're not going to drink tea out of delicate porcelain cups before you read my fortune in the leaves?'

Imogen snorted with laughter. 'Tea leaves? I don't have time for that! It's great big, steaming mugs made from respectable tea bags around here. Unless you want some of my herbal, non-caffeinated blends. Sorry if that disappoints you.'

'Not in the least.' Kim was still grinning. 'I'm just starting to discover winding you up is good fun.'

'Do you really think that's wise? For all you know, if you annoy me, I might rain down curses and conjure monsters to chase you.'

This time it was Kim who snorted with laughter.

'You think I'm funny?'

'Yeah,' she told her honestly. 'And I think the biggest danger I'm in around you is probably from overtiredness and hangovers, if last night is anything to go by.'

'I didn't give you a hangover, did I? I've got some tea that will help with that if I did.'

'No, I'm fine,' Kim reassured the other woman. 'But I also suspect if we'd had more bottles with us they'd have gone the same way as the first.'

'Maybe true.'

'Erm . . . you don't actually conjure monsters in here, do you?' Movement behind Imogen had caught Kim's eye. 'Only your bubble wrap appears to be alive.'

Imogen dove on the supernaturally active plastic. 'There you are. I thought you were in the kitchen asleep.' She pulled out the very unsleepy-looking kitten. 'Come say "hi" to Kim. She's going to help me make your home look pretty.' She struggled back to her feet, hampered by the wriggling cat. 'Nope, I'm not leaving you here by yourself. Too many of my plants would be bad for your tummy. And as nice as Kim and her brother are, we don't want to make a habit of visiting them at work, do we?'

'No, I'd much rather visit you here.' Kim leaned forward to tickle the kitten under the chin, breathing in the sweet smell of coconut and something flowery from Imogen's hair. It was only after a couple of seconds she realised what she'd said. 'Um . . . I mean I wouldn't want to see Bramble at Badger's Hospital because he was ill or hurt. Obviously.'

'Obviously.' Imogen nodded. 'But he's back in soon for his boosters, and to check his weight again. Anyway, come along Prince Bramble. Let's give Kim a tour of your castle and realm.'

Kim followed, playing along. The poor little stray definitely deserved some royal treatment. 'Ask his highness if this serf might be permitted to photograph his royal palace. I've got my tablet with me, so can do some live mock-ups if you like.'

'Oh wow, that would be brilliant. I thought I'd just show you the place and some paint catalogues, and you'd tell me which ideas were silly or not. I didn't expect digital mock-ups.'

'Well, you said you struggled with visualising things. I thought this might make it easier . . .' She hesitated, wondering if she'd overstepped the mark.

'It really will. Thank you so much for thinking of it.'

'It's not a problem. I like stuff like this. And, if you like my suggestions, it could be kind of cool seeing it come to life.'

'Make sure you save the pictures from today then, so we have before-and-after shots.'

'You might not even like my ideas.' Kim didn't know why she was arguing.

'I have a feeling I'm going to love them.'

'No pressure then.'

'No.' Imogen's eyes locked with hers. 'None at all. Just a feeling. Besides, you said you feel like you've known me for years already. Who better to help me design this place? I can't exactly ask Ryan. His apartment was fifty shades of beige before he had to soundproof it against Mallow.'

'Feeling like that, and actually knowing what you'll like, are two very different things.' Kim was already feeling the pressure starting to build.

'Kim, it's fine. You're just giving me some advice, and maybe showing me some ideas.' She squeezed her arm. 'Honestly, I consider this a huge favour, which I'm really grateful for. It'll be fine. Whatever you come up with is going to be perfect, I'm sure.'

Kim wished she had her confidence.

* * *

'Go on, say it.' Imogen knew Kim was holding back. 'I promise I'm not going to be offended.'

'It's just I'm a bit confused.' Kim pushed away her plate and reached for her tablet. 'You said you wanted to go for something peaceful and calming, but uplifting?'

'Yeah.' Imogen nodded.

'And you seriously think this colour scheme, with this pattern, is the way to achieve that?' She tapped the samples and paint charts Imogen had spread out.

'I told you I wasn't very good at this.' Imogen peered at the silvery blue wallpaper she'd picked, the colours she'd tried to match it with. 'The pattern reminded me of water, and I find that peaceful.'

'I can understand that, but . . .'

'Kim, just tell me.'

'I'm just worried if you put that up the whole double-height of the back wall, it could be a bit overwhelming and . . .'

'And?'

'And that by the time you pair it with the stark white you were planning for the rest of the walls it might look a bit like a swimming pool.' Kim blurted out the words, then ducked her head, letting her hair fall to cover her face as she fiddled with the tablet.

'Swimming pool? I thought white was clean and fresh, and water was soothing.'

'Well, it is, but . . .' She flipped around the tablet. 'Do you see what I mean? It's only a mock up on a generic room, but still . . .'

Imogen stared at the screen for a few seconds before creasing up laughing. 'I mean, I could add some palm trees and seagulls. Maybe even some sand and really go for a beach theme. Then I could sell beach balls, fishing nets and flip-flops.'

'Do you think there would be much call for that in Broclington?' Kim giggled. 'We're more than seventy miles from the coast.'

'Oh well, I guess it's back to the crystals, herbs and witchy-woo healing then.'

'Witchy-woo?'

'You can blame my brother for that one. But I find it kind of funny, so I let him get away with it, and only threaten him with curses every so often.'

'Are you, though? A witch I mean?' Kim's fingers were a blur on the tablet as she worked.

'Do you think I am?' Imogen found herself wanting to know the answer, to understand how the other woman viewed her.

'I don't think you would curse people. Not really. At least, not unless they were really, really bad. I think you're probably too nice for that.' She looked up from the tablet. 'At least that's the feeling I get from you. And I suspect if you could really curse someone, then anyone who pushed you far enough to try it would probably not be someone whose health and happiness I'd be too worried about.'

'You're probably right.' Imogen liked her answer. 'I wouldn't call myself a witch, not really. I certainly don't follow Wicca as a faith. I guess, if I had to pick a label — which I hate doing, by the way — I'd say I'm pagan-ish.'

'Maybe witch-adjacent?' Kim offered.

'Yeah, I'll have to remember that one. I like that.'

'So what does that mean? How did you get into all this?'

'Are you really interested?' Imogen leaned across to grab her mug and refill it.

'Yeah, I am.'

'Well, how I got into it is a much shorter story than trying to explain what it means.'

'Then start there.' Kim smiled as she accepted the fresh drink. 'If you don't mind talking to me while I play with your designs.'

'How could I possibly mind when you're doing me a massive favour?'

Kim smiled. 'Go on, talk to me.'

'In short, it was desperation.' Imogen wrapped her hands around her mug, trying to find the words to explain. They

42

didn't come any more easily when Kim stopped tapping at the tablet to look up at her, her bright blue eyes filled with compassion.

'If it's hard for you to talk about, tell me to butt out. I promise not to be offended.'

'No, it's all right.' Imogen tucked her hair behind her ears. 'I'd just finished my first year out of university as a physio when I started showing symptoms, but they were fairly easy to ignore at first, because they were so non-specific. Aching in the joints, general muscle pain, fatigue, mild digestive issues, minor skin irritations. Nothing that couldn't easily be put down to stress, or sequelae — long-term side effects — from one of the many infections you get exposed to when you're a student working in a healthcare setting.'

'But it was more than that.' Kim's gaze still hadn't left hers. 'Are you better now?'

'Yeah, most of the time I am, thank you.' She sighed. 'I have a connective tissue disorder that causes fibromyalgia.'

'I think I've heard of it, but I can't remember what it means. Sorry.'

'Nothing to apologise for.' She gave Kim a quick smile. 'I'm quite glad you don't know about it. It's not something you'd wish on anyone you cared about. Basically, it's a chronic disorder that affects most of the systems in the body. It can cause a range of symptoms, with widespread pain and fatigue being the most common.' It was easier for her to talk as if discussing a patient. 'And with that comes sleep disturbance, decreased balance and poor spatial awareness, and cognitive difficulties like "brain fog" and poor memory.'

'Oh, that sounds awful.' Suddenly Kim's hand was on her arm, warm and soothing. 'You said it's chronic? That means it doesn't really go away, right?'

'Unfortunately not.'

'You poor thing. Are you in pain now?'

Strangely enough, the unrequested sympathy, which would have usually bothered her, wasn't annoying from Kim.

'I'm a little stiff, but not as bad as I might've expected after spending the night in a field, drinking.'

'It was worth it though, wasn't it? To see a midnight ghost rainbow?'

'Yeah.' Imogen's eyes flicked back to where Kim's hand still rested on her skin. 'And to get to know you better.'

'Awww, that's really sweet.' Kim smiled and squeezed her arm. 'But for the record, next time you want to hang out, I'm good with wine in comfy chairs too.'

'Noted for next time.' Imogen couldn't help smiling back.

'Anyway . . .' Kim pulled her hand away and went back to tapping on her tablet. 'You were telling me your story. You got to the bit where you were diagnosed with a fairly shitty-sounding pain illness. But I'm not sure I understand how that links to your witch-adjacent behaviour.'

'Fibromyalgia is notoriously difficult to treat, and while it causes widespread pain, at the same time it doesn't.'

Kim shook her head, not understanding.

'Simply put, pain is usually a warning signal to your body that something is wrong. It's not always the case, like sometimes a headache is just a harmless headache, but more often than not pain is caused by something — like the warning you get if you touch something too hot, or sharp, it hurts and you yank your hand away. So in that way, the pain protects you from getting seriously harmed, or warns you that you are hurt so you get help.'

'Makes sense so far.' Kim nodded, her hair bouncing back and forth over the tablet screen.

'The problem with fibromyalgia is that, quite often, there isn't anything actually wrong, but you're still in pain. So because there's no stimulus for the pain — no sharp or too-hot object, no muscle that you're overworking — there's nothing to take away, and it can be really hard to effectively treat that pain. It often doesn't respond well to standardised analgesia protocols, either.'

'Meaning normal painkillers don't always work?'

'Meaning normal painkillers don't always work.' Imogen nodded. 'And it can become a bit of a downward spiral. You're in pain because your nerves and connective tissues are over-stimulated, but that in itself can cause the over-stimulation, which leads to more pain.'

'Pain that normal painkillers like paracetamol won't work on?'

'Uh huh.'

'Oh, poor you.' Kim looked up again. 'That sounds awful.' Again, the sympathy that would so often put Imogen on the defence didn't bother her this time. Maybe it was because Kim seemed genuinely saddened by the idea she was in pain. The honesty and kindness in her gaze made Imogen feel safer to open up more than she usually would.

'Yeah,' she admitted the thing that usually only people like Ryan knew. 'It can be pretty awful at times. But I'm luckier than a lot of chronic pain patients, because I found things that really work for me.'

'Ah, so this is where your witch-adjacent tendencies and beliefs come in. I'm guessing when conventional, modern medicine couldn't give you the pain relief you needed, you turned to . . . less conventional options?'

'Yeah.' Imogen grinned, glad Kim seemed to understand her. 'Pretty much spot on. I wasn't much more than a year out of uni, so I was still fairly used to the studying thing. My mentor at work was really good, and helped me look at other methods that would help — he was already trained in acupuncture and used it on other patients. Unfortunately that didn't really help me much, but it did open my eyes to the idea that there were a lot of options other than drugs out there, which weren't really working for me. The only ones that did were so heavy-duty that I couldn't take them and function. I couldn't drive, and I certainly couldn't work.'

'So your choice was give up, learn to live with the pain, find something else that worked, or drug yourself out of the career you'd only just started?' Kim watched her, her eyes wide.

'That's right, and I'm too stubborn for giving up or quitting.'

'I'm not sure taking the only painkillers that really worked for you is the same as quitting,' Kim repeated the argument that so many others had offered Imogen over the years. 'But I can understand that, if it wasn't what you wanted, why you'd fight and keep looking for better options. And you found them.'

'Yeah, I really did. A combination of targeted physiotherapy, different medication, emotional support and psychotherapy, and different pain management techniques gathered from all around the world, some more modern, and some rooted in history. Quite often I've found the most effective treatment plans — for chronic pain, at least — work with the body and the mind.'

'Is that like the chicken soup thing?' Kim glanced up from the tablet. 'You know, how scientists discovered a few years ago that chicken soup really can treat a cold?'

'Exactly that.' Imogen nodded, glad she understood. Not everyone did, and she'd had to deal with a lot of professional criticism over the years. 'The food we eat — or don't — can have a really important impact on our wider health. It's all about that holistic, wrap-around approach. And chicken soup is a great example. It has a compound called carnosine, which helps reduce inflammation in the upper respiratory system. You also get cysteine when cooking chicken in soup, which thins mucus. And sodium — salt — in warm liquids has a soothing effect on your throat. I think grandmothers the world over probably rolled their eyes and tutted when science "discovered" what they'd known for generations — that chicken soup helps when you have a cold. And when you start looking at the science behind how some drugs work, and where they come from, there's often a lot of proven treatments for ailments that support and complement more medicalised approaches. Like the gingerols and shogaols in ginger, which are known to help with travel and morning sickness — but without many of the side effects and risks of some pharmacological treatments.'

'That's really cool. So what else is there other than food?'

'All sorts. There's reflexology, acupuncture and Bowen therapy, all of which I'm trained in. And I do love crystal work and reiki too. Then there's things like mindfulness and psychological support, which I can refer people for.'

'How does counselling help with pain?'

It was a question Imogen got asked a lot, usually with different levels of belief, and sometimes anger — but Kim just seemed genuinely curious. 'It goes back to what I was saying about pain being a warning. You're mentally conditioned, for the most part, to avoid pain, or to stop whatever's causing it. To pull your hand out of the fire, whether metaphorical or real. When a person's body is put in a situation where they can't avoid that pain, or do much to stop or treat it, it can be scary. And it can trigger the fight or flight response, and anxiety or depression. Mindfulness and learning to recognise chronic pain as just that — chronic, rather than the panic danger warning — does seem to help some people to cope better with it.'

'Well, I can't say I totally understand it, but I'm glad you figured out what works for you.'

'Me too. And I trained to be able to help others too.'

'That is very cool.' Kim looked up and smiled shyly. 'Do you want to see what I've been working on?'

'Yes, absolutely.'

* * *

Nervously, Kim slid her tablet across the breakfast bar. 'What do you think?'

She tried not to hold her breath, but suddenly the offer that she'd thought was just an easy and friendly gesture had taken on a lot more weight. She really, really wanted Imogen to like her designs. She wasn't sure if it was because it was the first time she'd shared her work with the other woman, or because the shop clearly meant so much to her, or simply because Imogen was a new friend whose opinion was important to Kim. Regardless of the reason, her mouth was dry as Imogen flicked through the sketches she'd created, which now seemed hideously rough and unformed.

Imogen was silent as she stared at the screen, her face hidden by a curtain of curls.

'I mean, they're just rough. Too rough really. I should take them home and finish them off with a bit more time and finesse. They're really just working drafts.' She moved to pull the tablet back.

'No.'

Great. They were so bad Imogen wasn't even interested in seeing them developed into something more. Hot, prickly self-doubt flooded her again, and every bad grade, poor review and unsuccessful show came back in a wave of misery, reminding her exactly why she was back here playing receptionist for her brother. She just wasn't good enough.

'Kim, these are beautiful.' Imogen's voice was hushed, almost reverential.

'You don't have to say that just because I'm sitting right here.'

'I know that. I have to say it because they really are wonderful. You've captured exactly the feeling I wanted, and this—' she traced her finger across the image, not quite touching the screen '—is perfect. Now you've shown it to me, I can't imagine it any other way. Whatever made you think of it?'

'It was what you were saying, about the best approach being one that's holistic, and works with body and mind . . . and what with you being "pagan-ish", I thought a Celtic Tree of Life would be good. It's supposed to bind things together — the living and the after worlds, the conscious and unconscious . . .'

'. . . the mind and body?'

'Well, it's a bit of a tweak to the original symbolism. But, that said, the original Tree of Life would have had ten points. I think the image and symbol has been adopted and changed by so many cultures that the meaning has changed a bit, so it includes a lot of the things I think you might be wanting.'

'Like?' Those dark eyes were locked on her again.

'Like strength, healing, unity, peace and connection.'

'It's perfect.'

'And I thought, if you wanted to play with that image and those ideas a bit more . . .'

'Now you've said that, I do.' Imogen leaned closer, watching as Kim's stylus skipped over the screen quickly, grabbing the tools and colours she needed, setting up the layer before superimposing it across the image and picture she'd snapped of Imogen's main shop space earlier. The picture faded slightly, the background slipping into more muted tones, so the tree seemed brighter and more in focus. A few more clicks and the leaves took on the rainbow hues of early autumn, mixing deep, rich greens with vibrant golds, bronzes, russets, reds, browns and almost purple shades.

'Or something like this?'

'Hmm.' Imogen fiddled with a curl while staring at the screen. 'As an image, I like it. But I think I've always thought the Tree of Life would be green, and you know . . . livelier.'

'Fair enough.' Oddly, the critique from Imogen didn't hurt as much as it might have from another source. 'There was another idea I was half-playing with, but I didn't know if it might be a bit . . . much.'

'Would it take you long to show me?'

'Not really. Just a few minutes.'

'Long enough for me to make you another drink, and grab some more supplies?'

'Perfect.'

A few minutes later, Imogen was back with a basket full of herbs and flowers, and there was another steaming mug in front of Kim.

'No peeking!' Kim laughed, hugging the tablet against her chest as Imogen put down the drink.

'Fine, I'll just sit and pretend being patient is something I'm good at.' She huffed and pulled out a couple of flowers, weaving them together with pale pink ribbon, but when Kim looked up, she was grinning to herself.

Shaking her head, Kim went back to work. She couldn't say why, but she had a feeling Imogen was really going to like this option, so took longer than the few minutes she'd originally planned to make it more than the roughest of ideas. Plus, the slightly wicked part of her was enjoying teasing her new friend. But it was definitely the artistic pride that made her take time to smooth out her colour-blends a little more.

'You're doing it on purpose, aren't you?' Imogen murmured, her fingers still busy weaving and tying.

'What?' Kim widened her eyes as she looked up, completely innocent.

'Taking longer than you said.'

She shook her head, already fighting the smile tugging at the edges of her mouth. 'I don't know what you mean. I'm just wanting to present my ideas nicely. And if that happens to draw out the anticipation a bit . . .'

'Well, not like I can complain too much, especially when you're doing me a favour.'

'You really want to though, don't you?'

'Complain? no. I just want to steal your tablet and see what you're doing. Spare hand please.'

'What?' Kim was unsure what she meant.

'Can I have your spare hand please?' Imogen held hers out.

'Sure.' When her fingers touched Imogen's, for a few seconds tingles spread out across her hand, racing up her fingers and over her palm. Weird. She watched as Imogen tied the flowers and ribbons around her wrist, making her skin tingle there too. 'You made me a bracelet?'

'Yeah. And it might be sort of a little teeny, tiny midsummer spell.'

'You're putting a spell on me?' She wasn't entirely sure how she felt about that.

'Barely. Teeny tiny.' Imogen held her finger and thumb apart with the smallest of gaps. 'More of a good-luck wish than anything. Barely any more power than a wish made over birthday cake candles.'

'Birthday cake wishes can have a lot of power. Especially if you believe in them.'

'True.' Imogen smiled at her. 'Do you mind?'

'No. I don't think so.' She twisted her wrist back and forth, admiring the complex knots that held the plants in place. 'I recognise the lavender and rosemary, but not the yellow one. What's it for?'

'To bring good luck and love in the coming year. Lavender is a traditional herb for attracting love, rosemary is good for sweetness, and clarity, and the yellow is calendula, which has been used since ancient Roman times to help reduce inflammation and detoxify yourself. And without wanting to be rude, with what you told me about your last relationship, I think you're probably due some cleansing and sweetness — at least in the romance department.'

'You're not wrong there.' Kim laughed. 'So it's a good-luck-in-love charm?'

'Yeah. And, because it's midsummer, tradition has it that if you go to bed wearing it, or tuck it under your pillow, you'll see the face of your true love in your dreams.'

'That's a nice idea. Does it really work?'

'You could always try it and find out.' Imogen shrugged. 'Do I get to see your work now?'

'You're really not very patient, are you?'

'Nope. Never claimed to be. Can I see? Please?'

It was the please that did it. 'Of course you can.' She flipped the tablet around to share the image she'd been working on.

'Oh, Kim . . . this is lovely.'

'You really think so?'

51

'Yeah. I really do. So much so that I'm wondering if we can tweak it a bit . . .'

If it was as "lovely" as she claimed, then there wouldn't be any need to "tweak" it, but she kept the thought to herself and politely asked, 'What were you thinking?'

Imogen gave her an odd look. 'Kim, I really do like this. I was just wondering if there was a way you could extend some of the branches into vines or something, then have them weaving around the rest of the shop, all the way to the door, so they sort of catch people to draw them in?'

Kim nodded slowly, understanding. 'I think that could work. And we could maybe do similar with the roots. I wouldn't recommend it on the floor — it can be hard to keep patterns painted on floors without them quickly getting scruffy under people's feet . . . but maybe around the skirting boards, the base of any units you're installing?'

'Oh wow, that could be amazing.' Imogen's enthusiasm was contagious, and Kim could easily understand how she could engage with people in pain and convince them to try new things. 'It'd probably be really cheeky of me to ask if you'd mock that up to show me at some point, wouldn't it?'

'Yeah. It probably would.' Kim didn't know what it was about Imogen, but she really did find it hard to resist teasing her. 'Really, really cheeky in fact. Got any cake?'

'Cake?'

'Yeah. You know. Flour, eggs, butter, sugar . . . other yummy things all mixed up and baked in the oven until it's all fluffy and golden.'

'Oh, that's what they are. Thanks for the explanation.' She rolled her eyes, making Kim giggle. 'No, I don't have any cake. If I did I would have probably eaten it already.'

'Pity. I was open to bribery.'

'I've got chocolate. Would that do?'

'You don't keep cake around because you'd eat it, but you have chocolate.'

'You say that like it's weird.'

'Kind of is to me.' Kim shrugged. 'Chocolate is much harder to resist than cake.'

'Good, so it'll work as bribery then.'

'Yeah, probably.' Kim grinned, knowing that she didn't really need to be bribed, not when she was having fun finding something useful to do with her artwork. And if Imogen really did like what she showed her, enough to implement some of her ideas, then her art would be on display every day. Even if she didn't tell anyone it was hers and it was just a favour for a new friend, she still got a rush at the thought. 'I need to go back down and take some more pictures to superimpose the designs onto.'

'Whatever you need. I'll go grab the chocolate.'

* * *

When Imogen reached her still-to-be-finished shop floor, Kim was sat cross-legged among the chaos of unwrapping, using bubble wrap as a cushion, leaning over her tablet.

'I'm really sorry about the lack of any useful furniture. It's much more a "work in progress" down here than upstairs.'

'It's fine,' Kim reassured her. 'At least the floor here is better than at the vets. Doesn't matter how much disinfectant you use, I can't quite get past how many times it's been pooped, peed and barfed on.'

Imogen laughed, setting the tray on a box before sitting down amongst the chaos.

'Besides, I found myself a cute colleague.' Kim lifted up the tablet to show where Bramble had made himself comfortable between her crossed legs. 'I think we're friends again after his manhandling at the vets.'

'Give him some of these, if you want, and he'll probably love you until the end of time.' Imogen handed over a tin from the tray.

'Oh, yummy.' Kim prised the lid off and pulled a face. 'Fishy biscuits. Who's a lucky kitten?'

'If you ask nicely, he might even share them with you,' Imogen quipped.

'Yeah, I think not. He needs to put on weight anyway. Besides, I was promised chocolate, and that humongous bar happens to be one of my favourites.'

'Really?'

'Yeah, you've got good taste.' She grinned at Imogen. 'Now hand it over before I run out of energy to keep drawing.'

'Yes ma'am.' Imogen did as she was told, then started weaving more herbs and flowers together with different colour ribbons.

'More love spell bracelets?' Kim watched as Imogen's fingers twisted back and forth.

'Only a few. Most are for things like luck, protection, good fortune and similar. Things like the lavender and rosemary will dry and still hold well, even for a few months or more. They're pretty, and don't take a huge amount of effort or skill or cost me a lot to make, so I can give them away.'

'You could have fooled me. Your fingers are practically a blur. I'm pretty sure if I tried that I'd end up tying myself to it.'

'It's just practice.' Imogen smiled. 'And it's more impressive when I can find my crochet wand. I'm quicker with that.'

'Did you say *wand*?' Kim's eyes widened.

'*Crochet* wand. It's just a type of hook. You know, for working with yarn. Angela showed me how to use them, and I have to admit I'm a bit of an addict. She says I picked it up really quickly.'

'Well you would, wouldn't you? Given that you're witch-adjacent and it's a wand, it's pretty obvious you'd be good with it. At least it is to me.'

They worked in easy, companionable quiet, stopping every so often to give into Bramble's begging for more treats, or to snap off a couple more squares of chocolate. They'd eaten more than half the bar, Bramble had dozed off with a full belly, and Imogen had tied three more bracelets and started on posies, when Kim dropped her tablet to her knee and stretched.

'Wanna see?'

'Thought you'd never ask.' Imogen reached for the tablet. 'Oh wow. Kim, these really are lovely. And I love the butterflies you've added.'

'They're not butterflies.'

'They're not?' Imogen flicked her fingers over the screen, zooming in and out. 'No offence, but they look like butterflies.'

'I mean, they could be butterflies, if you want them to be.' Kim smiled. 'But I made one other change. So these are actually moths. Just something I thought of when I was heading down the stairs. Go back to the first image.'

Imogen flicked through the designs and studied the one Kim indicated. She smiled as she stared at the image, taking in new details every moment she looked at it. The tree was still there, but it had dropped lower, sinking more firmly into the ground, while its branches stretched up to the first floor of the building. The background had changed again, and this time the tree stood in semi-twilight, with the sun setting behind the trunk on one side, casting golden light over the scene. At the topmost parts of the tree, the wall darkened to soft blueygrey, and stars were flickering around the edges of the moon. Spanning across it all was a pastel, pale rainbow, which shimmered and glittered with magic, even in the small digital image.

'I mean, it's just an idea. Obviously I saved the original image. It will only take a couple of seconds to revert. It's just a silly idea.' She reached for the tablet again.

'Don't you dare.' Imogen held it out of reach. 'Please, Kim. I'd love to use these designs.'

'Really?'

'Really. Seriously, how do we do this? Do you email them to me along with your bill? Can you recommend anyone who can paint this for me?'

'Well, yeah. Me.' Kim's smile seemed hesitant, almost reluctant.

'I couldn't ask you to do that,' Imogen argued.

'You didn't. I offered. I mean, I can ask around and see who other people recommend locally if you'd be happier . . .'

'I just assumed you'd be too busy. I feel like I've taken up way too much of your time already. But if you're really willing, I'd much rather keep working with you. It's your design, after all. But take some time and think about it, and, if you're serious, then let me know your rates, OK?'

'We're friends, aren't we?' Her question threw Imogen a bit.

'I'd like to think so.'

'Then it's mate's rates. Cover my materials, then it's as much tea as I can drink, a good supply of cakes and biscuits. And maybe pizza if I'm working late.'

'That seems way too low for how good you are. You're under-valuing yourself, Kim.'

'No.' She shook her head. 'I just value your friendship more highly.'

'That's a really sweet thing to say.' Imogen wasn't sure how she was supposed to keep arguing, even though she wanted to.

'You only think that because you haven't heard my biscuit demands yet.'

'Oh, you have demands, do you?'

'Absolutely. Strict ones. None of that cheap supermarket crap, and no fruit ones. Double thickness chocolate dipped ones at the very least.'

'The ones I had from the café the other week were pretty good . . .'

'Even better. Especially if it's their salted caramel shortbread.' This time Kim's grin wasn't at all reluctant. If anything, Imogen thought it looked a bit wicked. 'And I did tell you that you're helping, right?'

'You saw my first idea. The swimming pool-cum-beach-shack look. What makes you think I can paint?'

'If you can load up a brush, slap it on the wall and stay in the lines, you can paint. Even my nieces can do that. I can draw it all out once the base coat is done, and then it'll just be like a big paint-by-numbers.'

'I'm still not sure about this, but I don't really feel like I can say no.'

'No. You can't.' Yeah, there was definitely a touch of wickedness in that look.

CHAPTER FOUR

'See, I told you that you could paint.' Kim stood back, hands on her hips as she studied their handiwork. She'd spent the first day washing the background colour and sky onto the wall at the back of the shop, then the next two evenings sketching the tree and another crawling around the floor, adding the roots to the skirting boards, sketching out templates for the furniture Imogen had given her measurements for.

Imogen had welcomed her warmly and easily, insisting that she made herself at home — joking that she didn't want to be the only one making drinks. And while it had felt a bit strange at first, wandering around someone else's kitchen and helping herself to "whatever she wanted", Kim had quickly felt completely at ease and happy.

For the last few hours, she and Imogen had been working to pick out the branches in shades of brown, with Imogen laying down the base colour and Kim adding in the highlights and shade. Working together, they'd already filled in the trunk and more than half of the branches.

'Like you said, I'm really just slapping it on the wall and trying to stay between the lines. The skill is all yours. It's you bringing it to life.'

'Maybe.' Kim shrugged. 'But it's going a lot faster with both of us working on it.'

'It's looking really good.' Imogen smiled and rubbed her back. 'It's going to be so beautiful.'

'Yeah. Are you doing OK?' Since Imogen had told her about her chronic pain, Kim was a lot more aware of her movements than most of her other friends or her family.

'You don't need to fuss over me.' Imogen shot her a knowing look. 'I'm fine. Just a bit stiff. I'm not about to go into a flare. This is fun, really.'

'You'd tell me if you were struggling? When I get into the zone like this, I can keep going for hours and forget to take proper breaks. And I don't want to . . .' She trailed off, not sure how to finish the thought without sounding patronising.

'You don't want to what, Kim? Force me to keep up with you and drive me into being sick?'

'Well, yeah.' She grimaced.

'Kim, I really appreciate you worrying about me, but you don't need to. I've been dealing with this energy-sucking demon for years. I know its tricks, its battle strategies and I can see its shadows. I know how to avoid letting it get its claws into me. I really am fine.'

'Sorry, I'm being condescending, aren't I?'

'Maybe a little.' Imogen shrugged. 'But I'm pretty sure you're only fussing because you care, so I don't mind too much. But I'm perfectly capable of telling you when I've had enough, OK?'

'You're sure?'

'Yeah. And right now I've had enough of this conversation, because focussing on my condition and the things it stops me from doing just makes me sad. I'm not willing to give it any more control over my life than it already has. Does that make sense?'

'Uh huh. So, basically, "shut up Kim".' She grinned.

'In the politest and nicest possible way I can say that to a friend who's helping me paint a giant tree across my store . . . yes. Shut up, Kim.'

'OK. But you're definitely sure you're OK and want to keep going?'

'Yes.'

'You're sure?'

'Yes, Kim, I'm sure. Is there something else you wanted to ask?'

'Actually, since you mention it, there is.'

'Right.' Imogen tapped the handle of the paint brush against her palm as she stared at Kim, waiting. 'And that would be?'

'What time are you ordering pizza? And do we need to talk about toppings?'

'Workwoman's choice. I'm assuming you can recommend somewhere as well?' She pulled out her phone and opened an app. 'Any of these?'

Kim leaned in to look at the screen. 'First one is pretty far away, so will take a while, if they'll even accept an order for delivery. Second has the best garlic bread, but is more expensive. Third is pretty good.'

'Second it is then. What do you fancy?'

'I'll eat pretty much anything.'

'OK, useful to know. But what would you actually like?'

'Whatever you want will be fine.'

'*OK . . .*' This time Imogen drew out the word. 'But if you were the one ordering, or you were the only one eating this, what would you pick?'

'Ham, red onions, double mushrooms and double cheese. Preferably on sourdough or deep-pan.' As soon as Kim said it, Imogen pulled a face. 'Which bit don't you like?'

'The mushrooms.'

'You don't like mushrooms?' Kim couldn't help but laugh. 'No. Why is that so funny?'

'Well, you're practically a witch. And mushrooms seem quite a witchy thing.'

'I think you're confusing them with toadstools. And I still don't like them. There's something weird about the texture, or the taste . . . I don't know. I just don't like them. Meat feast all the way for me.'

'Really?'

'Well, I'm going to be unhealthy, so I figure I might as well go all in.'

'I can eat meat feast.' It wasn't really her favourite — the spicy, greasy sausage thing wasn't to her taste, but she was more concerned with Imogen being happy.

'Or I can just ask them to do half and half. Is it the flat garlic bread, the dough balls or the twists you like?'

'The twists. With cheese.'

'And warm cookie dough?'

'You really do go all in when you go all in, don't you?'

'I'll take that as a yes.' She confirmed the order via the app and tucked her phone back into her pocket. 'And to answer your question, yes, I do. I don't really do half measures. When there's something I want, I put everything I have into getting it. Doesn't matter if it's a business, a relationship or dinner. I don't mess around.'

Kim smiled. 'That's quite an answer.'

Imogen shrugged. 'I don't have a lot of spare energy, so when I decide to do something I tend to commit completely. I know some people find it a bit full-on, but it's what works for me.'

'I think it's probably a good thing.' Kim collected some more paint on her brush. 'Maybe if I could put that much energy and commitment into something, I'd actually finish some of what I start and achieve something.'

'Maybe you just haven't found anything you think is worth that much of you yet.'

'Maybe.' Kim wasn't convinced. 'Or maybe my family are right.'

'How do you mean?'

Kim focussed on adding the curve into one of the branches Imogen had already blocked in. It was easier to talk about it when she didn't have to look at her. 'I'm one of those people who like to "try on a lot of different hats". That's how my mum puts it, on a good day. On a bad day I'm "worryingly indecisive". Dad just calls me a flibbertigibbet because I never really seem to settle on any one thing for very long. When I was younger, Jake and Cal would call me Bee . . . because I was always buzzing around from one thing to the next. I tend to be the type of person who does a lot of temp work. Usually in different places and different fields.'

'I suppose it could be a good thing to have lots of skills and interests.' Imogen's response seemed overly polite.

'Yeah, or jack of all trades and master of none. Depending on how you look at it. I'm not too great at the whole relationship thing either. I just seem to not have much luck in settling down the way most people do, and in a family full of ambitious people I stick out like a sore thumb. I've had more jobs in the last year than most people probably have in a lifetime.'

'I don't think there's anything wrong with not wanting to settle,' Imogen murmured quietly. 'I certainly don't intend on "settling down" with anyone less than my perfect, dream woman.'

'And that's what you're looking for, is it? Your perfect woman to whisk you off your feet?'

'I don't mind doing some of the whisking.' Imogen laughed as she painted in another branch. 'But yeah, I've done the short-term thing, and I'm hoping the next woman I meet will be more than that. I mean, don't get me wrong — I've had plenty of fun with "Miss Right For Now" and "Miss Bad But Oh-So-Good", but now I think, if I'm going to invest my energy in a relationship, I want it to be one that has the potential to be something serious.'

'Fair enough.'

'What about you?'

'I don't know,' Kim answered honestly. 'I'm not sure I've ever met anyone who I thought I could be that serious with. I mean, I'd like to . . . I think. I see what Cal and Jake have found, and the families they're creating, and I think I'd like that one day. But given my recent history that seems a bit of a pipe dream.'

'Hey, that reminds me . . .' Imogen looked up from the branch she was working on. 'Did you try the posy bracelet? Dream of anyone interesting?'

'No, I don't think it really worked.' She hadn't really wanted to tell Imogen that, but she'd asked. 'Unless you consider your cat "interesting". The only dream I remember was hanging out here and playing with him. Although . . . he is pretty cute. Maybe my perfect dream man has four legs, whiskers and a tail.' As if knowing he was being talked about, Bramble chose that moment to let out one of his stinky farts. 'Ugh, maybe not.'

'Manners, you brat-cat!' Imogen scolded, not quite able to keep her face straight.

'What about you?' Kim wanted to know. 'Did you dream of your perfect woman?'

'Yeah.' Imogen sighed and reached for more paint.

'Let me guess, she's a stunning blonde with a perfect smile, great boobs, fantastic hair and legs that go on forever.'

That prompted the laugh from Imogen she'd hoped for. 'I have no idea, but she sounds hot. You'll have to introduce me if you know her. More seriously though, it's the same dream that I've had on and off for a few years. When I'm asleep, it's the most wonderful dream. I know that I'm happy, and that she's sweet and kind and beautiful, and as crazy about me as I am about her.'

'That sounds lovely. So what's the problem?'

'When I wake up, try as I might — and believe me, I've really tried — I can't remember a single thing about her.'

'That must be really frustrating.' Kim sympathised, thinking that it would drive her crazy.

'Sometimes,' Imogen agreed. 'But at the same time, it's quite reassuring, because I know it will happen, and I know that when it does . . . it will be everything.'

'So you're saying you just have to be patient?' Amusement tugged at the edges of Kim's lips. 'You?'

'Yeah, I know.' Imogen laughed. 'I'm working on it, OK? I can be patient when it's for something worth waiting for.'

'Well, I hope you figure out who she is, and get to meet her soon.'

'Yeah, me too.'

'Before you sprain something trying to be patient.' Kim giggled when a clump of bubble wrap hit the back of her head.

* * *

They fell into an easy rhythm over the next fortnight, with Kim enjoying every spare moment she had painting in Imogen's shop. They'd finished the actual tree and roots in the first few days, and she'd been adding in details — painting in leaves, butterflies, stars and other things whenever she got the chance. She'd eaten her lunch there that day, holding the sandwich Imogen had made in one hand while painting a fairy with the other. That evening, she planned on finishing off the squirrel she'd started sketching.

She found that being around Imogen, working on the tree and being in the store gave her a sense of calm, of peace and grounding that she'd been missing for years. When she'd mentioned it, Imogen had just laughed and blamed the crystals — but Kim thought it was more than that. It was Imogen herself.

The only thing Kim didn't like was that Imogen kept wanting to pay for her work, even though it was the best fun she'd had in months — certainly since she'd come back to Broclington towards the end of last year this time, apparently to stay. She felt happy, perched on a stool, her palette of paint resting on a nearby shelf, while she finished adding in the different colours that made up the fluffy tail of the squirrel she'd been working on.

'Oh, he's fabulous.' Imogen brought her another steaming mug of tea, more than keeping up her end of the bargain with drinks, decent snacks and food. 'And I love the fairy. I can't believe how real she looks. You really are incredibly talented, Kim. And I do feel bad that you won't let me pay you.'

'You already bought me new brushes.'

'It doesn't seem enough for all the hours you've put in here.'

'I keep telling you, I'm enjoying myself.'

'And I keep telling you that, even so, I feel bad not paying you,' Imogen complained again.

'And I keep telling you that this isn't an argument you're going to win. I'm too stubborn.' Kim grinned.

'I think you underestimate how much "stubbornness" it takes to live with chronic pain and fatigue.'

'Nope,' Kim replied cheerfully, 'I'm not. I'm just betting on you being smart enough not to waste your energy arguing with me, when you know you're going to lose. I don't want to argue with you about this, Imogen.'

'So you'll send me your rates?'

'No. I'm just hoping you're going to stop asking. Because you're getting really annoying.' She shot her a cheeky look. 'So annoying, in fact, that I'm starting to feel tempted to take it out on your wall. I think this little squirrel would look good with devil horns and a pitchfork.' She waved the brush in what she hoped was a threatening manner.

'No, not my squirrel!' Imogen laughed. 'All right, all right, I give.' She held up her hands. 'I've got something for you, by the way.'

'Really?'

'Yeah. Hold your hands out and close your eyes.'

Kim hesitated.

'You can trust me. I promise it's not anything slimy or disgusting.'

'Sorry. The two brothers thing.' Kim gave herself a shake, put down the paintbrush and held out her hands, closing her eyes. She felt Imogen's hand, soft and warm, slide beneath hers, before something cool and heavy dropped into her palm. She closed her fingers over it as Imogen's hand drew away, leaving her skin tingling. She stayed there, her eyes still closed for a few seconds, letting the odd feeling of peace she had sink into her.

'You feel it, don't you?'

She certainly felt something, but she wasn't entirely sure what it was or where it was coming from — but it was nice. 'Something, yeah.' Slowly she opened her eyes, uncurling her fingers to reveal a pale pink carving of a crescent moon.

'Do you like?'

'Yeah.' She picked the carving up and turned it over, surprised by a flash of rainbows. 'It's really pretty, but um . . . what is it?'

'Rose quartz.' Imogen perched on the edge of the counter. 'It's a really good crystal for healing and unconditional love, and for recovering from the heartache of less-than-good relationships. And helping to attract healthy love into your life when you're ready for it.'

'Wow, a crystal can do all that?'

'Energy is energy.' Imogen shrugged. 'If I shone white light through a prism, it would split, right?'

'Yeah.' Kim just about remembered that much from science. 'Into a rainbow.'

'Exactly.' Imogen nodded. 'Well, light is just a form of energy we can see. So crystals can affect and transmute the energy around us. And they can hold energy themselves, and also raise your energy to different levels.'

'Really?'

'I believe it.' Imogen smiled gently. 'You could always try it.'

'I will.' Even if she wasn't convinced, she loved the sentiment behind the gift. She twisted it back and forth, admiring the rainbows. 'It's lovely. How much do I owe you?'

'You're kidding, right?'

'No, I can be your first sale.'

'Absolutely, completely, one-hundred-per-cent no.' Imogen crossed her arms over her chest. 'And since you've brought up the topic of owing money again, I still want to talk to you about this.' She flicked her fingers around the room, taking in all of Kim's painting.

'Don't make me threaten the squirrel again. I can give the fairies Elvis quiffs too!'

'OK, OK.' Imogen held her hands up in defeat. 'But you still aren't paying for the crystal.'

'Fair enough,' Kim agreed.

'But promise me, if you change your mind, or come up with any way I can repay you, or anything you need that I can help with, you'll let me know. OK?'

'OK,' Kim agreed, glad the conversation was finally over. And that she'd apparently won, and Imogen would forget all about it.

'Say the words, Kim. I wouldn't want you to think I don't mean it.'

'I promise if I change my mind, or think of something I need from you, I'll let you know. Happy?'

'For now.' She squeezed Kim's arm before heading to unpack more boxes.

Long after Imogen had moved away, Kim stared at the spot where the other woman's hand had rested — it was oddly warm, and tingled in a way that confused her. She guessed maybe there was something to the whole energy thing. She couldn't think of any other sensible, rational explanation.

* * *

'How's all the shop work going? Are you nearly ready for the big opening next week?' Ryan asked. 'Mallow, stop begging. She doesn't have anything you can eat. Do not give her any of your lasagne. There's garlic and onions in the sauce, and both can make her sick.'

'Sorry, girl.' Imogen frowned apologetically at the cockatoo. 'You heard what he said.' The bird whistled sadly and flopped down dramatically on the bottom of her cage, looking

67

utterly pathetic, like a starving, abandoned urchin. 'Are you sure, Ry-no? She looks so hungry.'

'She's conning you. She had some apple before you got here, and she's got freshly baked birdie bread in her bowl.'

Mallow replied with a loud, rude raspberry, followed by tutting and some seriously rude sounding muttering.

'Oi, you know Angela doesn't like you swearing,' Ryan scolded.

'How's her training going?' Imogen grinned as the bird muttered darkly and a toy went clanging across the cage. 'Asked and answered.'

'You were going to tell me how the shop's going, as you've stopped letting me in.'

'It's going really well, thanks. Painting is almost done, so I can start properly unpacking soon. And you can stop sulking. I want you to see the whole of the final thing in one go. No sneak peeks.'

'I know, I know. So you think you've come up with something really special?'

'Not me.' Imogen shook her head. 'It's almost all Kim's work. I did some of the really basic paint-by-numbers level stuff . . .'

'*You* picked up a paint brush? And did actual manual labour type painting?' He gasped in mock horror.

'Yes. It was actually kinda fun.' She smiled at the memory. 'Anyway, apart from me blocking in some of the basic stuff, it's all Kim's work. And she is phenomenal. What she came up with, and how it's turning out . . .' She sighed and shook her head. 'It's so, so much better than anything I could have dreamed of, even if I was given a century.'

Ryan paused, his fork halfway to his mouth. 'You really like her, don't you?'

'Yeah, I do. She's become a good friend really quickly.'

'Yeah.' He swallowed his mouthful. 'But you like-like her, don't you?'

'Don't know what you're talking about.' Imogen avoided the question.

'Yeah you do,' he argued. 'She's cute, and cool and funny. A bit edgy, and clearly creative. You've definitely dated women like her in the past. She's totally your type.'

'Except that she's not into women, and therefore is firmly and permanently in the friend zone.'

'But if she were that way inclined . . .' Ryan persisted.

'But she isn't.' Imogen shut the conversation down. 'What she is, is a really good friend. So I'm not even going to consider thinking about what you're suggesting.'

'Right. Sorry. But you blame me for wanting to see you happy?'

'Of course not. I love you for it. Even if you have turned into a meddling, nosey busybody recently.'

'I just want you to have the chance to find happiness like I have, Moggy.'

'Ugh, if I didn't love you so much I could really go off you.'

'Yeah, but you never will.' He pulled a face at her.

'Just do me a favour?'

'Anything. You know that.'

'If you're going to insist on setting me up with someone, at least make sure she likes girls first.'

'Yes, ma'am.'

* * *

'Hey.' Kim smiled at Imogen as she came out of Jake's room. 'How did my favourite little tabby do?'

'He was just fine.' She smiled back at Kim — that bright, warm smile that made her feel like she'd stepped into a sunny room. She had no idea how Imogen did it — how she made her feel like she was the only person in the room that mattered — but Kim was glad she did. 'A perfectly well-behaved little gentleman.'

'I'd expect nothing less.' Kim wove her fingers through the wire of the cat basket so Bramble could rub against them. 'How's your setup going?'

'Well, it's a bit boring when it's just me, Bramble and the radio, but we're getting there, thanks. Heading home for more of the same after this.'

'Sounds very sensible.' Kim brought up the bill on the computer.

'Yeah, well I've not had any better offers.' Imogen laughed. 'So it's just me, him, the microwave and more boxes this evening.'

'I might have a better offer.' As soon as the words had escaped, Kim wondered if they were the right thing to say.

'Sounds good to me.'

'You don't even know what it is yet.'

'No, but if it's with you it's almost definitely going to be fun. It usually is.' There was another of those bright, warming smiles.

'And now I'm worried I might have oversold it. It's just, once a month the Brockle's Retreat, our local pub . . .'

'Yeah, I know it.'

'Well, they do this steak meal deal. You buy two steak dinners, and they throw in a bottle of wine and dessert for free.'

'Sounds like a pretty good deal . . .'

'Yeah, it is, but given that most of my friends and family are coupled up . . .'

'Awww.' Imogen placed her hand over her heart. 'So you thought of me, your desperately lonesome damsel friend.'

'Now I regret saying anything.' Kim rolled her eyes.

'No, no. Sorry, it sounds like it could be fun.' Imogen's hand on her wrist sent a flash of tingling heat up her arm again. She really should ask about that reiki thing.

'Really?'

'Yeah.'

'OK. I'll . . . um . . . I'll . . .' For some reason she was finding it really difficult to concentrate.

'I could drop by the pub on my way home. See if they've got a table free?' Imogen offered. 'I think we both deserve a night on the town. Well . . . village.'

Book a table. That's what she'd meant to say. 'Yeah, that would be good.'

'Great.' Imogen's eyes were as bright as her smile. 'I'll text you what time.'

Even after Imogen had left, Kim could still feel the ghostly touch of her hand on her arm — a tickling distraction. When her phone buzzed and pinged a few minutes later, lighting up with Imogen's message, she couldn't have wiped the grin off her face if she'd wanted to. The rest of her shift passed in a blur, and she wasn't looking forward to finding out how many errors she might have made, but she almost skipped home, feeling ridiculously cheerful and optimistic for the evening.

Her good mood lasted right up until the point she stepped out of the bathroom — her hair glossy and make-up redone — and realised she had no idea what she was going to wear. Part of her was tempted to pull on her favourite treggings — the black ones with the subtle paisley pattern picked out in a slightly different shade of black, and the newish silvery silk turtle-neck that came high on her neck, but left her shoulders and part of her back bare. But then she worried about how well the silver really went with her pink streaks — and whether it would look like she'd tried too hard.

There were her trusty first-date jeans, which she always felt good in — and half a dozen tops that she could put with them, but then she'd be wearing a date outfit, which seemed weird for a meal down the local with her friend. But then again, maybe it wasn't that weird, to want to look nice when you were going out — even if it was just with a friend.

And it was just that — normal girly pride in her appearance, nothing more. The fact she ended up teaming her first-date jeans with the *Discworld* T-shirt Imogen had admired the day they met was just coincidence. It looked good with the purple not-quite-leather-but-still-cute jacket she wanted to wear, and her favourite biker boots.

When she'd finally stopped dithering over her outfit, she looked at her watch and swore. She'd spent longer getting ready for a slap-up meal with Imogen than she did any date, and now she was running late.

* * *

'I am so, so sorry.' Kim apologised as she slid into her seat at the table.

'It's all right, I was happy to wait.' Imogen closed the app she'd been fiddling with on her phone and smiled at the other woman. 'You look great. I can't help feeling a bit underdressed.' She fiddled with some of the folds on her slouchy jersey dress. It was comfy, and not exactly scruffy, but it looked like Kim was the type who dressed up for any occasion — surprising, as it wasn't what Imogen would have expected, but it was fun to learn more about her.

'Nonsense.' Kim shot her a warm smile. 'You look gorgeous.'

'Thanks.' Imogen reached up, untangling the tie that held her hair up, letting it cascade over her shoulders and down her back. Her hair could be annoying, and thick and heavy, but she had to admit it looked pretty good when it was down. 'There you go, is that any better?'

'No. Now you've gone from gorgeous to annoying.'

'How so?'

'Part of the reason I was late was that I have to stop and straighten my hair before I can let it down. Otherwise it's a frizzy, uncontrollable mess. You just pull out a hair tie and look like you've stepped out of a shampoo commercial.'

'I really don't.'

'You really do. I'm half-expecting you to start doing perfect hair flips any second.'

'You really are too sweet.' Imogen tucked her hair self-consciously behind her ears before reaching for the menu. 'Shall we order? I did think about it, but then realised I didn't know what you'd want.'

When their food arrived, Imogen glared at the giant mushroom sullying her plate.

Kim grinned at the look on her face and leaned over, fork already aiming for the offending fungus. 'Mind if I steal that?'

'Yup, please do.' Imogen wrinkled her nose, then picked up an onion ring and crunched into it happily.

'Do you want my onion rings?'

'I thought you liked onions,' Imogen argued. 'We don't have to swap just because you're eating the mushroom for me.'

'I like red onions.' Kim speared the golden loops and dropped them onto Imogen's plate. 'White onions have a funny aftertaste to me, and onion rings are always white. I've checked.'

'More for me, then.' Imogen giggled. 'Funny how the one thing on your plate that you dislike is one of my favourites.'

'I was just thinking the same.' Kim grinned back at her and chopped into the mushroom.

After a few moments of eating in companionable silence, Kim cleared her throat. 'You know, I'm feeling kinda sad.'

'Why, what's bothering you?' Without even knowing what the answer was, she knew she'd instantly want to fix it.

'Well, apart from a couple of sealing coats to protect everything, I think I'm pretty much done with your tree.'

'And that makes you sad because . . . ?'

'Because I've really enjoyed working on it.'

'I'm sure you can find other projects. In fact, I think you should.' Imogen narrowed her eyes at her. 'Only you should charge properly for it. Which is an argument we've still not finished. If you don't mind the unsolicited advice, that is.'

'From other people, I'd probably mind. But as it's you, I'll let it slide. But it's not just the painting.'

'No?' Imogen mentally tucked away the argument over Kim's lack of fees for another day — when her friend wasn't upset.

'No.' She fiddled with her fork, not meeting Imogen's eyes, which was weird.

'If you don't tell me what's bothering you, I can't help fix it.'

'Working on the tree was a good excuse to hang out with you.' Her answer did something unexpected to Imogen's energy, twisting and squeezing in the nicest way possible — a little like someone was enacting a healing or blessing on her.

She covered Kim's hand with her own, not in the least bit surprised that her fingers tingled when she did. She waited until Kim looked up, using the extra few seconds to mentally flip a coin between cheek and sincerity. 'You know, there's this really cool new invention called a mobile phone. You might not have heard of them, as they've only been around like . . . your entire life. And they're getting so clever nowadays that they're called "smartphones", and when you have one there's all these different ways you can contact other people.'

Kim laughed, shaking her head. 'You snarky bitch.'

Imogen just about managed to keep her face straight. 'You've got your consonants confused there, hun. I'm much closer to a witch than a bitch. Besides, I'm not sure I can compete with sliced-potato pillows. I've never been that good with a needle and thread.'

'It is a skill.' Kim laughed again.

'In all seriousness though—' she squeezed Kim's fingers before releasing her hand '—you don't need an excuse to hang out with me. Just give me a call, or drop me a message. Or even just drop by.'

'I can't just drop by uninvited,' she argued.

'That was me inviting you, Kim. Consider it a standing invitation.'

'Seriously?'

'Yeah. Now speaking of serious matters, I am seriously torn by the dessert menu. Obviously hot chocolate brownie is always tempting, but cookies and cream tiramisu sounds awesome too.'

'They're both pretty good.'

'Damn, I was hoping you were going to tell me one was awful.'

'Nope. I'd happily eat them both. In fact, shall we do that? Order both and share?'

'A woman after my own heart. Perfect.'

CHAPTER FIVE

Imogen tried not to pace nervously across the shop floor, failing miserably when she found her feet moving again of their own accord. She leaned against the counter, forcing herself to calm her breathing and draw in the energy of the sun as it streamed through the front window, bouncing off carefully placed crystals. The last thing she needed was to upset the balance of the space — especially when she'd worked so hard over the last few weeks to get it just right. But damn it, she was seriously nervous.

Even though the opening was going to be soft — with just a few of her long-standing customers, a couple of writers for health and spirituality publications, colleagues from physio teams, local yoga instructors and the leader of a nearby spiritualist church — she was still nervous. She started to wonder if she should have gone bigger and bolder, and invited the whole community — but she wanted to start slowly and give herself time to build her strength, while protecting her clients' health as well as her own. She'd even asked Ryan to stay away — or at least to leave his online persona behind, because she didn't need the extra attention that Maverick so often drew.

But as she stood there in the empty shop, half an hour before her guests were due to start arriving, she was second-guessing herself. She fiddled with her refreshment station, using the tongs to rearrange the snacks, then wiped them clean, and then contemplated ringing her brother and asking him to come after all.

She nearly jumped out of her skin when the newly installed bell on the door tinkled.

'Hi.' Kim smiled at her from behind a big bunch of fluffy-looking purple flowers. 'I know you're busy — but I just wanted to drop these off. Then I'm going to leave and let you be your amazing, awesome self and hugely impress everyone.'

'No pressure at all then.' Imogen bit her tongue. 'Sorry, what I meant to say was they're lovely, and thank you.'

'I was going to ask how you're doing, but I'm guessing I know the answer.' She gave the flowers to Imogen with one hand, hugging her with the other arm. 'You're going to be fine — better than fine — you're going to be brilliant and awesome, and your launch will go brilliantly and awesomely, and that's not me adding pressure, it's just me telling you what's going to happen.'

'Oh, you've taken up scrying, have you?'

'I don't know what that is . . . so, no. But I do know you, and you're going to be amazing.'

Kim's confidence in her was exactly the balm Imogen needed to soothe her anxiety. 'Thank you. And thank you for these too. They're lovely. A bit like amethyst. They're hydrangeas, right? You don't often see such a dark purple — they're very pretty.'

'Yeah, they're for promoting wealth and prosperity, which I thought was good luck for a new store . . . What?' Imogen must have given her a funny look. 'I don't know crystals, but I know a bit about flowers. They have a language all of their own. Mum used to drag all three of us out to help in the garden. Do you want me to put them in some water?'

'Yes please. Vases are . . .'

'Under the sink. I know.'

Imogen watched as Kim clipped up her stairs, and smiled to herself. She liked that Kim was so comfortable in her home, and knew where things like vases lived — even though they'd only been unpacked recently. And hearing her soft footsteps on the floor above gave her a sense of peace and happiness that left her feeling focussed and centred.

By the time Kim padded back down the stairs, the flowers cascading artfully from the vase, bouncing jauntily with each of her steps, Imogen knew her approach was exactly right for that moment in time. Kim's confidence in her lifted and buoyed her own.

'Is here OK for them?' Kim set the flowers on the counter, just above the computer, in a circle of crystals Imogen had set there a few hours previously — it was exactly where she had thought to put them as soon as she'd seen them.

'Perfect. Thank you so much, Kim.'

'You're welcome.' She adjusted the flowers, turning them to better catch the light, then grabbed her bag and headed towards the door.

'Do you want to stay?'

'You don't need me here,' Kim reassured her. 'You've got this.' She rested a hand on Imogen's arm. 'You're going to be awesome, but if you want to call me later and tell me exactly how brilliantly everything went, I'd love to hear.'

'Yeah, I will. And thank you, again.'

'You're welcome, again. I'll let you get on.' To Imogen's surprise, Kim leaned in and placed a soft kiss on her cheek. When she left, the scent of honey and fresh apples lingered in the air — tingling warmth lingered where Kim's lips had brushed her skin. A shadowy, ghostly touch of sweetness.

She walked around the store floor once more, stopping to adjust the odd crystal and tweak some of her goods and displays, then found herself standing by her computer, gently stroking the soft, velvety good-luck petals. How she'd gotten so lucky to have someone like Kim in her life, she wasn't sure, but she was incredibly grateful to the coincidental magic that had brought them together.

She smoothed her hair, shook out her skirts and straightened her top. She was ready. And Kim was right — it was going to be brilliant.

* * *

A couple of hours later, Imogen breathed a sigh of relief as she closed the door and flipped the sign over. She rolled her head, releasing some of the stiffness in her shoulders — all the tension she'd been carrying. She made it halfway across the floor before bursting into a fit of giggles.

The launch really couldn't have gone any better, with everyone seeming happy and enthusiastic, and lots of actual bookings, and promises and hints of future bookings — including interest in a pain management clinic at the local hospital, inspired by work she'd done for a neighbouring hospital trust. She definitely needed to give some major thanks to the universe — it had more than delivered, returning all her positive energy and affirmations many times over. Life was looking seriously good.

She'd barely made a dent in the tidying up when there was a tap at the window, and she looked up to see a familiar shape silhouetted behind the beaded curtain.

Imogen grinned as she unlocked the door. 'Have you been lying in wait, watching until everyone left?'

'No, I was just heading home and saw the shop empty. Have I timed it that well? Is it your coincidental magic thing again?'

'Yeah. Well, maybe not. I'd just started cleaning up.'

'I don't mind helping.' Kim followed her in. 'And while I do, you can tell me how brilliantly it went.'

'Sounds like you already know.' Imogen smiled at her.

'Really? That good?'

'Really, that good.' She laughed as Kim threw her arms around her in a tight hug.

'I'm so pleased for you! Congratulations!'

Imogen hugged her back, thrilled to have found someone who cared about her enough to be so genuinely happy for her. The change was almost as refreshing as her sweet-apple perfume.

* * *

Kim knocked at the door, and rebalanced the bags she carried.

'It's unlocked, come on in.'

She shut the door and trotted up the stairs. 'Happy awesome first week!'

'What's this?' Imogen looked confused.

'Your "Happy Awesome First Week" celebration.'

'That's really sweet of you.'

'I'm your friend. I'm supposed to be sweet to you.' Kim grinned. 'And it's only because I care about you, and respect you so deeply, that I remembered. Nothing at all to do with the fact that the day you opened your door — officially — also debuted my biggest piece of artwork to the world — or at least Broclington.' She leaned down to get out the plates. They'd eaten together so often that she knew where everything was.

'Ah, obviously. This smells amazing.' Imogen brushed aside the salad and nicked an onion bhaji from one of the foil containers. 'Ow, hot, hot!'

'Serves you right.' Kim shook her head, trying not to roll her eyes. 'Here, try this. Sweet lassi.'

Imogen took a couple of gulps of the drink. 'Thanks, that's much better. And delicious, by the way. What else did you bring?'

'Only the best chicken pasanda I've found within a thirty-minute drive. Definitely worth faffing around with picnic bags to keep it warm. And Peshwari naans.'

'What's Peshwari?'

'It's a naan stuffed with coconut, sultanas and almond — so it's sweet.'

'Sounds delicious.'

'My favourite.'

'And that—' Imogen perched on the worktop, taking a chunk of the bread while Kim dished up '—is the real reason we're such good friends. Because you have great taste in food, books and movies.'

'Oh.' Kim covered her heart with her hand. 'You wound me. You only like me for my food choices. And there I was thinking it was my winning personality.'

'Well, it doesn't hurt. You're not too bad on the eyes either.' She ducked as Kim threw a bag of salad at her. 'Didn't your mother teach you not to play with your food?'

'She tried to.' Kim stuck her tongue out. 'But I told you before, I'm the reason my parents have grey hair.'

'Yeah, and I still don't believe you're to blame. At least not totally.'

'Oh, you really should . . . TV or breakfast bar?'

'Breakfast bar, if that's OK. There's something I want to talk to you about.'

'Sounds serious.' Kim watched her, suddenly feeling a bit anxious.

'It's nothing to worry about,' Imogen reassured her, as if reading her thoughts. 'It's good news — I think.'

'OK, now you've really got my attention.' Kim pulled out the cutlery while Imogen grabbed extra plates and some kitchen roll. 'Am I going to want a drink with this?'

'Knowing you, probably.'

'So it is bad?'

'No.' Imogen reached over to squeeze her hand, sending another zap of tingly heat racing through her. 'But you almost always say yes to wine.'

'True.' Kim handed her the glasses, wondering what was going on.

'Sit, eat, I'll talk.' Imogen filled Kim's glass and handed it back. 'The short version — because I can see you're not going to enjoy your food otherwise — you know the hospital I'm doing the pain management clinic for?' She waited for Kim's nod. 'They're interested in seeing more of your artwork, with a view to potentially commissioning some. There's other people in the mix, obviously, but it's an invitation to submit ideas and a quote . . . if you were interested. They're accepting bids for the next couple of weeks.'

'What?' Kim froze, her fork halfway to her mouth, her mind reeling as she tried to process what Imogen had said.

'The trust has been doing work at the hospital, changing around some of the wards, adding space and reducing what's no longer needed — modernisation.'

Now she'd said it, Kim could remember both of her brothers talking about it — Callum when he'd been working there, and Jake when he and Evelyn had taken Summer for her follow-up scans, which had thankfully come back clear. 'I'd heard about it. A lot of work in the children's sections, right?'

'Yeah.' Imogen nodded. 'And the family rooms, the palliative centre, the wards. Almost all of it has been rejigged for better efficiency. When I was there last week, the physio lead asked me if I wouldn't mind attending one of the progress meetings. Obviously I said yes, partly because I'm nosy, and partly because being invited to something like that is a pretty big deal.'

'Wow.' Kim nodded, wondering what this had to do with her.

'And it was. It turns out he's really interested in learning more about pain management techniques that don't rely solely on pharmaceutical analgesia — it's an even bigger concern with minors than it is in adults, because the risks can be greater. And, apparently, it's been raised as a concern by CQC inspectors in a number of other areas, so they want to get ahead of the game locally.'

'Sorry, remind me what CQC is?'

'Care Quality Commission. They're the organisation who inspect healthcare. Anyway, the head of physical therapies mentioned my name and my complementary pain management clinics, and they want to team me up with some of their paediatric specialists, to see if we can work out a junior programme.'

'Oh, that's brilliant! I'm so pleased for you.'

'Thank you.' Imogen's smile was warm and genuine. Kim was just about getting used to the butterfly-flutter that she got whenever the other woman turned her full attention on her. She still didn't understand it, but she was starting to enjoy it.

'Anyway, as part of this meeting, they took a few of us on a tour of the site to show us the work that's been happening, and that led — fairly quickly — to a conversation about therapeutically informed environments, how things like colour therapy, and the settings in which ongoing treatments like physiotherapy and re-enablement work take place, can influence healing. Even follow-up appointments like the one your niece goes to are less stressful if it's a nice environment.'

'Yeah, hospitals can be pretty miserable places if you're not careful. I know everyone at the surgery worked really hard to make sure it had the right "feel" when they expanded services.'

'Smart move.' Imogen nodded. 'So, when they said they were launching a tender to commission the design and decoration of some of the children's wards and facilities, I showed them pictures of my shop.'

'What?' The fork froze again. 'You . . .' Her voice caught in her throat and she took a gulp of wine. 'You showed my paintings to the head of a whole hospital?' Panic tightened her stomach painfully. What the hell was Imogen thinking, showing her silly little fairies and sparkly rainbows to big important people like that?

'Please don't be annoyed with me.' Imogen's eyes were intense on hers. 'I think your work is brilliant.'

'Yes, but . . .' Kim pressed her lips together, thinking that Imogen was a very unusual person — and that highly paid hospital executives probably wouldn't share her eclectic taste — but not sure how to say it without risking offending her friend.

'And I'm not the only one.'

'They liked my work?' Kim couldn't believe she'd heard right.

'Enough that they'd be interested in seeing a bid from you. If you were interested in submitting something like that. The budget isn't huge, unfortunately, but it would certainly be more than what you let me pay you.' She poked her tongue out. Despite the shock reverberating through her, Kim found herself smiling at the familiar gesture Imogen had picked up from her. 'And the timeline is pretty flexible — to be set by the artist or designers, so long as it's completed before the reopening in six months.'

'You're crazy.' She shook her head, already thinking of all the reasons she couldn't possibly do this.

'Why? I've not committed you to anything, or made any promises to anyone. I just took advantage of a situation and shared the work of a promising local artist I know, who I thought could be perfect for the job.'

Kim snorted into her wine glass. 'Bloody hell, you make me sound like a professional who actually knows what she's doing.'

'I think you could be, if you stopped charging in biscuits, caffeine and takeaways. And if you wanted to.'

Kim shook her head, all the doubts and "nos" she'd heard before coming back in a wave of disappointment, reminding her of all the reasons Imogen was wrong. 'No. I just . . . don't think it's for me.' She shrugged sadly. 'But thanks for trying. I hope me saying no doesn't cause you any problems.'

'I don't see how it would.' Imogen shrugged.

They ate in silence for a few minutes. Or, rather, Imogen ate while Kim pushed her food around, her stomach rolling and her head spinning.

* * *

Imogen watched as Kim pushed the — frankly most delicious she'd ever tasted — bhaji across her plate. 'You know, I think

I'm buying into this red onion over white thing. These really are delicious.'

'Yeah, they're great.'

'So why aren't you eating them?' Imogen waited to ask the question that worried her until Kim looked up. 'Are you annoyed with me? Was I wrong to put your name forward? I probably should have spoken to you first, but it really was a spur-of-the-moment thing. I just saw the opportunity and thought it might be good for you. I'm really sorry if I overstepped.'

'No, you haven't. It's not that.' Kim looked so deflated that Imogen had to fight the urge to jump up from her seat and wrap her in a huge hug.

'Can I help?'

'It's just . . . I don't know . . . It would be amazing to do something like that, but I just couldn't.'

'Why not? You did a great job with my shop.'

'About a dozen reasons, just off the top of my head.' Kim stabbed at her curry.

'Do you want to talk about them? See if we can break them down at all?'

'Nah, it'd just be a waste of time.'

'Of course it wouldn't. Come on. Talk to me.'

'Really?'

'Really. I'm happy to see if I can help — if that's what you want. I mean, I don't want you to feel pressured, or like I'm trying to talk you into something you're really not that interested in doing. But equally, if you are interested, then I don't see why you shouldn't at least consider a submission. Not if I can help you overcome any of the "dozen reasons".'

'Well, for one thing, to submit an official bid to an organisation like a hospital, I assume you'd actually have to be a business — which I'm not.'

'You're probably right.' Imogen tore off another bit of the delicious bread and used it to mop up some of the sauce. 'But that's easily fixed. Just register yourself as a sole trader or small business.'

'You make that sound easy,' Kim complained.

'It is. When I did it, it took me a couple of hours to do the forms and cost about forty quid. I can't imagine it would be any more to register as a sole trader, if that's what you wanted. Registering a small business takes a couple of weeks if you post everything, but it's quicker online.'

'It's really that easy?'

'It was when I did it. Shouldn't think it would have changed that much, but we can look into it. What's the next problem?'

'Even if I set myself up as a company, there's no way they'd hire me because it's just me. It's too big of a project for one person. I've no idea how to tender for work, and I can't even begin to picture the designs. It's just too big.'

'Well, you could bid for one of the smaller lots, like the family room or sensory suites. I had a quick look at the paperwork, and there's nothing to say you have to submit to do it all. And the tender itself seemed pretty straightforward. Certainly no worse than ones I've seen in the past. Your brother or parents must have bid to the hospital trust at some point in the past, to be able to do the work they do. And as for the designs, I could take some pictures of the space for you when I'm up there next week. Or, even better, come up yourself and meet me for lunch or something. I'm sure if I asked, Bobbi could arrange access. She's the head of physical therapies, so my big boss for the pain management classes.'

'I couldn't ask you to do that.'

'You didn't. I offered.' She shrugged easily. 'She seemed really interested in the work I've done around the use of therapeutic environments in physical care. She even offered to link me up with some of the psychotherapy and psychology team, so I'm sure this wouldn't be a problem.'

'You'd really do that for me?' Kim's eyes were wide.

'It's just a quick email following on from a professional conversation. And you're my friend. Of course I'd do that for you.'

'You really think I should do this?'

Imogen sighed and put down her fork, trying to figure out how to answer the question. She knew what she wanted to say — what she wanted to scream and cheer for Kim to do — but she also knew that she had to choose her words carefully, to be fair. 'I don't know if that's really a question I should answer, because I don't think it's for me to tell you what to do. I know that you seemed pretty happy when you were working on my shop, and you've said you wanted to do things that are more creative. But, ultimately, you have to do what's right for you, so if you want to ask me if I think you *could* do it, then absolutely. But as to what you *should* do? I think you should do whatever feels right to you.'

'You make it sound so easy to know what that is.'

'For me, knowing what it is has always been the easy bit,' Imogen admitted. 'But having the courage, the faith and commitment to go after it — that can be harder.'

'What if I don't know what feels right to me?' Kim asked, in a voice so small that Imogen wanted to smack whoever had done whatever they'd done that made her friend doubt herself so much.

'I can try to tell you what it is for me, if you think that would help?'

'Yes please.' Kim's gaze was heavy and expectant.

'For me, you know, it's helping people better manage pain and improve their health and wellbeing, to be able to reclaim their lives. It's re-enablement, pure and simple.'

'But how did you know that was what you wanted to do?'

'I don't know how to explain it without sounding cheesy, so you're just going to have to put up with some clichés I'm afraid. It lights me up from the inside out. It inspires me to get up in the morning. It makes my pain seem less bad, and it's what I dream about — sad as that may sound.'

'It doesn't sound sad at all,' Kim reassured her as she finally started eating again. 'Or even all that cheesy.'

'Good. Because it's how I feel about it. And, in honesty, even if I couldn't make a living doing it, I'd probably still be involved, in some way or form. Because there's something in me that's compelled to do it. I guess, in simple words, it really is a passion.'

'Wow.'

'Yeah, and I'm really lucky to have been able to turn that into a career.' She spooned up the last of her curry, before glancing up at Kim. 'So, is there anything in your life that makes you feel like that?'

'Yeah. My art. But do you really, seriously think I could do it?'

'I think you're very talented, Kim. And I think if you really want to do this, you'll find a way to.'

'But . . . what if I can't?' She licked her lips. 'What if I try, and I can't make it happen? Imogen, what if I fail?'

'Well, there's always the risk that things can go wrong,' Imogen told her softly. 'The only way you can guarantee not to fail is not to try, but that guarantees you won't make it happen either.'

'That's quite zen of you. Are you part yogi as well as a little bit witch?'

Imogen was so glad to hear the teasing tone return to Kim's voice. 'Maybe. Some days I think I'm still figuring out what I am — that I'm just playing and making it up as I go along.'

'Well you're doing a much better job of faking it than I am.'

'I've probably just had a bit more practice than you. You certainly get plenty of practice faking being well when you have a chronic pain disorder.' She felt glum for a few moments before giving herself a shake — this wasn't about her. 'What if, instead of catching up on our series, we had a look at the paperwork? I've got it in my bag, if you wanted to, just to get an idea of the type of things they're asking for.'

'Yeah, but we watch the new episodes every Wednesday.'

'True,' Imogen argued, 'but this isn't the nineties. We won't miss it if we don't watch it right away, or even tonight.

It'll still be there tomorrow. If it helps to flick through the paperwork and talk it over, I'm here.'

'You really are a truly awesome friend.' Kim's words warmed Imogen through. 'If you really don't mind, then yes, I think I'd like to have a look. Shall we take it to the comfy seats?'

'We could.' Imogen grinned. 'But it's pretty comprehensive — meaning long, so we might need the breakfast bar.'

Kim rolled her eyes as she stood and grabbed both plates. 'You could have told me that before I agreed.'

'If I had, it might have put you off. If you're not interested, I think it should be for a better reason than being scared of a bit of paperwork.' She hid a grin when Kim's eyes narrowed.

'Scared? As if. Hand it over.'

* * *

'Imogen, light of my moon . . .'

'What do you want Ry-no?'

'Maybe I just want to check in with my wonderful sister and see how she is, to make sure she's in good health and better spirits?'

'Just ask me already so I can say no and go have my bath.'

'Seriously, are you all right? You're not having a pain flare? I can come over and make you grilled cheese and chocolate brownies if you are.'

'No, I'm fine thanks. And I already had dinner.'

'But you're having a bath? That's Imogen pain management one-oh-one.'

'I really am so lucky to have a brother like you,' Imogen told him honestly. 'But I'm fine. Sometimes a bath is just a bath. I'm managing my energy levels, doing my stretches, avoiding triggers and paying attention to warning signs.'

'So you're really fine?'

'I'm really fine,' she reassured him. 'Although I might be getting a little fed up of repeating myself.'

'Is it so wrong to call my favourite sister to see how she is?'

'I'm your only sister.'

'Even if I had a dozen sisters, you'd still be my favourite.'

'If I didn't already suspect you of wanting something, that would have given you away,' she said, laughing.

'OK. Maybe I do. Angela and I are in a bit of a bind. We were supposed to be — well, we *are* — hosting a donkey walk tomorrow, but we don't have enough volunteers. We've had two drop out last minute.'

'And you're asking me to help? On a Sunday? One of the few days off I actually have?'

'You know the donkey drove, and Petunia really seemed to take to you. And you might get lucky and see some badgers, or foxes.'

'I can see a fox anytime I want. I just turn up to the sanctuary with treats and whistle. Ruby loves me.'

'Ruby loves anyone who sneaks her sausages. Please, Moggy. The ticket revenue is money raised for Bill's — just think of the good karma.'

'It's amazing how much your belief in karma deepens when you're after a favour.' She rolled her eyes.

'You taught me well.' He chuckled.

'You knew I was going to say yes before you even called.'

'I hoped you would. Thanks, sis. See you at half-five.'

'Is dinner included in this event?'

'No. It'd be about twelve hours early. Or maybe late.'

'Huh?'

'Half-five in the morning, Moggy. It's a dawn walk.'

'I hate you.'

'Love you, too.' He laughed and hung up before she had a chance to complain further.

* * *

Bloody Jake and his bloody favours, Kim grumbled to herself as she stomped through the village. He'd called her the afternoon

89

before, croaking pathetically with a case of man-flu. She hadn't really been able to say no, especially when he explained that whatever bug had made him ill had hit Evelyn and Summer too — and he'd bribed her with a day off in the week. She was still grumbling, regretting how late she'd gotten up, when she reached the agreed meeting point where Ryan and Angela were already waiting, complete with their string of donkeys.

She waved to them and leaned against a tree, taking her phone out and flicking through her emails. She'd be nice and sociable later, when the donkey-walking guests arrived. For now, all she wanted to do was drink her second coffee of the day and hope the caffeine kicked in soon.

'If I'd known you were coming, I might have given Ryan less of a hard time. Maybe.'

'Hi.' Kim felt her morning grumps melt away under the warmth of Imogen's smile, as she leaned against the tree next to her. 'What are you doing here?'

'Collecting good karma, apparently.' She shifted against the tree trunk, kicking up one foot to get more comfortable. 'Or at least favours my brother is going to owe me. You?'

'Pretty much the same. Jake was supposed to be here, but he went and caught man-flu, and gave it to his fiancée and her daughter too, which means I've been guilted into getting up at ugly o'clock.'

'Not much of a morning person, huh?'

'Nope. Unlike you, apparently.'

'Oh no, I don't really believe in any time before 7 a.m. Later on days off.'

'Could have fooled me.' Kim looked her up and down, taking in her slim-fitting jeans, boots and oversized jumper in muted rainbow stripes, which was layered over a purple T-shirt, and matched the scarf holding her curls out of her face.

'Oh, I'm totally faking it. I don't even really like any time before 10 a.m. And at least you got organised enough for coffee. Just getting dressed and getting myself out the door was enough for me.'

'Survival mechanism.' Kim grinned and offered the mug to Imogen. 'You want?'

'You sure?'

'Yeah, it's my second one already, and you look like you need it more than me.'

'I could bloody well kiss you.' Imogen wrapped both hands around the mug gratefully and took a deep swig.

For a few seconds, Kim stared at her as she drank — her lips exactly where her own had been seconds before. Her heart raced at the thought of what Imogen had said. She knew it wasn't really an invitation, or even a suggestion — it was just an innocent turn of phrase. But the image it conjured was . . . Kim fiddled with her hair, tousling the streaky strands between her fingers and pressing them against her lips as her mind raced, trying to put together the pieces of a puzzle she didn't understand the shape of. The weird-but-nice tingling warmth that she felt so often when Imogen touched her, the way they laughed and fit so easily into each other's lives — as if they'd been together forever. The flush of heat she sometimes felt when their eyes locked, the way her stomach sometimes fluttered when they were together.

She wasn't gay . . . she definitely liked men . . . but did that mean she couldn't like women too? The idea was so alien to her that she wasn't sure what to do with it. It wasn't something that she'd ever really considered — but then again, she'd never met anyone like Imogen before.

As if knowing she was being thought about, Imogen looked up, her eyes locking with Kim's. There it was again, that flutter in her stomach, a feeling of slight breathlessness. She could feel her heart rate step up as heat rushed into her cheeks.

If Imogen had been an Ian or an Isaac, or any other guy, she wouldn't have questioned the feelings of attraction . . . but it was *Imogen*.

'Are you OK?' Imogen smiled at her, sending a rush of tingling through Kim.

'Yeah, just, um . . . what you said . . .'

91

'What . . . ? Oh—' Kim could see realisation hit as Imogen clapped her hand over her mouth. 'I'm sorry. My brain isn't in gear yet. I just meant to thank you for the coffee. Don't worry, I'm not about to pounce on you. For one thing, I know I'm not your type, and rejection is dreadful for the ego. For the other, I like you far too much to mess up our friendship like that.'

'Right.' Kim nodded, wondering how Imogen was so sure about "her type" when she was starting to question it herself.

'Have you thought about it any more?' Imogen's question jolted her out of her train of thought, snapping her back into the moment.

Kim didn't need to ask what she meant. 'Yeah, a lot. And if you're still willing to send that email to your boss . . .'

'I am.'

'Then I think I'd like to take a look at some of the spaces. I'm not promising that I'm going to come up with anything, but I have had a couple of ideas, and I'd like to see if they might work.'

'I'll get it set up,' Imogen promised.

'Thanks.' The approval in Imogen's eyes when she smiled at Kim sent the tingling into overdrive. Looking away was an impossibility. It could have been seconds or minutes — she stopped noticing time — before Imogen looked away.

'Come on, people are arriving. Looks like we're getting started.'

'Right.' Kim nodded again and headed over to take the lead reins of one of the donkeys, leaving Imogen to do the same. Her hand shook as she ran it down the stripe adorning the little donkey's back. 'Hi Petunia. You're going to be well-mannered for me today, right?'

The donkey headbutted Kim affectionately.

'Yeah you are, aren't you?'

'Petunia's always well-mannered.' Ryan waved to her. 'Now Ernie here—' he rubbed the ears of the donkey nearest to him '—he can be a bit cheekier, can't you, mate? Thanks for helping out, both of you.'

'It's OK.' Kim glanced over to where Imogen was helping a family introduce themselves to Poppy, a small chocolate-brown donkey who whuffled and snuffled happily. 'This actually might be quite good fun. Possibly even worth getting up at the crack of dawn.'

* * *

Imogen rested her hand on Poppy's shoulder and told her to "woah", just as Ryan had shown her. And, just like when it was Ryan or Angela asking, the little donkey stopped moving. She waited patiently, swinging her head around to peer at Imogen with huge dark eyes.

'Quietly now,' Imogen spoke softly to the family who were "walking" Poppy that morning. She pointed to where she'd seen movement. 'Look, over there.'

'Where? I can't see anything.'

'Just wait for a second.' Imogen really hoped that the movement she'd thought she'd seen was what they'd been hoping for. Whatever was rustling in the bushes was big — and it was close to one of Angela's release sites, which very few people knew about, so there was a good chance. She held her breath, not wanting to move in case she was right and scared off the one critter they'd all been waiting for.

A few seconds later, a black-and-white stripy head popped up between a patch of leaves.

'Look, it's a badger!'

The head disappeared almost as fast.

'Yes, that's a badger.' Or it was. 'If we're really, really quiet, they might come back.' Imogen crouched down. 'Shall we wait for a bit?'

After a few long minutes, there was another round of rustling, and Imogen was surprised when a small hand slipped into hers.

'Is that . . . ?'

'Yes, I think so,' Imogen whispered back. 'But let's stay super quiet and still so they know we're not going to hurt them.'

'OK.'

Sure enough, a minute or two later the black-and-white head reappeared, this time more slowly, the nose appearing to sniff at the air. A few breath-holding seconds later and a snout and head followed. The critter was probably only twenty or so feet away, and Imogen moved slowly to reach for the binoculars Ryan had jammed into her pocket earlier, handing them to the little girl, who was spellbound.

'Do you remember how to adjust these?'

'Yes, thanks. This is so cool.'

Imogen had to agree, as the family passed the binoculars back and forth, admiring the badger, who seemed to pose obligingly for them.

'Has it been hurt?'

'I don't think so,' Imogen replied softly, hoping that she was right. 'Why do you think that?'

'It's only got one ear.'

'That'll be Bella.' Ryan's group joined hers, moving quietly. 'She came to Bill's at the end of last year — we think she was side-swiped by a car. Our local vet, Jake, patched her up, and she spent a few weeks at the sanctuary recovering and being fed up before being released this spring.'

'One of your success stories, then.'

'Very much so.' Ryan looked around the group. 'And, if we're lucky, we might see her new friend. One of our other badger-spotting groups have reported seeing another badger over the last few weeks — so it might be that they're setting up a sett together.'

'Awww,' one of the members of the tour spoke. 'She's got a boyfriend.'

'That's presumptuous of you,' another argued. 'Maybe she has a girlfriend.'

'That could be true.' Imogen didn't miss the wink Ryan shot her as he explained. 'Sometimes lone badgers will come together in a group and all live together in what we call a "clan" or a "cete". They share each other's setts, feeding grounds and work together to look after cubs.'

'That's so cool!'

'Yeah, it is.'

The families fell silent, except for the odd fidget and the click of a camera lens, as they enjoyed watching Bella snuffle and wander about. They waited to see whether her friend would turn up, and if they would get a good enough look at them — and maybe take a few pictures — to decide whether it was a boyfriend or not. Even the four donkeys were quiet and surprisingly patient.

When the second badger finally made an appearance — after a few false starts that turned out to be squirrels — it was almost too exciting for some of the group, who had to be hushed — a few covered their mouths with their hands, or stifled gasps with their fingers.

Imogen had to admit, it was pretty magical.

CHAPTER SIX

Kim fired off a text to Imogen and scrunched her toes up inside her shoes, which squeezed them too tightly. They were a lot smarter than her biker boots, but a lot less comfortable. Then again, that was pretty much the same as her outfit, which felt like it restricted her movement, and the pins that had tamed her hair into something she hoped at least resembled professional.

She checked her skirt for the dozenth or so time, making sure it hadn't slipped round to make her look like she was a scruffy school kid. It was how it made her feel — the last time she'd regularly worn a fitted skirt and blazer was when it had been part of her uniform . . . and even then "regularly" might have been a stretch. Now she thought about it, she could remember spending a lot of time in detention for failing to meet the uniform rules.

'If it wasn't inappropriate for oh-so-many reasons, I'd be tempted to wolf-whistle.' Imogen greeted her with a grin.

'Yeah, I thought I'd step up the professional look for the day.'

'You look good.' As it usually did, Imogen's approval flushed warmth through her. 'You certainly look better than me.' Imogen gestured to her hospital-issue navy trousers and white polo shirt with a wry grin. 'Not much you can do with a uniform.'

'True.' Kim grinned, thinking again of some of the trouble she'd gotten into in the past for doing exactly that. 'But I like your braids.' She admired the complex twist and plaiting pattern that held Imogen's hair back.

'Thanks. Simpler than it looks, and I can't have it in mine or my patients' faces. Anyway, do you want to see the spaces now? The construction team are on lunch so we've got pretty good access. Then we can hit up the canteen.'

'Building site followed by hospital food — awesome.' Kim couldn't help laughing.

'Yeah, keep hanging out with me, I'll take you to all the best places. Besides, if we time it right, Bobbi should be heading down for lunch in about half an hour, in case you wanted to ask her anything.'

Kim swallowed, suddenly nervous. 'Guess it's a good thing I dressed up then.'

'Bobbi's lovely. You'll be fine. She's pretty excited to see what you come up with.'

'Gee, that doesn't add any pressure at all.' Kim rolled her eyes as she followed Imogen down a corridor and was zapped through a "staff only" door. 'You know, it's a bit strange seeing you in full-on professional mode, and in uniform.'

'Speak for yourself, Corporate Barbie!'

That made Kim snort with laughter in an entirely unprofessional manner. 'If anyone's a Barbie, it's more likely you than me — you at least have the boobs for it!'

'Yeah, but your eyes are blue like the OG Barbie dolls. And I'm just about resisting the urge to question the fact that you've clearly been eyeing up my boobs.'

'Not like they're easy to miss.'

'True enough.' She stared down at her chest for a moment before shrugging. 'Not like I can hide it.'

'And why would you want to? You're gorgeous.' Kim glanced down at her own chest. 'You know, this is a very, very surreal conversation. Boobs, Barbies and uniforms.'

'It's about to get even weirder.' Imogen grinned as she pinged them into another area of the hospital, this one swathed with plastic dust sheets. She signed in on a clipboard. 'We get to wear these.' She handed Kim a hard hat.

'Really?'

'Yup. You're lucky it's lunchtime. If there was active work right now, you'd have a lovely, subtle hi-vis jacket to add to your suit. I promised Bobbi. It was a condition of us getting access today — because if either of us get hurt she has to fill in an entire novel's worth of forms, which means she'd then stop liking me. Her words, not mine.'

'Well, we wouldn't want to upset Bobbi.' Kim jammed the helmet onto her head, wincing as one of the hair pins scraped her scalp.

'Nope. Especially as she's going to be on the selection panel.' She held up one of the plastic sheets. 'After you.'

* * *

'. . . and the sensory room could really suit a space theme, because then you could naturally have areas of darkness, which would work brilliantly with the fibreoptics they're weaving in, and it could be staged, so you have bright areas for the sun — obviously — and each of the planets, and it would tap in really well with increasing children's interest in science and engineering and stuff . . .'

Imogen nodded as she listened to Kim chatter away excitedly, her eyes sparkling as she described her ideas.

'And I do love the idea of turning the family room into a woodland scene, although I wonder if it's innovative enough. I mean, they're probably looking for something a lot more exciting and woke and on-trend, and I'm just not sure trees really hit those marks, but I could just *see* how the trees could wrap around the whole room, turning it into a sort of secret fairy grove, with the branches extending across the ceiling. It could look so cosy, especially as the guidance said the designer would lead on furniture and things, so long as it's available from their selected suppliers. I mean, I'd have to look, but I'm sure you could get earthy-coloured beanbags and mats and sofas and things. And maybe some of those huge swivelling cuddle chairs. And maybe even stools shaped like toadstools or something. I mean, I've never costed up things like furniture before, but it should be doable, right? It's just a big shopping list really, isn't it?'

'I'm sure you could do it.' Imogen gently pushed an empty cafeteria tray into Kim's hands as they made their way to the lunch queue.

'I'm sorry, I'm probably boring you chattering away with my ideas like this.'

'No, not in the least,' Imogen told her honestly. 'I'm really not very creative when it comes to that sort of thing. You saw my attempt at a peaceful, calming-but-uplifting vibe . . .'

'Yeah, your would-be swimming pool.' Kim grinned.

'That's the one.' Imogen smiled.

'So, what's good here? Anything?'

'Actually, yeah. Most of it's pretty good. And they make the cheesecakes fresh from scratch daily. Let's just say it's good I don't work here every day, otherwise I could do some serious damage to my figure.'

'Well that's dessert sorted.' Kim followed her along the line, adding things to her tray. 'And your figure is fine. Annoyingly perfect, actually.'

'Aww, you're too sweet.' Imogen refused to focus on that.

They squabbled briefly over who would pay, with Imogen winning as she waved her staff card and cited her discount. Then they found a seat by the window, overlooking the hospital courtyard.

'Thank you for this. It means a lot,' Kim told her earnestly.

'It's just lunch.'

'I didn't mean lunch. I meant all of this. Even the hardhat.'

'So, is there a way that I can ask without risking being pushy?' Imogen desperately wanted to know if Kim was going to be submitting or not.

'It's really helped.' She nodded. 'I'm feeling inspired, and seeing the rooms helps me feel more connected to it, like I can ground my ideas in reality. And like I maybe cheated a little bit.'

'How so?'

'Will you be giving guided tours to other prospective bidders?'

'No, of course not.' Imogen laughed. 'But it's a public building, and anyone can see the plans or ask to see the space too.'

'Oh.'

'But I certainly won't be telling them about the cheesecake.'

'Kim? I nearly didn't recognise you, so dressed up!' A slim blonde with stunning green eyes waved as she approached. 'What are you doing here? Are you OK?'

'Yeah, I'm fine.' Kim stood and gave the woman a quick hug. 'Just having lunch with a friend.'

'And you couldn't think of a better venue?'

'I heard about the cheesecake.' She laughed. 'This is Imogen Finnegan. She's opened the new store in the village. Imogen, this is my soon-to-be sister-in-law, Evelyn. She and Jake are getting married in . . . how long is it now?'

'Less than two months, and coming far too quickly.' She reached out her hand. 'Nice to meet you, Imogen.'

'You too.' Evelyn's hand was warm and firm. 'I had hoped to do so sooner, but there never seem to be enough hours in the day!'

'Tell me about it.' Evelyn laughed. 'I'd meant to drop by for the opening, but got sidetracked by patients, the surgery, my family . . .'

'Still, at least we've met now.'

'Yeah. So, would that be Finnegan, as in Ryan Finnegan?'

'Yeah, he's my big brother. But please don't hold that against me.'

'It's all right, we like Ryan.'

'So do I, most of the time.' Anyone who spoke well of her brother was good in her book — especially when they knew him as Ryan instead of his online persona. 'And congratulations on the upcoming wedding.'

'Thank you. It's pretty busy, planning a wedding alongside all the work we're doing at the surgery, but it's wonderful as well.'

'Evelyn's a community nurse in the village,' Kim explained.

It all clicked into place. 'Right, so you're involved in the practice changes that have been rolled out. I've been following the work you've been doing online. It's really impressive, and the focus on re-enablement directly in the community, bringing it back to primary care to reduce the pressure on secondary, is brilliant.'

'Thank you. We think so. And we're hoping it's going to change things for the better.'

'Seems that way to me,' Imogen agreed.

'I've heard some good things recently about your new clinic.' She smiled. 'I'd love to stay and chat, but I'm due in a multi-disciplinary care planning meeting, which is much more of a mouthful than the actual work involved, but useful and important.'

'Feel free to drop by anytime,' Imogen offered, glad to find a potential ally. 'I'm here a few days a month, but otherwise I'm usually in my store. Unless I'm with a client, the kettle is always on.'

'Thanks, I'll do that. Or I can probably get your number from Kim?'

'Yeah, that works too.'

'Thanks. We'll catch up. Nice meeting you, Imogen.'

'Yeah, you too.' She waited until Evelyn was well out of earshot before turning back to Kim. 'She seems nice.'

'She's lovely. And her daughter Summer is the sweetest thing.'

'Summer? One of the kids who helps at Bill's?'

'Yeah.' Kim nodded. 'Have you met her?'

'No, but Ryan has a lot of good things to say about her.'

'She really is amazing.' Kim smiled. 'Especially when you consider what she's been through.'

'Oh?' Imogen ran her spoon over the top of the cheesecake, gathering up the creamy goodness.

'You've heard of Summer's Christmas?'

'About Santa coming in August?'

'Yeah. It's a big fundraiser, we raise a small fortune every year. The first event was for her. She was sick, and needed treatment that was only available in America. So the village came together to raise the funds.'

'Wow, that's amazing. And she's all better now? Ryan didn't mention her being sick.'

'Yeah, she's in extended remission. And planning to become one of the youngest vets ever.'

'That really is wonderful.'

'Yeah.' Kim smiled. 'We may have only met her a few years ago, but she's a Macpearson through and through. And Evelyn is like the sister I always wanted.'

'So, if she's so lovely, can I ask why you didn't tell her about the tender? I mean, feel free to tell me to shut up and stick my nose back in my cheesecake — I won't be offended — but . . . I am curious.'

'I don't know,' Kim replied. 'I adore her, it's just . . . you know about the projects she's working on with my brothers. I'm just me with my little art ideas that probably won't ever get anywhere, just like me.'

Hearing Kim sound so down on herself, and her dreams, hit Imogen hard. 'Why are you so negative? You seemed a lot more certain about this all a few minutes ago.'

'I've always been the family screw-up.' Kim shrugged and smashed her cheesecake into the plate. Watching her abuse the confectionary forced a decision that pulled Imogen right out of her comfort zone.

'You asked me for my opinion. Do you really want it?'

'Yes please.'

'You were really excited about this a few minutes ago. When you were looking at the spaces and talking about your ideas, you lit up. You did an amazing job in my store, and you said your dream was to make beautiful, artistic things.' She reached across the table to squeeze Kim's fingers. 'I know I've not known you all that long, but you really don't strike me as a "screw-up", not in any way, by any definition of the phrase. I think you could create something really beautiful here. And, more than that, I think if you don't try because of an old view of a previous version of yourself, you'll always wonder what would have happened if you had tried.'

Imogen was surprised when Kim flipped her hand over so their palms were pressed warmly against each other. She squeezed back, sending waves of heat racing up her arm.

'Can you answer me something else?' Kim asked.

'I can try.' She forced herself to look away from Kim's eyes, which had locked on hers.

'How is it that we've only known each other for a matter of weeks, and you seem to know me better than anyone else? Sometimes myself included.'

'I guess I'm just good at reading people. Or maybe we really have known each other "forever", or at least longer than this lifetime.'

'Maybe.' Again those bright blue eyes locked on Imogen's, making it just a little bit harder to think straight. 'You really think I should do it?'

'Yeah.' Imogen nodded. 'I do. But I don't think it should be because I've said that . . . I think, if you're honest with yourself, it's what you really want, and that's why I think you should submit.'

'You're probably right.'

'Only probably?' Imogen raised both eyebrows, silently challenging Kim.

'Definitely a little bit. Like maybe half . . .'

'I'll take that.' Imogen grinned.

CHAPTER SEVEN

Imogen hung up the phone with fingers that shook. Then, for good measure, she picked it up and smacked it down again — harder this time, but it didn't help. She hadn't really expected it to. That stupid, small-minded, vicious, backwards-thinking harridan. And . . . as *if*.

She tried to think more logically . . . This wasn't the first time she'd encountered such out-and-out, ill-informed, arrogant, self-absorbed bigotry, but the place that . . . *person* . . . had taken her hatred was somewhere she'd managed to avoid for many years. She'd started to think — to hope — it had been buried and smothered out by a wave of rainbows, education and pride celebrations that flooded the country, carried by her community and thousands of proud allies.

How stupidly naive she'd been.

That was the problem. She'd relaxed, so the attack had caught her completely off-guard. Things had been going so well, for so long, that she'd gotten complacent and left herself open to hurt.

Knowing that, and trying to take on some of the responsibility, didn't help. She shouldn't have to be responsible for other people's narrow-minded prejudice, and that thought just made her angrier. The anger that coursed through her was so intense that her skin exploded in goosebumps as adrenaline numbed her extremities. Her stomach rolled, trying to reject the coffee and bagel that had been her breakfast. She took a few deep breaths, trying to settle her stomach and emotions. It wasn't working — she flicked burning tears from her cheeks.

She stalked over to the door, snapped the latch shut and flipped the sign. The very last thing she wanted right at that moment was to deal with anyone else. She wasn't even sure she could deal with her own company at the moment — she could already feel the adrenaline rush of anger fading to leave a dull, nagging warning in her joints. Wonderful. Just fucking wonderful. She knew damn well that stress, and emotional distress, could trigger a flare — but knowing that didn't make it any better. If anything, knowing that the vicious vitriol she'd just listened to was going to have a lasting impact, ruining the rest of her day, just made her angrier. It was so unfair.

She knew she needed to let the energy go — that holding onto it was only going to be toxic and make her feel sicker for longer — but it was hard to just "let go" of such unfairness and downright cruelty, which would almost certainly go unpunished. Well, at least until karma caught up with her. The problem was, as much as Imogen did trust karma, she hated feeling helpless.

The woman hadn't made any actual threats to Imogen's person, so all she could really report her for was a bit of name-calling, which she hadn't any evidence of, and therefore the police could do very little about. Even if it was technically a hate crime.

She — and all of her clients — had every right to choose who to be treated by. For whatever reason they wanted. And if their reasons were vicious, angry, bigoted bull, then all Imogen could do was try and not stoop to the level of hoping that Mrs Molvaney's bunions persisted in hurting her for many more years. At least, she could try.

She took a deep breath and grabbed one of her lepidolite towers from the display shelf. The purple-lilac crystal, often known as purple mica, had the perfect energy for promoting calm and tranquillity, helping her to rebalance her battered emotions, and it was sturdy enough to take the misery and abuse she really needed to throw at it. Afterwards, she'd either cleanse it, or keep it — which was always a dangerous temptation when she got beautiful stock in.

She sat on the bottom of the stairs, next to the squirrel that Kim had threatened with devil horns, and sighed. Pulling out her phone, she would send a quick apology message. Kim didn't need to see her in this state, and it wasn't like she was going to be any fun anyway. She was just going to gather her energy, drag herself upstairs and curl up with a blanket or three until she felt better.

* * *

Kim knocked at the door and waited. After a few moments of total silence, she tried again, this time louder. When the shop door finally opened, Imogen looked worse than Kim had ever seen her. She was pale, drawn and had dark circles under her eyes, and her hair was falling out of the messy bun it was in — not in the cute way.

'Hey.'

'You didn't get my text?' Imogen leaned heavily against the doorframe. 'I'm really sorry, Kim, but I don't think I'm going to be very good company today. Would you mind dreadfully if we postponed?'

'Actually yeah, I would mind. Because I'm worried about you. And I did get your text, so I brought soup. And ginger tea. And now, looking at you, I'm wondering if I should have brought my dad or brother too. Should I call them?'

'No, thank you.'

'I can call Liv, if you'd prefer a woman.'

'It's not that.' Imogen shifted, wincing. 'I don't need a doctor. It's just a flare-up.'

Oh hell. Kim stared at Imogen, trying not to let the horror she felt show on her face. Her friend looked like she'd been partying for three days straight and developed the devil's own hangover, then been dragged through a hedge backwards and beaten up for good measure. Just looking at her hurt. 'This is fibromyalgia?'

'Yeah.' Imogen nodded tiredly. 'And I don't mean to be rude, but I really need to go back upstairs.'

Kim could see she was starting to shake. 'Let me help.'

'I'll be fine. I just need to rest.'

'You don't look like you'll even make it upstairs.'

'I'll manage, I always do. Just lock the door and post the key back through, would you?'

Kim watched as she walked back across the store, very slowly, limping as if each step hurt. She hesitated for a moment, thinking that maybe she should back down, but then saw Imogen stumble. She caught herself, but that was enough to make Kim's decision, so she locked the door from the inside and raced to Imogen. She slipped one arm round her waist, and used the other to drape one of Imogen's over her shoulders. 'Come on, let me help.'

'I really will be OK.' Despite her arguing, she leaned against Kim.

'How are you going to get upstairs? Planning to crawl?'

'Wouldn't be the first time.' Her sigh tickled Kim's neck, sending weird goose pimples running over her skin.

'Yeah, well, that's not happening today.' Or ever again, if she had anything to say about it. But she'd settle for Imogen letting her look after her right now. 'Come on, let's get you upstairs and I'll put the kettle on. OK?'

'You really don't need to do this.' Even Imogen's voice seemed weaker and more wobbly than usual.

'No, but I want to. And I'm not having any more arguments about it.' She tightened her arm around Imogen's waist as they headed up the stairs. 'Couch or bed?'

'Um. Couch, I think.'

'You sure?' She didn't sound it.

'Yeah. I don't think I can handle being put to bed by you.'

'What?' Kim laughed.

'Sorry, the whole brain-to-tongue-filter-thing breaks down sometimes when I'm flaring.'

'So you say things you shouldn't? This could be interesting.' She lowered Imogen gently to the couch. 'Now what can I do to help? Have you taken your painkillers? Heat's supposed to help, right? Do you want tea or a hot water bottle? What about blankets? Have you got one of those weighted blanket things? Do they work for you? When you're comfy, I can make you some food. Some people say sweet things help — the energy boost thing. Are you one of them?'

'You've been researching my condition?'

'Well, if asking at the surgery about it is research, then yes. But don't worry,' Kim jumped to reassure her, 'I didn't say it was you, just that I knew someone who had it and wanted to know more about it so I could better support them.'

'You really said that?'

'Yes, and I meant it. So, what can I get you?'

'I really am fine now.'

Kim looked at her for a few moments, then grinned. 'Well, I could do with a cuppa. So, do you mind if I put the kettle on?'

'You really can be stubborn.'

'Not like you weren't warned. Now, do you want tea? Hot water bottle?'

'Yes please. That would be good.'

'All right. Is there anything else I can get you?'

'Haven't you got anything better to do?'

'Nope. Not really,' Kim told her cheerfully, 'so you might as well sit back, hush up and let me look after you for a bit.'

The last thing she expected was to see Imogen's shoulders heave as she burst into tears, doubling over to sob on her knees.

'Hey, Imogen.' Kim didn't hesitate to sit next to her, stroking her back and trying to soothe her friend. She leaned down, stroking Imogen's curls out of her face. 'What's all this about? Please tell me how I can help.'

She mumbled something that Kim couldn't understand. 'You can talk to me. Please let me help. Come on, sit up and tell me what's wrong. Please?' Imogen didn't fight when Kim lifted her back upright, but she wasn't sure if it was because she was glad Kim was there, or if she just didn't have the energy to fight. But when Imogen collapsed against her, tears coming hot and fast, she wrapped her arms around her, rocking and shushing.

It took a few painfully long minutes before Imogen calmed enough to look up and start making sense. 'Sorry, I didn't mean to do that.'

'It's OK,' Kim reassured her.

'No, it's not. You don't deserve this.'

'Honestly, it's fine. I mean, you're annoying, but fine.'

Imogen's face crumpled again as she stared at Kim. 'Great. Now I'm annoying too.'

'Yeah. But that's a me problem. I always get annoyed at girls who can pretty-cry.'

Exactly as she'd hoped, Imogen looked up, confusion overwhelming whatever had upset her. 'What?'

'When I cry I go bright red and blotchy — it's like a snot-monster exploded. My eyes swell up and I look like I've gone a couple of rounds in a boxing ring. You, on the other hand, cry pretty. You're all pale and interesting, with your eyes all big and glossy, and just a little flush in your cheeks—' she handed Imogen a box of tissues from the coffee table '—and the very tip of your nose.'

'You're just being nice.' Imogen sniffed and blew her nose.

'Nope, I'm really not. You're sickening. No one should be allowed to look this good when they're crying, unless they're an actress. It's just not fair on us snot-monster mere mortals.'

Imogen snorted with laughter, drying her eyes. 'You really are too nice to me.'

'Nah, not even close.' Kim gave her another squeeze, careful to be gentle. 'Do you want to tell me what's wrong?'

'It's nothing. I'm just being silly.'

109

'If it's got you this upset, then it's not silly,' Kim promised her. 'And whatever it is, if I can help, I really wish you'd tell me.'

'It's not you who caused this, if that's what you're worried about. There's no guilt, so you don't have to stay.' Imogen pulled away.

'Oh good. Thanks for telling me that. But I was planning on staying because my friend isn't well, and I thought I might be able to help. Now, if you're OK for a few minutes, you're going to tell me where your hot water bottle is, and I'm going to fill that up, make drinks and then you can tell me what's going on, OK?'

'OK.' Imogen's smile was watery, but still there, so Kim headed out to the kitchen.

* * *

Imogen tucked the hot water bottle behind her back, low against her often-problematic sacroiliac joint, and accepted the tea from Kim with a smile that only felt a bit wobbly. She really was one of the most amazing people she'd met in a long time. She wrapped both hands around the mug, letting the heat sink into her joints. It was hot — painfully so, really — but it hurt less than the pain of the fibro. So long as she struck the careful balance between the heat hurting and burning her skin — again — she'd be OK.

'So, do you want to talk?' Kim settled on the couch opposite her. 'Or should I be scared to suggest that, given your lack of mouth-to-brain filter?'

'I think I can just about manage to keep my foot out of my mouth. Especially given how stiff I am today.'

'Well, glad to see your sense of humour is returning, even if it is a bit darker than usual. I'll take that as a good sign.' She tucked her feet up, getting more comfortable, and for a brief moment Imogen envied her ease of movement. Not because she'd ever, ever want Kim to experience the pain she did, but just because — on days when her condition was this bad — it was easy to forget what it was like to move freely and without pain.

Imogen chased the thought away and took a deep breath. 'I lost a patient today.'

'Oh, I'm so sorry to hear that. Was it expected? Not that it makes it much easier, but somehow it's worse when it's not, if that makes sense.'

For a few seconds, she couldn't make sense of Kim's question. 'No, I didn't mean "lost", like died. I meant "lost" as in she just doesn't want to be treated by me anymore.'

'Right, sorry. I'm used to that meaning something different with the surgery. I'm guessing, from the impact it's had on you, that it's not because she's made some sort of miracle recovery.'

'No. She just doesn't want to be treated by someone who's gay.'

Kim's hands were warm on her knee. 'She's an idiot, and you're better off without her. And it's completely her loss, because you're bloody brilliant at your job.'

'That's nice of you to say.'

'I'm not being nice,' Kim argued, her fierceness surprising Imogen. 'Just honest.'

'You're going to make me cry again,' Imogen warned. 'And I'm really not much of a crier.'

'Could have fooled me,' Kim teased her gently.

'I meant usually.' She rolled her eyes. 'And I'm usually better at managing my triggers, and not letting shit like this bother me, but I'm just feeling a bit tired, and hormonal, and she caught me off-guard.'

'And that's triggered this?'

'Yeah.'

'I hope whatever was wrong with her is something really painful and long-lasting!'

'Kimberly!' Imogen was equal parts shocked and touched. 'You can't go wishing ill on people.' She tried not to think

111

about how hard it had been earlier for her to not hope for something very similar.

'Why not? She deserves it for doing this to you.'

'Because she didn't do this to me. Fibromyalgia and tiredness and it being the wrong time of the month did this to me. And because she isn't worth the risk of negative karma to yourself. You shouldn't wish pain on her.'

'If you say so.'

'I do. Please just leave it alone, Kim.'

'All right,' she grumbled, clearly far from happy.

'I think I might put a movie on or something.'

'Is that going to help?'

'It might do if it's funny.' Imogen wasn't ready to admit to Kim that it was her presence that was really helping take her mind off everything bad. She didn't want her to feel like she had to stay.

'I like funny movies.' Kim pulled the blanket off the back of the sofa and draped it over Imogen, leaning close and filling her nose with that fresh honey-apple scent. 'Have you eaten yet?'

'I made cereal for lunch.'

Kim regarded her with shrewd eyes. 'But did you actually eat it?'

'Some of it.'

'Right, then I'm raiding your kitchen while you pick the film. Anything you really fancy? Like I said, I did bring soup. Albeit from a shop — but it's posh-shop soup.'

'I'm not exactly good company right now. In fact I'm probably just about the worst hostess possible.'

'You still don't get it, do you? Doing nothing with you is still more fun than doing almost anything with anyone else.'

She said it so matter-of-factly — that sweet, kind, mind-boggling, unexpected expression of affection — that it left Imogen gobsmacked, with no idea how to respond.

'Are you kicking me out? Because — and forgive me for being rude here — you don't look like you've got the energy.'

Imogen shook her head, unsure of whether she wanted to hug Kim or scold her more. She really was the best kind of pest there was.

'No? I didn't think so.' She grabbed the remote control from the table and passed it to Imogen. 'Now, again, is there anything you fancy?'

'There's some of that caramel popcorn you like above the oven.'

'Soup followed by caramel popcorn. Score.' Kim sauntered back to the kitchen.

* * *

'Kim, I really appreciate your help, but if you need to get off somewhere, it's fine. I really am going to be OK.'

Kim finished her soup and pushed away the bowl, then laughed. 'And leave you to eat all this popcorn? Not a chance . . . More seriously, Imogen, if you want me to go because you'd rather be asleep or have a bath or something, then tell me. I'm not going to be offended. But if this is you just fussing because you're worried about me seeing you when you're less than your best, or some other similar nonsense, then forget it. I'm more than happy to sit here, scoff all your treats and keep you company for a bit while we find out if this dude—' she flicked her fingers at the screen '—is smart enough to realise blondie is actually in love with him. My guess is he will, but not for at least another thirty or forty minutes.'

Imogen stared at Kim for a few seconds, trying to force her thoughts past the fog in her brain to figure out how she was supposed to respond. She was used to dealing with her condition and managing it so that, for the most part, it didn't eat up whole chunks of her life. She was used to dealing with all sorts of responses, ranging from being told she should "just exercise it away", or that it "was all in her head" or, worse, being accused of lying to seek attention because she "looked too well to be as ill as she made out".

So she'd gotten used to dealing with it by herself — even Ryan knew to leave well alone when she was mid-flare, or risk having her melt down in tears or lose her temper with him. She was used to making apologies and excuses when the condition flared to disabling levels and she was forced to give in to it, which invariably meant letting people down.

What she wasn't used to was someone cheerfully bursting in, rearranging their plans to look after her, coddling her in blankets, making her food and making her laugh. She wasn't used to someone who looked at her, saw her flaws and weaknesses, and just accepted them with pragmatism and good humour.

'Well?' Kim nudged her. 'You going to share that popcorn?'

'Yeah.' Imogen handed over the bowl. 'Here you go.' She sighed and settled back, snuggling into the sofa cushions.

What felt like a few seconds later she opened her eyes again, and it took a few breaths of honeyed apple sweetness for her to reorient herself. The leads from the film were frozen on her TV, paused in the middle of a passionate embrace — clearly they'd figured things out. In her sleepy state, she was tempted to snuggle more closely against Kim. As soon as the thought escaped from her dreamy self into consciousness, she moved, forcing herself upright.

'Hey, sleepyhead.' Kim smiled at her. 'Are you feeling any better?'

Imogen blinked a few more times, trying to figure out the answer. 'Yeah . . . I think I am. Sorry.'

'For what?'

'Falling asleep on you. Literally and figuratively.'

'Nothing to apologise for. You obviously needed it.' She dropped her tablet to her lap. 'I've fed and watered Bramble, and sorted his stinky box out.'

'Thanks.'

'You're welcome. Do you want anything?'

'Depends . . . Have you been working on your hospital submission?' Imogen pointed to Kim's tablet.

114

'Yup. Want a peek?'
'Definitely.'

* * *

Kim stopped on the way home to pick up the groceries her mum had asked for. She'd just grabbed the milk, and was heading to the next aisle for bread before joining the queue for the till. Even if she'd wanted to avoid hearing it — which she really would have preferred — Mrs Molvaney was broadcasting her opinions at a volume any town crier would envy.

'. . . she's one of them. It's not right, it's just not. Having one of them in our village doing something like that.' Kim didn't need to see the woman's face to picture her nose scrunching up as her lips pursed. Disapproval like she'd sucked a lemon was pretty much the woman's go-to expression. She idly wondered who had attracted the sour-sucking look today.

'It shouldn't be allowed. We should have been warned. Consulted with, before they let one of them open a business like that.' Molvaney didn't wait for comment from her small audience made up of Kerry, who was behind the till, and the other would-be customers waiting to pay, but Kim's attention was instantly caught. She couldn't think of many new businesses in the village . . . except for Imogen's.

'Honestly,' the foghorn of accusation went on, 'letting a gay treat decent, unsuspecting people like us without any warning. Touching people and calling it medicine. I'll tell you for nothing I cancelled my appointment as soon as I found out what she really is.' Kim saw red as the woman carried on, spreading lies about one of the best people she knew. The realisation that this — or someone very like her — was who had caused Imogen's flare the week before sent shards of anger through her.

'And I suggest you all do the same. You can't trust people like that. Lord only knows where her hands have been, or the types of depraved things she does with them.'

115

'Who exactly are you talking about, Mabel Molvaney?' Kim snapped. 'It wouldn't be Imogen Finnegan, would it? Who has just opened her complementary therapy store . . . The same Imogen Finnegan who is a highly trained, qualified, experienced and dedicated medical professional? And one of the nicest people I've ever met? Would it be her you're talking about?'

The woman didn't answer, which infuriated Kim even more. She didn't often say mean things — but when she did, she at least had the guts to say them to whoever had annoyed her. She prided herself on never saying anything behind someone's back that she wouldn't say to their face. 'Well? Is it Imogen Finnegan you're slandering? Because she's the only person I can think of who's opened a new business here recently and who also happens to be gay. Not that it should be any of your business.'

'It's my business if she's touching me.'

'Why? Because she likes women instead of men?'

'Well . . . yes.'

'I'm curious.' Kim's voice was softer and calmer now, which would have had most people who knew her starting to panic and look for a retreat. 'Have you ever refused treatment from my brother?'

'Kimberly . . .' Kerry had known her long enough to recognise the tone. 'Do you think maybe you've said enough?'

'I'm only curious.' Kim fixed her eyes on the older woman. 'Come on, Mrs Molvaney, answer the question. If you got sick or injured, would you refuse treatment from my brother? Or my dad, come to think of it.'

'No, of course not.'

'But their sexual preferences are towards women too.'

'Yes, but they're doctors.'

'Yes they are — highly trained medical professionals, who have taken an oath dedicating themselves to the care of their patients.'

'It's not really the same though, is it?'

116

'Because Imogen is "only" a physiotherapist? So it's physios you have a problem with. Does that extend to nurses like Evelyn, and other healthcare professionals like Millie? I'm pretty sure she's been looking after your daughter and grandson, hasn't she?'

'Yes, but that's different.'

'Right, so it's only people like physiotherapists whose romantic attractions interest you. Is that what you're saying?'

'Well, no, but . . .'

'Oh please, explain it to us. I'm sure we're all just waiting to hear what else you have to say.'

The stupid woman gaped at her, not knowing what to say now she had been confronted.

'Do you think, maybe, that the problem isn't them, and it's really you? That it's not Imogen who's the problem, but it's really your stinking, small-minded, bigoted attitude? For the love of all that you consider holy, what is your problem with gay people? Do you think that you're so incredibly irresistible that she wouldn't be able to help herself? She's a medical professional — who has been through the highest levels of DBS clearances, by the way — not some sort of sexual predator.'

'I never said that!'

'No, you just implied it. At the top of your voice, in the middle of the village shop, intent on spreading your gossip and vitriol throughout the community Imogen's wanting to support.'

'She's got you there, Mable.' Kim didn't recognise the voice, but was glad of the support. 'You did do that. And it is a bit old-fashioned thinking.'

'You're older than me!' Mable snapped.

'Apparently I'm old enough to know better. Perhaps you have some growing up to do.' Kim wished she knew the speaker — the older woman wasn't someone she recognised, but she loved her in that moment for sticking up for her friend. And for what was right and fair. 'Really, she deserves an apology.'

'I'm sorry if you took offence.' Mable didn't look up from her nails.

'I took offence because you were being offensive,' Kim responded, trying not to snap. 'By rights, it's not me you should be apologising to, it's Imogen. But I doubt you will, because I don't think you have the guts to.' Still irritated, she held up her purchases so Kerry could run up her total, then slapped a note down on the counter before stalking out.

'Kim!' Kerry's voice barely slowed her. 'What about your change?'

'Stick it in the charity pot, Kez.'

She made it to the end of her street before realising she was far too wound up to want to sit at the dinner table making polite conversation with her parents, so she grabbed her phone and fired off a message to her friend Millie, hoping she'd be up for a drink.

* * *

Two days later, Imogen stopped by the vets on the way back from the hospital. Thankfully, she seemed to have timed things perfectly and the waiting room was empty. Kim smiled at her as the door swung closed.

'Hello. I wasn't expecting to see you today.'

'Have you got a couple of minutes, please?'

'Sure.' Kim walked around the desk to lean against it.

'Is there anywhere private? Just for a couple of minutes.'

'Sure.' Kim gave her an odd look, walked to a door and keyed an unlock code before holding it open. The supply closet was a mix of cleaning products, medications and veterinary equipment. It was small, and smelled strongly of disinfectant, but if she was about to have an argument with her friend, then it was a better place than the public reception.

'Are you OK?' Kim closed the door and leaned against it.

'Yeah.' Imogen thought she'd ordered her thoughts on the drive here, but now she struggled to know where to start. 'I, um, heard you had a bit of a run-in at the shop.'

'Can't say I'm surprised — out of interest, who told on me?'

'A patient in my pain clinic.' Imogen wasn't going to say more than that, and hoped Kim knew better than to ask.

'Which means I don't get to ask who has a big mouth.'

'No, not really. But it doesn't matter.' Imogen jammed her hands into her pockets.

'You're annoyed with me.' Kim sounded surprised.

'No, I'm not. I'm worried about you.' Imogen fidgeted. 'It's not that I'm not grateful — I am. And I really like that you wanted to defend me, but please don't do it again.'

'Why not? She was disgusting and out of order. She had no business talking about you like that! She's such a vicious, nasty cow!'

'Kim, please don't be angry over this.'

'Why not? You could sue her for slander if you wanted.'

'Probably not.'

'You didn't hear her.'

'No.' Imogen ditched the fidgeting, this time wrapping her arms around herself. 'But I got given a pretty good blow-by-blow report. Kim, I really don't want you making enemies on my behalf. I don't need you to fight my battles, especially ones this silly and pointless.'

'Pointless? I don't think challenging bigoted, dangerous views is pointless. What's wrong with you?'

'I just don't think it's worth the stress and trouble it will cause.'

'How can you say that?'

'Do you think it's the first time I've had to listen to people say stupid, bigoted, small-minded crap like that?'

'No, but—'

'Kim.' Imogen caught her hands. 'It's not worth it to me. You know fibro limits my energy, so I pick my battles carefully. People like that just aren't worth my time or effort. It's that simple to me. Do you understand? I can't waste energy getting as angry as you are now. And I don't want you to, either. I know you don't have the same limits that I do, but

119

I don't think it's healthy to carry this much anger for any length of time.'

'I don't know how to let it go.'

'Do you think the person who said all these things has given it anywhere near the thought you have?'

'Probably not. I'm not sure she's capable of that much intelligent thought.' Kim snapped the words out.

'Kim, please, try to find a way to let it go. Don't let her nasty words poison you, OK?'

Kim nodded, drumming her fingers against her thigh. After a few seconds, she looked up, her blue eyes still sparking with anger. 'I understand what you're saying, I just don't know how to do it. I'm not exactly known for my brilliant and even temper.'

'Really? You don't say?' Imogen grinned. 'Maybe take a couple of deep breaths and focus on something happier. Something more positive?'

'Sorry. I can't think of anything positive enough right now.'

'Can I try something?' She adjusted her hold on Kim. 'Place your fingers here, over your pulse point. Feel it hammering away?'

'Not good?'

'Not ideal. Now, focus on that hammering, feel it in your fingers and your wrist, and let it slowly drop back while you focus on something happy.'

Kim gave her a look of irritation, mixed with disbelief.

'Don't knock it until you've tried it. Give me the benefit of the doubt for a few seconds, OK?'

Kim rolled her eyes, but shut them and looked like she was concentrating. After a few moments, Imogen felt the pulse in her wrist start to slow, and a few seconds later Kim opened her eyes.

'Feeling any better?'

'You're going to be annoying about this, aren't you?' Kim flashed her a grin that was much more like her usual, sarky self.

'Would I do that?' Imogen smiled back, glad to see her friend feeling better. She'd meant what she said — the last thing she wanted was for the stupid, thoughtless words of one idiot to hurt anyone she cared about.

'Oh, so you're not even a little bit smug about the fact you were right?'

'Nope.' Imogen crossed her arms over her chest.

'So I've completely and totally misjudged you?' Kim teased as she opened the door. 'The words "I told you so" aren't burning on your tongue? Not at all?'

'That wouldn't be very professional of me, would it?'

'Nope. But how badly are you wanting to say it?'

'Pretty badly,' Imogen admitted with a grin.

'Know it all!' Kim poked her tongue out.

'Hey, I worked long and hard to know that much!'

'Well, since you're so clever, how about coming to the pub on Friday? It's quiz night, and we need help to maintain our winning streak.'

'Oh, this is the thing Ryan's been trying to get me to go to.'

'You don't like quiz nights?' Kim gave her an odd look.

'I don't dislike them,' Imogen answered. 'I'm just not very good at general knowledge. And I've been pretty busy setting up a new business. It does take up a lot of time, you know.'

'But you're set up now . . .'

'I am,' Imogen agreed.

'And it's really good fun. And our team could use the extra help.'

'Ryan said that too.'

'So you'd be making your brother happy as well as me, and having good fun.'

'You're not going to let this go, are you?' Kim shook her head. 'All right, all right. If I'm feeling OK, I'll come. And that's as good as you're getting.'

'Good enough for me.' Kim stopped even trying to hide her grin.

'*If* I'm feeling OK,' Imogen repeated.

'You will. I'll see you Friday. If not sooner.'

'If not sooner.'

Imogen was still smiling when she climbed back into her car.

CHAPTER EIGHT

'Hey, you made it!'

Kim spun round in her seat and waved to Imogen, who flicked her fingers in greeting.

'Come on, Moggy, hurry up and sit down, they're about to start.'

'Keep calling me that and I can turn right back around, Ry-no.'

'Don't drive her off, Ryan.' Angela poked him. 'You said she's good at literature and mineralogy.'

'Am I?' Imogen pulled a face.

'Better than he'll be.' Kim grinned. 'This is Harry, local police sergeant, and his wife Marie. Millie here is our community nurse and midwife, and we're missing Callum and Liv tonight, but you know the rest.'

'I do.' She greeted Harry, Marie and Millie with polite smiles and waves.

'Shove over, Jake.' Kim wriggled away from her brother. 'Make some room. Unless you've found time to pick up a book that isn't a medical manual. Come sit, Imogen.'

'I'll have you know, Summer and I also read fairy stories . . . complete with all the voices,' Jake complained, moving over. 'Good to see you again, Imogen. How's the kitten?'

'Getting into mischief. So, exactly as he should be. Nice to see you as well. You too, Evelyn.'

'Yes, you too.' The blonde smiled at Imogen as she sat down. 'And now I'm not rushing off, maybe we can actually talk this time.'

'Sounds good.'

'You drinking or not, Moggy?'

'Drinking, if I have to put up with you! Seriously though, knock off the nickname would you?' She leaned over to grin at Angela. 'I don't know how you put up with him.'

'He has his good points.' Angela smiled. 'For one, his sister and bird are pretty cool.'

'You know you love me really.' Ryan wrapped his arm around Angela, pulling her in tight and kissing her cheek.

'I really do.' Angela snuggled against Ryan, making Imogen smile. She really was thrilled for her brother, even if she did think Angela was out of his league. Imogen only hoped someday she'd meet the woman from her dreams, and that she'd look at her the way Angela looked at Ryan.

She chatted easily with the group around the table until the quiz started, laughing along with everyone, and trying to contribute as best she could. But, for the most part, she just enjoyed the company. When a question about the Sto Helit family, and where they would be most likely to be found, came up, Kim's eyes locked with hers and she smiled hugely.

'Oh no,' Ryan teased. 'It's that crazy book series you like, isn't it? You've found someone else who believes the world is flat, haven't you?'

'I don't believe in the *Discworld*.' Imogen giggled, rolling her eyes at her brother.

'No, that would be stupid,' Kim agreed. 'It's just good fun. And really well written.'

'Thank you.' Imogen held her glass up in cheers.

'Just don't get the appeal.' Ryan shrugged.

'That's OK.' Imogen shrugged back. 'I don't get the appeal of all your videos and social media stuff either.'

'And if you did, your business would be busier and even more successful.'

'And if I was any busier, I wouldn't be able to keep up.' It was an old argument, but one Imogen was used to. She was lucky to have a brother who cared about her enough to keep challenging her to do more — but also respected her enough to accept when she told him she was happy as she was. And she really was.

Ryan had found a place where he could truly be himself. Sat around that table, with people who had welcomed her so warmly, and Kim, who shared everything so openly with her, she really hoped this could be the place for her too.

* * *

'So what you really want to do is paint walls?' Kim's date asked.

'Yeah.' She nodded. 'But, like, pictures and murals.'

'Is there really much call for that? I mean, what's wrong with just a nice, clean white wall and some photographs? Or better, a large-screen TV?'

'It's about creating a particular environment and feeling,' Kim tried to explain, wondering why she was struggling to find the right words with this man, who she'd scored an eighty-seven per cent match rating with, so much more than she did Imogen. 'Like to make a shop feel more magical and inviting, or to help children feel less scared in hospital.'

'I'd think a good seventy-inch TV and playing cartoons would achieve that,' Blake argued. 'Especially if you hooked up a games console.'

'True.' Kim didn't really want to argue when she was on a date, but she couldn't help thinking that he was completely missing the point. Where was the wonder, the imagination, the comfort in a TV? She was saved from the awkward silence by the arrival of their food.

'Would you like my onion rings?'

'Why did you order them if you don't like them?' Blake, her very good-looking, very polite, very nice and very perfect — on the app, at least — date asked.

'I didn't order them, exactly,' Kim explained. 'They just came with the meal.'

'You could have asked them to change the meal. You do know that, right?'

'Yeah, but it just seems more complicated.' Kim couldn't help thinking that Imogen would have already snagged the crispy onion rings off the plate. Probably switching them for mushrooms. She also would have laughed at the joke she'd made about their waitress — Susan — that had gone straight over Blake's perfectly coiffed head.

She sighed inwardly, finding herself wishing they'd only met for coffee instead of a whole meal. He was pleasant enough. But that was it — there was no spark between them, and clearly they didn't share a lot of interests, or sense of humour, so there were a lot more awkward silences and conversation about the weather and how nice the place was and what a varied menu they had than she would ever want on a date.

She found herself wondering what Imogen was doing right then — probably she'd be playing with Bramble, or settling down with a book after a long week. Having seen her when she was in the midst of what she casually referred to as "just a fibro flare", and realising how crippling it could be, Kim understood why her friend put so much emphasis on protecting her time and energy. And while Kim didn't have pain or illness as a consideration, she was starting to wonder if she should start being a bit more protective of her own time.

But, instead, she forced herself back into the moment, making more polite conversation, and tried not to compare him to her friend. Especially difficult when the dessert menu came out and she found herself thinking Imogen would definitely have shared plates. And a lot more laughs. The more she thought about it, the more she realised that she would rather be with Imogen than Blake, or anyone even vaguely like him. The thought flung her into a spiral of confusion, and left her even quieter than before . . . on the outside at least. Her mind was screaming at her, demanding she pay attention to something she didn't understand how to even think about.

She politely refused the offer for coffee, or more drinks, and paid her share of the bill as soon as she could without being rude. But she was pretty sure neither of them would be rushing to contact the other and arrange a second date. That became even more obvious when he politely shook hands with her and wished her a good weekend — with no mention of a call or message to come. Which was fine by Kim.

She called Imogen on her way back to her car.

'Hello, should I ask how the date went?' Just the sound of her voice made Kim relax.

'Given that it's not even nine and I'm calling you while walking to my car? Probably not.'

'Was it that bad? Didn't look anything like his profile?'

'No, he did. He was very nice.'

'So . . . ?'

'He thinks walls should be crisp-white and covered in TVs, doesn't get Pratchett jokes, or share desserts. Just lots of polite conversation, awkward pauses and zero sparks. We shook hands very politely a few minutes ago and neither suggested a repeat event.'

'Oh dear. Do you want to come round?'

'See, you get me.' Kim unlocked her car. 'See you in about half an hour.'

* * *

'Wow.' Imogen opened the door and tried not to gawp. Kim was wearing jeans that fit her perfectly, with a velvety top beneath her jacket that was almost the exact shade of blue as her eyes — which were slightly smoky and seemed bigger and brighter than usual. Her lips were pale pink, and had a subtle shimmer that she found hard to look away from. She had to force herself to step back and hold the door open, reminding herself that Kim was her friend. Her very, very good friend who had just finished her date with a man, and who would definitely never be anything more than a friend.

'You like?' Kim gave a little shimmy and twirl.

'You look gorgeous,' she answered honestly. 'And your date was an idiot if he didn't see that.'

'You know there's more to things like this than looks. There just wasn't any connection. To be honest, I have better chemistry with you than I did him.' She slipped off her jacket, and Imogen had to remind herself how to swallow. What was she supposed to do with a comment like that? And she hadn't realised, until Kim chucked her jacket over the banister, that the back of her top was made entirely of sheer lace. 'Mind if I put your kettle on?'

'Course not. You know where everything is. Help yourself.'

'Tea?'

'Yeah, red leaf please. I don't fancy a caffeine hit right now.'

Kim did as she was told, making herself at home as usual. Imogen couldn't help but smile as Kim put the mugs down on the coffee table, scooped up Bramble, apologising to the grumbling kitten, before flopping down next to Imogen.

'Want to talk about it?'

'Not much to say really. Just no click at all.'

'Maybe you're just having a bit of a bad patch. Weird energy in your life, or something. Do you still have that rose quartz moon I gave you? That should be good for helping to attract love into your life.'

'Yeah, it's in my windowsill. That's right, isn't it?'

'Which way does your window face?'

'I'm not sure. I don't think I've ever checked.'

'Well, what time of day does the sun hit, and from which side?'

'Oh, duh.' Kim laughed, then muttered, moving her fingers in the air as she figured it out. 'North-east-ish . . . I think.'

'Well, that should be fine, as the sunrise will hit it. If you're wanting to attract new love energy into your life, putting rose quartz where the new day's light lands is ideal.'

They fell into an easy silence for a while, which Kim eventually broke. 'Why is it that sitting here quietly with you is so much easier, and nicer, than with anyone else?'

'Because we're best friends and there's no pressure or expectation between us. For example, you don't care that this T-shirt is probably ten years old and used to be a lot more purple than grey, or that these leggings now have holes in them, courtesy of our little friend there.' She flicked Bramble's whiskers gently, making him grumble and swat playfully at her. 'Or at least if you do care, you keep your judgement silent.'

'Nah, it doesn't bother me at all. And I think maybe you're right.' Kim shifted to lean her head against Imogen's shoulder. 'Can I ask you something?'

Imogen was flooded with Kim's warmth and sweet scent. 'Of course.'

'Even if it might be something that might be a bit personal and offensive?'

Imogen took a deep breath, then turned to face Kim, thinking she had a pretty good idea what this question might be. 'Are you asking it to be offensive, or because the answer is something that's important to you?'

'Obviously the latter. I wouldn't ever want to offend.'

'Then I'm not going to be offended, am I? Hit me.'

'When did you . . . I mean . . .'

'Kim, just spit it out.'

'How did you decide you were gay?'

Imogen took a deep breath, sipping her tea to buy herself some time. She knew she needed to be really careful in what she said over the next few minutes. Her gut told her what Kim was really asking — or maybe she just hoped she knew — but, at the same time, the last thing she wanted was to push her with assumptions. And there were at least a couple of things she needed to clear up.

'OK, so first off, do me a favour and don't ever ask anyone that ever again.'

'Shit, I have offended you.' Kim buried her face in her hands. 'I'm sorry. Please forget I said anything.'

'No,' Imogen tugged her hands away. 'It's OK. I said you should spit it out, and you did. I'm not offended, but someone who didn't know you so well might find the way you phrased your question a little . . . well, offensive. It's just not the best way you could have asked. For one thing, it's not something you decide, like you pick your hair colour. Despite what some people seem to think, I don't believe sexuality is a choice. I didn't wake up one morning and decide I wanted to like girls, and I'm not going to wake up one day and decide otherwise either.'

'So if you're gay, you're gay, and if you're straight, you're straight? That's it and there's no movement on that?'

'That is a gross over-simplification.' Imogen took another sip of her drink. 'And I mean gross in the massive sense of the word, not the disgusting one.'

'OK.' Kim nodded earnestly, while Imogen tried to order her thoughts.

'To answer your question, a lot of people will have different opinions, but, personally, I think it's a spectrum. Some people are attracted to people of the same gender, and some are attracted to people of the opposite gender. Or other genders. And I think that some people are very firmly fixed within their point on the spectrum, like me, while others can move around on it.'

'Right.'

'But to answer your original question, when did I first *realise* that I'm attracted to other women . . . wow, probably around eleven or twelve. I think I'd just started secondary school.'

'That young?'

'Well, when did you decide that you liked boys?'

'I don't think I ever really decided . . . Oh, I see what you mean. Sorry.'

'It's fine.' Imogen squeezed her fingers. 'You'd have to do a lot worse than some clumsy phrasing to offend me.'

'You really are awesome.' Kim squeezed her hand back.

'You're pretty awesome too.' Imogen settled back against the cushions. 'You know, when we were kids, how we all had crushes on bands and actors and celebrities?'

'Yeah.'

'Well, while all my friends were obsessing over boy bands, I had pictures of Kylie on my wall.'

'Kylie, huh?'

'Yeah.' Imogen chuckled. 'She's gorgeous, talented and always comes across as being genuinely nice.'

'Plus the gold hot pants probably helped.'

'I cannot believe you just said that!' Imogen squealed.

'Am I wrong?'

'No,' she admitted, blushing. 'But just so you know, the only thing currently saving you from a pillow beating is Bramble.'

'He's a lovely boy.' Kim cuddled her furry protector closer.

'Only boy I've ever snuggled with like that.' Imogen laughed.

'So, I guess it's normal that this . . . realisation . . . happens when you're young?'

'I think for some people, yes. And I think it's getting easier and easier for people to be aware — and supported to explore — their identities and preferences at younger ages. I mean, there's still a lot of prejudice and ugliness out there, but generally speaking I think it's better.'

'You mean that Molvaney idiot.'

'Not just her.' Imogen's mood dropped through the floor — she had to bite the inside of her cheeks to keep from crying, remembering other people with very negative views — ones who mattered to her a lot more than a loud-mouthed village gossip.

'Whoever it was—' Kim's hand was warm on her wrist '—I'm really sorry.'

'Thanks.' Imogen concentrated on her tea, giving herself time to re-bury the feelings she worked so hard to keep down. Even now, years later, her parents' reaction still hurt.

'Do you want to put on a film or something?' Kim asked after a few minutes of quiet.

131

'Sure. Anything in mind?'

'How about *The Delinquents*, or *Street Fighter*?'

'If you're looking for Kylie films, *Moulin Rouge* was good too.'

'Oh, you want to watch a film with your teenage crush?' Kim looked at her with wide-eyed innocence, just about suppressing a grin. But if the way her lips twitched was anything to go by, it was a close thing.

'Bramble, come here, sweetie.' She picked up a pillow. 'Auntie Kim's in trouble!'

* * *

Kim's mind was spinning so much that she struggled to focus on the film. After a while — and a few toe-tapping numbers — she cleared her throat. 'Imogen?'

'Yup.' She paused the film and looked at her, making Kim think she'd been waiting for her to speak again. Perhaps she'd not done such a good job feigning interest in the characters as she'd thought.

'So, the people who move up and down this spectrum thing?' She picked her words carefully, really not wanting to offend Imogen, but still really wanting to ask the question. 'How do they know?'

'Well, I can only tell you what I'd guess at, and what friends have told me . . . but it's usually that they start being attracted to people who are outside their usual sphere of attraction. People different from who they usually like.'

'Right, so like, if you suddenly started eying up Ewan McGregor instead of Kylie?' She flicked her fingers at the screen.

Imogen laughed. 'I suppose so, but I don't think that's ever really going to happen for me. I feel pretty firmly set at my end of the rainbow. For one thing, I'd really miss boobs.'

'And I guess Mr McGregor in gold hotpants just isn't your thing.'

'I could go off you just for making me think of that image! The hairiness, all the jiggly bits in the wrong places. Just no.' She shuddered. 'Just not my thing at all.'

'Sorry.' Kim laughed.

'You're really not, are you?' Imogen shook her head, trying to clear the mental picture. 'Although, it's not always like that,' she added quietly.

'How do you mean?'

'Well, we're talking about someone's overall attraction changing — a complete slide along the spectrum. But for some people I've known, it's not that they stop being attracted to the types of people who they liked last week, last month or last year. It's more that they are drawn to one individual, specific person outside their normal sphere of attraction.'

'Right.' Kim's breath caught in her throat. 'So does that mean they're gay then? If they're suddenly attracted to someone of the same sex?'

'Maybe. Or bi, or pan, or any of the other identifiers or labels in the rainbow. In some ways, I think the labels are given too much importance.'

'How so?'

'Well, I'm lesbian. I like women. Always have done, and probably always will. But that's not my whole personality, there's so much more to me than the people — the women — I'm attracted to. And I don't really want it to be the biggest label people see when they look at me. And don't for a second think it's because I'm ashamed of who I am. I'm not at all. But how would you like it if the first thing anyone thought about when they looked at you was your sex life? I'd rather be known for being kind, for my sense of humour, my skills at pain management, even my crazy, comb-eating curly hair . . .'

'Or your witch-adjacent tendencies.'

'Exactly. I've always thought the obsession with what happens in other people's love lives is a bit sad. I mean, so long as it's consensual and legal, and no one gets hurt, what business is it of anyone else? Unless you're mutually interested in pursuing a sexual relationship, I'm not sure it's anyone else's business really.'

'That makes sense.' Kim nodded. 'But does that mean you really do want to beat me over the head with your cushion for asking this stuff?'

'No, it's OK. You're asking generally, and for a reason. Not specifically or offensively. Or because you're just bored and nosey.'

'Thanks, I really appreciate that. But if I annoy you, you'll tell me, right?'

'Kim, it's me. Of course I will.' She giggled. 'And I really can hit you with a cushion if you like. In case just telling you is too subtle.'

'Gee, thanks.' Kim rolled her eyes.

'Not a problem. I'd do the same for any friend. Ask your questions.'

'Is there a certain age it tends to happen at? The moving up and down the spectrum thing?'

'As I said, I can only answer based on what others have told me and what I've seen — but I don't think so. I mean, that TV presenter had been married for three decades and had children before coming out in his sixties.' She paused and took a sip of her wine. 'And if it's that "one person" situation, then I guess it would happen whenever you met them, regardless of your age.'

'Makes sense.' Kim chewed her bottom lip, trying to figure out what she was supposed to say or think or feel next. She really appreciated that Imogen was happy to sit by her quietly, giving her space — but making her feel supported — while she tried to work out what it was she wanted to say. 'Thanks for letting me ask all this. And not getting offended when I say stupid things.'

'I think when we're as good of friends as we are, you probably don't need to say thank you this much.'

'Mum says something similar — that you don't need to thank family.'

'Hmm. I think family can be a bit trickier.' Imogen didn't say any more, but it did make Kim wonder what had happened in her past, and whether there was anything she could do to help put the smile back on her face. She really did hate seeing Imogen look sad.

She knew if she stopped to think about it, she'd chicken out, so she took a deep breath and just went for it. 'What evenings do you have free next week? Or what are you doing tomorrow? Do you want to do something together?'

'Yeah. I was just going to do boring life admin stuff tomorrow, like laundry, and I've got clients Monday and Tuesday evening, but am free on Wednesday. What were you thinking?'

'Um, I hadn't actually thought further than asking you out. We could do brunch tomorrow — if your life admin stuff doesn't take too long. Or dinner and a movie mid-week. Or afternoon tea up at one of the hotels, then a stroll round the grounds if the weather holds?'

'Sounds good,' Imogen replied. 'Shall we put the film back on?'

'Yeah.' Kim snuggled back into the pillows, beaming, and tried to focus on the screen.

CHAPTER NINE

It took Imogen a lot longer than it should have to pay attention to the nagging voice from the back of her mind. She could have blamed it on being distracted by Kylie zipping around the screen dressed as a strutting fairy, but in truth she was a bit blind-sided. Even if she'd been the type to idly fantasise about her friends — which she wasn't — she'd never dreamed that Kim would . . .

But the more she thought about it, the more she realised that Kim's invitation might be more than just friendly, and that it felt different from other times they'd made arrangements. And the more Kim's comment — which she'd originally thought was a throwaway remark — rang in her ears . . .

'Kim?' She paused the film again. 'I just need to check something.'

'Is everything OK?'

'Yeah, I hope so.' She pressed her lips together tightly, aware that, this time, it was her who needed to be really careful in how she asked things. She took a deep breath and just went for it. 'What you just said about "asking me out". Was that just a weird turn of phrase I'm reading too much into, or did you mean it in a different way to when we've hung out before? Maybe in a way that's more than friendly?'

136

'Maybe the second option.' Kim winced, but then looked up at her with a shy smile that was beyond adorable.

'OK.' Imogen kept her tone gentle, hoping that she could soften the blow. 'In that case, I'm really sorry, but I'm not sure we should go out tomorrow.'

'No?'

Imogen shook her head slowly. 'I don't think it's a good idea, because I think we probably need to talk a bit more. Don't you?'

'Probably. But I'm not sure I know what to say,' Kim admitted.

'If it helps, I might have a guess about some of what this is about?' Imogen murmured softly.

'Really?'

'Maybe.' Imogen sent a quick prayer to anyone who might be listening, to help make sure she wasn't about to screw up one of the best friendships she'd ever had. Her instincts told her she was probably — almost certainly — right, but that didn't mean she wasn't terrified. 'I like you, Kim. I really do. You're my best friend, but I wouldn't be honest if I didn't admit there have been a few times when part of me wondered if we could be something more. But I respect you, and value our friendship, too much to want to endanger that.'

'I understand.' Kim's words were quiet, and she cuddled Bramble more closely against her.

'I'm not sure you do,' Imogen replied. 'I don't want to put words in your mouth, or any pressure on you, but some of the things you've said tonight . . . Kim, would it be completely arrogant of me to think that maybe some of your questions were about me?'

'You're not arrogant, Imogen.'

Not the quartz-clear answer she was hoping for, but it was enough to give her the confidence to continue. 'And would I be totally out of order to ask if maybe I wasn't the only one who'd wondered if there might be something more?'

'You're not,' Kim confirmed. 'At least, I don't think you are. This is all pretty new to me. You're my best friend too,

137

Imogen, and I adore pretty much every moment I spend with you.'

'At least that much is simple.'

'I'm not sure the rest of it is,' Kim continued, 'because it feels like a lot more than that. I honestly feel like if someone offered me the choice between touring the Taj Mahal and visiting the pyramids on the way back, or just sitting on your couch with you pretending to watch a film that neither of us are paying attention to, then it's you. Hands down, every time. And that scares me and excites me, because I've never felt like that about anyone before. I've never felt so . . . grounded, like I am when I'm with you. There's never been anyone who excited me so much that I'd rather be with them than off exploring something or somewhere else — because being with them felt like way more of an adventure than anything else I could think of.'

'Wow.' Imogen wasn't sure what to say.

'And I'm not even finished,' Kim added. 'I've been thinking about this for weeks, on and off. But, even now, I'm not sure how much I should say or not.'

'You should tell me everything you think you want to tell me, because I'm the last person who will judge you.' Imogen told her honestly.

'Just remember, you asked for this,' Kim warned her.

'I will. Tell me everything.'

'The thing is, what's going on between us — and I don't totally know what it is — but whatever it is, you're right, it feels like it might be a lot more than friendship, because there's this heat and want that I can't explain. I'm not walking down the street and looking at women thinking "yeah, she's cute," except in the objective way that I'd tell Evelyn or Liv that they look nice . . . not in a fancy-them and want-to-touch-them type of way . . . it's just you who makes me feel like that. When it's you, I want things that I never thought I would want — things I'm only just starting to understand. You excite me, Imogen, and that scares me, because I don't

138

know how to deal with this. And I don't know what I'm sup-posed to think or do or say.'

'And you figured this out on your date tonight?'

'Oh, that makes me sound terrible.' Kim grimaced. 'It wasn't all tonight. I've been thinking about it for a while now. But maybe it finalised some things for me.'

'Did you figure out anything else? Like what you might want to do?'

'Yeah, I think so.' Kim looked away.

'Do you want to tell me what? I'm not a mind-reader.'

'Are you sure? Sometimes I wonder.'

'My instincts are pretty good most of the time, but that's it. So, want to tell me?'

'I can't.' Kim sighed.

'Why not?'

'Because it wouldn't be fair to you.'

'I'm not sure *that* seems fair.'

'No, it definitely isn't.'

'I mean you deciding what's fair to me or not. Why don't you tell me what it is you want, and I'll tell you whether it's fair.' She took Kim's hand in hers, gently stroking her palm. 'I'm a big girl, Kim. Whatever it is, I can take it.'

'I think I want to kiss you, but I've never done this before, so I'm worried that I'd be using you to . . . I don't know . . . figure something out about myself. Which wouldn't be fair.'

'Do you think you'd be using me? Is that what you think is happening here?'

'No.' Her voice was a hushed whisper. 'I think I might be falling for you. Which is weird and confusing, and exciting and terrifying and wonderful all at the same time. Except — what if I'm wrong, and I'm not attracted to women — to you? And instead I hurt you and ruin our friendship. Because I remember you saying that you wanted your next relationship to be serious, and I don't know if that's something I'm in a position to offer.'

Imogen's head was spinning, and her heart racing by the time Kim had finished. She knew she could make it easier for

Kim by taking back what she'd said about wanting her next relationship to have, at the very least, the potential to be serious. She could just make it all about having fun, taking the pressure off them both. But she had to admit that Kim was right. 'I understand. And you're right — I don't want to risk messing up our friendship.'

'But it's so hard to know if what I'm feeling is real, or just a fantasy, because I've never felt like this before.' The look of confused misery on Kim's face was enough to make Imogen's decision for her.

'Come here.' She leaned forward and caught Kim's face gently between her hands.

* * *

'What are you doing?' Kim's eyes were wide.

'Hopefully simplifying things. I'm going to kiss you, if you'll let me.'

'How is that simple?' Kim squeaked.

'Well, either there's nothing here and we shrug and go back to being friends, or there is something and then we have something to talk about.' She leaned forward, pausing so close that Kim could feel her breath hot against her lips. 'Unless you want me to stop?' Imogen was scant inches away from Kim, her gaze hot and intense. 'Tell me what you want.'

'I don't know.' Kim gasped.

'Do you want me to stop?' She stroked Kim's hair and tucked it behind her ear, smoothing it back from her face.

'I don't think so?'

Imogen went to pull away, but Kim grabbed her arm, holding her there. 'You don't sound very sure. You have to tell me what you want. Because I have to do something, whether it's pull away, or kiss you — there's a decision here.'

'We could just stay here. Not moving and not deciding.' Kim suggested, knowing it wasn't really an answer, but wanting to delay what felt like a monumentally huge and quite probably life-changing decision. Despite what Imogen had said, she felt pretty sure going back to being just friends wasn't going to be as easy as she made out.

'All right.' Imogen pulled back slightly, making Kim want to whimper and pull her back closer again. From the smile Imogen shot her, she knew exactly how she felt as she twisted in her seat, kicking her feet up beneath her. 'Let's press pause then. We can just sit here, and talk about nothing important, while you figure out what you want.'

'Yeah, that works.' Kim twisted round, matching Imogen's position. She reached for Imogen's hand again. 'Just for a couple of minutes?'

'As long as you need.' She looked down to where Kim's fingers were gently stroking hers. 'I probably shouldn't tell you that feels really nice, should I?'

'Maybe not.' Kim kept stroking her fingers, letting her touch travel over Imogen's palm. She bit back a giggle when Imogen shivered, glad to see she was very much affected by Kim's presence and touch. 'But I'm glad you're enjoying it too.'

'Yeah?'

'Yeah.' With a hand that shook slightly, Kim reached up and slid her fingers along Imogen's jaw, tracing over her cheek and tangling gently in her curls.

Imogen leaned back in, resting her arm across the back of the sofa, and pushed Kim's hair back. 'Do you think we've waited long enough?'

'Yeah, I think so.' Kim's breath came too fast with excitement and anticipation as Imogen lowered her mouth to hers. She was gentle at first, brushing her lips softly against Kim's in a breathy, sweet motion that flushed tingles through every part of her. After a few seconds she pulled away, holding Kim's face in her hands while she studied her — searching for confirmation in her eyes.

Kim didn't want to wait — she had no hesitation left. She tangled her fingers in Imogen's curls and pulled her back against her, kissing her warmly and using her tongue to part her lips — needing to taste her and fill another of her senses with Imogen's essence.

A few dozen heartbeats later, Imogen pulled away, and brushed one final, sweet, gentle kiss against her lips before slowly letting go of her. She stroked Kim's cheek and the edge of her lips with a tender thumb. 'Well? Did it do anything for you?'

Anything? Was she kidding? Pretty much every nerve ending Kim had was tingling, and she could barely think of anything but Imogen. 'Yes.' Her voice came out breathless. 'You?' She forced the word out nervously — she suddenly realised there was a chance that Imogen hadn't felt the same.

'Oh yeah.'

'Really?' Relief loosened Kim's tongue.

'Really. Very much so.' The smile Imogen gave her was beautiful — like the sun coming up, the clouds parting after rain, midnight rainbows and every other cheesy cliché she'd ever heard. Even in her own mind, Kim's thoughts were ridiculously giddy.

'So . . .' Imogen leaned against her own hand, her elbow propped on the back of the sofa and her fingers disappearing into her soft curls — the curls that Kim longed to bury her own hands in. She wanted to twine them around her fingers and hold Imogen close to her. The thought shocked and excited her, and she realised she had no idea what Imogen had just said — but she was watching her expectantly.

'I'm really sorry,' Kim confessed. 'You just asked me a question, but I've no idea what.'

Imogen laughed and shook her head. 'I said, it's pretty clear to me there's something here, and did you want to talk about it?'

She should say yes. They should definitely talk. It was the sensible, smart, mature thing to do. But when Imogen caught her eye, the last thing she felt like being was smart or sensible. 'I don't know. I think I might be a bit bored of talking.'

'Yeah?' Imogen's smile in that moment was even more perfect than da Vinci's greatest masterpiece.

The thought, combined with the relief, made Kim laugh. 'Yeah.' She bit her bottom lip, and felt a thrill of heat when she noticed Imogen's gaze drop for a moment. 'I can think of something much better to do.'

'We really should talk.' Imogen's words contradicted the way her hand slipped back around Kim's neck, the heat in her gaze as she drew her closer again.

'We will,' Kim promised, breathless. 'Just . . . later.'

'Later,' Imogen promised, the word hot against Kim's lips. 'Before anything gets too serious.'

'Uh huh.' Kim was barely listening as her lips melded back against Imogen's, heat flushing through them both.

* * *

'Stop it.' Imogen laughed, trying not to squirm as Kim slipped her arms round her waist and kissed the back of her neck.

'Why?' Kim's breath was hot and tickled in the nicest possible way, sending bolts of desire racing down her spine.

'Because I can't think straight when you do that, and if you don't let me concentrate I'm going to scorch the milk, which will make for a disgusting drink.'

'And you did promise me the "best hot chocolate I've ever tasted". It would be a shame to ruin that.' She gave Imogen a quick squeeze, before letting her go and reaching for the mugs. 'And I guess we should talk still.'

'Yeah.' They'd delayed the conversation — Kim had proven very insistent — in favour of staying on the sofa, wrapped up in each other and acting like teenagers. And as glorious as that had been, she was under no illusions that there were conversations they should probably have — no matter how much she'd like to keep ignoring them.

Imogen added some more of her spice blend to the milk, before slowly stirring in the cocoa and melting in the dark chocolate. She whisked the mix together, slowly drizzling in honey before realising there wasn't anything else she could do. So she ladled it into the big mugs, handed the squirty cream and marshmallows to Kim, and set the hot chocolate down on opposite sides of the breakfast bar — deliberately putting some space between them.

'Did I develop cooties in the last few minutes?' Kim regarded her with amusement.

'You're the one who teased me at midsummer about how irresistible you are . . . I'm just trying to give myself a chance.' She was only half-teasing, and the flush that swept over Kim's cheeks made Imogen quite grateful for the expanse of wood and steel between them. 'You look really pretty when you blush.'

'No one looks pretty when they blush.' Kim rolled her eyes.

'You do,' Imogen insisted. 'When you turn pink, your eyes look even more blue.'

'It's a Macpearson thing.' She shrugged off the compliment. 'Cal and Jake have them too. Nothing special. This really is delicious, by the way.'

'My own spice blend. And I wish you wouldn't do that.'

'What?' Kim's eyes — the gorgeous bright blue of the most expensive kyanite crystals — looked confused over the top of her cream-laden mug.

'Shrug off compliments like you don't deserve them.'

'I don't do that . . . do I?'

'Enough that I've noticed. And if you pushed me, I'd have to say it's one of the few things about you that I don't like.'

'I didn't even realise I was doing it.'

'I know, and I think that might be the thing that bothers me the most.' She reached out and took Kim's hand. 'You are smart, creative, kind, funny and sarky as anything, and incredibly sweet and beautiful. When you don't see, and treat, yourself like that — then yeah, it bothers me.'

'Wow. You really think I'm all those things?'

'Yeah. I really do. And more.'

'Wow. That's, um . . .' Kim took a deep breath. 'You're amazing, Imogen, in so many ways. The fact that you think all those nice things about me . . . it's a bit . . . much. I don't really know how to take it.'

'As a compliment. That's sort of the point. I know you see yourself as the black sheep of the Macpearson clan, but you're really not. Not following a medical or clinical route doesn't mean you're anything less than them. So maybe take the compliment, smile and say thank you?'

'OK.' She smiled. 'Thank you.'

'You're welcome. It wasn't that hard, was it?'

'No, I guess not. Might have been quite nice, actually.'

'Get used to it. Because unless you tell me not to — and have a damn good reason for it — I plan on paying you a lot of compliments. Which I guess brings us back to "later", and the conversation we've both been putting off.'

'Yeah.' Kim nodded. 'Awkward conversation time.'

'I'm hoping it's not going to be that bad.' Imogen took a deep breath. 'You're really important to me, Kim, in so many ways. You're my best friend, and I don't want to do anything to risk that relationship. But at the same time, I really like you. More than I have done anyone for a long time — maybe ever. And it doesn't seem fair to not tell you that. But, whatever happens next, I really don't want to screw up our friendship.'

'I completely agree. We're friends no matter what. If I was my niece's age, I'd offer to pinkie-swear to being BFFs.' She giggled, then shrugged and held out her hand. 'Screw it, maybe I'm nowhere near as mature as I should be.'

'Maybe I'm not either.' Imogen knew she was grinning like an idiot when she wrapped her little finger around Kim's, squeezing tightly.

After a few seconds, Kim reached over to wrap her other hand over the top of Imogen's. 'I agree about the rest of it too. I like you too, which still feels really weird to say, but I'm quite excited to see where this might go. And I do mean that, it's just . . .' She looked away.

'You know there's nothing you can't say to me, right?' Imogen squeezed Kim's hands back. 'I don't want you to ever think you have to hold back, or do something crazy to please me, like give up bacon. OK?'

'OK.'

'Kim, I really do mean that.' Imogen needed to make sure Kim really understood. 'I like you for you, Kim, just as you are. And there's nothing you can't tell me, OK?'

When Kim looked up, Imogen was a little saddened to see surprise in her eyes.

'You really mean that, don't you?'

'Yeah, I really do. So what was the "just" you were hesitating to say?'

'Just that . . . um . . . that this . . . being with someone like you . . . it's all new to me.'

'I know that,' Imogen reassured her. 'I know you probably have some things to think about and figure out, and decisions to make, but the last thing I want to do is put pressure on you. So if this . . . the idea of us . . . is something you want to explore further . . .' and she really, really hoped it was '. . . then anything that happens — and I'm not assuming it will — but if it did, it would be at your pace. OK?'

Kim nodded slowly, then looked up and grinned — mischief in her eyes. 'Just to make sure I've got this right . . . you're saying you're going to be patient?'

'Yep.' Imogen pressed her lips together, trying not to laugh.

'You, who are one of the most impatient people I know, are going to be patient?'

'I also told you I'm trying to do better, especially when it's something worth waiting for.'

'Are you saying I'm worth waiting for?'

There were so many ways Imogen could have answered that question — including telling Kim she was quite possibly

146

the woman she'd been waiting most of her life for. But that wouldn't be fair, and would definitely be putting pressure on her. So instead she opted for honest, but simple. 'Yes. I think you might be.'

'And I get to set the pace that suits me best?'

'Yes.'

'Right.' Kim pulled her hand away, making Imogen want to swallow her words. 'So, if I decide I want to grab these drinks and take them back to your much comfier, much snugglier couch, then you're going to come with me? Because that's the pace I want to set?'

Imogen grinned, shaking her head as Kim did exactly that. This woman was going to drive her crazy.

CHAPTER TEN

Kim groaned when her phone started buzzing and beeping, making Imogen pull away and break their oh-so-delicious kiss. 'Ignore it.'

'The whole reason you set the thing was to make sure you got back to Badger's Hospital on time,' Imogen argued with her.

'Yeah, but that was before I realised I'm not going to get to see you tonight or tomorrow either,' Kim grumbled as she thumbed her phone into silence, then threw it across the picnic blanket they'd spread out in the shop's poor excuse for a garden. 'If I'd realised there would be so much work this year involved with Summer's Christmas, I would have refused to help. I'd much rather stay here with you.'

'You'd have said no to your family — and all the other organisers — just to spend time with me? No, you wouldn't have.'

'You're right. I wouldn't have. And rebuilding the community centre is a really good cause. But that doesn't mean I have to be happy about it, especially when it means less time with you.'

'I know.' Imogen's hand was warm on her waist, even over her T-shirt. 'But I like that you considered it, even for a few seconds. And I'm sorry we've struggled so much to get together this week.'

Kim shrugged. 'I know you have a business to run. And I've been busy being "volunteered" for organisation and setup this week. I should probably learn to say no a bit more.'

'I think it's wonderful that you're so involved with your community.'

'Yeah, but if they'd asked me this week, when I knew about you, I probably would have refused,' Kim told her honestly.

'That's really sweet.' Imogen stroked her cheek gently — the touch sent tingles racing throughout Kim. '*You* are really sweet. And I can't wait until we can spend some proper, uninterrupted time together.'

'Me either.' Kim leaned forward on her knees to place another kiss on Imogen's beautiful, sweet mouth. For a few delicious moments, Imogen pressed warmly against her, kissing her back. It was almost scary how easily she could have lost herself in kisses and touches like that. Almost.

'No.' Imogen pulled slowly away. 'As much as I want to stay here in the sunshine with you, I have clients this afternoon, and you probably have a surgery's worth of patients and owners to organise.'

'Ugh, don't remind me. Jake's holding a pet-grooming clinic this afternoon, and for all that I'm supposed to be working admin, I usually get dragged into it. I'd much rather stay here with you.'

'Aww.' Imogen placed her hands over her heart like the best of dramatic soap stars. 'You'd rather be with me than washing smelly dogs. Be still my fluttering heart. I don't know how to handle such sweet words.'

'Shut up.' Kim threw a grape at her. 'I bring you lunch and you take the piss out of me. Some gratitude.'

'If we had more time, I might be tempted to try and convince you to let me show you how grateful I can be.'

Kim knew she was just teasing, and wouldn't try to pressurise her into anything she wasn't really ready for, but the hot promise in Imogen's eyes sent delicious shivers down her spine, leaving her tingling in the most intimate of places. From Imogen's grin, Kim was pretty sure she knew exactly the effect she was having as she trailed her fingers up and down Kim's wrist.

'You really should go.' Imogen lifted Kim's hand up to her mouth, letting her lips follow the trail her fingers had just created, sending fire racing after the shivers she'd created earlier — before letting go and pushing herself to her feet. 'Come on. I'll see you at the weekend.'

'Yeah, along with the rest of the village and thousands of other people.' Kim usually enjoyed the weird summery-Christmassy mash-up that was the hugely successful fundraiser. But this year she found herself resenting the time it would keep her away from Imogen. The fact that it was partly — mostly — her fault didn't really make her feel any better about that.

She knew Imogen was being respectful and giving her the space they both knew she needed to figure out this new version of herself. They also both needed time to figure out who and what they were to each other in this new version of their relationship, without the pressure of other people's expectations, eyes or opinions. All of which was good and sensible, but sometimes she wished she lived in a big city again — where no one cared who she was, what she did or who she did it with. She'd felt lonely when she'd lived like that, but there were times — like now — when she would have appreciated the anonymity.

'Come on.' Imogen helped pull Kim to her feet. 'I'll clear this up. You have pongy puppies waiting for you.'

'Thanks.' Kim rolled her eyes. 'But it's not the dogs who are really the problem. Cats come to this clinic too. You're a cat owner. You know how much fun that job is.'

'Maybe I should kiss you now then, while you're still in one piece.'

'Sounds good to me.' Kim made the best possible use of the thirty or so seconds she had left before she really, really needed to head back to work, or else she'd be so late that even running there wouldn't get her out of trouble. It was a good thing her brother couldn't exactly fire her. At least, not without getting into a pile of trouble with their parents.

'Go.' Imogen unhooked Kim's hands from around her waist, and kissed each hand in turn. 'I'll see you at the parade or fete.'

* * *

Come the weekend, Imogen stared around in amazement, not quite believing what she was seeing. Angela had told her the event was big, but hearing that and seeing the little village crammed full of people was a very different thing. If she hadn't seen it for herself, she wasn't sure she would have believed how many people could fit into Broclington.

'Wow. This is . . . incredible.'

'Yeah, Angela said it was popular.' Ryan grinned down at her. 'But this is something else. You ready?'

'Right, sorry.' She fiddled with the camera. 'OK. In three, two, one . . .'

'Hellooooo, Rickheads!'

Imogen watched through the little screen as her brother pasted on the Smile he was so well known for, switching into his online persona. It really was quite amazing that he could switch to Maverick Star so easily. But she was glad that he dropped the persona on and off as easily as he did now — like she would change shirts — because for a few years she'd struggled to know how to handle "Rick" taking over, and had gotten more and more worried about her brother. She'd convinced him to go to rehab, but it hadn't really helped change his behaviour. Thankfully, his wake-up call hadn't destroyed anything that couldn't be repaired, healed or rebuilt, and meeting Angela had turned out to be the best thing that could have happened to him. She was so grateful to the universe for bringing them together.

She looked around while he did his piece to camera — she was used to being his film crew from time to time. The whole village had been decked out as if it was Christmas — trees, lights and decorations waved in the gentle breeze and sparkled jauntily in the Summer sunshine. All around her people were dressed in festive finery and sparkles, with Christmas hats and headbands, paired with T-shirts, shorts and flip-flops. She was glad she'd listened to Kim's advice — although it had seemed weird at the time — and was wearing a sparkly T-shirt, snow-flake earrings and tinsel in her hair, along with her cut-off shorts and trainers.

Ryan started to wrap up the video just as a marching band struck up a noisy, cheerful version of jingle bells. The crowd roared and cheered so loudly it almost drowned out the music. The noise was so loud, so filled with expectation and excitement, that it was palatable.

'Thanks.' Ryan took the camera from her and flipped it round, filming the scene for himself. After a couple of min-utes, Imogen got to see exactly what all the noise was about. A sleigh, pulled by half a dozen men dressed in black-and-white sport kits, antlers and stick-on noses, appeared around the corner. Santa wore a bright red Hawaiian shirt over equally bright red shorts, under his more traditional, unbuttoned red and white fur coat.

Following along behind the sleigh were a group of chil-dren carrying donation buckets and dressed as snow prin-cesses, fairies and elves, escorted by a couple of adults who looked only slightly less excited to be there.

'Oh my Goddess.' Hardly able to believe her eyes, she whipped out her own phone, aiming at the petite elf, helping to marshal the children into some sort of order. The red and green streaks in her hair — matching the stripes of her over-the-knee socks — bounced in time to the music.

She couldn't believe Kim hadn't told her about this — and definitely wanted photographic evidence. Kim paused in front of her, grinning hugely. 'There's a fee for photos you know.' She shook her bucket. 'Otherwise you might end up on the naughty list.'

'Yeah, we know Santa really well,' the sparkly snowflake-girl by her side added.

'Well, I'd better donate then.' Imogen pulled out a handful of change from her pocket and dropped it into their buckets.

'Thank you! Happy Summer's Christmas!' the snowflake trilled.

'Yes, Happy Summer's Christmas!' Kim's eyes locked with Imogen's for a few heartbeats — she flashed Imogen a smile and a quick wink as they danced away.

Imogen hadn't realised Ryan was paying more attention to her than his own filming until he nudged her arm. 'Was that Kim Macpearson under those rosy cheeks and elf ears?'

'Yeah.' If she didn't say anything more than that, maybe Ryan would leave well enough alone — for once.

No such luck. 'Really? Kimberly Macpearson?' Ryan grinned and nudged her again. 'I didn't even know she's . . . you really are full of surprises. So much for "just friends", huh?'

'Ryan, just don't.' She shook her head, not wanting to talk about it.

'Aww, c'mon, Moggy. Dish the dirt. We always used to gossip about girls.'

'Ry-no.' She used his old nickname. 'I mean it. Please leave this alone. It's really new and . . .' She trailed off, not totally sure how to finish. She wasn't sure what it was with Kim, but she knew she didn't want to gossip about it. Especially in a public setting.

'Oh wow.' Ryan's voice was lower this time as he studied her, all trace of Maverick gone. 'She's the reason you're so happy lately? I thought maybe it was that your business was going well, and you were feeling settled and happy here.'

'I am.'

'Yeah, but it's more than that, isn't it? You're serious about her.'

Imogen shook her head. She'd not even had this conversation with Kim — she'd barely let herself think about it. As much as she loved her brother, he wasn't the first person she should have this conversation with. 'We're just enjoying each other's company while figuring some things out.'

'All right.' Ryan flung his arm around her shoulders as they watched the rest of the parade dance, drive and shake their fundraising buckets. 'Play it coy if you like, but I know that look on you. It's OK though, you know you can trust me. I won't say anything.'

'Thank you.' She did know she could trust him. Even when he was being a bit of an idiot as Maverick, she always knew he had her back.

'And if you do want to talk . . .'

'I don't.'

'Yeah, but when and if you do, you know you've got my ear.'

'Thanks. You're a good brother.'

'I have my moments.' He grinned at her, the cheeky, slightly irritating glossy smile that so many millions of people apparently followed online. 'Now we better get our behinds over to Angela and the stall before everyone else beats us there.'

'Yessir!' She mock-saluted him.

'Careful. If you annoy me enough, I just might set the animals on you.'

'Yeah, yeah. Sure you will.' She laughed as he led them out of the crowd and round to the large village park. The cricket pitch and pavilion were now swamped by a large marquee and what must have been miles of fairy lights. Rows of brightly coloured stalls covered in Christmas decorations stretched out across the park in every direction, and the delicious scent of fried food, roasting meats, barbecues and doughnuts filled the air.

'This is incredible. I had no idea it would be so big.'

'Yeah,' Ryan agreed. 'I saw the videos from previous years and helped with the setup, but it's still majorly impressive. Are you regretting not having a stall of your own?'

'Maybe a little.' She contemplated her answer. 'But I did make up some freebies and leave them with some cards at the community stall. And I'm still not sure I could have managed it this year without tiring myself out. If I pick up more than a few new clients at once I'll be struggling with my bookings anyway. Right now with the hospital, and the clients who moved with me, I've got more than enough to keep me busy. Maybe next year when I've got more help and am better established.'

'How is the recruitment going?'

'I've had a couple of interesting applicants. Good feeling about one of them in particular. He's coming back in for a second interview and to do a bit of a trial next week.'

'Fingers crossed then. Come on. Come meet our racers.'

* * *

The sun warmed Imogen's muscles as she bent down to scoop up Frostfur — a small, lean ferret whose brown fur was tipped with white, making her look like she was cold and frosty, instead of as warm and wriggly as she really was. Imogen cradled the ferret in her arms, letting the animal brace her forepaws against Imogen's arms while she snuffled around, taking in all the different smells and noise going on around them.

Most animals would have been nervous to be surrounded by so much noise and chaos, but all of the ferrets Angela had picked out seemed to thrive on the attention, sticking their muzzles under every pair of hands that reached for them, happily showing off. A few times Imogen had struggled to keep hold of Frostfur, as the animal found a particular person more interesting than the others and tried to make a break for it. At first, Imogen was worried she might hurt the small creature, but Ryan was right — they were a lot tougher than they looked, and clearly loved the job they'd been picked for.

Imogen worked her way around the crowd, handing out purple tokens in exchange for cash, and making sure no one did anything to Frostfur that might irritate her enough to nip — but she was easy-tempered and seemed happy to meet new people.

Imogen smiled as the buzzer sounded, letting the crowd know they were just minutes away from the race, and it was time for Ryan, Angela and her to load the ferrets into their starting cages. Frostfur almost leaped into her cage — eager to get started. Imogen had a pretty good guess that anyone holding a purple token would soon be trading it in for prizes — cans of ale for the adults who wanted them, and packets of sweets for the children and everyone else.

She took the stakes, trading more donations for tokens, then sat down on one of the chairs inside the pen they had created. She watched Angela and Ryan work the crowd, building their excitement. The ferrets thrived on the energy too, playing and showing off in their starting cages, climbing around and twisting in the small space.

A few minutes later, Ryan — in full Maverick mode — worked up the crowd even more, running a countdown until he and Angela — in a well-practiced move — lifted the gate that penned the ferrets into their start cages. They shot off down the thirty feet of coloured drainpipes to loud cheers, and Imogen stood up, ready to try to catch them when they reappeared. She'd already learned they had to be fast, because — just like Angela and Ryan told the crowd — the furry critters loved the tubes, and would happily dive back into them to disappear out of reach.

As Imogen had expected, Frostfur beat the other ferrets to the first viewing point — a break in the tubes where the drainpipes were joined with wire. Thirty seconds later she was in the middle — a larger box, also made of chicken wire. The brown ferret — her brother — in the second tube was just behind her, and beat her into the third and final box.

'Remember,' Angela called out to the crowd. 'It's all four feet on the grass at the same time for the win.'

Imogen laughed as Frostfur stuck her nose out of the winning end of the racecourse — much to the delight of everyone holding a purple chip — then proceeded to sit and carefully wash her whiskers while the crowd laughed, groaned, shouted and whistled. The albino ferret, running tube one, popped his nose out first, then slowly climbed out to balance on the edge of the tube, before performing a 180 that would be impossible for almost any other animal and disappeared back up the tube. He reappeared in the starting cage only seconds later. The wild-coloured ferret in tube four had stopped moving in the middle box, and appeared to have decided a sunny snooze was in order.

After another minute or so with none of the competitors exiting the course, Angela walked over and nudged the sleepy ferret with her finger. It batted her fingers with his front paws, before jumping up and racing down the tube. All four ferrets were now at the winning end of the course, popping their noses in and out of the tubes.

At first, Imogen thought the animals might have been nervous and put off by the noise and smells of the crowd, but she had soon learned that these ferrets were incredibly intelligent — more so than most cats or dogs — and not only thrived on the attention of so many people, but played up and showed off to get even more.

Eventually, after a little more booing and groaning, and a lot more encouragement, it was Frostfur who put all four feet to the grass first and was scooped up by Angela to be shown off and cheered as the victor, while Imogen and Ryan scooped up the other three ferrets — which included dismantling lane four, to convince the ferret who had returned to sunbathing that it really was time for him to have a snack break while the B-team of ferrets took over.

* * *

Kim waited until the crowd around the ferret racing dispersed before approaching. 'Hey, Angela, looks like you're drawing good crowds again this year!'

'Yeah, the gang is doing good trade. But we always do — beer, gambling, fluffy critters and a lot of laughter, all while helping an animal rescue charity. Who wouldn't get on board with that? And of course, Maverick helps. Are you coming in? Ryan and Imogen are just putting away the team.'

Kim thought about it for a few seconds, then nodded. 'Sure. Do I get tips on who to bet on?'

'Nope, because it's almost guaranteed that as soon as I make a recommendation, that'll be the ferret who turns around halfway or decides to have a nap in the middle of a race.' She moved the fence open for Kim, giving her a quick hug when she walked in. 'I'm loving the outfit, by the way.'

'Yeah, I'm pixie Kim today.' She laughed. 'It was parade and bucket rattling duty or the first-aid tent — and I couldn't handle the thought of hours in a hot tent, playing nursemaid to people who should have paid attention to what their kids were eating, remembered to use sunscreen or kept their fluid intake up.'

'Wow, don't hold back on my account.' Angela giggled.

'What? I never claimed to have a good bedside manner. Just one of the reasons the family business was never going to be for me.'

'I don't know, from what I hear you can be pretty nice when you want to be.' Ryan grinned as he came back out. 'Ouch.'

'Oh, I'm sorry, did I accidentally tread on your foot?' Imogen glared at him. 'So terribly sorry.'

Kim gave Imogen a puzzled look, but she only shot her a small, slightly nervous smile back. She was trying to reassure her, but something was clearly bothering her. It became even more obvious when Ryan pulled Angela aside on some flimsy pretence of an excuse.

'What's going on?' Kim asked, somewhat nervously. Imogen sat down in one of the chairs behind the drainpipe racetracks, where it was relatively quiet and away from the crowd, and motioned for her to take the other.

'I know we said we'd give . . . us . . . time and space and privacy, but my brother is annoyingly perceptive when it comes to me, and I've never really been able to lie to him.'

'Oh, so he knows.'

'Yeah.' Imogen nodded and winced. 'He guessed. I'm sorry.'

'For not being able to lie to your brother? I'm not sure there's anything to apologise for there.' Kim tried to reassure her. 'My friend Millie can be like that at times — irritatingly perceptive.'

'If it helps, I trust him, and he's promised not to say anything. And I believe him. He won't gossip.' Imogen rolled her eyes. 'I probably can't stop him from ribbing me, but that's fairly normal for us. But I am sorry.'

'It's OK . . .' Kim hesitated. 'But we should probably let him know it's OK to tell Angela too.'

'You're sure?'

'Not really.' Kim really wanted to reach out and touch Imogen, but she wasn't ready for that yet. 'But I'd hate it if someone told me something and then made me keep it a secret from someone I cared about.' She met Imogen's eyes, hoping that her meaning was clear.

'Yeah. I wouldn't be too keen if Ryan asked me to keep things from you.' Imogen smiled, making Kim wonder — again — if she could read her mind. 'You look adorable, by the way. The pointy ears are seriously cute.'

'Thanks.' Kim giggled. 'You look good in tinsel.'

'Thanks. I've missed you this week.' Imogen's words made her feel all warm and gooey.

'Yeah, me too.' As soon as she'd said the words, she realised how incredibly true they were. She'd really missed the ease and sweetness of being around Imogen. 'I don't suppose there's any chance I can see you later? What are you doing tonight?' she asked hopefully.

'In all honesty, as much as I really want to say yes, I probably shouldn't. But what are you doing tomorrow?'

'Playing "auntie" in the morning for a couple of hours and looking after Summer and Sarah, but nothing much in the afternoon. So whatever you had in mind.' She didn't really care what Imogen suggested, so long as it could include her.

'I'm probably going to be taking things easy . . .' Imogen warned her. 'I was planning to head home tonight, take a very long, very hot bath, and then do my sensible-but-boring stretches, but I'm probably still going to be a bit tired tomorrow.'

'So just chilling?'

'I don't want to risk a flare. I've got quite a busy week.'

'I wasn't complaining.' Kim jumped to reassure her. 'Just like I'm not complaining all that much about the fact you basically just told me you're washing your hair instead of seeing me tonight. Like it isn't one of the oldest, and worst, excuses possible.'

'Kim, it's about condition management, it's not like . . .' Kim lost the battle to keep from grinning and Imogen shook her head. 'You're teasing me.'

'Yup. So tomorrow afternoon? You, me, some binge-worthy boxset?'

'You're really OK with that?' Her eyes were bright and hopeful, and her lips curled into that soft smile that Kim found so irresistible.

'I can't think of anything I'd rather do,' Kim told her honestly.

CHAPTER ELEVEN

Imogen sighed happily as Kim twisted round on the couch, her knees pressing tightly against Imogen's thigh as she pulled her more firmly against her, kissing her more deeply. Kim's fingers traced up and down Imogen's bare arms, stopping at the thin straps of her top and bra before tracing up and down again, teasing goose pimples from her skin.

She held her breath when Kim's fingers scraped over straps and stroked along her collarbone, dipping into the hollows there before moving lower, gently exploring. When those fingers quested back up to slip beneath the straps, sliding them down her arms, Imogen dropped her hands away from Kim's face to make it easier for her, letting her slip the fabric lower and bare more of her skin.

Her skin tightened and tingled under Kim's fingers, sending fire racing through her, and Imogen twisted her own fingers around the throw on the sofa, pulling the fabric tight with the effort of not grabbing Kim and ripping every stitch off her. It was slow, sweet, exquisite torture as Kim nuzzled against her neck, kissing and teasing the skin there before working back down, slowly and tentatively at first. When she found an extra sensitive spot that sent a shiver through Imogen, she giggled

161

and paid it more attention, clearly enjoying making Imogen squirm. After long, delicious, almost painful moments, Kim kissed her way back to Imogen's mouth.

'Are you OK?' Kim slid her hands down to Imogen's, where they were still fisted in the blanket. 'You are enjoying this, aren't you?'

'Of course I am.' Imogen giggled as Kim unwound her fingers from the cover. 'I'm just trying to make sure I don't break my promise to you. About making sure I don't push you too far too soon.'

'I'm sorry, I must be driving you crazy.' Kim apologised, half-laughing.

'Yeah, you are. But it's OK. I told you that this is going to be at your pace.'

'You sure?'

'Yes.' Imogen caught one hand and kissed Kim's open palm, enjoying the other woman's shiver. 'Besides, I'm already planning my revenge.'

'You are?' The quiver in Kim's voice sent another flush of heat through Imogen.

'In great detail.' Imogen leaned forward and placed a teasing kiss on Kim's lips.

'Should I be scared?'

'Very,' Imogen promised. 'Do you want to know what I'm planning?'

'I think so.' Kim nodded, her eyes darkening with excitement to sapphire.

'When you give me the word . . . the look . . . when you decide you're ready . . .' Imogen slid her other hand along Kim's jaw to cup her face, leaving her fingers resting just behind her ear. 'I want to explore every single inch of you, until I find every single one of these sweet, sensitive spots you have.' She let her fingernails graze the spot she'd kissed earlier, eliciting a breathy moan from Kim as she squirmed. 'Just like this one here. Do you want to know what I'll do then?'

'Tell me.'

'I'll use them to please you, driving you crazy until you come apart in my arms, beneath my hands, beneath my lips, again, and again.' She punctuated her words with soft kisses. 'And again, and again, until you can't even remember what day of the week it is.'

Kim swallowed hard. 'I can't tell if you're teasing me or not.'

'Maybe I am.' Imogen teased Kim's bottom lip with her own mouth, even though she was partly torturing herself too. 'Maybe I'm not. But like I said, whenever you're ready.'

'Thank you,' Kim whispered the words against Imogen's skin. 'For being so patient with me. I know it can't be easy for you.'

Imogen kissed Kim again, this time much more sweetly, then slowly drew away, sorting out her top as she did so. 'You're right, patience is not something that comes naturally to me. But like I said, I'm pretty sure you're worth the wait. Besides, I have to admit that I quite like this whole making out like teenagers thing.'

'You're not just saying that?'

'No. I'm not. There's something really fun and kind of sweet about it.' She kissed Kim one more time before pushing herself off the sofa.

'Where are you going?' Kim caught her hand.

'Kitchen.' Imogen kissed her fingers. 'If I can't have you, I'm at least getting something sweet.' She loved the way such a simple gesture and a few words could bring an adorable pink flush into Kim's cheeks. She didn't think she'd ever tire of it. The thought surprised her, but the more she thought about it, the more she realised how true it was. She found herself humming as she put the kettle on and opened up a bag of cookies she'd bought yesterday.

'Just popping to the bathroom, if that's OK.'

'Of course. You know you needn't ask.'

Imogen took a few extra minutes to start dinner in the slow cooker, throwing in mince, vegetables and seasonings.

She cheated, of course — the vegetables were from a packet in the freezer, bought pre-chopped — but Imogen was happy to trade the extra financial cost for the energy and time it saved her. Yet another little thing, another little trick, that helped her manage her condition better. To someone else, peeling and chopping a few vegetables was the work of minutes — not something to even consider, but to her it was another little bit of energy she could save for something more important, more interesting or more fun than crying over onions.

By the time she'd finished, Kim still wasn't back. Imogen gave her a few more minutes before gently knocking on the bathroom door. 'Not wanting to bother you, but are you OK?'

'Um, yeah. But do you have any . . . girly things?'

What? The question didn't make any sense. 'The only guy who comes up here is Ryan. Probably ninety per cent of everything I own is "girly" in at least some way.'

'I meant like monthly girly things.' Even through the wooden door, Imogen thought Kim sounded tense. 'I had a quick look, but . . .'

'Right. Sorry. Grey tin, shelf under the basin.' She waited a few seconds, then winced when there was a thump, followed by what sounded like soft cursing. 'You OK?'

'Yep. Fine thanks. Just need a couple of minutes.'

'OK. Shout if you need anything else.' She thought Kim sounded even more tense than before, but decided to leave her to it. She obviously wanted some privacy to sort herself out. Not that Imogen blamed her — periods really could suck with their timing. She headed back to the living room and started scrolling through the channels to find something to watch other than the clock.

It was nearly ten minutes before Kim came back, her face bright red — and not in the adorable way — one hand shoved in her pocket and the other wrapped around her waist like she was trying to protect herself.

'Kim? Are we OK?' Imogen reached out to her, trying not to let panic bite too hard when she shied back. 'Do we need to talk about something?'

'This is so awful,' Kim groaned.

'I mean, periods aren't exactly my favourite time of the month, but it's really not that bad.' Imogen tried to reassure her, while trying to figure out what was really going on. It seemed like a massive over-reaction to her.

'I wish it were just that.'

'Tell me? Whatever it is, I'm sure we can fix it.'

Kim took a deep breath. 'When I was getting the things, I knocked something over in your bathroom.' Her words were fast and jumbled together, and Imogen was struggling to understand her. 'And when I picked it up it fell apart and I was worried I'd broken it, so after I put it back together I turned it on to make sure I hadn't broken it and now I can't turn the frigging thing off.'

When Kim finally took another breath — while Imogen tried to figure out what she was talking about — she realised she could hear an oddly familiar sound. One that didn't belong in this room. When the realisation hit her, she clapped her hands to her mouth, biting the inside of her cheeks and screwing her eyes closed so she didn't burst out laughing.

After a few seconds, she thought she might have finally gained control of herself, and she held out a hand that only shook slightly with held back laughter.

'By the sounds of it, I'm pretty sure you've got my friend Rosie in your pocket.' Imogen figured talking normally might make things easier for Kim. 'And she comes apart for cleaning — so you almost definitely didn't break her. It.'

Kim wouldn't look at her as she pulled her hand out of her pocket and dropped the toy into Imogen's outstretched hand. Imogen couldn't help but notice Kim had turned pretty much the same shade as the bright pink cause of her embarrassment. 'It won't turn off.' Kim ground the words out from between clenched teeth.

'Yeah, it's a pleasure lock. So you don't accidentally turn it off in the heat of things. You have to click, click, hold . . .' The buzzing stopped almost instantly.

'I'm so bloody embarrassed.' Kim's voice was muffled by her hands.

'If anyone should be embarrassed it should probably be me. It's my toy. And if it helps, it was clean. I promise I always sanitise all my toys before I put them away.' Imogen tried to make it better in any way she could think of.

'I'm not sure if that helps, to be honest,' Kim grumbled, but she did look up. 'Toys? As in plural.'

'Yeah.' Imogen laughed. 'I've got a box of them under my bed.'

'I don't know how I'm supposed to respond to that.'

'However you want.' Imogen shrugged. 'They're just sex toys. I mean, I like sex, Kim. Whether it's with a partner, or by myself. I'm not ashamed to admit that. And frankly the endorphins from an orgasm have some brilliant analgesic properties — they're great painkillers. And if my nerves are going to be overactive and buzzing, I'd much rather it was with pleasure than pain.'

'I can't believe we're having this conversation.' Kim shook her head again. 'In fact, why are we having this conversation? Why was it in the bathroom?'

'Because Rosie's waterproof, never fails and is really good fun in the bath.' Imogen laughed.

'You said you were having a bath last night.' Kim chewed on her bottom lip.

'Yeah, I did.' Imogen felt her own blush start as she realised where Kim's thoughts were heading.

'Did you, um . . . do you ever think of me? When you're . . . you know . . .'

Imogen took a couple of steps towards Kim, then reached out and took her hand, just touching her fingertips. She looked up and met Kim's eyes. 'Would it bother you if I did?'

166

'Um.' Kim fiddled with Imogen's fingers. 'I think it might bother me more if you didn't. Is that weird? I mean, we haven't even . . .'

'Yeah, I've thought about you,' Imogen admitted, stopping Kim's spiral. She slipped her arm around Kim's waist to draw her closer. 'What about you?'

'What about me?'

Imogen smoothed Kim's hair away from her face. 'Have you ever thought about me like that?'

'Maybe,' she admitted, turning pink again.

'And?'

'And what?'

'And did thinking about me like that work for you?'

'Yeah,' Kim replied, her cheeks now scarlet.

'Good.' Imogen leaned in to brush a kiss against her lips.

Kim pulled away and sighed heavily. 'I should probably get going anyway.'

'Am I pushing you too much?' Imogen was worried. 'Is this too much, too soon? If it's the vibrator, you can consider it gone. I'll chuck it in the bin.'

'No. You don't have to do that. I meant I should go because . . . you know . . . I'm on my period.'

'And?'

'And that means we can't do . . . anything.'

'Like what?' Imogen demanded. 'Like we can't sit on my couch and talk, or binge-watch TV? Maybe snuggle a bit?'

'Yeah, but that's it. We can't do anything more than that. And in a couple of hours I'm probably going to be in pain, and grouchy, and you're not going to want to be around me. I'm not going to want to be around me. I should just go home, take some painkillers, curl up and wait for the worst of it to be over.'

'OK.' Imogen nodded. 'You're probably right. You should go.'

'OK.' Kim folded her arms back around her own waist.

'But only if that's what you really want to do. If, on the other hand, you'd like to stay here, I hope you know you're more than welcome. And that I keep an unhealthy amount of chocolate in the place. And, in case you've forgotten, dealing with pain is quite literally my job. And I'm really quite good at it.'

'It's your day off, and you should be resting,' Kim argued. 'You don't want to be looking after me.'

'It's just a period, Kim. I've been dealing with them for more than half of my life.'

'I'll just go home. Honest.'

Imogen took a deep, calming breath before replying. 'Kim . . .' She paused. 'Do you have a middle name?'

'Elizabeth.'

'Pretty.' She smiled, before putting her hands on her hips. 'OK. Kimberly Elizabeth Macpearson, you can bloody well stop that right now.'

* * *

If Kim hadn't already been leaning against the wall, she would have taken a couple of steps back under the ferocity of Imogen's frustration. She wasn't sure what she'd done, but whatever it was she knew she'd do anything she had to in order to make it right. 'Stop what?'

'Stop putting yourself down. Stop acting like any time you're even a hair's breadth less than perfect, you become some sort of burden. It's OK to be you, Kim.' Imogen reached out and stroked her cheek. 'You've already seen me in full-on flare mode, and the first thing you did was look after me. Can't you accept that maybe I want to look after you too? That it's OK for you to be you, even if you are a bit grumpy. That you don't need to change, or try to be someone you're not, because I like *you*, Kim. Just as you are. OK?'

'OK.' Sure, whatever she wanted. It was just one of those things people said without really meaning it. People always wanted her to change.

'Kim, I really mean this. You understand that, right?'

168

'I do.' Her response surprised her almost as much as Imogen's words.

'Good.' The kiss Imogen brushed against her lips was light and gentle, but so filled with emotion that Kim found herself having to blink back tears. 'Are you OK?'

'Yeah. Just feeling a bit hormonal and soppy. Sorr—' She stopped mid-sentence from the look on Imogen's face. 'Yeah. I'll be fine. Are you sure it's OK if I stay?'

Imogen nodded, that soft smile Kim liked so much appearing. 'Yeah, it's more than OK. Sit down and give me a couple of minutes?'

Kim made herself comfortable on the couch, watching as Imogen headed to the kitchen. A few minutes later, she came back and placed a loaded tray on the coffee table. 'One more thing.' She was back less than a minute later, half-hidden behind a bundled-up duvet. 'I know we've got the throws in here, but I find my duvet more comforting.'

'I get that.' Kim accepted the cover from her and spread it across her legs, leaving room for Imogen next to her.

'Hey.' Imogen grinned at her as she sat down, tucking her feet under the covers. 'Fancy meeting you here.' She reached over to grab the tray, pulling it into her lap. 'So, paracetamol and ibuprofen, in case you want them. Chocolate, for obvious reasons. The popcorn you like. Between my kitchen cupboard and store I've got about half a dozen different tea blends that might be helpful, depending on your symptoms.'

'So this is you in professional mode?' Kim grinned, teasing as she grabbed the popcorn. 'Over-the-counter painkillers, treats and kitchen witchery?'

'Oh, this is me just getting started. I also have heating pads and cooling pads. And this—' she held up a pale-grey, smooth crystal the length of her finger that was wider at one end '—is a massage wand, in case you'd like me to do some reflexology on you.' She put the crystal in Kim's hand. 'Moonstone, because it's brilliant for helping balance feminine energies. And, from the ancient techniques that are over

four thousand years old, to one of my newest, coolest toys . . .'
She held up a sleek black box.

'Exactly what type of toy are we talking here?' Kim eyed
the box suspiciously.

'Not *that* type.' Imogen smacked her knee playfully. 'I
mean, I wouldn't not recommend that type of endorphin rush
as a good painkiller. But this—' she flicked the box open '—is
the very latest in pain management technology. My Bluetooth
transcutaneous electrical nerve stimulator.'

Kim shook her head.

'Most people just call them TENS machines.'

'Is that like the things that zap you with electricity?' Kim
pulled a face.

'Yes, but it's only a very small electrical current. And it
can temporarily reduce, or interrupt, the pain signals between
the targeted area and the brain, which relieves pain and relaxes
muscles.'

'Have you tried it? Does it hurt?'

'This is actually my personal one,' Imogen reassured her.
'I use it quite a lot. But there's new pads for it in the box if you
wanted to try it. And no, it's not painful. If you're not used to
it, it can be a bit uncomfortable at first, but I find them very
effective. And I like that it's drug and chemical free, and it can
be used alongside other things as needed, without having to
worry about drug interactions and similar.'

'Will you show me how to use it?'

'Of course.' She put the tray back on the table. 'Is your
pain usually worse across your back or lower stomach?' Imogen
snapped the pads off the control unit and replaced them with
new ones.

'Tummy. Definitely.'

'Can I . . . ?' She tugged at the bottom of Kim's T-shirt.

'Of course.'

Imogen gently slid the fabric out of her way, rolling Kim's
leggings down. 'About here?' She trailed her fingers over Kim's
skin, a couple of inches below her belly button.

'Uh huh.' Kim's breath caught in her throat.

'OK.' Imogen peeled the protective backing off the pads and pressed the gadget gently but firmly against Kim's skin, then slipped her clothes back into place. Imogen wriggled for a couple of seconds, pulling out her phone and unlocking it. 'Like I said, this model is a Bluetooth one, so everything is controlled from the app. I think there's fifteen different levels of intensity and about a dozen different patterns. Here.' She handed over her phone. 'But maybe start out lower, as you're not used to it.'

'Thanks.' Kim picked a pattern at random and nearly dropped the phone. It felt like someone was flicking elastic bands all across her lower abdomen and she squirmed uncomfortably. 'I don't think I like this.'

Imogen peered at the screen. 'Try seven or eight.'

'Really? Isn't that going to be stronger?' She gritted her teeth as the thing changed, dragging pins and needles over her skin.

'Trust me.'

The flicking, prickly pins turned to a buzzing that seemed deeper, but a lot more comfortable. She sighed and settled back into the sofa cushions.

'Better?'

'Yeah.' Kim nodded, still getting used to the odd sensation. 'This could work.' She leaned forward, then bolted upright with a yelp as the vibrations zapped across her skin.

'Sorry, I should have warned you — you might want to be careful how you move around while you get used to it. Changes in position can change the direction of the charge. Was it painkillers you were after?'

'No.' She shook her head.

'Popcorn?'

'Of course.' Kim laughed and caught the bag Imogen threw at her. 'Thanks.'

'Anything else I can get you?'

'No.' She leaned forward — this time more carefully — and pressed a piece of popcorn against Imogen's lips. She waited patiently for her to part them, her eyes not leaving Imogen's, her fingers not moving, as Imogen finally did. 'I'm actually feeling pretty good right now.'

Imogen chewed and swallowed, still grinning. 'Does this mean you're not going to mock my kitchen witchery?'

'Maybe.' Kim leaned back in, another piece of the sticky-sweet popcorn in her fingers. 'Or maybe I just like teasing you.'

'You do, huh?' Imogen slid her hand around Kim's wrist, holding it in place while she kissed each fingertip in turn. 'You realise I might just be tempted to return the favour?' The look in her eyes as she gently nipped a finger sent shivers racing up and down Kim's spine.

* * *

'Ooh wow.' Kim's breathy moan as she flopped back against the cushions told Imogen she'd hit the right spot. 'That's incredible.'

'How about this?' Imogen smiled to herself as she worked her thumbs under and round Kim's ankle bones, hitting the points she knew best relieved monthly cramps. Kim's answering groans were everything she needed to know. And it definitely didn't make Imogen think thoughts that would be completely inappropriate with anyone else — like briefly wondering about the other situations that might make Kim make sounds like that.

'I don't know what you're doing, but please keep doing it.'

After a couple of dozen sweeps around Kim's ankles, Imogen shifted position, letting one foot drop into her lap so she could use the cool, smooth moonstone wand on Kim's instep.

'Seriously, that's incredible. How does you rubbing my feet help my back stop hurting?'

'This "foot rubbing" is reflexology. It's been used for around four thousand years, and works on the idea that every part of the body is connected, so stimulating the nerves here—' she twisted the wand again, eliciting another delicious sigh from Kim '—can influence how other bodily systems are working and help get your energies back into harmony.'

'It's absolutely working.' Kim sighed again.

'Does this mean no more teasing me about kitchen witchery?'

'You made a lasagne in a slow cooker. A good one! That's definitely some sort of magic.'

'Modern-day witches' cauldron. You'd be amazed what you can learn to cook in those things with a few tweaks and some creative thinking.'

'Or witchcraft.' Kim wriggled and yawned, her feet still in Imogen's lap. 'Just like what you're doing now.'

'I told you, it's reflexology. Thousands of years of teaching based on how qi — energy — works within the body.'

'It's amazing. I could happily fall asleep right here.'

'You're welcome to, but my bed's a lot comfier,' Imogen didn't realise what she'd said until Kim pulled her feet away and sat up, crossing her legs as she did so.

'Did you just ask me to stay over? Like a sleepover?'

'Yeah. I guess I did.' Imogen dug the crystal into her palm nervously. 'What do you think?'

'I think . . . I would like that.' Kim rolled forward onto her knees, bringing her much closer.

'Yeah?' She stroked Kim's cheek before kissing her.

'Yeah, I would. Unless you've changed your mind?'

'No, I haven't.' The more Imogen thought about it, the more she realised how right it felt. 'I'd like you to stay, if you still want to.'

Kim nodded. 'So, you're going to lend me some pyjamas, right?'

* * *

'I can't believe you don't have proper pyjamas,' Kim laughed when she came out of the bathroom, tugging at the T-shirt and shorts Imogen had lent her.

'What would I need them for?' Imogen shot her a wicked grin that made Kim tingle all over. 'Either I'm alone so I don't need them, or . . . I'm not alone and I don't want them. Don't worry, I've found something more sleepover-friendly for myself too. You done in the bathroom?'

'Yes thanks.' Kim tried not to think too much about what Imogen had just said. She definitely shouldn't be thinking about what Imogen did or didn't usually wear to bed. Not when they were having an almost completely innocent sleepover. But it was very, very tempting to muse, along with wondering what else Imogen could do with those highly trained, magical fingers.

Instead of thinking about it, she pulled back the surprisingly heavy covers, wincing as her stomach cramped again. Bugger. 'Immy?'

A few seconds passed before Imogen stepped into the doorway, her fingers tangled in her hair as she braided it. 'What did you just call me?'

'Um . . . Immy? Sorry.' She pulled a face.

'Don't be. I think I like it. Definitely better than what Ryan calls me. Did you need something?'

'The pain machine stopped. Don't worry, I can wait.'

'Don't be silly.' Imogen carried on twisting her curls into a braid. 'My phone's by the bed.' She called out the pin code as she headed back to the bathroom.

'Thanks.' Kim sat on the bed and dialled in the number, at the same time wondering how many people in her life she'd give unfettered access to her phone. Certainly not her brothers or parents . . . but Imogen? Maybe. She quickly opened up the app and dialled in the settings she'd discovered she liked best, relaxing as the pulse started.

'Hey, Kim?' Imogen peered back round the door, this time holding a toothbrush. 'All my patient details are locked in a secure app, so feel free to nosey through the rest of my phone if you like.'

'I wasn't going to snoop!'

'Not really snooping when I say you can do it.' Imogen disappeared again, leaving Kim staring at the glowing screen. She flicked through a couple of apps before opening up the camera, thumbing through pictures, grinning at the ones taken in the last few days. She laughed at the video of herself dressed up and dancing in pointy ears with the stripy skirt of a pixie-elf creature.

After a few seconds of thought she switched the camera into portrait mode, smiled into the screen and took a couple of shots. She'd leave them there for Imogen to find later. She put the phone down, tucked her feet under the edge of the covers and looked around the room. It was giving off serious late 1980s vibes. All it needed was some boyband — or Kylie — posters to really complete the look. She wondered if the room had been so purple when Imogen moved in, or whether she'd chosen it. Remembering how Imogen's initial design for her store had turned peaceful and uplifting into swimming pool, she suspected the colour might be recent.

She looked up when Imogen came back in. 'Hey. Is this side of the bed OK? I can move.'

'It's fine. I usually end up on this side anyway.' She dragged back the rest of the covers and climbed onto the bed, then rolled on her side to look at Kim. 'I've had a really good weekend.'

'Yeah, me too.' Kim rolled to face her. 'And this feels nice. Even if this is a little weird.'

'Is it that weird?'

'I was just trying to remember if I've ever slept with someone before actually *sleeping* with them.'

'Huh.' Imogen chewed her lip. 'Now you mention it, I'm not sure I have for a long time either. And not with anyone like you. But I don't think this—' she wriggled closer '—is weird. It feels easy.'

'Did you just call me easy?' Kim narrowed her eyes and pursed her lips together — mostly to keep from laughing.

'Yes, I did.' Imogen slid an arm around her waist. 'But I meant it in the nicest possible way. Things just feel really comfortable and easy with you — between us.'

'I know what you mean.' Kim trailed her fingers up and down Imogen's arm. 'I feel it too. But isn't it always like this?'

'How do you mean?'

'For you. Isn't this feeling normal when it's . . .' Her assumptions shattered as Imogen shook her head, smiling as she finished the thought more slowly, regretting the words almost as soon as she said them '. . . two women?'

Imogen was still shaking her head, her lips bitten tightly together.

'Oh stop it,' Kim tutted. 'Just laugh at me already. I know you want to.'

'Sorry.' Imogen buried her face in the pillow and still failed to muffle her laughter.

'You done yet?' Kim pulled a face, too comfortable to move. 'I'm suddenly feeling really silly. I knew things felt different, but I've never been with a woman before, so I thought that was the difference. You're saying it's not?'

'Not for me, no.' Imogen stopped laughing for long enough to look at Kim, propping herself up on her elbow. 'But I've also never been such good friends with someone first, like we are. I've usually tried to keep friendship and romance separate.'

'But not with me?'

'You said it yourself.' Imogen leaned over to kiss her. 'You're just too damn irresistible.'

'You're never going to let me live that down, are you?' Kim groaned.

'When you have so much fun tormenting me?' She kissed her again. 'Not a chance.'

176

CHAPTER TWELVE

'OK then.' Imogen finished showing Kai around. She'd had a good feeling when they'd first met and chatted — and was glad that she still felt the same at their second meeting. And he'd turned up and still seemed pretty eager, and competent, so at least she hadn't scared him off. 'So what do you think? Do you fancy working a couple of hours and seeing how you get on?'

'So I'm getting the trial?' His grin and enthusiasm were contagious. 'Do I get to ask how many others there are? Just trying to gauge the competition.'

'Right now, just you.'

'Awesome. You must really like me, then.'

'I had a good feeling about you,' she admitted. 'But that can be revised if you annoy me.'

'Oh well, if you don't hire me it won't be a total loss.' He grinned again.

'Oh?' Imogen wasn't sure she liked the sound of that. Even though it was only a part-time role, she was still hoping for someone with commitment. She knew it was a bit much to ask for passion and dedication for her store, but she'd thought he was a bit more interested than that. She started to worry that maybe she'd read him entirely wrong.

'No. If you don't hire me, I figure there's more chance of you saying yes if I ask you out.' He grinned at her again, and she realised what it was about him that she liked — his cheeky, teasing confidence reminded her of some of her favourite people. He could have been pushy, verging on offensive even — except his smile and energy was so polite and genuine that it would have been hard to take his words as anything other than complimentary.

'You should probably focus more on trying to impress me into hiring you, not dating you,' Imogen warned with a grin. 'The latter would be a waste of your time. I'm neither single, or your type.'

'Pity.' He shrugged good-naturedly. 'But if you were single, what makes you think you wouldn't be my type?'

'I just assumed your type would be people who are actually interested in men. Unlike me.'

'Damn. Did you hear that?'

'Hear what?'

'The sound of men's hearts breaking all over the county.'

Imogen just about got her hand over her mouth before cracking up laughing. She really hoped Kai worked out, because she knew working with him would be good fun. 'I'm going to let that one slide. But be careful how you speak with customers, OK? I quite like the banter, but not everyone does.'

'I know,' he replied soberly. 'It's a sad world where you can't brighten someone's day by paying them a compliment, but I understand. Hardly the first time I've worked in retail . . . and yes, I know there's more than just retail in this role — but I get customer service. You can trust me with your shop-baby, Imogen.'

'I believe you.' She nodded.

'Besides, I'm not going to screw you over. You might curse me or something.' He grinned at her.

'Nah, I don't curse people as a rule. It's not worth the negative karma.' She grinned. 'Any other questions?'

'Where's the kettle and biscuits?' He caught the look Imogen shot him. 'You said you had a new client consultation in—' he checked the clock '—about half an hour. I assumed part of the job is greeting your clients, making them drinks and making sure they're comfortable — while not flirting with them too much.'

'Through here.' Imogen beckoned him through to the back. 'My consultation room, toilet and washroom.' She pointed them out. 'And kitchenette. I live upstairs, and currently keep some storeroom space there, but wouldn't expect you to be up there.'

'No, you need your own space,' Kai agreed. 'I assume that includes your client records? Upstairs behind the locked door?'

'It does.' Imogen nodded.

'Good. One less thing for me to worry about then.' He flashed her a wink. 'I can just stay down here and play with your crystals and customers.'

'Just don't scare any of them off.' Imogen tried not to roll her eyes. The more he talked, the more he reminded her of Ryan. If Ryan favoured motorbikes and ink over social media and animals.

'Will do my best, boss. Do you need some quiet time to prepare for your client? I can go be nosey and familiarise myself with more of your stock. And see if there's anything I want to haggle and cheek you for a staff discount on. I get one, right?' He flashed her another grin.

'Try not to spend all of your wages before you've earned any.' Imogen headed to her consultation room and shooed him back into the shop.

She heard soft voices a while later that went on for a few minutes before turning into laughter, followed shortly by a knock at her door — although it was open.

'Hey, boss.' Kai held his arm out to an older woman who — despite her brightly coloured fleece — Imogen would best describe as grey. Everything about her — skin, eyes, how she moved — seemed tired and dulled, as though she walked under a great cloud. 'This is Trish Roberts. Trish, meet Imogen. Boss, Trish is currently under treatment at the hospital for stage three breast cancer. Her pathway is curative — and she's absolutely going to kick its arse, right, Trish?'

'Doing my best.'

Imogen's heart went out to the woman. Even the watery smile she gave Kai as she sat down looked like it was painful.

'But she's been having a hard time with some of the side effects, haven't you, lovely?' Kai asked quietly.

'Yeah. Sometimes feels like the treatment is competing with the illness to try and see which can make me sickest first.'

'I'm really sorry to hear that.' Imogen held out her hand. 'But it's nice to meet you, and we'll see what we can do to help.'

'Thank you.' Trish nodded.

'Right. I'll leave you two ladies to chat, and I'll go brew up some of that ginger and liquorice tea I was showing you. That way you can try it here before you buy any to take home. And I'll see if I can't rustle up some biscuits while I'm at it.' Kai quietly closed the door, leaving Imogen feeling more than a little impressed with him. Not only had he made a new client feel relaxed, but he'd also gathered enough information — in the space of a few minutes — to be able to make what seemed to be a meaningful contribution. It could, of course, be luck that made him suggest one of Imogen's favourite teas for treating nausea in her collection — but somehow she didn't think it was.

'Is it OK if I call you Trish?' She focussed on her new client. 'We tend to keep things fairly informal here.'

'Of course.'

'Do you want to tell me a bit about what's brought you here today? Which side effects are bothering you the most?'

'None of them are much fun, but the sickness and the neuropathy are the worst.'

'Have you discussed these with your care team?' Imogen always insisted on working alongside medical teams wherever they were involved.

'Yeah, but the medications to counteract the side effects of the treatment have their own side effects, and I end up

180

feeling like I'm running in circles. And I really don't have the energy spare for any running. I'm six months into this treatment plan, and have at least another six months to go.'

'So what about the side effects?' Imogen pushed gently.

Trish's sigh sounded bone-weary. 'The anti-sickness make my mouth really dry, which makes everything taste even worse than the chemo, and I get dizziness and chills. And the painkillers make me so drowsy I'm not safe to drive and can barely make it through a couple of pages before nodding off.'

'You like to read?' Imogen would focus on the positive for a few moments.

'Yeah, to my grandkids, but it's getting harder every week. If I take the meds I'm not in pain, but I'm so out of it that I struggle to focus.'

'Bit of a sense of detachment, maybe?' She didn't like to put words in her client's mouths, but she did want to get to the bottom of how best to help Trish.

'My grandson, Mark — he's ten — he says I'm a regular space cadet. It would be funny if it wasn't so true. I just really want to not be in pain, but also not be so doped out of my mind that I can't enjoy time with my family. I used to be really good at crafts, and I worked as a seamstress for years. It's bad enough I can barely hold a crochet hook, let alone thread a needle. I can handle that. But,' she sniffed, 'not being able to play with my grandkids? That's almost as bad as the bloody illness.'

'I completely understand.' Imogen pushed a box of tissues towards her with one hand, and rested her fingers lightly on Trish's for a few seconds.

'I know it's a long shot, but my cancer nurse — Karina—' Imogen nodded, recognising the name '—she mentioned you'd helped one of her other ladies — that's what she calls us, her ladies — so I figured it was worth at least the cost of meeting you.'

'Well, I'm glad to hear Karina's passing on my details.' Imogen smiled. 'But I want to start by reassuring you that

181

the only cost today is your time. Well, that and anything Kai might convince you to buy on the way out.'

'Do you think you might be able to help me at all?' Trish gritted her teeth for a few moments and took a couple of deep breaths. 'I don't mean to put any pressure on you, but I'm pretty desperate.'

'There's definitely a few things we can look at trying—' Imogen was interrupted by Kai's knock. 'And with timing so perfect you'd have thought we practiced it, here's Kai with some of them.'

'Sorry I was a bit longer. I popped to the shop for some ginger biscuits. They're not as strong as the ones I make, but they're the best I could find at short notice.' Another good point for him in Imogen's book.

He placed the tray on the little table and shot Imogen a wink before leaving.

Imogen took her tea and settled back into her seat, waiting for Trish to do the same. 'If it's OK with you, I'd like to just sit here and drink our tea while we chat a little more about the things you might like to try with me.' She waited patiently while Trish sipped her tea and nibbled at the gingerbread. Within minutes her colour was starting to improve, and Imogen made a mental note to ask Kai what else he'd added to her tea. She wasn't going to say anything in front of a client, but it smelled slightly different to normal.

'Can I ask something?'

'Whatever you want. This is your time and your space,' Imogen reassured her.

'Is this going to be very expensive? Only I've had to cut my hours at work with the treatments so far . . .'

The question Imogen hated to answer — because she hated that she had overheads and couldn't give every treatment away. 'Well, it is more than a packet of pills, yes — but there's options and discussions we can have about that. There's also funding that you can probably access through the NHS — that's called a Personal Healthcare Budget, which your GP or someone at the hospital can help arrange. On top of that, some of the work I'm going to suggest we might be able to do within the confines — and funding — of the pain management clinic at the hospital, depending on what works best for you.'

'OK.' Trish nodded, looking a lot less grey.

'But we can talk about that later. First, how about we see what we have in my skillset that can offer you some relief? And if we can find something that helps you, then we can figure out the rest from there. How does that sound?'

'Good.' Trish nodded. 'That sounds really good. I actually feel quite optimistic about this.'

* * *

When Kim skipped into Imogen's shop a few days later, she definitely hadn't expected to be greeted by a tall, broad-shoul-dered man, dressed in denim and leather, with dark ginger hair tied back in a short tail. Ink traced up his arms to disappear beneath tight sleeves, under a much-patched and studded open leather waistcoat. When Imogen had told her she'd hired some help, she hadn't expected someone who looked quite like this.

'Welcome to Fairy's Botanica. I'm Kai and I'd love to know how I can help you today. Can I interest you in a cup of tea? It's an orange, jasmine and ginger oolong blend — won-derfully relaxing and good for boosting the immune system.'

'I thought something smelled good. But I was actually looking for Imogen.'

'She's just with a client, but she should be finishing up shortly. And is there anything — anything at all — that I can help with in the meantime? It really would be my pleasure.' His hazel eyes twinkled as he grinned.

Kim shook her head, and was still working out how to respond when Imogen appeared.

'Hey.' She flashed Kim a smile that sent warmth racing throughout her body. The look in her eyes when they locked on Kim's told her she was feeling the same.

'I brought lunch.' Kim held up the bag she'd packed that morning.

'Sounds good. But you don't have to do that. I do have a whole kitchen upstairs. And a mini one down here.'

'I know, but I wanted to.' Kim smiled, meaning every word. She liked looking after Imogen, even if it was just little things like lunch — which was actually a really good excuse to see her. And she highly suspected that Imogen was much better at looking after her clients and patients than she was herself, and often skipped proper meals.

'Let me just see out my last client. She's taking a few minutes to rest and make sure of her balance after treatment. Bowen therapy can sometimes make you feel a little dizzy,' she explained in response to Kim's questioning look, before turning to Kai. 'And she'd like a packet of your jasmine tea to take home.' She headed back to her consulting room, then paused. 'And Kai? Don't flirt with Kim please. Otherwise I might have to reconsider my "no cursing employees" rule.'

Kai shrugged and shot Kim an apologetic grin. 'Sorry. It was just a bit of good-natured fun. I don't mean anything by it, I know you're not interested. Leastways, not in me.'

'She told you.' Kim felt her eyebrows shoot up in surprise. It made sense that someone who worked with Imogen and saw her on a daily basis would know — eventually. But she was shocked Imogen hadn't discussed it with her first. It was one thing when it was Ryan and Angela — she was hardly going to ask Imogen to lie to her brother — and she knew Angela well enough to trust her, but this was someone she didn't know at all.

'Nope. And she didn't have to.' Kai shook his head. 'As soon as she stepped out here, your aura lit up.'

'You're teasing me.' Kim pulled a face.

'Hers changed too, in case you're interested,' Kai murmured as he weighed out some tea.

'Really?'

'Yeah. I mean, boss-lady is a pretty warm and friendly type anyway. Makes sense with the work she does. But when she spotted you just now, her energy changed and became softer. Almost glowy.'

Kim must have pulled a face, because Kai laughed. 'You don't believe in auras?'

'In honesty, this whole way of thinking is quite new to me,' Kim admitted, watching as Kai measured out tea leaves. 'I grew up in a family who are very clinical in their thinking and approaches. I only had my first reflexology session very recently.'

'And?'

'Total convert. And I might be in love with those TENS machines.'

'But auras are where you draw the line?' He fixed her with an odd look.

'I'm still new to all this. I'm not sure I've worked out what I believe in or don't yet.'

'Auras are real enough that I could tell — just by looking — that you and Imogen are . . . hmm.' He folded his arms and looked at her for a few seconds. 'Well, you're a lot more than friends, but as to what? I think you're still figuring out what the rest of that answer is.'

There was no way Kim was buying the act. 'She told you. This is a wind up.'

Kai shook his head and held up his hand. 'Scout's honour.'

'I'm not sure I believe you were ever a scout.' Imogen laughed as she joined them, followed by her client. 'But I will leave you to settle up with Jane here, and book her next appointment.' She patted her client's shoulder. 'Remember, drink plenty of water — or tea — for the rest of the afternoon, and try to rest if you can.'

She turned to Kim with that brilliant, beautiful smile. 'So you said you brought lunch?'

'Chicken pesto wraps.' Kim held up the bag.

'Sounds great. Weather's nice. Garden?'

Kim followed her through to the courtyard. Imogen grabbed her wrist as she stepped into the sunlight, spinning her round and into her arms.

185

'Hi.' Kim giggled as Imogen stroked her cheek. 'I've missed you the last few days.'

'I've missed you too.' Imogen leaned in to kiss her. 'What are you doing this weekend?'

'Hanging out with you?'

'Really good answer.' Imogen drove any questions she might have had about Kai right out of Kim's mind.

'You think so?' Kim wrapped her arms around Imogen's neck.

'Uh huh.' Imogen lowered her lips to Kim's again, sending scorching heat through her.

* * *

Imogen glanced at Kim again, starting to feel worried. Despite Kim's reassurances, she was pretty sure something was wrong: Kim was fidgety, almost anxious or on edge. She was doing her best to hide it — which bothered Imogen even more, the idea that Kim felt like she had to hide something from her. Obviously she'd give her the space she clearly needed, but she hoped Kim knew that she really meant her offer of support — for whatever the problem was.

'I need to use your bathroom.' Kim untangled herself from Imogen's arms, and stood, gently putting Bramble on the floor, who shot off to his basket.

'You know where it is.' Imogen paused the movie that she was pretty sure neither of them was watching at all, levered herself from the sofa too and headed for the kitchen. Maybe Kim was having second thoughts about things. About them. The idea scared her, but she wouldn't blame Kim if that was it.

She felt a bit guilty — worrying that the pressure she'd put on Kim had contributed to whatever it was that was going on for her. It was so tempting to try and take back what she'd said about wanting a serious relationship — to just not worry about the future and give in to the teasing heat . . . because that was still there. It would only take a few words for Imogen to make it all about sex, and having fun, and take the pressure off them both. But at the same time, she knew she'd be lying and that — as tempting as it was in the short-term to just say screw it and get on with screwing — it also seemed like the fast-track to hurting them both, and ruining a really good friendship. She didn't want to lie to either of them, even if it would have been easier in the short-term.

So she'd just have to suck it up, pull up her big girl panties, and carry on taking her frustrations out on Rosie in the bath.

'Immy?'

'I'm making drinks. Tea or coffee?' She opened the fridge. 'Um.'

'I can do hot chocolate, or there's more wine. What do you what?'

'You. I want you.'

Imogen looked up and froze, suddenly forgetting how to breathe. Kim stood in the doorway wearing a shy smile and a purple lace negligee that clung to her curves, moulding itself over her small breasts, the curves of her stomach and hips, and everywhere else that Imogen wanted — no, *needed* — to have her hands. It ended far above Kim's knees. Somewhere else she desperately needed her hands and lips.

'Are you going to say something?' The soft shiver in Kim's voice forced Imogen to unstick her tongue from the roof of her mouth. 'Anything?'

'Oh my Goddess,' she breathed the words as a prayer. 'Are you serious?'

Kim laughed. 'No, I just bought this, snuck it into your flat in my bag and changed in your bathroom in case I got bored of your TV choices.' She rolled her eyes and Imogen knew she was done for. Only Kim could stand in her kitchen in smoking-hot lingerie, snarking at her, and be all the hotter for it.

'I might need you to pinch me or something because I'm pretty sure I'm dreaming.' Imogen forced herself to remember how to move, how to stand and close the fridge door. 'You look like a dream come true.'

'I was going for cute.' Kim shrugged.

'You left cute standing in the dust miles back.' Imogen finally got her limbs to remember themselves and pulled Kim against her, letting her fingers trace over the pattern of the purple lace that kissed her skin. 'You are phenomenal. Stunning. Breathtaking.'

'So you like it then?'

'Like isn't even close to how I feel about this.' She brushed Kim's hair from her shoulders, letting her fingertips tease the sensitive skin there, before sliding her hand around the back of her neck to draw Kim in for a kiss. 'If you were any hotter—' she whispered the words into her ear '—I'd be seriously worried about spontaneous human combustion.'

Kim giggled, pressing against her. 'Do you have any idea what you do to me when you say things like that . . . ?' She moaned as Imogen's lips traced down her neck.

'I've got a pretty good idea.' Imogen traced her spare hand down Kim's arm, loving the goose pimples that decorated her skin. She stopped when she found Kim's hand in a fist behind her back, wrapped around something bulky. 'What's this?' She pulled Kim's hand out to reveal a familiar flash of lurid pink.

'Um . . . insurance?' Kim turned almost the same shade and refused to meet Imogen's eyes.

'Should I be offended that you're doubting my skills enough that you borrowed my vibrator?'

'No!' Kim's gaze snapped up to meet hers, her eyes flashing. 'It's not for you . . . I mean. I wanted it, to be sure . . .' She shook her head before burying her burning cheeks against Imogen's shoulder.

'Kim, sweets.' Imogen slid her fingers beneath Kim's chin and made her look up at her. 'Is this why you've been so anxious all evening? We don't have to do this.'

'But I really want to,' Kim argued. 'And you said Rosie never fails to . . . you know . . . for you. I wanted her for backup.'

'I'm pretty confident we're not going to need her.'

'Yeah, but you know what you're doing. I . . . don't. I really want this to be good for you too, Immy.'

'Oh.' Realisation dawned for Imogen as she stared at Kim. 'Wow. Kim, you . . .' She pulled her back close, kissing her hard and parting her lips with her tongue. It was that or risking words slipping out that were too big and too scary to say right then. But even though Imogen muffled the words with the kiss, they bounced around her mind.

* * *

Kim's heart hammered against her ribs as she took Imogen's hand and tugged her towards the bedroom, still amazed that this was happening. Or about to happen. Part of her was nervous — terrified — but at the same time it felt so utterly right that she was surprised it had taken so long.

Imogen's eyes had raked over her, hot and needy as they'd taken in every inch of skin and lace. She felt more desired and excited than she could ever remember feeling before. And it gave her the confidence to wrap her fingers around Imogen's hand and pull her towards the bedroom. Goose pimples tracked over her skin, making her feel hot and cold and tingly all at the same time.

Heat flashed through her when Imogen paused by the bedroom door and caught her between her arms, trapping her against the wall. She stroked Kim's hair back from her face and studied her closely. 'As much as I really, really want to do this — and I do, more than anything — we can still stop right now.'

'Why?' Kim tangled her fingers in Imogen's curls.

'Because this is a really big deal.' Imogen pulled back slightly, and Kim immediately missed her touch, fighting the urge to whimper. 'Up until now we've really just kissed . . .'

'We've done a bit more than "just kiss", unless you forgot the other night.'

'Believe me, I haven't.' Imogen grinned. 'But kissing and . . . playing, even sharing a bed, as wonderful as it is, is quite different, and a lot easier to take back than going all the way.'

'I won't want to take anything back,' Kim told her honestly, pulling Imogen's hands around her waist, tucking them behind her back so she stood in her arms. 'I've been thinking about this, and I really want it. You have been incredibly patient, which I'm really grateful for . . . but I think we've waited long enough.'

'You're sure?'

'I really, really am.' She kissed Imogen again. 'I'm just a bit nervous, too.'

'You think I'm not?'

'It's not your first time with a woman,' Kim pointed out. 'You know what you're doing.'

'True.' Imogen did that thing that felt so good — when she tucked Kim's hair away from her face and stroked the skin behind her ear and down her neck. 'But it's my first time with you. And you do know what you're doing. You know what feels good to you. How you want me to touch you.' She smoothed her hands down Kim's back, making her gasp and squirm. 'Just touch me like that.'

Kim slid her hand around Imogen's neck before kissing her deeply, pressing tightly up against her, before pulling away. 'So if I want to do that, you're OK with it?'

'Yeah, very OK.'

'And this?' Kim slid her fingers into Imogen's hair to find the clip holding it up.

'Yeah.' Imogen smiled as Kim loosened her hair, letting it cascade over her shoulders and down her back.

'How about this?' Her fingers were tentative and almost hesitant as she ran her hands down Imogen's, then reached down her thighs, gathering up her dress as she inched her fingers slowly back up.

'Definitely.' Imogen kissed Kim again, then traced a line of heat along Kim's chin and down her neck, before lifting her

arms up and letting Kim peel her dress over her head. 'Can I .
. . ?' She teased the lace down over Kim's shoulders, following
her fingers with her nose and lips before tracing her fingers
down over her breasts.

Kim let her head fall back as Imogen's lips and tongue
scorched a pathway lower — kissing, teasing, licking and
sucking, leaving Kim shaking with the need for more. She
whimpered and shoved her hand in her mouth when Imogen
gave her exactly that, kissing lower down her stomach.

Imogen stood and pulled Kim's hand away from her
mouth, replacing it with her lips. 'Sweets,' she breathed the
words into Kim's ear, 'you don't need to hold back from me.
Give me everything. Please?' She nipped Kim's neck, making her shiver and squirm breathlessly. 'Everything.' Imogen
caught Kim's face in her hands and kissed her again, making
her knees tremble and her body ache in the most delicious,
needy places. She waited until Kim's eyes met hers, then kissed
her again, this time slowly and sweetly, in a way that stole her
breath.

Kim half-fell and half-sat on the edge of the bed, parting
her knees so she had space to pull Imogen close to her — still
slightly shocked that this was happening, even as she tangled
her fingers amongst Imogen's curls. She didn't think she'd
ever tire of doing that, of feeling the soft waves and twists
in her hands, as she pulled Imogen tightly against her and
surrendered to her lips. The long, sweetly scented, coconutty
curls reached almost to Imogen's waist, surrounding Kim
and clouding her senses in the most delicious way. She traced
one hand back up Imogen's spine, only to be thwarted by
her bra strap — and fingers that shook. After a second and
third attempt she grumbled, pulling away from their kiss to
try again.

She swore softly. 'How is it I can do this behind my own
back without even thinking?'

Imogen laughed in her arms and kissed Kim again. 'It's
because you're not used to thinking about it. And forwards

is backwards to you.' She tucked her hands behind her back, still kissing Kim, and peeled away the satin and lace, letting it drop down one arm, then the other, to land on the floor. She drew away from Kim, moving back half a pace.

'Oh wow,' Kim murmured. 'You are so beautiful.'

'I was thinking the same about you.' Imogen rested her hands on Kim's shoulder, letting her take her time.

At first Kim's touch was tentative and nervous, but when Imogen groaned happily and pressed against her hands, Kim tugged her sharply against her, giggling as they toppled onto the bed, Imogen's hair falling all around her. She tangled herself in Imogen happily, losing herself in her scent, her taste, the feeling of her skin and her touch as Imogen did her best to keep her promise, and drive her totally crazy.

* * *

Imogen shivered as Kim trailed lazy fingers over her ribs, skimming the incredibly sensitive skin of her breast, before stroking up her throat. Imogen caught her fingers and kissed them, before dragging her tired and deliciously aching body over to face Kim, lazily twisting a leg through hers.

'Well?'

'Well what?'

'Well, can you remember what day of the week it is?'

Kim looked at her strangely for a few seconds before cracking up laughing. 'I think I can just about figure it out.'

'Oh, in that case you should probably come here.' Imogen drew her closer. 'I did make you a promise.'

'You more than kept it.' Kim grinned. 'I didn't know my body could do . . . that. I mean, I knew in theory women were capable of multiple times . . . but knowing that and experiencing it . . . that often . . . wow.'

'Yeah, benefits of not needing to wait for certain anatomy to recover. Plus I kind of think it's Mother Nature's way of paying us back for the misery of periods.'

'That's a brilliant way to look at it.' Kim flopped back against the skew-whiff pillows.

'So you didn't miss . . . other things . . .' Imogen was pretty sure she knew the answer, but in that moment of quite literal naked vulnerability, she felt a bit nervous, like she needed to check.

Kim giggled again, making Imogen tense.

'You're seriously asking me that?' Kim shook her head in disbelief. 'Immy, I didn't miss a thing. It . . . you . . . amazing.' She giggled again. 'I might just about have remembered it's Saturday, but I lost count of how many times it was amazing for me.'

'I think it might technically be Sunday by now.'

'See what I mean?' She squeezed Imogen's fingers, before her face fell. 'It was OK for you too, right?'

'OK isn't even close to a good enough description,' Imogen promised her, kissing her fingers again and making a decision. 'There's something I want to ask you.'

'Sounds interesting.' Kim propped herself up on her elbow.

'I've got to go away at the end of the month for a couple of days, just a trade show that some of my favourite suppliers attend. I usually go down the night before, then do a couple of hours at the show on the Saturday, and then stay down overnight as it's quite a drive. That way I don't wear myself out.'

'Or risk triggering a flare.'

'Exactly. And I thought maybe . . . if you wanted to come too, and you can say no if it's too much too soon . . . But, I thought we could extend it and be there Friday, Saturday and Sunday night?'

'So you're asking me on a mini-break?'

'Yes. With a few hours of work thrown in for me, but yes. I am.' Imogen watched Kim closely, trying to figure out her feelings. 'I know I said I wasn't going to push you, and I'm aware that this might be sort of pushing, but I can't help but like the idea of spending a weekend with just you and me, and a load of people who we don't really know and who aren't part

193

of our lives, and whose opinion we don't have to think about. I just thought it might be nice for us to have some time and space together, where you and I can just try being us. Outside of this building.' She realised she was starting to waffle and bit her lips together, suddenly nervous.

'I'm making things hard for you, aren't I?'

Imogen sighed. 'I'm not going to lie to you and say this is the easiest relationship I've ever been in. I'm not used to having to hide my feelings, and I'm not that good at it — as you found out via my brother at Summer's Christmas. But, as much as I want to walk through the village holding your hand, and kiss you under the tree where we watched rainbows in the dark, I understand this is new for you, and I'm not going to push you to take steps before you're ready.'

'I really appreciate that.' Kim slid her hand around the back of Imogen's neck and leaned over to kiss her gently and sweetly. 'And I'd really like to go with you. A weekend away with you sounds lovely.'

'I haven't told you where it is yet,' Imogen warned, already suspecting that Kim wouldn't care.

'Oh yeah, I should probably have asked that.' The gorgeous pink that Imogen found so adorable flushed across Kim's cheeks.

'Sandown racecourse. It's in south-west London, not far from the Surrey border.'

'Well, it's not the seaside, but that doesn't sound bad. If you let me know the hotel, I'm sure I can find something to do while you're working.'

'I hadn't actually booked anywhere yet. I wanted to make sure Kai was onboard and settled before I left him in charge, and convince Ryan to look after Bramble. And I was hoping I might need to book for two.' She grinned. 'I usually just stay at whichever business hotel has the best rates, just somewhere to crash and sleep. But I thought if you said yes that we could have a look for something a bit nicer? Maybe a cutesy bed and breakfast or similar?'

'That sounds good. And I've got some points and loyalty discounts run up on a few travel websites that we can use to upgrade . . . if you wanted to?'

'You don't have to do that.'

'I know, but I'd like to. I can see us lolling around in huge fluffy robes in some spa hotel.'

'Well, when you put it like that, I'm not going to argue . . . at least not too much. If you're sure?'

'I am. And I can drive too. That way you'd be less likely to tire yourself out, right?'

'Right. And that would be great.' Imogen smiled.

'And that way, you'll have more energy for other things that are far more interesting than driving down the motorway.' This time Kim's grin was impish.

'Oh, you've got plans have you?'

'I might have.' Kim tugged her closer, sliding her hand down Imogen's back, making it very clear exactly what she had in mind.

* * *

'I was thinking about going shopping next weekend to look for my wedding hat.' Kim's mum took the salad that Kim had just finished chopping. 'Do you want to come with me? It's ages since we've had a girly shopping day.'

'Oh, I would have loved to, but could we make it another time? I'm going away next weekend. I was going to tell you later.'

'Anywhere nice?'

Kim froze, staring at the grain of the chopping board — thick, heavy, solid wood. It was the perfect opening, and her mum had always tried to be supportive. She was going away with Immy — just the thought of it made her smile — and she wasn't ashamed they were together at all. She just wasn't sure how her mum — or the rest of her family — were going to take the news. In truth, Kim felt like she was still getting to know the new version of herself.

'Kim? Are you OK, love? I asked what you were planning.'

'Sorry, yeah.' Kim shook her head, making her mind up. Even though she was still getting to know Kim 2.0, she already liked her. And she very definitely liked Imogen.

'Bit of a spa weekend with my girlfriend.' Kim forced herself to focus on the chopping board. If she did that, she might be able to control the nerves while she waited for her mum's response.

'Oh, that's a pity.' Julie went back to chopping the other vegetables.

Kim looked up, bemused. That was it? She'd just told her mum she had a girlfriend — that she was dating a woman — and the best she could come up with was "that's a pity".

'I'm sorry, what?'

'Well, you've been staying out such a lot lately, I'd been starting to hope that maybe you'd found a nice gentleman you were seeing. I do want so much for you to be happy, Kim. To find your someone special like your brothers have.'

'And the only way you think I can do that is with "a nice gentleman", right? It doesn't occur to you that there could be any other option? Another way that I could be happy? You just want me to find a man and settle down and be taken care of so you don't have to worry about your little black sheep.' She didn't know how it was her mum could always go from being kind and supportive to winding her up in a couple of breaths. She knew she didn't mean it, but it didn't make the frustration any easier.

'You don't need to get snippy with me about it.' She smacked the knife down.

'Why not? It's the truth, isn't it? Come on, Mum, you might as well admit it. I've always been the odd one out. Of all of us, I know I'm the one who has worried you and Dad the most. Even when Sarah's mother walked out on her and Cal, and even when Jake was racing around the world trying to cure a kid of cancer, who wasn't his — I know it was me who worried you more.'

'Kim, that's not fair . . .' Julie started.

'No, but it's not untrue either.' She met her mum's gaze, not wanting to back down. Not this time. Especially not when she'd just told her about Imogen. 'Is it?'

'Not completely, no,' Julie admitted quietly. 'But me and your dad, we just want to see you settled and happy. Whatever that looks like for you. It's what we want for all three of you. And I think if you were being honest with yourself, you'd admit you've always been a bit restless.'

As much as she wanted to, Kim couldn't really argue with that.

'So yes.' Julie reached across to clasp her daughter's hand. 'If you want to accuse me of worrying about my baby girl, I'm not going to apologise for that. But I will apologise if me or your dad have ever made you feel like an outsider in your own family. We never meant it. We just wanted . . .'

'Me to settle down and stop being a pain in your arse?'

Her mum's nose wrinkled at the crude term, but she still laughed. 'I wouldn't really have put it quite like that . . . but yes. In some ways, I know it's our fault. After Callum and Jake maybe we were a bit . . . complacent. We thought we were prepared for another child, but you . . .'

'I know.' Kim rolled her eyes. 'If you'd had me first, I'd be an only child, and I'm the reason your hair is grey.' She'd heard it all before.

'If you gave me most of my grey hairs, you certainly gave me my laughter lines too.'

'Really?' She hadn't heard that before.

'Yes, really.' She patted Kim's hand before letting go. 'But you're right, your brothers were a lot . . . easier . . . if that's the word you want to use. They both figured out what they wanted to do with their lives early on, and fixed on those goals, which made it easier to know how to support them. We've always wanted to support you, Kim. I just don't think we've always known quite how to do it when you flit between ideas and relationships so quickly.'

She tried not to take it personally, not to remember how often she'd been called flibbertigibbet by her dad and brothers for doing exactly what her mum had just described, but it was hard — especially when she knew her mum was right. As much as she might like to argue that it was creativity and self-expression, she knew her track record was very flibbertigibbet-y at times. But that didn't excuse her ignoring what she'd said about Imogen. 'Mum, did you hear what I'd said about why I can't go shopping with you?'

'Yeah. You've booked a spa weekend with a friend. Remember to take flip-flops, won't you? So many people we've treated have picked up fungal infections or a verruca wandering around places like that.'

Kim shook her head. As much as she loved her family, sometimes they really were impossible to talk to. 'Yeah, Mum, I'll pack some sliders.'

CHAPTER THIRTEEN

Imogen stretched luxuriously under the covers, wriggling her fingers, hands, wrists, toes and ankles in turn before testing her legs, back, arms and neck.

'You good?' Kim came out of the bathroom wrapped in a towel, her hair damp around her shoulders from the shower. She kissed Imogen before sitting at the dressing table.

'Yeah I am, thanks.'

'No stiffness or pain from the drive yesterday? Or last night's activities?'

'Barely even noticeable.' Imogen grabbed Kim's pillow and tucked it behind her head, propping herself up more comfortably. She grinned at Kim, who met her eyes in the mirror as she started brushing her hair.

'Are you just going to lie there and watch me?'

'Yeah. That was my plan. Do you mind?'

'Of course not.' Kim smiled at her in the mirror. Then she squeezed some lotion out of a tube and rubbed it over her hands, before leaning down to start smoothing it up her leg. Imogen swallowed hard when Kim's hands slid over her knee, pushing the towel higher as her hands encircled her thigh, rubbing the cream over the skin that she already knew was soft and smooth.

When Kim started on her other leg, Imogen couldn't think of a reason that she should keep resisting, so she threw back the duvet and rolled to her knees. She crawled to the end of the bed near Kim. 'Come here.'

Kim twisted round on the stool and stood up. 'Do you want something?'

'I do, as a matter of fact.' She hooked a finger into the top of Kim's towel and tugged gently, pulling her close.

'Oh. Is it anything I might be able to help with?' Imogen wasn't sure how Kim managed to pull off innocent and wicked at the same time, but it looked really good on her.

'Yeah, funnily enough it is.' Imogen tugged at the towel again while Kim wrapped her arms around her neck.

'I thought you wanted to get to the show early . . .' Kim murmured and pushed Imogen's hair aside, then kissed and nuzzled down her neck.

'Uh huh. But I found something I want more.' She kissed Kim, loving the way she arched against her. 'A lot, lot more.'

* * *

Kim found one of the few tables left in the restaurant and claimed it quickly, setting down her bags before ordering a pot of tea. She looked up a few minutes later when Imogen walked in and had to catch her breath. Imogen looked beautiful as she stood there, looking around. The afternoon sunlight caught her hair, making it look even glossier and silkier than usual, and it kissed her skin golden. But it was nothing to the smile that lit up her face when she spotted Kim and made her way quickly through the busy room.

'Hey.' She leaned over the table to kiss Kim before sitting down. 'Looks like you've had a good day.'

'Better than my credit card.'

'Show me in a minute. Have you ordered yet?'

'Only drinks. I wanted to make sure we got a table. I thought you might want to sit down to eat rather than do takeout.' She handed her the menu. 'How's your back?'

'Fine thanks.'

If Kim hadn't been watching her so closely — if watching Imogen hadn't become one of her favourite new habits — she might actually have believed her. Instead, she waited patiently for Imogen to order, added her own food, then glared at her.

'How's your back really?'

'Grateful for the chance to sit down,' Imogen admitted with a sigh. 'Started twinging a bit earlier, but only really started to hurt the last half-hour or so.'

'Is there anything I can do to help?'

'It's not that bad,' Imogen reassured her. 'And I'll be fine after a bit of a rest. I'm just a bit achy where I've been walking around a lot.'

'This event is a lot bigger than I'd expected,' Kim replied, reaching over the table to squeeze Imogen's hand. 'Are you sure you're OK?'

'I'm sure I *will* be. Distract me. Tell me what you've been up to.'

'Shopping.' Kim grinned. 'This place is a lot more interesting than I expected. I thought it would all be very trade-oriented, but it's actually pretty cool.'

'Don't tell me I'm tempting you to the witchy side of life,' Imogen teased. 'You're not going a bit alternative, are you?'

'I think I already was a bit, don't you?' Kim pulled one of her bags into her lap. 'Look at this.' She retrieved a ball of yarn that was shaded like expensive fluorite, shimmering from deep purple through to violets and blues, then to turquoise and emerald. 'It's bamboo. I'm not sure I even knew that you could make bamboo into wool. And it's all hand-dyed, so every batch is slightly different.'

'Very pretty.' Imogen stroked it. 'Are you planning on taking up knitting?'

'Not a chance. I tried my hand at textile art and wool work in college. It didn't go well. But given how much Angela loves to crochet, and that it's her birthday soon, I thought it would make a nice gift. And I can't imagine she would have bought something like this for herself — so I got enough to

201

make a shawl or cardigan . . . at least, that's what the stall holder said.'

'It's beautiful. And very Angela. I'm sure she'll love it.'

'And I bought myself a really pretty skirt — hand-dyed again, so completely unique. Oh, and this bracelet.' She held her wrist out.

'That's really pretty.' Imogen lifted her hand up to look more closely, then brought Kim's fingers closer to her face. 'And you smell amazing.'

'Honey, vanilla and a touch of cinnamon. There was a group offering massages, and . . .' she leaned in closer '. . . I taste as good as I smell.' She laughed when Imogen's eyebrows shot up. 'Don't worry, I checked it was edible first.'

'Good.' She let Kim's hand drop to the table, still cradled in hers. 'I wonder if they sell their blends as well.'

'They do.' Kim grinned. 'I bought this one and another. Cocoa and cherry blossom. I figured I knew a talented woman who might be willing to show me how to enjoy them.'

'Yeah, I might have an idea or two.' Imogen nodded.

'Thought you would.' Kim bit her lip for a second, thinking, before pulling her hand away. 'I bought something else too. A book.' She pulled the book to the top of the bag, and let Imogen see the title and image of intertwined female silhouettes.

'*The Violet Tantra*?' Imogen kept her voice low.

'I thought it could be fun to try.' Kim shrugged, deliberately keeping things casual.

'Kim, sweets, you know there's more to . . . the topic that book covers . . . than just fun, right?'

'Yeah, I do. I . . .' Kim was interrupted by a waiter arriving with their food. 'Later, all right?'

'OK,' Imogen agreed. 'Later.'

* * *

By the time they got back to their hotel that evening, Imogen was struggling. She did her best to hide her wince as she sat down, but the nagging twinge from earlier had escalated to full-on, hot, twisting knife pain at the base of her spine that radiated across her hips and down her thighs. The TENS machine had barely taken the edge off, and she was starting to think she'd have to take the heavy-duty, knock-out painkillers that rarely seemed to work.

'You're in pain, aren't you?' Kim asked as she shut the hotel room door.

'I'm all right.' Imogen forced herself to smile and reassure Kim.

'Would you like to try that again?' Kim sat on the bed next to her, moving slowly so as not to jostle her. 'Immy, I know what you're doing, and you can stop. You don't need to hide this from me, to mask it — you can be honest — I can handle this.' She slid her fingers beneath Imogen's. 'I'm here, and I'm not going anywhere. I see you, Imogen. All of you.'

Imogen's throat tightened as Kim's words settled and took root inside of her. She had spent so long doing exactly that — masking and hiding the effects of her illness, not giving herself any other choice than to be strong and beat the pain, the stiffness, the fatigue and the brain fog every day, and not be a bother to others — she wasn't sure she knew how to let herself be weak around another person.

She didn't know when the first tear fell — the first sob caught in her throat and surprised her. But Kim had seen it, and had already reached over to cup her cheek, stroking away the tears with her thumb. She shifted, slipping to kneel on the floor in front of Imogen, her hands holding Imogen's tightly. 'It's OK. Let it out. I'm not going anywhere.'

She didn't know how long it took her to calm down, but by the time she could breathe without her gasps turning into sobs, there was a pile of wet, soggy, gross-looking tissues at her side.

'Still think I cry pretty?' She attempted a smile.

'Yeah.' Kim handed her another tissue. 'You're still beautiful.'

'You're biased.'

'Maybe,' Kim admitted. 'But if it helps, at 4 a.m. the other night, when you were snoring and drooling, I found you a lot less attractive. If you hadn't rolled over when I prodded you for the umpteenth time, I was contemplating putting my pillow over your head.'

'What?'

'Not to hurt you or anything.' Kim laughed. 'Just so I could get some quiet for a couple of minutes.'

'Should I worry about closing my eyes tonight?' Imogen pulled a face.

'No.' Kim laughed again. 'If I was going to bash you with a pillow I'd have done it before. How are you feeling now?'

'A bit silly. I don't know why I got so upset. It's not like this is even the worst my pain gets.'

'If I were to hazard a guess, I'd say maybe it's not just the pain making you cry.' Kim wrapped her arms awkwardly around Imogen in a gentle, careful hug. 'Maybe it's the fact that you spend so much of your time just dealing with it, that you don't give yourself the time or space to acknowledge that the amount of pain you deal with isn't normal or fair, and that you are a freaking rockstar just for getting out of bed every morning, let alone being the sweet, kind, lovely, successful person you are.'

The fierceness of Kim's words made Imogen well up again. 'You really think that?'

'Yes. You are amazing.'

'If you keep being this nice I'm going to cry again,' Imogen warned.

'And if you need to do that, I'll be right here. Though I might move off the floor before my back starts hurting too.'

'I don't know what I did to deserve you,' Imogen told her honestly.

'I already told you. You're a rockstar.' She leaned down and kissed her softly. 'Now, if it's OK with you, there's something I've been thinking about since I booked this room. And I'm thinking now might be fairly good timing.'

'What's that?' Imogen really hoped it wasn't anything she'd need too much energy for. Even the thought of getting changed and walking to wherever they planned on eating dinner felt like planning a marathon. An uphill one.

'Nothing that will take much energy, if that's what you're worried about.' Kim kissed her again before stepping away.

'And you accuse me of reading *your* mind.' Imogen started bundling up the pile of gross, damp misery next to her.

'Maybe you're rubbing off on me.' Kim chucked a prob-ably-not-real leather folder onto the bed next to her. 'I'm thinking room service, those big fluffy robes they've left for us, maybe a pay-to-view movie, and you might have noticed that rather large bath in the next room.'

'You want to stay here, watch TV, order room service and have a bath?'

'Yeah. Although I'm not too fussed about the order. So long as it's with you.'

Imogen watched, shaking her head as Kim bustled around the room, shaking out the robes and tidying up, pausing to smile at her every so often. And Kim thought Imogen was the awesome one.

* * *

Kim shifted, leaning over to put her wine glass carefully on the bathroom floor before sighing happily and leaning back against Imogen, cocooned by her arms and the warm water and bubbles. 'This is utter bliss.'

'Yeah,' Imogen agreed. 'Absolute perfection. I want to take this bathtub home with me.'

'I'm afraid it won't fit in my car. Or your flat.'

'Spoilsport.' Imogen flicked bubbles at her.

'I'd say pragmatist.'

'Fine. *Spoilsport.* But when I buy a house, it's definitely going to need room for a bath like this.'

205

'You're not staying where you are?' Despite the warm water and Imogen's arm loosely around her waist, a cold snap shot through Kim.

'The flat's just a rental. The lease on it and the shop can be separated, and longer term I think I want a proper home. Something with a bit more character, and space for a garden that's more than the patio, or the tiny patch of grass and weeds that came with the shop. And now I'm adding a roll-top bath to the list.'

'Oh.'

Imogen pulled Kim's wet hair from where it clung damply to her neck, placing a kiss there. 'But just in case you're worrying . . . I've set my business up in and around Broclington. Ryan — the single most important part of my family — is there too.' She stroked Kim's cheek. 'Along with some other very important people. I wasn't planning a move any time soon. And when I do, I can't see it being very far.' She brushed her lips against Kim's, sending tingles up and down her spine — her stomach flipped and squeezed.

It felt so easy and comfortable, half-floating and half-cuddled in Imogen's arms, and she knew she didn't want to move. Maybe ever. She took a deep breath. 'Do you think now would be a good time to talk? About the book I bought today?'

'Yeah.' Imogen's arm tightened around her waist. 'Kim, like I'd started to say earlier, tantra is about more than fun . . . about more than sex . . .'

'I know.' Kim nodded and twisted, slightly awkwardly in the water. It wasn't exactly comfortable, but she managed to move so she could look at Imogen properly, her feet dangling over the edge of the bath. 'I do understand that. I read the cover, and I talked to people on the stall — who were very informative.' She felt a blush start to warm her cheeks even more than the steam already had, but she carried on. She needed to say the things that had been rattling around her mind. 'From what I understand — and I'm sure you'll correct me if I'm wrong — it's about forming a deeper, more spiritual connection. At the soul level. Deeper than just the physical.'

'Yeah, that's about right.' Imogen nodded, her arm still tight around Kim, her eyes intense. 'The word "tantra" means woven together. And that's what it's about — weaving together the spiritual and sexual, and putting emphasis on emotion and intimacy in sex.'

'I understand,' Kim promised. 'And I think I'd still like to try. With you.'

'Really?'

'Yes.' She forced herself to breathe, to not hold her breath. 'What do you think?'

'I think finding Bramble, needing a vet and meeting you was a gift from the universe. And I think it makes it easier to tell you this.' Imogen wove her fingers around Kim's. 'I'm falling for you.'

'Really?' It was Kim's turn to not know if she could believe her good luck.

'Yeah.' Imogen nodded. 'I'm already a bit in love with you.'

'A bit, huh?' Kim cupped Imogen's cheek with her free hand, grinning so much that it was hard to kiss her — but she managed.

'Yeah.' Imogen pulled away an inch or so, her grin matching Kim's as she caught her breath. 'A bit. Probably about half.'

'Wow.' Kim dragged her feet back into the tub, twisting so she could straddle Imogen and buried her fingers in Imogen's hair. 'This OK?' She worried about Imogen's back.

'This is perfect.' Imogen slid her hands around Kim's waist and pulled her closer.

'So, half in love with me?'

'Yes. At least.' Imogen nuzzled against Kim's neck, making it hard for her to think. 'And I'd love to try tantra with you. I just can't promise I'll be very good at it.'

'Why would you think that? You're amazing at . . . things like that.'

Imogen shrugged, her shoulders and breasts moving against Kim. 'In case you hadn't noticed, I tend to get pretty carried away with you. You warned me — you're just too irresistible.'

Kim kissed Imogen again, and again, pressing more tightly against her, using the movement of the water to get more than a bit carried away.

It wasn't until much later when they were dry, warm and snuggled under the crisp hotel covers, Imogen already asleep, that Kim found a semblance of something close to courage.

'Immy?'

Imogen shifted in her sleep, snuggling deeper into her pillow, but didn't respond.

Her being asleep made it easier. 'I'm falling for you too, Immy.' Kim whispered the words, trying out how they felt to say. 'I think I'm a bit in love with you too.'

Imogen shifted again, her arm draping comfortably around Kim's waist. 'I'm really glad you wanted to tell me, but I kind of already knew.' She tugged Kim closer, fitting perfectly against her like she'd been designed to be there.

* * *

'Hang on a minute.' Evelyn reached across the table and grabbed a stack of expensive cards. 'We've run out of the RSVP cards, but still have all of the direction and hotel cards left. What's going on?'

'Oh no.' Kim covered her mouth as she looked around the table, hoping she hadn't done what she was almost certain she had. Grimacing, she reached for the last envelope she'd stuffed, undoing the ribbon that held it closed. Yup, there it was. Two RSVP cards and nothing to tell guests where they were supposed to be or how to get there.

'Shit. I'm sorry, Evelyn.'

'It's OK.' Her future sister-in-law smiled.

'Yeah, but I'm messing up your wedding stuff.'

'Kim, it's fine,' Evelyn promised. 'And at least they're not glued shut. We'll just untie them and do it again. It doesn't matter. And even if they were glued, it still wouldn't matter. Jake and I are going to have the perfect wedding, whatever happens.'

'How do you sound so sure about it?'

'Because I am sure. Because invites, and flowers and dresses and good weather . . . it just doesn't really matter. Don't get me wrong, all that stuff is nice, it'll be beautiful and lovely and make for wonderful photos, but whatever happens it's going to be perfect because Summer will be there and Jake and I will be married at the end of the day.'

'That is such a good way of looking at it.' Kim opened up another of the invitations she'd put together incorrectly.

'Thanks. I think so. And I'm marrying into a pretty great family too.'

'Yeah, us Macpearsons have our good points.' Kim smiled.

'You really do. Even if attention to detail isn't one of them.' Evelyn reached for another envelope and started working on the knot. 'So are you going to tell me what's got you so distracted?' She gave her a sly look over the blue knotted satin. 'Or should I ask who?'

'You've been talking to my mum.'

'Often. We get on really well. But I would admit, purely coincidentally, that she might have mentioned that she's been seeing a bit less of you than usual, and suggested I could ask about it tonight.'

'Oh for the love of . . .' Kim let her head drop to the table. 'She's sent you to spy on me.'

'She has not!' Evelyn argued — a bit too vehemently for Kim to believe.

'Uh huh. Sure she hasn't.' Kim rolled her eyes, knowing that it was exactly the type of thing her mum would have "suggested", in the nicest possible terms, and that she would have kept making those suggestions until Evelyn gave in.

'OK, yeah, she might have,' Evelyn admitted. 'But is it OK if I'm curious too? Kim, you've seemed so happy the last few weeks, and the work you did in Imogen's store is beautiful. If there's someone new in your life who's even partly inspiring any of this, then I'd really like to meet him. In fact, why don't you bring him to the wedding? I mean, unless you don't want to. No pressure if it's still too new . . . but if you'd like to, then anyone who makes you smile this much is more than welcome.'

'Thank you.' Kim's thoughts bounced around like crazy while she fiddled with another ribbon, fraying the edges until Evelyn took it away from her.

'We're friends, right?' Kim asked.

'Of course we are. And in four weeks we'll be sisters too.' Evelyn put the invitations to one side, giving Kim her full attention. 'What's going on?'

'Can I tell you something? Without you judging me?'

'I'll do my best,' Evelyn promised.

'I am seeing someone.'

'Why do you seem nervous telling me that?'

'Because the person I'm seeing is a bit different from my usual type.' Kim phrased her answer carefully, remembering how her mum had refused to acknowledge it.

'Without wanting to be rude, maybe that's a good thing,' Evelyn mused aloud. 'It's not like you have the best track record in relationships. Though I'm hardly one to talk before meeting your brother.'

'I think it's a good thing. But when I tried to tell Mum about it, it didn't go so well. In fact, she did the thing where she basically ignored me and pretended I'd not said anything. Like she does when she's annoyed with me but doesn't know what to say.'

'Oh.' Evelyn frowned. 'Oh, please don't tell me he's married or something awful like that.'

'No, of course not! Eww. Do you really think I'd do that?'

'No, I don't. But I can't think of many things Julie would be so set against. She's always been so welcoming to me.' She hesitated as another thought occurred to her. 'He's not a criminal or something, is he?'

'No.' Kim laughed. 'Definitely not.'

'What's the problem with him then? Or what does your mum think the problem is?'

Kim took a deep breath. 'What if he isn't a he?'

'What do you mean?' Evelyn's brow wrinkled in confusion, then her eyes widened in realisation. 'Oh. Right. So she . . . Oh, sorry. Is it they? I can't make that assumption nowadays, can I? Um. Sorry, I should be handling this better. Give my brain a couple of seconds to catch up.'

'It's OK. It took me a while to figure it out too. And yes, "she" is right.'

'OK.' Evelyn nodded. 'So you weren't expecting this?'

'No.' Kim smiled. 'I wasn't expecting anyone like her at all.'

'And that's the smile I meant.' Evelyn hugged Kim round the shoulders. 'So, when do I get to meet her? This woman making my nearly sister-in-law smile like that?'

'You already have. It's Imogen.'

'Oh, I like her. She's good to work with. Really knows her stuff and is great with patients. Her pain management clinic has been a real boon to the re-enablement programme here.'

'Yeah, she said it's going well.'

'It is.' Evelyn nodded. 'So, um . . . when you told your mum, what did she say?'

'Nothing.' Kim tried not to growl her frustration. 'She completely ignored it and carried on the conversation like I hadn't said anything.'

'I know I don't know her as well as you do, but that doesn't sound like the version of Julie I'm used to. What exactly did you say to her? Is there any chance she misunderstood?'

'I said I was going to a spa with my girlfriend.'

'Kim, I sometimes refer to my female friends as "girlfriends". Maybe your mum just thought you were saying something like that.'

'Do you really think so?' Kim was dubious.

'I think that if you didn't say something like "Mum, I'm dating a woman," then it's possible that she misunderstood, or just completely missed it. Your mum is a very kind and

211

compassionate person, who adores her family and is incredibly supportive of your happiness.'

'The problem is . . .' Kim sighed and leaned on the table. 'Sometimes she has different ideas of what happiness should look like. Especially when it comes to me.'

'But she might not actually realise what you've said,' Evelyn argued, annoyingly reasonable. 'So, do you want me to add her as your plus one?'

Kim nodded slowly, thinking. 'Obviously I'll have to ask her, but yeah. I think I'd really like that.'

'Well, when you do, you can give her this.' Evelyn pulled out the invitation with Kim's name on it and added Imogen's next to it.

Kim studied the neat handwriting. *Kimberly and Imogen.* She smiled as she ran her fingers over the letters pressed into the expensive paper, thinking how good they looked together. 'Thank you.'

'Why don't you see if Imogen wants to come to the Macpearson Sunday lunch? Let the family get to know her. You know the door is open to everyone. I think it's especially going to be open to Imogen.'

'Yeah. I'll talk to Immy.'

* * *

'Are you Imogen?' The man who snapped at her from inside her own shop doorway might have been attractive — if he hadn't been radiating so much anger that she was pretty sure she'd need to smudge the entire building.

'Yes, I am. How can I help?'

'You can stop spouting your claptrap and selling your . . . your . . . snake oil. Who the hell do you think you are? Putting people's health at risk to line your pockets, making money off their misery and illness? People like you disgust me.'

'She is the owner of this establishment,' Kai snapped back. 'Who the hell are you to come crashing in here mouthing off like that?'

212

'Kai, it's OK. I've got this, thanks.'

'You sure, boss?'

'Yes.' Imogen nodded firmly. Unfortunately it wasn't the first time she'd encountered people who disagreed with her beliefs and treatment protocols — usually before they knew anything about it. 'Although he does have a good point.' She fixed her eye on the angry man. 'May I ask who you are?'

'I'm Trish Roberts' doctor. And the person she brought this to.' He yanked a sheaf of papers out of his bag and stormed across the store to smack it on the counter in front of them both, making Kai bristle.

Imogen rested a calming hand on Kai's arm for a second — the last thing she wanted was for him to get annoyed as well — and picked up the papers. She recognised them instantly — she'd helped enough patients complete them over the years. 'It's a standard application form for Personal Healthcare Budgets.'

'Yes, one with your name on it. This is the third of these I've had in as many weeks.'

'I'm still not sure I understand what the problem is.' She had an idea, but unlike the man filling her store with discord, she tried not to jump to conclusions.

'The problem is you abusing sick and dying patients to scam money out of the NHS, while flogging them stories and promises you can't keep!' His blue eyes blazed angrily at her.

'I don't make promises I can't keep. My treatment protocols are proven and evidence-based . . .'

'They're dangerous hokum.' He shook his head. 'People like you disgust me.'

'Maybe if we could take the time to discuss things—'

'I'm not interested in hearing about your so-called evidence base. Pull your head out of your rabbit hole. And leave my patients the hell alone. I won't be signing this or any others.' He stormed out, leaving his papers and bad energy behind.

Imogen took a deep breath, forcing herself to try and be calm, to return to the moments before Sir Poorly-Informed-Loud-Mouthed-Grump-A-Lot had stormed in to ruin her day.

Kai gestured to the forms. 'May I?'

Imogen nodded, not trusting herself to speak as he picked up the forms and scanned them.

'Well, the address is the Broclington surgery. What a well-informed ray of sunshine he was.' Kai shot daggers after the man. 'Want me to curse him for you?'

Imogen burst out laughing. 'Thank you, but no. The likes of him aren't worth the negative karma. Clearly he's already got his own problems. I'll have to go and phone Trish.'

'Will you still be able to treat her?' Kai busied himself with tea and herbs. 'She seemed so nice.'

'Of course I will.' Imogen nodded firmly, her mind already racing ahead. 'It might be that one of the oncology team at the hospital are willing to sign the forms. And if not, I'll treat her pro-bono.'

'Can you do that?'

'Benefit of being the boss.' Imogen winked. 'My rules. Besides, she's already been unlucky enough to get cancer and have to fight for her health. She shouldn't need to fight for treatment as well, just because she got lumbered with a doctor like that.'

'Do you know who he is?' Kai continued glaring.

'Not a clue. Haven't met him before.'

'Let's hope you don't have to again!'

'From your lips to the Goddess's ears,' Imogen agreed fervently. 'Is that one of your calming teas you're brewing?'

'Yes, ma'am.' He put down the tea leaves and picked a large lump of mangano calcite off the shelf. It was a beautiful piece — twice the size of her hand — with the typical translucent properties of calcite making it seem to glow with pink softness. Perfect for promoting peace and tranquillity, offering soothing from traumas, it radiated energy similar to a hug from a best friend.

She didn't say a word as he folded it into her arms, but raised her eyebrows in question.

'I thought you could use a hug. And if I gave you one it would border on being unprofessional and bring us one step

214

closer to you breaking my heart.' He posed like the lead in a soppy seventies drama.

'I thought I'd told you to stop flirting with me.' She laughed despite her words.

'No, you've told me it's pointless and a waste of my time, but it's still amusing. And made you smile. I'll go make us tea.'

'Thanks. I think we're both going to need it.'

She tucked the crystal into the crook of her elbow and drummed her fingers against the countertop as Kai left to boil the kettle. Nope. It was no good — she was going to have to smudge the whole place before she felt better again. Sighing, she pulled out her sage brooms.

CHAPTER FOURTEEN

Kim tightened her grip on Imogen's hand as they walked up the street.

'We don't have to do this.' Imogen pulled her to a halt. 'If you want to change your mind we can go back to mine and eat sandwiches in bed.'

'Don't you want to do this?'

'Kim, sweets.' Imogen looked into her eyes. 'I would love to meet your family. But if you want to turn around right now, I'm still going to be happy to spend the day with you. There's no pressure.'

'I want to do this.' Kim nodded.

'Are you trying to convince me, or yourself?'

'Maybe a bit of both.' Kim winced. 'I'm just nervous.'

'You said Evelyn was happy for you . . . for us.' Imogen wanted to reassure her. 'And that she thought your mum's under-reaction was probably her not understanding what you'd said.'

'Yeah.' Kim gnawed at her lip. 'But she might be wrong.'

'What do you want to do, Kim — go in or go back to mine? Whatever it is, I'm going to support your choice and keep my hand in yours. But the longer we stand here talking about it, I think the more likely it is that the decision will be made for you.'

'Please make the decision for me.'

'I didn't mean me, sweets. Telling you what to do isn't really us, is it? I just meant this isn't a very long street, and if your family are all due at roughly the same time . . .'

'Oh. I see what you mean.' Kim nodded. 'Are you sure you want to do this? Us Macpearsons en masse can be pretty full-on.'

'I'm not in the least worried.'

'At least one of us isn't.' Kim sighed. 'You did make frangipane.'

'I did.'

'Really posh-sounding frangipane.'

'If you think pear, honey and cinnamon is posh, then I guess I did.'

'It would be a shame not to share it, after all the effort you put in.'

'True.'

Kim smiled at Imogen in the way that made her feel like the most important person in the world.

'OK. Let's go shake up the Macpearson clan a little. And don't say I didn't warn you.' Kim gave Imogen's hand one last squeeze before opening the garden gate and letting herself in the front door. Within seconds two young girls burst into the hallway, accompanied by two dogs who seemed to be competing with the girls to make the most amount of noise possible. Imogen grinned, and took a hasty step back — it was that or risk being knocked over by the crazy welcome.

'Aunty Kim, Aunty Kim!' The girls chattered excitedly about dresses and fairies and all things sparkly while the dogs yapped and charged around.

'OK, OK, enough.' Kim knelt down, and was nearly flattened, before the dogs raced to sniff around Imogen's legs. 'Tilly, Sparks, *down*!' Kim ordered, and was promptly ignored.

'Hello, love.' An older man wandered in from the kitchen. 'Tilly, Sparks, enough. Sit!' The dogs promptly hit the floor, tails wagging excitedly.

'I don't know why they never do that for me,' Kim grumbled. 'Hi, Dad.' She gave him a quick hug. 'This is Imogen.'

'Your mum said you were bringing a guest.' He held his hand out. 'Nice to meet you, Imogen.'

'You too, Dr Macpearson.' Imogen shook his hand politely.

'Round here you've got three people who answer to that name. And it'll be four if Liv changes her name. Tom is easier.'

'Thank you.' Imogen smiled, already warming to the man.

'Girls, have you said hello to Imogen properly or did you forget in all the excitement?'

'It's OK. I'm pretty excited too. It smells amazing in here. I'm looking forward to dinner.'

'You should.' The older blonde girl with bright green eyes nodded seriously. 'Nanna makes the best roast dinners ever.' She held out her hand. 'I'm Summer.'

'It's very nice to meet you.' Imogen shook her hand seriously.

'I'm Sarah. Did you bring cake?' The younger-looking dark-haired girl with the same blue eyes as Kim stared at the cake tin.

'Yes, I did.'

'You didn't have to,' Summer added. 'Nanna always makes crumble. But I'm glad you did! Me and Sarah love cake. What did you bring?'

'It's a pear, honey and cinnamon frangipane.' Imogen grinned and leaned down. 'It's like the spongey bit on the inside of a Bakewell tart.'

'Oh wow. Granddad loves Bakewell tarts, don't you, Grandad?'

'I might be partial to them.' Tom nodded and shot Imogen a wink. 'And this sounds like a very special one.'

'What about you?' Imogen knelt to Sarah's level, opening the tin to show her the contents. 'Do you like Bakewell tarts?'

'Yeah, but they're not my favourite. They're really nice, but not as good as Brockle cakes.'

'Is anything as good as Brockle cakes?' Imogen laughed and held out the tin. 'Do you want to do me a favour and take it to your Nanna?'

'Sure. Come on, Sarah.' The girls ran down the corridor, followed by the dogs, who had clearly worn out their patience.

'I'd say that was a success.' Tom grinned. 'And as much as I love my wife's crumble, your frangipane sounds delicious.'

'Then I'm glad I made it.'

'Come on through and meet the others. They're in the kitchen.'

Kim smiled back at Imogen, who nodded at her and winked, before following her down the corridor to the bright, noisy kitchen. Jake and Evelyn were already sat at the table, setting out table mats, cutlery and crockery, while two other people worked at the counter carving meat and dishing up vegetables, but both paused to smile and greet her.

The kitchen was filled with amazing smells, and looked like something out of a lifestyle magazine. Somehow it managed to blend the chaos of a busy, multi-generational family — complete with dogs — with gorgeous design to feel warm and comforting. For a few seconds, Imogen felt a pang of something. It wasn't envy, exactly, but there was a definite pang of sadness that she didn't have this with her parents.

She shook her head, forcing the thought away, as Kim smiled at her. 'Imogen, this is my mum, Julie, and Liv, my brother Callum's fiancée.'

'And my new mum.' Sarah wrapped her arms tightly around Liv's waist, grinning up at her.

'It's nice to meet you.' Liv carefully put down the dish of carrots she'd been holding and held her hand out to Imogen.

Julie placed a covered dish on the table, then wiped her fingers on a cloth, which she threw over her shoulder to hold her arms out to Imogen. 'We're a hugging house. It's nice to meet you. Welcome to our home.'

Imogen let herself be folded into the hug, and returned it happily, thinking how lucky Kim was to have a family like this. The knot of tension she hadn't realised she'd been carrying released a bit. She'd really wanted this family to like her — to make things easier for Kim — and it was looking like things were off to a good start.

Julie released her with a smile.

'Take a seat, Imogen, and help yourself.'

'Thank you, this all looks so delicious.' Imogen accepted the plate of stuffing offered to her.

'Where's Cal?' Kim asked.

'House call,' Liv said. 'But he told us not to wait for him as he didn't know how long he was likely to be. But he did say not to let you and Jake scoff all the potatoes.'

'Not likely.' Julie placed a heaped bowl of golden, steaming, crunchy-looking potatoes on the table.

'And while we get stuck in, why don't you tell us about this guy Kim's been seeing?' Julie asked. 'I'm hoping you've at least met him. I can't get a word out of her about it, but we know she's seeing someone.'

'Evelyn? Are you OK?' Liv rubbed the other woman's back as she choked on her drink.

Kim's eyes met Imogen's, filled with panic. Beneath the table, Imogen wrapped her fingers around Kim's and stroked her thumb, trying to offer reassurance. However Kim wanted to handle this, she was going to back her completely.

* * *

Kim took a deep breath and reached for her glass. Suddenly her mouth was incredibly dry, and her hands felt shaky. She'd thought about this for weeks, trying to figure out the best combination of words, then imagining everyone's reactions — because if she could, then maybe she could minimise the negative fallout.

'Well? Have you met him?' Julie persisted.

'Um.' Imogen's hand tightened around hers, and Kim knew she was wondering what to do. There really was only one thing she could do, and her mum had given her the perfect opening.

'There . . . um . . .' Kim took a deep breath. 'There isn't a guy.'

'Come on, Kim,' her dad grumbled from the top of the table. 'You're out more nights than you're in. When you're here, you're distracted for the most part. And you're walking around with that silly grin on your face. If you're not seeing someone, we should book an appointment and run some bloods on you.'

Great, now her mum was looking worried too.

'Just tell them, sis. It'll be fine.' Obviously Jake had heard from Evelyn, but rather than it annoying Kim, she found it reassuring. Especially when her brother shot her a cheerful wink. He was behind her, at least.

'Tell us what? What's going on? You're not pregnant are you?'

'No, no. Why would you go there?' Kim shook her head.

'Well, you are acting a little oddly, love,' her dad continued. 'And you do look like you've put on a little weight.'

'If she'd put on weight,' Liv joined in now, 'it's Kim's business.'

'Well, I am her doctor . . .'

'No, you're her father. If she sees anyone nowadays it's usually me or Evelyn or Millie. But, in my professional opinion, Kim looks healthy and happy to me.'

'But you've not known her as long as I have . . .'

'Obviously not, which is why she's on my list and not yours.'

'Not everything is medical, you know,' Jake joined in.

Kim turned to Imogen while her family discussed her. 'Regretting coming yet?' she whispered.

'Not one bit.' Imogen gave her hand a squeeze as the conversation around them took another turn.

Kim shook her head, not knowing whether to laugh or cry. 'OK, enough. Dad, I love you, but I do not want to

221

discuss menstrual cycles and whether or not I look bloated, thanks all the same.'

'What's bloating and what does it have to do with bikes?' Sarah asked.

'Bloating is how you feel when you've eaten too much cake and not enough fibre and vegetables,' Liv replied. 'And it's not related to bikes.'

Kim saw Imogen smother a grin.

'Enough, please.' Kim held up her empty hand. 'Yes I'm seeing someone, but . . . um . . .' She took a deep breath before ploughing on. 'But it's not a guy. It's Imogen.' She lifted their joint hands above the table and looked at Imogen, whose smile gave her all the encouragement she needed to carry on. 'Immy and I . . . we . . . have been dating. It's been a couple of months now, and we really like each other.'

The silence that descended around the table stretched out between Kim's heartbeats, making each of them echo and boom. Surely someone was going to say something?

'Well, I think it's wonderful.' It was Evelyn who broke the awkward quiet. 'Anyone who makes Kim smile like she has been lately is good in my books.'

'Hear, hear!' Tom agreed.

'Guess this means we'll have to rearrange the seating charts again for a plus one?' Liv asked, ever the organiser.

'We can do it easily,' Julie replied. 'If it's appropriate?'

'I already told Kim she should ask Imogen.' Evelyn smiled. 'What? She only spoke to me a couple of days ago. And it wasn't my business to discuss, except to tell Jake I wanted to invite Imogen to our wedding. Which she is still very much welcome at.'

'I have the RSVP in my bag.' Imogen smiled. 'I just wanted to make sure the offer still stood after today.'

'It very much does.' Evelyn nodded.

'Then, yes please.'

'Awesome! We can help with your hair,' Sarah told her very seriously. 'We've got hair glitter, and tiaras and chalks that dye it for like one day.'

'We could give her matching streaks to Auntie Kim!' Summer added, bouncing in her chair. 'You have very pretty hair. Like Esmeralda.'

'Imogen's is more curly,' Sarah argued. 'I bet the fairy crystals would stick in her hair better than yours.'

'Esmeralda?' Imogen asked Kim in a whisper.

'Disney princess. It's better than what I got. Apparently my hair is like Mulan's when she was pretending to be a boy. Only with better colours.'

'Well, I'm glad you're all happy about this.' Jake tapped his knife against the edge of his plate thoughtfully. 'I'm not sure I am.'

'What do you mean?' Kim stared at her brother, feeling shocked. The last person in her family she thought would have a problem with her and Imogen was Jake.

'I just feel like it goes against the natural order of how things are supposed to be.'

'What do you mean?' Kim repeated, her mouth dropping in shock, mirroring expressions around the table.

'Jake . . .' Their mum's tone was quiet, but the warning was clear to everyone.

'It's all right, Mum. I've just got some questions. I'm interested in understanding this new and important person in my sister's life. That's OK, isn't it?'

Kim nodded stiffly, her fingers tightening round Imogen's.

'I think everyone round this table are wondering how this happened. Because — and no offence meant here, Imogen — but you are hot. Like the girls said, Disney-princess beautiful. And I already know you're smart and funny, and you run your own business. What on earth are you doing with my weirdly dressed, geeky, bratty little sister?'

'You utter bas—'

'Little ears,' Jake interrupted her with a grin. 'Manners, remember.'

Kim picked up a bread roll, but Imogen placed a hand on her arm, and leaned over the table, beckoning Jake closer. 'You, Jake Macpearson, might be considered funny if you

223

put on a funny hat and funny tights, but as you apparently wouldn't know a joke if it got up and gave you a much-needed haircut, I doubt it.'

Kim slapped her hand across her mouth to keep from laughing. She looked back and forth between her brother and girlfriend. When Imogen waggled her eyebrows at him, she couldn't help it and started snorting and giggling, setting the whole family off laughing.

'Ugh.' Jake shook his head. 'Don't tell me you watch that silly programme too. It's ancient.'

'I absolutely do. *Blackadder* is hilarious and more than stands the test of time.' Imogen grinned. 'And by the way, if she wasn't your sister you'd see that Kim is all kinds of Disney-princess beautiful . . . And that you, sir, are a pompous wobble-bottomed dullard!'

'Wobble-bottomed!' Sarah giggled, clapping her hands.

'Hey, I thought I was your favourite!' Jake complained.

'Yeah, but Imogen's funny. Tell us some more! Please?'

'OK, OK . . .' She looked at Kim. 'How does the cannibal brain one go?'

'The one about someone being so silly and empty-headed that if a hungry cannibal cracked their head open, they wouldn't find enough brains to spread over a cracker that was very, very small?' She watched as Sarah and Summer worked out the insult and creased up laughing.

Imogen tapped her arm gently. 'Where's the bathroom please?'

'I'll show you.' She wanted a couple of moments alone with her anyway.

'I can't believe you *Blackadder*-ed my brother!'

'He deserved it.' Imogen giggled. 'And I don't get the impression your mum would have liked you throwing food at him.'

'Nope.' Kim led the way upstairs, pointing to the right door, but caught Imogen's hand. 'You're brilliant. Thank you.'

'Nothing to thank me for. But are you OK?'

'Apart from planning to put something gross and squelchy in Jake's desk drawer? Yeah, I'm good. I'm really sorry about him thinking he's funny.'

'It's OK,' Imogen promised. 'You've met my brother, you know I understand.'

'Yeah, well . . . I'm still contemplating introducing Summer to coffee to get my own back.'

'Stick with squelchy gross things. I like Evelyn, and caffeinating her daughter wouldn't be fair to her. It's clear that your family love you a lot.'

'Yeah, they do. And about that?' She slid her hand over Imogen's cheek. 'It's a lot more than a bit. Much more than half.'

Imogen wove her fingers through Kim's hair and kissed her gently and sweetly. 'For me too. I'm definitely more than half in love with you.'

* * *

Imogen paused at the end of the hall, checking that her hair and dress were smooth before heading back into the kitchen.

Oh no, please not him. She couldn't see his face, but the hair, the set of his shoulders and the voice were too familiar. Even though he was calm this time, all of the happiness she'd felt a few seconds ago drained from her, as surely as if she'd walked unprotected into a curse circle.

'Immy.' Kim held out her hand. 'Come meet my brother, Cal.'

Imogen swallowed hard and pasted on her brightest smile. The same one she used when patients swore blind that they had done every single one of the stretches and exercises she'd given them and still seen no improvement, when they both knew they were probably fibbing.

There was a moment when he first turned around that Imogen thought it might be OK, that maybe he'd gotten over what happened earlier, but she saw the moment that he recognised her and his bright blue eyes hardened.

'What the hell are you doing here?'

'Callum! That is no way to speak to a guest.' Julie's voice lashed across the room like a whip. 'Kindly remember your manners and apologise to Imogen.'

'Apologise to her? Are you kidding? Do you have any idea who she is?'

'She's our guest.' Tom's tone was calm but firm. 'So either find your manners or take your meal into another room.'

'Daddy, why don't you like Imogen? She's really nice and funny.' Sarah's face had fallen, and Imogen felt bad for being part of the reason why.

'Do you want to tell them or should I?' He glared at Imogen.

'Callum and I had a disagreement of a professional nature. He disagrees with my approach.' As tempting as it was to drop him in it and complain about his attitude, he was Kim's brother — she needed to get on with him.

'That's how you're going to sell it, is it?' He folded his arms, still glaring. 'That I just happen to disagree with your approach? You're not going to mention that you're a money-grabbing con artist peddling false hopes and falser cures?'

'You are bang out of order.' Imogen ground her teeth together, trying her hardest not to lose her temper. That she felt it would be completely justified made it harder to control the urge to give him a verbal slap.

'I'm out of order? That's a bloody joke.'

'Daddy? What's going on?'

'Adult conversations that you'll find boring. Take Summer and go play in the other room.'

'But Uncle Callum . . .' Summer added her complaint.

'Go, please. Both of you. Now.'

The air was tense and awkward as the girls scrambled to obey.

'Well, at least they're not here to witness whatever this is.' Liv shook her head, staring at Callum. 'What's going on? Are you OK?' She rested a hand on Callum's shoulder, clearly worried.

'You still don't know who she is, do you? You've all sat here and eaten with her without having a clue who she is.' He shook his head, glaring at her in disgust. 'All those Personal Healthcare Budget applications we've been getting recently, the ones for all the bullshit woo-woo stuff? It's her that's behind them.'

'What?' Julie looked around the table.

'You know how we've been seeing an increase in applications from patients to use personal care budgets for . . . let's be polite and say "alternative therapies" . . .'

'Complementary,' Imogen couldn't help but correct him.

He barely glanced at her. 'Whatever. Anyway, she's the one behind them. Just another charlatan milking people's pain and suffering and despair for every penny they can get. And this one has found a way to rinse some extra cash from the NHS for her brand of woo-woo bullshit.'

'Woo-woo bullshit?' Kim clenched her fists so hard that her nails must have been digging into her palms. Imogen rested a hand on her wrist, trying to calm her. She failed miserably. 'Maybe if you climbed down off your ivory pedestal once in a while you might actually see there's more to life than the end of your stethoscope and medical degree.'

'Kim, that's hardly fair . . .' Liv started.

'No, it's all right,' Callum interrupted her. 'My sister clearly has something to say. Why not let her?'

'Why? It's not like you would listen to me. Or anyone else without their gold star medical degrees.'

'And what's that supposed to mean?'

'That you, Callum, can be a close-minded arse who has a history of being so arrogant and so bad at listening to anything but his own internal monologue that it nearly cost you the best relationship you've ever had. Half the time your daughter comes to me rather than talk to you, and I'll bet the rest of the time she goes to Liv.'

'It's normal for little girls to want to talk to other girls. And besides, I'd rather be what you call "close-minded" than a

227

gullible idiot who fritters away all her time and money chasing nonsense crap that never amounts to anything — which is why you're back living with our parents at your age.'

'Gee, why don't you tell me what you really think?' Kim shook her head, feeling disappointed but not surprised by Callum's reaction.

'I'm not all that surprised you've bought into her—' he flicked his fingers at Imogen, as if shaking off something unpleasant '—brand of . . . hokum bullshit. But I'm surprised the rest of you welcomed her. Especially you, Liv.'

'Why especially me?'

'Because the latest patient she tried to con was one of yours.'

'You're reviewing my patient files now? Really?' Although Imogen didn't know Liv well, she knew that look and tone of voice. Liv wasn't impressed with her fiancé or — if Imogen had to guess — having her work overseen.

'I wanted to see how many of these requests you'd had.'

'And you didn't tell me because . . . ?'

'I was dealing with it.'

Tom stood up. 'I'm going to go check on the girls. Callum, you shouldn't be reviewing other doctors' files without due cause. In this instance I really do think you're in the wrong, and have some apologies to make. I expect this argument to be well and truly over by the time I get back.' He paused by the door. 'I have to admit to being very disappointed in your manners. Yours too, Kim. I wouldn't blame poor Imogen if she decided never to speak to us again.'

'Just one more thing.' Liv waited until Tom had left the room. 'Do I get to ask which of my patients this involved, or is that something you're "handling" too?'

'Don't let it concern you.'

'Your sister may have a point about you being arrogant. I thought we'd broken you of that habit.' Liv's words were short and clipped, and even to Imogen it was clear she was annoyed. 'This is one of my patients we're talking about, and I want to know who.'

Imogen could see another argument brewing between Liv and Callum, which made her feel incredibly guilty — she hated conflict, especially when she was the cause of it. But she wasn't going to back down when a patient's health was at stake.

'A middle-aged lady with cancer.' Imogen wouldn't reveal the woman's identity — that wasn't fair — but she thought the case notes discussed in abstract were probably OK. Just about. 'She came to me because she was struggling with some of the side effects of treatment.'

'And you sold her some bullshit line — no doubt about magic herbs and crystals being better than chemo — convinced her that your route was best and she should abandon all the nasty, painful drugs and their yucky side effects in exchange for your "magical potions". And when I interceded to protect another of my patients from your brand of quackery, you went over my head to the hospital and complained about me!' Callum slammed his hand down on the table.

'Is it true, Imogen?' Julie asked softly. 'Are you the one behind the increase in patient funding requests for alternative therapies?'

'Complementary,' Imogen corrected again, wondering why she was bothering. 'But yes.'

'The patient we're talking about,' Liv said, 'she has stage three breast cancer and is struggling with nausea, loss of appetite, dizziness and fatigue? And neuropathy so bad she can barely hold a pen?'

'Yes.'

'Last time I saw her, she asked me about the statistics and long-term survival rates for women with her type of disease. I've been trying to catch up with her onco team to discuss better support options. Do you really think you can help her?'

'Yes,' Imogen told her honestly.

'If anyone can, it's Imogen.' Evelyn stuck up for her, earning a grateful look.

'Of course she bloody can't,' Callum fumed. 'She's peddling snake oil!'

'You should look at some of her treatment protocols,' Evelyn argued. 'They seem really effective.'

'No offence, Evelyn, but this is a bit out of the sphere of expertise for just a nurse.'

'Excuse *you*,' Evelyn snapped. 'You know damn well I'm a lot more qualified than most nurses. Especially when it comes to managing cancer treatment side effects. And even if I wasn't, there is no such thing as "just a nurse".'

'You know what he means,' Liv tried to smooth things over.

'Yes I do. I know he's being an arrogant arse. Again.'

'He's just trying to protect our patients,' Liv sided with Callum.

'Maybe they don't need protecting in this instance,' Jake waded into the argument. 'There's a lot to be said for taking a more holistic approach in treatment, and if the patient really is struggling and Imogen can help . . .'

'Really, Jake? You're going to get involved with an opinion?'

'I am a doctor, Callum.'

'Of animals.'

'Oh, here we go again.' Jake folded his arms, matching Callum's stance and glare. 'You do know veterinary medicine is a lot more specialist than your daily job. Remind me, Cal — how many surgeries did you perform this week? I have to be able to do everything you and Liv and Dad do, and surgery, over a dozen different species without half the resources you have. And my patients can't even tell me where it hurts.'

Imogen winced, recognising an old grudge when she heard one, feeling dreadful that her presence had triggered it all. It was like watching a car crash in slow motion — and still not being able to do anything to stop it.

'Yes, you're just a regular Dr Dolittle.'

'Shut up, Cal. Kim's right, you really are an arse.'

'I think everyone needs to stop talking, right about now.' Julie tried to smooth things over. 'Why don't we all sit down, let this nasty scene go, and we can make some tea.'

'Oh yes, tea. The magical cure-all for everything from alopecia to cancer to Zika virus! Let's all have a lovely cup of tea. Should we add some crystals to it as well, Imogen? What would you like to charge?'

'Callum!' Evelyn gasped. 'That's out of order.'

'What? You know I'm right. If teas and crystals and herbs and whatever other nonsense she flogs worked, we could have just poured that down Summer's throat and given her some magic beads or something instead of having to waste a fortune sending her to America.'

'Callum, that's enough.' Tom came back into the room at just the right time to hear the latest dig — and see Evelyn dissolve into tears in Jake's arms. 'You are beyond out of order.'

'I've had enough.' Jake was clenching his jaw. 'Dad, will you please ask my daughter to grab her things and Tilly? We're going home.'

'Kim,' Imogen kept her voice low, 'I think I should go too.'

'No, you definitely shouldn't,' Kim argued.

'Oh yes.' Callum's eyes snapped back to Imogen. 'The grifter herself.'

'Don't call her that!' Kim snapped at him. 'And you need to take back what you said about Summer before you cause any more problems.'

'The problem is her, abusing sick and dying patients to scam money out of the NHS, while flogging them stories and promises she can't keep!' His blue eyes blazed angrily at Imogen.

'I don't make promises I can't keep. My treatments help people.'

'So do sugar tablets in some cases, but I won't be prescribing them for cancer! People like you do more harm than good — people like you kill patients of mine with your lies and money-grabbing scams!'

'Don't talk to her like that!' Kim spat the words out angrily.

'Kim, it's OK.' It wasn't, but Imogen couldn't bear the argument happening around her — or because of her.

'It's not even close to OK.' Kim shook her head before glaring at her brother again. 'Say what you like to me — about me — I don't care. But don't talk to her like that.'

'You're defending her? Why? What's going on? Why *is* she here?'

'She's my girlfriend.' Kim's words didn't fill Imogen with the usual sense of joy and pride, instead they left her feeling cold and slightly sick — which wasn't helped when Callum laughed rudely.

'Girlfriend? So you're gay now? Of course you are.' He laughed again. 'It's all the rage. Why wouldn't you suddenly decide you're gay?' He looked around the room. 'What? Can't you see this for what it is? Just Kim being the Bee again. Another rebellious fad that will disappear into the wind and leave other people to clear up her mess. This relationship — if you can even call it that — is as fake as her so-called girl-friend's so-called cures.'

'That's what you think, is it?' Kim challenged her brother.

'No. It's what I know.'

Imogen barely had a chance to register what was happen-ing — let alone react enough to stop it — before Kim grabbed her and kissed her. In any other situation it would have been a wonderful kiss — sweet, sexy and demanding — but in that moment, and knowing the reason behind it, Imogen was left feeling cold and a bit distant.

As soon as Kim pulled away, Imogen stepped back. She stared at her feet for a few breaths, trying to calm and centre her-self to get through the next few minutes of her life. 'Julie, Tom, thank you so much for inviting me into your home. The food was delicious. I'm really sorry for all the drama and discord that my presence has caused. I hope the rest of your day improves.'

She walked from the room in a slight daze, blindly stuffed her feet into her shoes and fumbled with the door. She made it to the garden gate before hearing Kim calling her name. She kept walking, tucking her hands firmly into her pockets.

* * *

'Immy.' Kim raced after Imogen and grabbed her wrist, but Imogen kept walking. 'Imogen, will you please talk to me?'

She stopped a few paces later, then looked back to check they were away from Kim's home. 'Will you promise me something?'

'Of course.' Kim nodded eagerly.

'The next time you're going to kiss someone, do it because you bloody well want to. Do it because you're so compelled to touch them that you think you'll scream, or cry, or explode if you can't. Do it because everything in your body is aching, and your mind is screaming to kiss them. Not to prove a point to someone else.'

Kim clapped her hand over her mouth as Imogen's words sunk in. She really was a first-class idiot. 'Is that how I made you feel?'

'Yeah.' Imogen nodded tersely. 'And I'm not interested in being part of your rebellion against your parents, or whatever that was. I'm better than that, Kim. And until a few minutes ago, I thought you were too.'

'I'm sorry. I won't ever do it again.'

'No, I'm the one who's sorry,' Imogen replied sadly, the tone of her voice sending ice through Kim. 'Because I don't think I can do this.'

'Do what? Immy, you're really worrying me now.'

'I can't be the reason another family is torn apart. I'm sorry, Kim. I'm just not worth it.'

'Imogen, are you breaking up with me?' The question was ridiculous — there was no way that could be what was happening — she had to have misunderstood or misheard. There was no way they could have gone from saying they loved each other to breaking up in a few short minutes because of her brother's hissy fit. It was too absurd for words.

Imogen nodded, not meeting her eyes. 'I'm sorry, Kim. But your relationship with your family is important.'

'My relationship with you is important,' Kim argued fiercely. 'You're important to me.'

'It's been a handful of weeks . . .'

'Nine weeks. Nine wonderful weeks . . .'

'Yeah.' Imogen nodded sadly. 'But it's still not worth destroying your family over. I'm sorry, Kim. Be kind to yourself, OK?'

Her words sounded so horribly final that Kim couldn't bear it. 'Immy, please don't do this.' She could feel tears streaking down her cheeks, and her nose was already bunging up, but she didn't care.

'Kim, this really is for the best.'

'How can anything that hurts this much be "for the best"?' Kim demanded.

'Because there are plenty of other girlfriends — and boy-friends — out there just waiting to meet you. You only have one family. Goodbye, Kim.' Her first steps when she turned to walk away seemed hesitant, giving Kim hope.

Enough to make her run in front of Imogen and try again. 'You don't know what you're talking about!'

'Don't you think it's odd that you've never heard me mention my parents? Or any of my family except for Ryan? And no, you don't need to try and remember when I did, because I definitely haven't.' Her voice was flat and dull.

'I guess I never really thought about it.'

'No. Because you don't have to. Because you have a family who love and adore you, even if your brother could do with a serious bit of self-reflection. And that's so, so important. It's worth fighting for. And do you know how I know that? It's because I don't have it. I don't have a family who love and support me and would fight for me. Because when I needed them the most — when I came out — they rejected me. Ryan was the only one who stood by me.'

'Immy, I'm so sorry . . .'

'Thank you. But I didn't tell you because I want your sympathy. I told you so you understand that I know what I'm talking about. I caused a huge schism in my family, Kim. A great big rift, because I couldn't be the person they wanted me to be. Because they couldn't accept I'm gay. My parents have barely spoken to me for my entire adult life. They didn't speak to Ryan for years either when he supported me. Your family aren't like that, Kim. They genuinely do want what's best for you.'

'And what if you're what's best for me?' Kim had to keep trying.

'How can I be any good for you when I'm the problem? When I'm the person — the thing — that just caused this huge row? Kim, your family love you. I'm the problem in this equation, and I'm the one thing that's easy to remove. I'm so sorry Kim, but don't destroy your family over me. I'm really not worth it.'

Tears blurred Kim's vision as Imogen walked slowly, painfully away.

CHAPTER FIFTEEN

Imogen woke up wincing, her pillow already damp with tears. It seemed appropriate — she couldn't actually remember if she stopped crying before she fell asleep. Waking up feeling like her eyes were filled with grit, and on a wet pillow, seemed about right.

She wriggled her fingers and grimaced — then gasped in pain. Not only were her hands aching and swollen, but her eyes and nose burned too. Her hands and wrists were no better, and rotating her ankles and trying to raise her knees sent burning knives stabbing into her lower back — which only matched her ribs when she tried to take a deep breath.

She wanted to move, to drag herself out of the damp, miserable and painfully lonely bed. To swallow a few of the extra strong painkillers and muscle relaxants that her doctor prescribed for days like this, which she usually tried hard to avoid because she hated the way they made her feel. But she hated how she felt anyway, so maybe the meds wouldn't be that bad. The problem was, she wasn't sure if she really deserved to feel better, and she was very sure she couldn't find the energy or motivation to actually move.

She ignored the burning, gritty pain and let her eyes drift shut. More tears tracked down her cheeks to soak into her pillow. If she kept her eyes closed for long enough, she hoped she could fall back to sleep and stay that way until the pain went from intolerable to merely agony.

It might have worked, except that the ache pounding behind her ears got louder and louder, until she realised that it wasn't just in her head. 'Please shut up and go away,' she groaned. 'Whoever you are, please just go away.'

Mercifully, it stopped and she sighed in relief. But her relief was short-lived when the thumping pain was replaced by her phone bursting into life. She closed her eyes and waited for the noise to stop. Perversely, within seconds of it finally not torturing her, it started again — seemingly even louder than the first time, although she knew that wasn't actually possible. When it stopped again, it was barely for thirty seconds before starting again.

Whimpering, Imogen forced herself to stretch enough to grab it off the bedside table, the effort leaving her panting. It stopped ringing before she could answer it, but true to pattern it started again a few seconds later.

'Morning, boss, glad you answered. I was starting to get worried.'

She closed her eyes again. 'Sorry, Kai, I overslept.' It was easier to say that than explain what was really going on.

'OK, if you're still getting dressed, you could drop the keys out the window. Assuming we're still opening today?'

'Yeah, let's do that.' She closed her eyes for a few seconds, relieved the decision had been made without her having to put any effort into it. She just didn't have the energy for that

'Is that going to be soon?' Imogen jumped — she must have dozed off, which was incredibly unfair and ironic when she had spent most of the night desperately trying to get some sleep. 'Yep, sorry.' She levered herself out of the not-exactly-comfort-able-but-less-painful-than-moving spot in the bed, taking the covers with her. She staggered across her living room to the kitchen, glad there was no one around to see her struggling.

She pulled the spare keys out of the kitchen drawer and hobbled over to the window. She tugged the blanket more tightly around her shoulders before leaning out, waving to Kai and dropping the keys out to him. 'I'll be down in a bit.'

'Take your time. I'll open up and put the kettle on.'

'Thanks, Kai.'

She didn't want to know how long it took her to drag on some clothes and make it downstairs — the fact that she did it at all was a win. But it felt like less of an achievement when Kai took one look at her and grimaced.

'No offence, but you look dreadful.'

'Don't worry, you can't catch this.'

'Good to know. Was it at least a good night?'

Imogen shook her head. 'I'm not hungover. This is what a fibro flare looks like for me.'

'Wow, for me to look that rough it would have been a bloody good night. You look like you're owed a few.' When Imogen didn't have anything to say in reply, he carried on. 'I have to admit, I'm wondering if you're well enough to be down here working. You can leave the store to me today if you like.'

'That is really tempting,' Imogen admitted.

'Have you got any one-to-ones today?' He flicked through the diary.

'No.'

'Then why don't you head back up? I can bring you up tea and some crystals — if you don't mind me being in your living space.'

'I don't mind.' She shook her head slowly. 'But I'm not sure crystals are going to help today.'

'How would you feel about a minute or two of total unprofessionalism so I can give you a big hug? You look like you could use one.'

'I think you're probably right.'

Kai stepped towards her and wrapped her in a big, gentle hug, letting her tuck her head against his shoulder. He was so warm, and solid, smelling of the woody, creamy, slightly spicy sweetness of sandalwood and the heavy scent of leather. She breathed in again, feeling the tension in her muscles starting to recede.

238

'You know, you really should consider training in reiki or Bowen . . . you've got great energy for it.'

She felt his chuckle deep in his chest. 'You know, I had been thinking about that. But we can have that conversation another time because — and I say this with the utmost respect — you look bad enough to scare customers away.'

She didn't fight much as he shooed her back upstairs. She would have been lying to herself if she'd said she didn't need the extra sleep, but at the same time she really could have done with the distraction of customers to keep her from thinking. Thinking was too painful.

She woke up a couple of hours later when there was a knock at the door — this time the internal one that led to the stairs and store. Groaning, she pulled herself to her feet. 'Kai, you don't need to keep checking on me. I'll be fine.'

'Not Kai.' Ryan's voice echoed back to her. 'But I have been talking to him.'

Imogen opened the door and gave him the best smile she could manage.

'Ick. Kai said your aura was all grey and limp. I didn't know what he meant, but now that I see you, I get it. You do look kinda wrung out.'

'Gee thanks, Ry-no.' She limped back to the couch and pulled her blanket back around herself. 'Nothing I like better than hearing I look as bad as I feel.'

'Damn, Moggy. I was hoping it was going to be a "not as bad as it looks" moment. Good thing I popped into the bakery.' He pulled out a familiar box. 'I got you Brockle cakes . . . I'm putting the kettle on.'

'If you like.'

'I was telling you—' he headed to the kitchen '—not asking.' He was back a few minutes later, with plates, forks and steaming cups.

'Thanks.' Imogen tried not to wince as she reached for a mug.

'So, are you going to tell me what's wrong? Because this looks like more than a "normal" flare to me.'

239

'The short version is Kim and I . . . well, we aren't any more.'

'I'm so sorry, Moggy. Do you want to tell me what happened?'

'Not really.' Imogen sighed and stabbed the cake.

'But do you think it might help?'

'I had dinner with her family.' Imogen sighed. 'And though it started well, it ended badly. They're never going to accept me, and I can't do to another family what I did to ours, so I broke up with Kim.'

'I am so, so sorry. But Imogen . . .' the fact that he didn't call her Moggy told her how serious he was '. . . you didn't do anything to our family. They did it to themselves, and to you.'

'Whatever.' Imogen shrugged, then regretted the movement as the pain intensified in her back. 'However you spin the story, the result is the same.'

'I have to admit, I'm surprised — and fairly disgusted — with the Macpearsons right now. I had thought they were pretty liberal and welcoming to everyone. I didn't think they'd be homophobic.'

'Oh, it's not the fact that I'm a woman they have an issue with.' Imogen glowered at her cake again. 'It's the fact that I'm a holistic therapist.'

'That's a bit close-minded of them.'

'In fairness, Jake and Evelyn were really nice and supportive.' Imogen wanted to be fair.

'I'm not surprised.' Ryan tucked into his cake. 'From what I've seen of how Jake works, he usually takes a holistic approach to caring for animals.'

'Yeah, but that turned out to be part of the problem.' Even the cake wasn't improving her mood. 'Jake and Evelyn tried arguing with Callum — but he had no interest in listening. Callum said some really unkind things to Kim and Evelyn, and then it felt like everyone was arguing with everyone else. It got really vicious.'

'Sounds to me like Callum's the one with the problem,' Ryan pointed out.

240

'But they're a close family, Ryan. I can't pull them apart. I can't be the reason another family gets into arguments that could tear them to shreds.'

'Imogen, they're adults — you can't take on responsibility for their behaviour.'

'But when I know I'm the cause of the arguments? That I can just end them by removing myself from the situation? I can take responsibility for that.' She felt the tears start to race down her cheeks. 'I can't destroy another family, Ryan. Not when I can so easily walk away.'

'Is it really that easy?'

'No. No it isn't.' Tears choked her voice in her throat. 'It's the hardest thing I've ever bloody done.'

'Oh, Moggy.' Ryan gathered her up in a gentle hug, being careful not to knock or squeeze her aching body. 'Sometimes you're too bloody nice for your own good.'

* * *

Kim slammed the door and stomped up the stairs, not caring about taking off her shoes, greeting her parents or anything else. She'd been more miserable in the last week than she'd ever remembered feeling before.

If it hadn't been for Jake turning up that morning — declaring that he'd had enough, threatening to dump cold water all over her and her bed — she probably wouldn't have made it into work. Not that she thought she'd actually been much use . . . But she'd done her best, given that Jake and Evelyn had been the only ones to really stick up for her and Imogen.

She sighed and wrapped herself in her dressing gown, then pulled out her phone for some doom-scrolling, which she really hoped would be enough to properly numb her mind. She swore softly when she heard her mum's footsteps on the stairs, hoping she was heading for the bathroom, but betting that — given her luck — she wouldn't be.

'Kim, love.' There it was, the polite but unignorable tap at the door. 'I hope you're decent because I'm coming in.'

'It's all right, Mum, I'm decent.'

'Good.' She came in and put down two mugs on Kim's dressing table, before pulling the stool over to the side of the bed. 'Because I need to talk to you.'

'I'm not really feeling very talkative.'

'OK. Then I can talk, and you can listen. Love, you've not been like yourself this last week or so. Since the meal with Imogen. You've been far too quiet, and you barely come out of this room. We hardly see you anymore.'

'Not much different from last week then.' Kim shrugged, remembering her mum complaining much the same. 'At least I'm home now.'

'But you're miserable.' Julie patted Kim's knee.

'I miss her, Mum.' All of Kim's stubbornness and defensive grumbles dissolved under the tears she'd told herself she wasn't going to continue shedding. 'I really, really miss her.'

'Have you tried calling her?'

'Yeah.'

'And?'

'And she answered, and it was awkward and uncomfortable and . . .' She sniffed deeply, not caring that it was disgusting. 'It was miserable and broken. It made me miss her even more. But she's adamant about this, which somehow makes me like her even more.'

'It takes a strong person to stand up for what they believe in when push comes to shove.' Julie nodded and took a sip of her tea. 'Have you spoken to your brother?'

'You know he dragged me out of bed and off to work today,' Kim grumbled, avoiding her mum's gaze.

'And you know damn well that I'm not talking about Jake. Have you spoken to Callum?'

'I'm not sure I'd have anything polite to say to him.'

'Kimberly, that is uncharacteristically unkind of you,' Julie warned.

'He started it,' Kim snapped back, still furious with Cal for everything he'd cost her. She wasn't sure she'd ever want to

speak to him again. She knew she sounded whiney, and probably a bit immature, but she didn't care. She missed Imogen
so much that it physically hurt, and it made her grumpy and
mean. 'Will you be having this conversation with Jake too? I
know damn well he's not talking to Callum either, because I've
been screening the calls he didn't want to answer today, which
is about as much fun as it sounds! You said I'm not behaving
like myself — when did Callum turn into such a miserable arse?
He was disgusting to Imogen, and I can't believe the way he
spoke to the rest of us. Seriously, Mum, I thought he'd calmed
down and stopped being quite such a dick when he met Liv.'

'Kimberly . . .' her mum warned again. 'You know I don't
like you talking about your brothers like that.'

'Yeah, well maybe I didn't like how Callum spoke to me.
Or my girlfriend. Or Jake and Evelyn and pretty much everyone else. And I still can't believe what he said about Summer.
But I don't see you kicking his arse over it.' Kim flopped back
on her bed and stared at the ceiling, wondering briefly if it
would be more or less painful if the roof collapsed on top of
her than this constant nagging ache of missing Imogen.

'There might be things about this situation you don't
understand,' Julie added gently.

'I understand that he started a massive row with my girlfriend — yes, Mum, my girlfriend . . . because that's what
Imogen is.' The tears choked her again. 'Was. That's what
Imogen was.' After a few more seconds of deflated misery she
huffed, rolling over to glare at her mum. 'So, these things I
don't understand, the ones that apparently give Cal a free pass
to be a total jerk to all of us, and blow up what was possibly
the best relationship I'd ever had — are you going to tell me
what they are?'

'They're to do with a patient.' Julie smoothed her daughter's hair back.

'Right, so that means no.'

'Not without breaching patient confidentiality.' Julie
shook her head. 'But it's enough to say there was a self-styled

243

alternative therapist involved who did a lot of harm to a patient.'

'But Imogen isn't like that,' Kim protested. 'She's properly trained and qualified, and she runs clinics at the hospital.'

'Really? I don't think I knew that.' Julie frowned. 'I really don't feel that we got to know Imogen properly at all.'

'And whose fault is that?' Kim glared at her mum.

'You really don't think there's any hope?' Julie asked quietly.

Kim flopped back on her bed and put her pillow over her face, feeling like her heart was breaking all over again.

* * *

The following week, Imogen dragged on her hospital uniform — and dragged really was the right word. Everything felt like it took far more effort than it should, stripping her of what little get-up-and-go she had left. She'd had a colleague cover her clinic the previous week. But it felt like it would be more effort to log on, find a sub, call them and explain why she needed the cover, and what the clinic needed to cover, rather than just suck it up and do it herself.

Fibro could be so weird that way — sometimes the effort of getting through the day seemed less than the effort of calling people and explaining things. Although, of course, she was well aware that the second option came with a hefty helping of guilt, which always made her feel worse — and plenty of time to think, and stew, and miss Kim even more than she had when she woke up in the night. 3 a.m. really was a cold and lonely time, but she wasn't sure that 3 p.m. would be that much better, and it was this thought that had driven her out of bed and into her shower.

She'd been in a minor flare since that awful meal and the fallout. "Minor" because she was a lot better than she had been when Kai had chased her out of her own store, but she still had a low-grade fever, dull aches throughout her body and the pervasive feeling that she was trying to wade through sludge, which dragged her back at every step and added unbearable weight to her limbs while filling her mind with fog that made it hard to think. About anything except missing Kim.

She made it through her clinic without any foul-ups, managing to get her notes updated before the dull ache behind her eyes turned into a deep, throbbing pain, sucking away what limited energy she had left. She closed down her case notes and logged out of the system, ignoring the flurry of emails. Nothing was marked urgent, and she could always log on later from home if her guilt outweighed her fatigue.

She'd made it almost to the main hospital doors before hearing someone call her name. She pasted on her most professional smile as she turned around, hoping it would be something quick so she could escape back to her flat — and probably a long, hot bath.

'Hey, Imogen.' Evelyn's smile was so warm and genuine that Imogen felt herself relax and smile properly.

'Hello.'

'It's been ages.' Evelyn reached over to give her wrist a quick, friendly, reassuring squeeze. 'How are you doing?'

'I'm fine, thanks.'

Evelyn shot her an amused glance. 'That the answer you want to stick with? I don't want to take sides, but — in case it helps — I'm still pretty mad with Callum too. And I'm hoping we can still be friends.'

Imogen had to bite the inside of her cheek for a moment before trusting herself to speak again. 'I'd really like that.'

'Good. So, how are you really?'

'I . . . will be fine.' Eventually. She had to believe that was true, and that the aching pain of Kim's absence would fade, and that she'd stop hating the empty side of her bed. 'Anyway, enough about me. How are you?'

'I'm good thanks. Busy, of course.' Evelyn fell into step alongside Imogen. 'Between here, the surgery, Summer and Jake — not to mention the wedding planning — I barely have time to stop. But I'm good.'

'I'm glad to hear it.'

245

'Speaking of the wedding . . . you know your invitation still stands. We'd love to have you there.'

'Thank you, but I don't think that would be the best idea.' Imogen pulled a face.

'You might be right, but I would have welcomed you. Callum was . . .' She shook her head, irritated. 'He was out of order.'

'Yeah, he was.' And she was still furious about it. 'But I don't really want to talk about it. I just don't have the energy.'

'That's fair enough. You know, you can ask,' Evelyn added gently.

Imogen didn't need to ask what Evelyn meant, or how she knew. 'How is she?'

'I think she's much the same as you. She's been pretty down, but I think she's going to be fine. Given time. They say it's a great healer.'

'They do,' Imogen agreed. 'Although, personally, I've always preferred a more proactive approach. And crystals.'

'Yeah, you've still not totally sold me on those.' Evelyn laughed.

* * *

'Jake?' Kim peeked into his office and held up two steaming mugs. 'Can I have a word?'

'Of course.' He eyed the coffee suspiciously. 'Is this a drop-everything-and-take-a-break kind of word?'

'Yeah.' Kim took a deep breath. 'I want you to start looking for my replacement. Urgently. As soon as possible.'

'Kim, you don't have to quit. You don't have to run off again. We can sort out this mess with Callum.'

'You think I'm running? That this is about Callum?'

'That's not it?'

'No. I wasn't planning on running, Jake.' She glowered at her brother.

'Sorry — but you do have a bit of a history of . . . um . . .'

246

'Were you going to say something like "being a bit of a flibbertigibbet"?'

'That's Dad's term, not mine,' Jake complained, before wilting under her glare. 'It might have been something a bit like that. Sorry.'

'It's OK.' Kim grinned.

'You're a brat.'

'So I've been told. Mostly by you. For years.' She took a swig of her coffee. 'But I'm not running this time, Jake. And this isn't about Callum and Imogen.'

'Is it me? Have I done something to upset you?'

'No, it isn't about you, either. It's not about anyone else, it's about me.' Kim smiled. 'It's actually a really great opportunity.'

'Are you going to tell me what it is?'

'I got another job.' She grinned cheekily at her brother and stuck out her tongue. 'One that's going to be much better than working for you!'

'Still being a brat. So, how did you get a job at a toy factory? That was your dream job when you were little, wasn't it?'

'I'm surprised you remember that. It's not quite a toy factory, but I am going to get to play with some really cool stuff. A few weeks ago, I put in a bid to the hospital as part of their ongoing remodel. And I just found out that it was successful. I won the bid, Jake. I'm going to be decorating the two sensory rooms on the new children's wing.'

'Wow, that's amazing! Congratulations!' Jake gave her a hug. 'I didn't even know you were interested in doing stuff like that.'

'I'm hoping to make this my career,' Kim admitted quietly, before wondering what she was doing. She held her head up and shook back her hair. 'Actually, screw that. I'm *going* to make this my career. I'm good at painting, Jake. And it turns out I'm good at understanding the feelings, tone and environment that someone wants to create, and translating that into paint and images that can turn an empty space into somewhere that's welcoming, inspiring, uplifting and a little magical. And that's not me being arrogant, Jake — that's what the selection committee said about my work. About me.'

'That's great. I really am pleased for you.'

'But?' She could hear the unspoken word in his voice.

'You're really annoying at times, you know that?'

'Of course I do. You tell me at least once a week.' Kim poked her tongue out at him. 'But?'

'But I have to admit I'm quite surprised. I mean — and please don't think I'm being unkind here — you've gone from floating around between things, not really committing to much of anything, to bidding for and winning an NHS contract.'

'You missed out that I set up my own business as well. Not bad for the family flibbertigibbet, is it?'

'No, not bad at all. Well done, sis.' He raised his mug in salute. 'But seriously, where the hell did all this come from?'

Kim studied her drink for a few moments before answering honestly. 'Imogen.'

'Imogen?'

'Yeah.' Kim nodded. 'I know it probably sounds a bit crazy, because we weren't together all that long — but she changed me, Jake. For the better.' She bit her lips together, refusing to cry. She'd done plenty of that over the last two weeks.

'Do you want to talk about it?'

'Yeah?' Kim desperately wanted to talk, but it seemed like such a big thing to drop on Jake — especially when he was so busy with his own family and relationship. 'Even if I don't really know how to say it without being cheesy?'

'Go for it.'

'I'm not sure I ever really saw myself like you and Callum — like someone who would have some life-changing love story. I just didn't ever really see myself as someone who would "settle down", because I don't do "settling". But with Imogen? I didn't feel like I was "settling" for a moment. Not one single moment. And I've never felt like that before. Can you understand that?'

'Yeah, I really can.' Jake smiled in that wistful way that Kim knew meant he was thinking about Evelyn and Summer.

'Sometimes the right person changes everything, before you've even realised it's happened. Is that what you're saying happened with Imogen?'

'Yeah. I've been thinking about it a lot recently, and I think that the thing about Imogen was that she really saw me — everything about me — my dreams, passions and hopes, but also my fears, shames and doubts. I feel more settled because Imogen helped me figure out who I am, who I want to be and how to go after my dreams. I'm not even sure I truly knew what my dreams were until Imogen helped me have the courage to realise them — and she helped me figure out one of the pathways I could take to make them mine. It was like she shone a light on me and saw every part, and she still loved me. And you know what? She helped me love myself more too.'

'Wow.'

'I know. I did warn you it was cheesy.' Kim felt her cheeks start to flush.

'No, I don't think it's cheesy,' Jake reassured her. 'Well, maybe a little bit. But I can understand it. I feel the same about Evelyn and Summer, because they helped me turn into a better version of myself.'

'Nah, you were always pretty awesome, Jake.'

'So are you. I mean, for a girl,' he teased.

'Gee, thanks. But you're wrong. I don't think I was. But it was so easy to be with Imogen, and for the first time I wasn't trying to change myself to be what someone else wanted me to be, or what I thought they wanted me to be. The really sad thing is I don't think I even realised I was doing it all the time. But Imogen saw it, and challenged me on it. She helped me to realise it wasn't making me happy, because I wasn't really being me. But . . . I think I'm starting to figure out who I am, and do you know what? I kinda like this new version of me. I think, given time, I might even learn to love myself. If Imogen could, and she really did, then I must be someone at least a little bit special, because she's phenomenal. Dazzling.'

'You really did love her.' Jake's mouth hung open. 'Evelyn said she thought you were serious but . . .'

'But what?'

'But I thought the whole you and Imogen thing was just another Kim flight of fancy.'

Kim rolled her eyes. 'Imogen is — was — my best friend, and so, so much more. She's been so influential in my life, but in such a positive and healthy way.'

'I'm really sorry, Kim. No wonder you're so angry with Cal.'

'How do you forgive someone who ripped apart the most important relationship in your life? Could you forgive anyone who hurt Evelyn like that?'

'Not easily, no. I've barely forgiven him for the Summer comments.' Jake sighed. 'Is it really hopeless?'

'Imogen has a real problem with the idea of causing arguments within a family. And nothing I can do or say changes how Callum reacted, or the fact that she's right, half the family aren't talking to the other half. Have *you* stopped screening his calls yet?'

'We're on speaking terms. Well, we're being cordial.' Jake shrugged. 'It'll blow over eventually. It always does between us — we've been arguing the vet versus doctor thing for years. What he said to Evelyn was a pretty low blow, but she's a lot more forgiving than I am. She's talking to him at work, but I don't think there's much chance he's getting an invite to dinner any time soon.'

'So Imogen was right to be so upset.' Kim frowned and tucked her spare arm around herself, trying to comfort herself. 'Callum's reaction to her has caused a rift.'

'You were right when you called him out on his behaviour, on how often he lets his temper get the better of him. Liv jokes about how bad the first two impressions he made on her were. Most people try to make the best first impression, with Cal it took three.' Jake shook his head. 'He's old enough to take responsibility for his own actions and sort himself out. I'm much more worried about what's happening between you and him. And you and Imogen.'

'Thanks to Cal, there isn't a me and Imogen, and I don't see how there can be.'

'I'm so sorry, sis.' He threw an arm around her shoulders.

'Thanks. I should probably get back to work.'

'Yeah, I hear your boss can be a real slave-driver. And I should probably get on with drawing up an advert for a new receptionist.'

'You're really not mad at me for that?'

'No, I'm proud of you. And I can't wait to see your work. What you did in Imogen's store was beautiful. I'm excited to see what you can do with a decent budget. Besides, I think there's more than enough bad feeling in the family right now.'

'Yeah. Thanks, Jake.'

'You're welcome. And whatever I can do to help, I will. If you need to pick up some part-time hours while you're setting up your business, you know who to ask.'

'Thanks, Jake.'

'But maybe not as a receptionist. You're better at animal care and grooming than you are administration, which isn't really hard because you are a truly dreadful receptionist.'

'Gee, thanks, Jake. You're just too kind.'

'Always happy to help out my little sister.' He grinned. 'Go on, go try to do some work that doesn't involve messing up my files.'

'Sir, yes, sir!' She flicked him a cheeky salute and turned around, relieved at how well the conversation had gone. She really couldn't handle the thought of being out of sorts with Jake as well.

'Hey, Kim?'

She turned back, worried he'd changed his mind. 'Yeah?'

'Your business — what's it called?'

'Colours of Imagination.'

'Oh, I like that.'

'Yeah. Not bad for the family flibbertigibbet, huh?'

* * *

Jake stared at his office door for long minutes after Kim left, his mind churning over the conversation they'd just had. He felt bad — he'd underestimated Kim's feelings for Imogen and hadn't realised how much pain she was in. In some ways, he'd been as bad as Callum, making assumptions and not bothering to talk to his sister.

After a few more minutes of self-recrimination and thought, he picked up his phone.

'Ryan, hey, mate. You got a couple minutes? Remember that favour you owe me? For breaking a load of data protection rules and handing over the sanctuary's billing info?'

'Yeah, of course.'

'I'm calling it in.'

'What do you need?'

'How's your sister?'

'Imogen's pretty torn up,' Ryan replied. 'I think she's been fighting with a fibromyalgia flare since it happened, although she keeps denying it, but it's pretty obvious she's hurting.'

'Yeah, Kim's more miserable than I can ever remember seeing her. I don't think I understood how serious Kim was about Imogen until now.'

'I hadn't totally appreciated it either,' Ryan admitted. 'But Imogen's been really upset and on edge. And, frankly, she's kind of scary in this mood. Please tell me this favour is going to fix this?'

'I hope so. Either that or I'm about to make things ten times worse, and then I'll have Kim and Evelyn mad at me.' He grimaced at the thought of just how miserable they could make him if they really wanted to. 'What do you say? You in?'

'Risking pissing off my sister, who's already a bit scary? She knows most of my darkest secrets — and that's just her — some of her friends are decidedly witchy, and scarier than her.'

'And?'

'Sure, why not? I've had a good life. What do you have in mind?'

Jake kicked his feet up onto the desk and explained.

* * *

Imogen gave in to the hammering at the door and flung it open, then gaped at her visitors. 'What on earth are you doing here? Aren't you supposed to be a bridesmaid?' She looked Angela over, taking in her hair, make-up and parts of a dress not hidden by her coat. 'Hang on, you are bridesmaid. Oh no, please tell me nothing happened at the wedding.'

'Nothing that wasn't supposed to,' Ryan reassured her. 'Jake and Evelyn are happily Mr and Mrs, and, when we left, Summer was just starting to drag people onto the dancefloor.'

'So why are you here and not there?'

'You know how, traditionally, the bridesmaids are there to look after the bride, and basically be her maid and do whatever she needs?' Angela asked as Ryan gently, but firmly, pushed Imogen to one side and walked in.

'I thought it was to protect against vengeful spirits, and to confuse jealous suitors who might try to steal away the bride and sully her innocence?'

'Is it really?' Angela's eyes were wide.

'She'd know.' Ryan shrugged. 'Anyway, you're missing the point, Moggy. You RSVP'd to be a guest at this wedding, but you're here and not there.'

'You know exactly why that is.' Imogen shook her head.

'But the bride and groom have requested your presence,' Ryan explained.

'And we're not supposed to go back without you.' Angela was grinning.

'No.' Imogen crossed her arms. 'I really can't.'

'I'm pretty sure they really meant it,' Ryan argued. 'Except for the bit about throwing you over my shoulder if you refused.' He shot Angela a worried look. 'Evelyn was kidding about that, right?'

'Probably.' Angela nodded. 'But Evelyn was pretty clear that she really wanted us to bring you back.'

'Why?'

'Because you're her friend,' Ryan answered. 'And because she wants you there.'

'I really don't want to,' Imogen argued.

'It'll be OK. I promise.'

'Why aren't you letting this go?' Imogen stared at him, suddenly feeling suspicious.

'Because, Moggy, this is something I really think you should do. This community is important to you, and you can't keep avoiding everyone.'

Angela slipped her arm through Imogen's and tugged her towards the bedroom. 'And we're under strict instructions to take you back with us.'

'I don't even think I have anything to wear to a wedding,' Imogen complained, hoping that would be a good enough excuse to get her out of this — but she should have known better.

'I'm sure we can find something.' Angela all but man-handled her through the door and reached for her wardrobe. 'Do you mind?'

'Help yourself.' It seemed like she wasn't getting any choice in the matter. She'd just sneak in, give her card and gift to the happy couple, along with her congratulations, and then creep back out. It would be fine. And it was less effort than arguing with Ryan, who could out-stubborn all of Angela's donkeys when he really wanted to.

'This is really pretty.' Angela pulled out one of Imogen's favourite long skirts — a silky number painted in swirling shades of purple, green and blue. 'What do you usually wear with it?'

'Just a tank top or jumper. Something simple against the pattern.'

'This scarf could work well.' Angela spread out a scarf from one of the hangers. 'And it looks nice and long.'

Imogen flopped down on her bed and dragged a pillow over her face. Maybe if she stayed there long enough, her uninvited guests would get bored and leave.

'She's got silver shoes and a bag that would look pretty good.' Ryan leaned against the doorframe. 'I gave you those two Christmases ago. Jewellery?'

Imogen waved her hand towards a box, but still didn't sit up.

'Oh, I like this bangle. It looks solid enough that we can use it to help secure the scarf as a top.' Angela sounded much more excited than Imogen felt. 'And this choker is beautiful. It's so magical-looking. What is it?'

'Happy puppy stone,' Ryan chuckled.

'What?'

Imogen sighed. 'That's what he calls labradorite.'

'What's it good for? Apart from being really pretty.'

'Protecting against negativity. Helping boost your energy.' Imogen sighed and sat up. 'And for emotional resilience and healing the spirit.'

'Sounds like a good one to wear tonight, then.' Angela draped the cluster of stones around Imogen's throat. 'Definitely.' Angela nodded. 'Come on, let's get you ready.'

'I really don't want to do this,' Imogen complained again.

'And we still really think you should. Come on, Moggy — it's not going to get any easier because you've put it off.'

'If I put this off for long enough, the reception will be over.'

'Imogen Finnegan, you might be good at being stubborn, but I have years of experience dealing with you. Do you really think you can out-stubborn me when I put my mind to it?' Ryan folded his arms across his chest. 'Especially when you know I'm right.'

'Come on, Imogen,' Angela cajoled. 'It might even be fun.'

'Sure it will.'

'Well, there's an open bar. So it'll be more fun than arguing with me,' Ryan pointed out.

'OK, OK.'

* * *

'I really am so happy for you and Evelyn,' Kim told her brother, trying not to let the tears she could feel welling up escape and ruin her make-up. Even waterproof mascara had a limit, and she didn't want to spend the rest of the day looking like a panda and ruining wedding photos. Not that anyone would really be looking at her. She followed Jake's eyes across the room to where Evelyn had bent down to talk to Summer and adjust the crystal head-piece woven through the little girl's curls, her silvery-grey gown pooling out around her feet.

'She's incredible, isn't she?' Jake smiled goofily. 'They both are.'

'They really are,' Kim agreed. 'And they look beautiful.'

'I know.' Her brother fiddled with his new ring, twisting it around his finger. 'Moments like this, I can't believe how lucky I am.'

'I really am so, so happy for you both.' Kim bit the inside of her bottom lip to keep it from trembling. She absolutely would not do or say anything that would take away even a moment of his happiness — and that included breaking down in front of him. It wasn't his fault she and Imogen were over — she lay the blame for that firmly at Callum's feet, and her parents' for not telling him to shut up.

She'd done well to find lots of other people to socialise with throughout the day, hoping it looked like she was taking the opportunity to catch up with people she hadn't seen in a while, and not that she was proactively avoiding her brother and parents. She'd smiled and posed nicely in the pictures when needed, and the meal had been fine, as she'd had Summer and Sarah to amuse her, along with Liv to chat to.

It had been a beautiful and highly emotional day seeing Summer, Jake and Evelyn finally, officially become a family.

And so long as she focussed on how happy she was for them — and she really, truly was — then she would just about be OK.

She realised Jake had said something, and started guiltily. 'Sorry, what?'

'I asked if you'd dance with me.'

'You want to dance with me?' Kim was surprised — it was a bit out of character for Jake. He'd usually prefer to take the mick out of her.

'One-off offer for a one-off event. I'm only ever getting married this once.' He smiled over at his new family — the two girls he'd just committed the rest of his life to.

Kim groaned. 'You really are nauseatingly happy.'

'Yup. I know. I'm disgusting. Come on.' He held out his hand.

'You really trust me not to tread on your toes?'

'Hmm. Maybe not.' He grinned. 'Let's hit the bar first, just in case I need some painkillers.'

* * *

Imogen hadn't been close to convinced that what she was doing — what Ryan and Angela had pretty much strong-armed her into — was a good idea. And when she saw who was waiting outside the hall, she was tempted to turn tail and run.

'Don't you dare,' Ryan warned as they pulled up.

'What?' He narrowed his eyes at her, and it didn't take a psychic to read the message — he knew exactly what she was thinking, and he knew that she knew. But she still shook her head. 'Ryan, I can't . . .'

'When have you ever backed down from anything? Least of all Callum Macpearson.'

She knew exactly what he was doing — trying to goad her — but it didn't stop it from working, annoyingly.

'How about we meet you in there?'

'I could go off you.' She glared at her brother, who just shrugged. She shook her head, got out of the car and

257

straightened her shoulders. She'd just hold her head high and walk right by him. She wouldn't even acknowledge his presence — there was no way she was giving Callum Mac-grumpy a third opportunity to have a go at her.

'Imogen, can I please have a minute?'

She took a breath, shook her head slightly and carried on walking.

'Imogen, *please*. I know I've been a total arse, but for Kim's sake . . .'

She hesitated, pausing by the door.

'I know saying sorry won't be anywhere near good enough, but I really would like to apologise. Because, I realise now, that what you and Kim had was far too special and important. I — or anyone else — should never have been allowed to come between you.' He seemed contrite, or at least he was doing a good impression of it . . . and he knew where to hit her weak spot: Kim.

'Thirty seconds. After that, whether I ever have to listen to you is my choice. OK? And I really do mean ever again.'

'More than fair.' He nodded. 'Imogen, my reaction to you — both times — was unforgivable, and I know that. But I'm hoping you're a much better person than I am, and that you might consider forgiving behaviour that I couldn't.'

'You're asking me to be the bigger person? That's pretty low.'

'Bigger, better, smarter, kinder, more empathic. Pick whatever term you want. But yes. I'm really hoping so.'

'And why should I? Fifteen seconds.'

'Because I'm not here to make excuses — just to apologise profusely and completely, and promise to do my best to never speak out of turn to you again. Or just to not speak to you — if that's what you prefer. But I don't want there to be any more hurt because I'm a big idiot-head — as my daughter put it. In case it helps, I really do feel awful for the pain I caused Kim. And you. And I know I'm out of time, but I really am so very sorry. But if there's anything you can think of that I can do to undo some of the damage I've caused, I hope you'll tell me what it is.'

His bright blue eyes — so similar to Kim's — seemed sincere. Imogen wavered, wanting to believe somehow it could all be OK. But what he'd said — the arguments he'd caused — had been so vicious. And she didn't know how to deal with that, not without understanding more. Her eyes flicked over Callum's shoulder to Ryan — the traitor — who gave her a hopeful grin and a thumbs up.

'You could tell me why you reacted so badly. Help me to understand.'

'You want to hear my excuses?' Those familiar blue eyes widened in surprise.

'I think reasons can be different from excuses, and if I understood why you reacted the way you did, maybe I'll find it easier to trust your apology.'

'That's fair enough.' He gestured to one of the benches in the garden. 'Um . . . do you want to sit?'

He fidgeted as they sat, and it occurred to Imogen he was nervous too — which made her feel a bit less on edge.

'So, in case you hadn't noticed, my sister is right. I really can be a close-minded, arrogant arse.' Callum folded his arms across his chest. 'But I do really regret it.'

'Especially when you're completely in the wrong?' Imogen couldn't help the jibe.

'Yeah.' He nodded. 'Especially then. Right . . . explanations.' He fidgeted some more, running his hands through his hair. 'There was a situation involving a patient, so obviously I'm limited to what I can tell you . . .'

'I understand.'

'He was young . . . not that there's a good age to get something like he did . . . but he was far too young.'

Imogen nodded sadly, knowing what Cal was getting at. 'It seems to be that way too often.'

'It shouldn't have gone the way it did. His parents thought it was just the flu or something like that. They hadn't

259

expected cancer. But we caught it early, and everything was looking promising. He was on a curative pathway.'

'I'm scared to ask.' Imogen had a horrible feeling about where this story was going.

'His parents were desperate — they turned to social media to "research" different treatments.'

Imogen winced.

'Unfortunately they found some that they liked the look of. They were convinced that it would be better for him, especially when compared to the side effects of the chemo, so he wasn't throwing up or losing his hair, or feeling so tired.'

'So they thought it was working?' Imogen was starting to get angry. 'Should I ask what this "treatment" was?'

'Homeopathy. With acupuncture, meditation, dietary changes and mistletoe infusions.' Callum bit out the words angrily. 'By the time his parents were willing to listen — and we'd managed to track them down — there was nothing to be done but refer to hospice.'

'Oh, Goddess bless.'

'Yeah.' Callum hung his head.

'So when I rocked up into the village and you started to get forms for *complementary* therapies, you reacted emotionally, from a place of potentially unresolved vicarious trauma, instead of logically and calmly.' Callum's head snapped back up to look at her. 'What? Are you surprised that I actually sound like I might know what I'm talking about?'

'There is no good way I can answer that, is there?'

'Not that I can think of.' Imogen found herself fighting the urge to smile. 'But Callum? I'm not hocking some alternative quackery. My therapies are complementary, and I'm a qualified physiotherapist and fully registered complementary therapist. I keep my professional development and clearances up to date. I spent years dealing with my own fibromyalgia, which doesn't respond well to most medications, so believe me when I say I'm something of an expert on chronic pain. I've studied it and lived it. Which is why the hospital hired

260

me. I usually try to work holistically with patients — with the local care teams and GPs.'

'You mean when they're not being arses?'

That time Imogen did laugh. 'They're not all that bad. Some of the locals are positively welcoming. Friendly, even.'

'I deserved that,' Callum agreed, surprisingly amenable. 'And I genuinely really am very sorry. I have been told I make a dreadful first — and sometimes second — impression.'

'Whoever told you that, I'm probably going to agree with them.'

'My much nicer and better half.'

'I knew I liked Liv.' Imogen grinned.

'Still can't believe she puts up with me some days. Even my daughter loses patience with me. And she's right too. But it is something I'm working on.'

'Not being an arse?'

'Yup, and I probably deserved that,' he admitted. 'I have a bad tendency of jumping to conclusions at times. I don't always give people the benefit of the doubt, and my temper can be a lot shorter than it should be. I've had lectures from both Liv and Jake this week on how badly I screwed things up between you and Kim. And I daresay if my sister was on speaking terms with me, she'd have given me an earful too. I really am sorry, Imogen. And if you'll let me, I'd like to try and help make things right.'

'Thank you for explaining things,' Imogen added quietly. 'It does help to understand where you're coming from. And I won't repeat anything you said. Except for maybe the arse comments. It's so rare one of you high-and-mighty doctors actually admit you're in the wrong.'

'If you're taking the piss out of me, can I hope it's because you're thinking about potentially forgiving me?'

Imogen sighed, studying her fingernails for a second. 'Angry energy isn't helpful for anyone to carry around. You screwed up, you had reasons, you've apologised and explained. I think it's probably best if we all try to move on from it. I'm not planning on going anywhere, and it would be helpful if the local doctors didn't block me too much. Even if they can't be supportive of my work.'

'I will contritely and humbly look at any of the research papers or evidence base you'd be willing to send me.'

'You might regret that,' Imogen threatened. 'Some of my methods — like reflexology — have been around for thousands of years. That's a lot of studies and evidence. And I'm not sure I believe the "humbly" bit.'

'I'm working on that too.' Callum shrugged, still looking repentant. 'Do you think I could buy you a drink. Inside?'

'I thought it was an open bar?'

'Well, maybe fetch you a drink, and give the barman an overly generous tip?'

'OK.' Imogen guessed she could be the bigger person. 'I wanted to give Jake and Evelyn my congratulations.'

* * *

Kim giggled as Summer and Sarah skipped faster and faster, dragging her round in their sugar-and-excitement-fuelled dance as they got giddier and dizzier.

'Macpearson, Macpearson, I'm a Macpearson!' Summer sang happily as they span round and round.

'Yes, you are.' Kim scooped her up and kissed her on the nose. 'And we couldn't be happier, could we Sarey-fairy?'

'Nope.' Sarah grinned at them both. 'Summer's the best cousin-fairy-BFF ever!'

'Well, I'm glad you agree.' At Callum's voice, Kim's mood plummeted. She refused to look at him. 'Nanna is looking for you both. I think she wants more princess photos.'

'Will you be OK, Auntie Kim?' Summer hesitated, watching her.

'She'll be fine,' Callum reassured the little girl. 'Go on, don't keep Nanna waiting. I promise to behave.'

Kim started to walk away, still not feeling like she had anything to say to her brother.

'Kim.' His hand on her wrist stopped her, but she still didn't want to look at him. 'Can I have this dance?'

'You've got to be kidding.' She glared at his hand holding her.

'How about me, then? May *I* have this dance?' Imogen stepped out from behind Callum.

'Imogen?' She couldn't believe what she was seeing — who she was seeing.

'I don't understand.' Kim's eyes flicked to Callum, too scared to hope that what she wanted to happen might actually be happening.

'Imogen and I talked. She's decided to give me another chance. A third one.'

'Really?'

'Yeah.' Imogen offered her hand to Kim. 'Can we talk? Maybe while we dance?'

As much as Kim wanted to say yes, she found herself hesitating, the pain still fresh in her mind.

'Kimberly.' Callum squeezed her wrist, demanding her attention. 'If you only ever listen to me about one more thing in your life ever again, please let it be this. You've been happier and more settled recently than any of us have ever known you to be. If Jake's right, and Imogen is even partly the reason for that, then you'd be stupid to let anyone stand in your way. Even me.' He took Kim's hand and placed it in Imogen's. 'And you're really not stupid, sis.'

With that, he walked away, leaving them holding hands. She looked up and met Imogen's eyes — the usual flush of heat hit her as the rest of the room dimmed around them.

'Please?'

'Sure.' Kim tried not to hope for too much as she followed Imogen back to the dance floor.

'You look absolutely beautiful,' Imogen told her as she slid her arm around Kim's waist.

'Thanks.' Kim felt the heat spill into her cheeks as she took in Imogen's outfit. 'You look gorgeous too.'

263

'Thanks.' Her soft smile was as irresistible as always, but it dropped away far too quickly. 'I messed up, Kim. I let the bad experience with my parents influence how I reacted to your family — especially Callum. I was so busy trying to make sure I didn't cause another family to split up that I hurt you instead. You don't have any reason to forgive me for that, or to trust me again, but I really am sorry.'

'You really mean that, don't you?'

'Yes. I'm sorry I let my fear destroy one of the best things that ever happened to me, and I'm sorry I hurt you. And I really hope that, one day, you might be able to forgive me — and trust me enough — that we could be friends.'

Kim took a deep breath. 'I'm sorry, but I don't want to be friends with you, Imogen.'

'I understand.' Imogen swallowed hard and stepped away, her lips pressed in a tight line as she looked at the floor. 'Then, I guess this is goodbye.'

'Immy? Do you remember what you said to me after the argument?'

'I said a lot to you. Most of which I'm not proud of and I'd rather you forgot.' Imogen sighed.

'At least some of it was good,' Kim insisted. 'You told me that the next time I was going to kiss someone, I should do it because I wanted to. Because I'm so compelled to touch them that I think I'll scream or explode or cry if I can't. That I should do it because I was aching to do it. Not to prove a point to anyone else.'

'Are you making a point here, Kim?'

'Just making sure you understand this.' She stepped close to Imogen and slipped her hand around her neck, before brushing her lips gently against Imogen's.

Imogen gasped and froze for a couple of heartbeats, then wrapped her arms tightly around Kim's waist and kissed her back — hard — pouring so much emotion into the gesture that it left Kim's knees wobbly and weak. She could have sworn that she'd seen stars for a couple of moments, behind the spinning disco lights.

'Kim . . . I . . .'

It thrilled Kim to know she could leave Imogen speechless. 'Yes?' She grinned, stroking Imogen's cheek.

'Please tell me that wasn't a goodbye kiss? To make sure I know what I'm missing.'

'No. It was because I wanted to. Is that OK?'

'Definitely.' Imogen nodded.

'And if I want to keep doing it? And things like this?' She wound her fingers through Imogen's. 'Is this OK too?'

'More than.' Imogen lifted their joint hands to kiss Kim's fingers. 'But are you sure about this?'

'If Cal can get third, fourth, fifth, sixth and probably twelfth chances, I think you can get a second one, Immy.' She giggled. 'Besides, this last three weeks aside, I think these last few months are the happiest I've ever been. You're good for me. You bring out the best version of me, and you gave me the confidence to pursue a future I'd barely dared to imagine . . . I won the bid, by the way.'

'That's fantastic! I'm so pleased for you.' Imogen gave her a joyful hug.

'Thanks.' Kim tightened her arms around Imogen's waist, enjoying the feeling of warmth against her. It felt so good and so familiar to be back in her arms, Kim didn't ever want to let go. 'For the congratulations, and for your help. You know I couldn't have done it without you.'

'Nonsense.' Imogen scoffed as they fell into step with the music, half-dancing and half-swaying. 'It was all your skill and vision.'

'You gave me the confidence to try,' Kim argued. 'You convinced me that it was worth the risk — that I should aim for the stars, because even if I missed them I still had a chance to catch the moon on the way back. You were the one who told me if I didn't try, then I'd always wonder.'

'For what little input I gave you, I was happy to help.'

'You really did help a lot,' Kim insisted.

'Well, are you going to tell me how the bids went?'

'I didn't get everything I asked for, but I caught the flipping moon, Immy. I won the bids on two of the sensory rooms, and I already told Jake to start looking for my replacement.' She giggled again. 'He didn't seem too upset — said I was a terrible receptionist.'

'I'm so freaking proud of you.' Imogen's adoration was hot and fierce in Kim's ear, sending a delicious shiver down her spine — and making her take a chance even bigger than setting up her own company.

'But the moon isn't enough for me this time. I want the whole galaxy of stars, or nothing.' Kim met Imogen's eyes squarely.

'And what are your stars, Kim? What's the galaxy you're aiming for?'

'You. Us. Walking off this dance floor together, and staying that way. Professionally I feel happier, more excited and more fulfilled than I ever have done. But personally? I'm miserable. I miss you, Imogen. I miss us.'

Imogen caught Kim's face between her hands and leaned in, hesitating less than an inch from her lips — so close that Kim could feel her breath as she spoke. 'If I could, I'd scoop every star out of the sky to give you.' She brushed her lips against Kim's gently, before pulling back, watching Kim for her reaction. Whatever she'd hoped for, she must have seen it, because her mouth was back on Kim's in a heartbeat — hot, sweet and far more insistent — deliciously demanding.

'I found them first!' Kim was only vaguely aware of the gleeful cry.

'Ugh, they're doing kissy faces. Yuck!'

That was enough to break them apart, though Kim kept her hand on Imogen's waist. 'There is nothing wrong with two women who care about each other kissing, Sarah.' She scolded her niece gently, thinking that the sooner she got used to it, the better.

'Oh, it's not 'cause you're both girls.' Summer rolled her eyes at her cousin. 'She just thinks all kissing is gross.'

Imogen shrugged, clearly amused. 'Give it a few years and you might change your mind and discover you quite like "kissy faces" after all.'

'A few years?' Evelyn joined them in a flurry of silvery lace and smiles. 'Please don't let her grandfather hear you say that. I don't think Tom plans on letting either of them date until they're at least thirty!'

'Congratulations, Evelyn. You look wonderful.' Imogen let go of Kim to hug her friend.

'Thank you.' Evelyn smiled — the epitome of bridal happiness. 'And I'm so glad you came. Please make this special day even better and tell me you're talking about kissing because you and Kim have sorted things out and are back together?'

'Yeah.' Imogen slipped her hand back into Kim's. 'I think we have.'

'We definitely have.'

EPILOGUE

Kim cuddled closer to Imogen, sliding her arm through hers as they walked back from the Brockle's Retreat pub.

'Do you mind if we cut through the park?' Imogen asked.

'Sure.' Kim sighed happily. 'Any particular reason?'

'Just thought it would be nice.' Imogen checked she had the things she needed in her bag. She held Kim's hand until they reached the park gates, where she stopped and turned. 'I know this is going to sound really strange, but can you wait here for a bit please?'

'Um . . . OK?'

'Thank you.' Imogen kissed her quickly on the cheek. 'Maybe just count to ten slowly, then come on in?'

'What are you up to?' Kim's confusion was clearly visible, even in the near-darkness.

'It's a surprise. Trust me?'

'Always.'

'Brilliant.' Imogen clicked her phone torch on and headed through the gate. 'Actually, maybe count to twenty.' She raced down the path to set things up, leaving Kim looking slightly bemused.

It only took Imogen a few seconds to make her way to the tree, shake out the blanket from her bag, find the cable she'd tucked up earlier and connect it to the power bank from her pocket. She was just trying to crack the seal on the bottle — and grumbling at her uncooperative fingers — when she heard Kim's footsteps.

'Oh, Immy, this is beautiful.'

'I know it's not exactly midnight rainbows . . .'

'I think rainbow fairy lights in our tree are pretty special.' Kim smiled at her. 'Is that mead?'

'Yeah, but I can't get the bloody thing open.' Imogen held it up. 'My hands have stiffened up. Sorry.'

'Sorry?' Kim took the bottle and cracked the seal easily. 'This is amazing. Our first non-date night, recreated.'

'Yeah.' Imogen sat down, arranging her skirt around her legs.

'I feel like I should warn you about me.' Kim settled next to her.

'Oh really?'

'Yeah, it's only fair.' Kim nodded. 'I mean, you have great manners. The perfect lady. I bet you even have another blanket for us to share.'

'I do.' Imogen pulled the blanket out.

'See, that's why I should warn you about me,' Kim told her seriously — though Imogen could see the edges of her mouth twitching with amusement. 'I am definitely the type to try it on with someone who has had a few drinks.'

Imogen burst out laughing. 'That sounds like it could be a promising end to an evening.' She leaned forward to kiss Kim, then leaned back against the tree trunk.

'This really is wonderful.' Kim took a sip from the mead before handing it back to Imogen. 'And exactly what I needed after a week covered in hospital construction dust. Thank you.'

'You're more than welcome.' Imogen took her own swig of mead. 'It's going well though, at the hospital?'

'It really is.' Kim grinned as she took the bottle back and settled next to Imogen. 'I'm loving every second of it. Even trying to mark up all the points for the electrics, and the billion and one holes for the fibre-optic star scene, while they plaster the rest of the walls. It's going to be so amazing, Immy.'

'Of course it is.' Imogen kissed Kim's fingers. 'You are amazing. But actually, I wanted to ask you something.'

'Yeah? What's that?'

'Well, you know how I keep telling you that you shouldn't change anything about yourself to try and please other people?'

'Just one of the many reasons why being with you is so awesome.' Kim smiled at her.

'Well, there is one thing I'd like to change about you.' Imogen reached into her pocket.

'It's my hair, isn't it? You don't like the blue.' Kim shrugged. 'I'm still not totally sold on it.'

'I told you I loved the purple before — and this blue catches your eyes. But it's not your hair, Kim.'

'Is it my new boots . . . ?'

'Kim, sweets—'

Imogen held up her hand, palm open — to stop Kim from running through the list of her insecurities, and also to show her the crystal keychain dangling from her finger. 'I want to change your address . . . for at least some of the time.'

'What?'

'It's the key to my flat. I had it cut before the . . . argument. I'm saying I want you to feel as much at home there as I do, to come and go as you please. Because you being there, Kim, that's what really makes my flat feel like a home.'

'You're saying you want me to stay over more often?' Kim reached for the key.

'Yeah, if that's what you want.' Imogen had to push down the worries and nerves that screamed at her — they'd only been back together a couple of weeks — and she really didn't want to scare Kim off by moving too fast. But, at the same time, she knew exactly what she wanted, and she wanted to make sure Kim understood it too.

She watched nervously as Kim fingered the cascade of tiny crystal stars that made up the keyring, squinting in the moonlight. 'These pink ones are rose quartz, right?'

'Yeah.' Imogen nodded.

'Which is for love.' Kim nodded to herself. 'I can't make out the other ones though?'

'Rainbow moonstone,' Imogen murmured quietly.

'Which has a meaning I assume you're about to tell me?'

'Creativity, balance. And reuniting lost lovers.' Imogen grinned. 'And there is this ancient tradition . . . if you give your lover moonstone under a full moon, the passion you share stays strong for as long as the moon is in the sky.'

'I like that one.' Kim played with the crystals again. 'So you really are offering me the stars — and the moon.' She leaned forward to kiss Imogen — slowly and sweetly, but still leaving them both breathless.

'Does this mean you'll think about bringing some things to my flat? So you're not trying to cram everything you need into an overnight bag, or racing back to your parents' to shower and change?'

'Is this your way of telling me you don't like me borrowing your clothes?' Kim bounced the key up and down in her palm, driving Imogen slightly crazy. She wished she'd just answer her already!

'Now you mention it, yes — I do have a bit of an issue with you wearing my clothes. It's not fair how much better you look in some of them than I do. They're supposed to be *my* clothes.'

'Shut up.' Kim laughed and leaned over to kiss her again. 'You know your boobs are much better than mine.'

'I know you don't need the uncomfortable underwires I do. And I know that if I moved into the gym at work and gave up half my favourite foods, not to mention this,' Imogen reached for the mead, 'I still wouldn't have legs as good as yours.'

'I love your legs as they are. And I love how easily you do that.' Kim gave her one of the smiles that sent shivers of heat racing over Imogen's skin. 'How you make me feel like someone special.'

'Pretty easy when it's you. You *are* special. So, would you think about it? Maybe moving some of your things into my place?'

271

'I don't know.' Kim sighed, and the sound cut through Imogen. 'I mean, you know how disorganised I can be . . . Living between two places sounds worse than overnight bags. I'll never know what's where, I'll spend all of my time going back and forth trying to find things.'

Damn. She had pushed Kim too fast. 'You're right. I hadn't thought of it like that.' Imogen tried not to be stung by the rejection. But as flimsy as Kim's excuse was, she wasn't going to call her out on it.

'I think it would probably just be easier if I had everything in one place, don't you?'

'Yeah. Sure. That makes sense.'

Imogen looked away and took a deep gulp of the mead.

'Immy? How do you feel about it?' Kim nudged her. 'I mean, I don't have to move everything, everything . . . but probably most of it. Maybe some of the smaller bits of furniture too . . . I don't have much like that, but maybe a set of drawers and a wardrobe . . .'

It took Imogen's brain a few seconds to catch up with her ears. 'Wait . . . are you saying you want to move in with me?'

'Yeah.' Kim nodded. 'I think I am. Unless you think it's too soon. I mean, I know we've only been back together since the wedding, but—'

Imogen interrupted her with a kiss, sliding her fingers around Kim's neck to bury them in her hair. She kissed Kim slowly and deeply, letting go of all the worries she'd had, just concentrating on kissing her best friend, losing herself in her touch.

'So, is that a yes?' Kim grinned at her.

'Yes. Bring whatever you want. I want you to be happy in my flat . . . in our flat. Move things around and change things up. I really want it to be your home too.'

'Does that maybe extend to redecorating?' Kim asked cheekily. 'You know I love purple — I wore it in my hair for long enough, but . . .'

'You don't like my bedroom?' Imogen exclaimed. 'But I thought I'd done such a good job matching it all up.'

'Oh, you really did.' Kim tried not to laugh. 'But that's part of what bothers me. Having the walls, the carpet, the bedding and the curtains all such similar shades is a bit overwhelming.'

Imogen buried her hands in her face, laughing. 'I did warn you I had awful taste in interior design.'

'At least it doesn't extend to the women you date,' Kim pointed out with a grin.

'Yeah, I definitely have better taste in people than paint.' Imogen teased Kim with another soft kiss. 'Do whatever you want to make yourself feel at home. Move things around, bring in your own things, redecorate if you want.'

'Really?'

'Yes. Whatever makes it feel like home for you.'

'You do that plenty.' Kim smiled and kissed her. 'But, now you've said it, I am thinking about some of your paint choices, and I'm just itching to pick up a paint brush. Are you sure you'd be OK with that?'

'Yes,' Imogen promised. 'Like I said, whatever makes you feel at home. Actually—' she held up her hand again '—just promise me you'll leave the shop alone? No sneaking moustaches on my squirrels or painting devil horns and pitchforks on my fairies!'

'No, you've got it the wrong way round. The squirrels are getting the devil makeovers!'

'No.' Imogen shook her head, trying not to laugh.

'Spoilsport.' Kim stood up. 'Are you going to turn off these lights?'

'We're going already?' Imogen asked.

'Yeah.' Kim held up the crystal keyring. 'I've got a new key that I really want to try out.' She held out her hand to help Imogen to her feet. 'And, as pretty as it is here, I'm starting to get cold. I can't help thinking that it might be more fun to finish this bottle somewhere more comfortable . . . like bed?'

'Oh, so you're inviting yourself to mine, are you?' Imogen teased as Kim pulled her closer.

'Oh, I've got my own key now.' She grinned wickedly and kissed Imogen. 'And instructions to come and go as I please. And I definitely plan on coming . . .'

'Oh my Goddess, you're incorrigible.' Imogen laughed and buried her face in Kim's shoulder.

'Yup, and you love it.'

'I really do.' Imogen looked up and smoothed Kim's hair back from her face. 'And I love you too. A whole lot more than half.'

'Of course you do. I've been telling you I'm irresistible all along.' Kim giggled, then sobered. 'But seriously, I love you too, Imogen. You were probably one of the last people I would have ever imagined saying that to, what with all your hippy-dippy nonsense . . .'

'Hey!'

'Sorry.' Kim wasn't in the least bit repentant. 'But you were exactly who I never knew I needed. You've made me a happier, brighter, more confident and better version of me.'

'No. You did that all yourself,' Imogen told her honestly. 'You were always amazing. You just needed to see it.'

'I needed someone like you to help me see it,' Kim replied quietly. 'And I'll be forever grateful to you for doing that.'

'Forever's a long time, Kim.'

'I don't know.' Kim brushed her lips against Imogen's. 'With you, I'm starting to think it might not be long enough.' She laughed at herself. 'Sorry, that came out a lot more cheesy than it sounded in my head.'

'I think it was pretty perfect.' Imogen squeezed Kim's fingers.

'Oh good.' Kim grinned. 'Do you want to pack up these blankets then, and head back to yours before I ruin the moment with something else that's super cheesy?'

'No.' Imogen bent down to grab the blanket, then threw one end of it to Kim, who automatically helped her fold it.

'No?' Kim folded the blanket in half lengthways.

'No.' Imogen stepped towards her and gathered the blanket into her arms. 'But we can go back to our home.' She kissed Kim again, her lips soft and sweet from the mead.

'Yeah . . . definitely a lot more than half.'

THE END

ACKNOWLEDGEMENTS

Well, I did say we'd be back in Broclington soon! It's been so lovely writing this fourth (!!) book, and getting to know some of the original village characters so much better.

This series is always so much fun to write, and I truly hope you enjoyed reading it just as much! Without you wonderful readers, this series wouldn't exist — so always the biggest thank you goes to you for picking it up, downloading, reading or listening — I'm always pleased to welcome you back into my made-up world!

As ever, no book ever gets written without a lot of help. So on to thanking the truly brilliant people who have helped this time . . . Stephanie Carmichael, who runs the spectacular Enchanted Realm in Newcastle and online, thank you for helping reignite my love of all things sparkly and crystals — and teaching me so much. Even if I now do have way more things to dust. And for introducing me to mangano calcite — which really *does* feel a bit like a hug . . . Told you I'd write a crystal store into one of my books one day!

As to Imogen's health conditions — these are ones I very much know on a personal basis. And if you know me in the real world or in social media, we've probably talked about it at some point — especially if you're a spoonie. So to all those making up the fibromyalgia and hypermobility communities thank you — for the advice, support, safe space for complaining, and ongoing hope and inspiration. Butterfly hugs to you all, fellow spoonies and weary travellers. Keep on fighting, it's worth it — even if we do have to rest sometimes.

And, as mentioned in the dedications, thanks to the people who walk our journeys with us, buoying us up when we're tired and low, and keeping us going when we're too tired and in too much pain to keep going by ourselves.

And, on a personal note, thanks to my own, real-world Little Village surgery, and the amazing team there who keep me going. And really do listen to their patients.

As always, thanks need to go to Emma GH who first saw this book as a half-imagined synopsis and scribbled first chapter which she encouraged me to give life to. Still sad to not be working with you any more — but thrilled for your success!

And thanks to Becky Slorach, who picked this up partway through, and has been so supportive of this book, and the characters within it. I'm well aware that a lot of the topics are sensitive, and I'm truly grateful to the team at Joffe and Choc Lit for supporting this story.

There's so many to thank in this team for bringing this book to life, so as always . . .

. . . Thank you to Sarah, who is so supportive and good-humoured during edits. Hopefully I've got timelines straight now! And thank you for sharing such support.

Of course, thanks to Becky and Kate — who make sure everything is where it should be, when it should be. And to Tia who is teaching — and challenging me — about social media. Brockle cakes would never have been baked without her . . . I'm equal parts excited and nervous to see what the next challenge is!

And, of course, thanks to the wider team at Joffe including Jasmine, Abbie, Claire, Hanna, Sasha, Gemma and Tia. Also to the tireless proofreader Becky Wyde, who makes sure those late-night writing errors don't make it into your reading!

Also to my amazing cover designer Jarmila Takač, who created such beautiful artwork — big thank you for bringing this one to life.

And a huge thank you to the wonderful ARC readers, bloggers and reviewers who help tell the world about these books.

Always, thanks go to my Choc Lit sister authors — who write, laugh, commiserate and celebrate together.

And the biggest thanks of all go to my family: to Alex who still makes me endless hot drinks, keeps me strong when I'm in a flare and struggling, and who introduced me properly to astronomy, and helped me learn about midnight rainbows and find one (yes, they really exist!).

And to Dad, who listens to me complain and lifts me up when I'm down, and reads all my stories — even though they're definitely not his genre!

ABOUT THE AUTHOR

Ella's long-standing addiction to the written word started so long ago that she struggles to remember a time when reading wasn't an important part of her life — and she's wanted to be a writer since she realised that it was actually a job.

She has a BA Hons in Communication, Authoring and Design, and won the Floella Benjamin Award from the SWWJ in 2019, and works as a Bid Writer by day. She also has a hypermobility disorder, which comes bundled with other health conditions including fibromyalgia, chronic pain and chronic fatigue. But she considers herself to be very lucky to have a wonderful support system around her, who she is grateful for every day, and who help keep her going.

Ella grew up on the outskirts of London where fairies left surprises at the bottom of her grandma's garden, so it isn't surprising that she still looks for magic in everyday life — and often finds it. She now lives in Warwickshire (where there are probably more fairies).

She shares her house with her husband, who introduced her properly to astronomy, and makes her endless hot drinks and doesn't complain (too much) when she forgets to drink them, and their small parrot, who likes to critique her work from his favourite spot on the keyboard.

If you've enjoyed this book (hopefully you have if you're still reading!), please spend a couple of minutes to leave a review and tell your friends about *Midnight Rainbows*, and Broclington in general — it's one of the best ways for authors to meet new readers.

To find out more about Ella, follow her on social media:

Twitter:@EllaCookWrites

Instagram: @ellacookwrites

Facebook: WrittenbyElla

THE CHOC LIT STORY

Established in 2009, Choc Lit is an independent, award-winning publisher dedicated to creating a delicious selection of quality women's fiction.

We have won 18 awards, including Publisher of the Year and the Romantic Novel of the Year, and have been shortlisted for countless others. In 2023, we were shortlisted for Publisher of the Year by the Romantic Novelists' Association.

All our novels are selected by genuine readers. We are proud to publish talented first-time authors, as well as established writers whose books we love introducing to a new generation of readers.

In 2023, we became a Joffe Books company. Best known for publishing a wide range of commercial fiction, Joffe Books has its roots in women's fiction. Today it is one of the largest independent publishers in the UK.

We love to hear from you, so please email us about absolutely anything bookish at choc-lit@joffebooks.com.

If you want to receive free books every Friday and hear about all our new releases, join our mailing list here: www.joffebooks.com/freebooks.

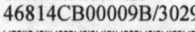